A MESS OF A MAN

A. M. HARGROVE
& TERRI E. LAINE

DEDICATED

This is dedicated to the fans of Cruel & Beautiful who wanted to read Ben's story.

ACKNOWLEDGEMENTS

We'd like to send out a HUGE thank you to all our readers for taking a chance on us with *Cruel and Beautiful*. Never did we dream our novel would shoot to the top the way it did and it was only because of you, dear readers. When the requests for more books began pouring in we knew we had to tell Ben's story. Although we didn't go through the cases of tissues as we did in **C&B**—translate, we still cried—it wasn't nearly as ugly. So again, we'd like to thank you and hope we continue to fill you with our heartwarming novels.

There is a group of people who deserve our deep gratitude, namely our beta readers. Their patience with us during this project is deeply appreciated and without their input, this book would not be what it is. So here's one big squishy-huggy thank you to the following people: Jill Patten, Andrea Stafford, Kristie Wittenberg, Kat Grimes, Heather Carver, and Nina Grinstead. You ladies ROCK!

We're also blasting a hearty THANKS out in shouty caps to Nina Grinstead at Social Butterfly PR for pulling together an AHH-Mazing marketing plan that included lots of punch, bells, and whistles (and maybe some alcohol, too). She worked her ass off and did one bad ass job. Nina—you are the bomb! And thanks for putting up with me (Terri) and my many back and forth messages, lol <3 ~ Terri ;)

We'd also like to thank to Rick, Julie, Mary Beth, Terrie, and Amy at Red Coat PR for all their behind the scenes action, too. GO RCPR!

Finally, we want to thank Lisa Christman of Adept Edits. This lady was not only fun to work with but polished up our manuscript like gold. Thanks for the Sam-isms!

PROLOGUE

THERE IS FINALITY TO THE SOUND of the door closing behind her. A sort of tormenting peace knowing the end has come. It's not like I should have expected things to go on this way for long. How could they? The few people I let into my inner circle have dropped out of my life or let me down.

One evil word has taken on the role of judge, jury, and executioner to those closest to me. Why should this be any different?

My hand presses against my forehead to ease the crushing headache insisting on making its presence known. It's only a matter of time before everything will splinter—like the exterior of my empty heart.

I stare holes in the walls as if I can still see her, the one I let in. The sun rises and sets with her inner and outer beauty, blinding me with something I don't dare name because it scares me in ways that bring me hope—hope I've never had before. Every time I'm with her, I know dawn will come. Now that she's gone, darkness has blocked the sunlight seeking entrance through my window.

Sweeter than peach cobbler, she hardly has a bad thing to say about anybody—until now. Her parting description of me, beginning with ass and ending with hole, reverberates through my hollow heart, as I stand here entrenched in my spot. I'm not even

1

shocked, as this isn't the first time I've been on the receiving end of that sentiment. I'm only surprised because I don't think I've ever heard her so much as mutter a single curse word before. And the first time I do, it's aimed squarely at me.

My hands tighten around a tumbler filled with amber liquid before I toss back its contents hoping for oblivion or something close to it. This road is so familiar. Only this time is different. I never cared like I do now. She means more to me than a quick fuck. Hadn't I been about to tell her just that? How could things have gone wrong so fast?

Her parting condemnation of my character mocks me as it slashes across my chest drawing blood, as was its intent. My heartbeat slows and echoes from the other side of the chasm created between us when she unknowingly ripped my heart out of my chest and left with it.

Yet the door between us continues to dare me to cross over its threshold and make things right. Something seemingly so simple, yet the hardest thing I've ever had to do. As if that weren't enough, my best friend disapprovingly glowers at me from beyond the grave making me miss his presence more than ever before. He'd been my compass, my right hand man, my voice of reason when it came to situations like this.

Inexorably alone, I watch my life implode into a wasteland from my bad decisions. I can fix this. The letter he wrote in his final days itches to be in my hand. The worn lines of the paper I've unfolded and refolded so often are in a drawer next to my bed. But I'm not strong enough to go get it. It doesn't matter. How many times have I read the damn thing? A hundred? A thousand? His poignant thoughts and advice are tattooed on my brain, as deeply as the image of his dying face as he took his last breath.

When the fuck will I get that picture out of my head? And when will I stop needing him to talk me off the ledge, goddammit? How the hell am I supposed to fix this thing between her and me without him? "Why the fuck did you have to die? Friends aren't supposed to die on each other. And you know I suck at this shit!"

The words echo off the walls as I continue to grow roots into the floor like an unwanted weed.

I can practically hear him shouting, "Get off your ass and stop her, you idiot!"

But I can't. I've died a million deaths since the day he left this earth.

"If you were still here, I wouldn't be in this shit storm," I choke out as if his memory were tangible.

What I wouldn't give for him to be here now. Anything. Because if he were, I'd know anything is possible. Especially everything I want to have with her. His death is only a reminder that dreams don't come true.

Don't be a dumbass. You can still fix this.

Although I cling to his memory like the air I need to breathe, I choose to ignore his unspoken advice. Instead, I stubbornly stay embedded to my spot because nothing can change the outcome. It's a truth she and I know will haunt me until my last breath. And it's created a wall between us I'm unable to climb ... even if you gave me a damn ladder.

I've never been much of a risk-taker when it comes to matters of the heart. I can fill a bank account to a number with many zeros behind it from my astute choices in the market. But I can't be a man a woman stays with. Hadn't I warned her about that too?

Unable to see past my own shitty existence, I long for her to come back. I want to believe it's all been some kind of mistake and I can forget what I know to be true. As the seconds continue to tick by, the inevitability that things are really over sinks in. My window of opportunity quickly closes as fast as her car door slams and the engine fires to life.

She's so close, yet miles away. The longer I let the minutes expand between us I know distance won't make the heart grow fonder. But maybe it's for the best. Love, or whatever masquerades as it, just isn't enough for the dirty, fucked up truth. Right when things were better than I ever expected, facts messed it up.

Groaning, I launch the crystal glass worth a small fortune at the door I can't seem to force myself towards. A beautiful show of light plays off the shards as they cascade down in an explosion of fireworks. Visually, it's what I feel inside as desolation constricts and then obliterates my chest because the best thing I ever had is gone ... leaving me with only the certainty I'm meant to be with her.

"I love you," I whisper for the first time and in place of goodbye. I can only pray we both survive what's to come.

ONE
BEN

---◆---

THE MUDDLED SKY IS A REFLECTION of the state of my life as I watch my best friend's casket being lowered into the ground, gone forever. Drew, at twenty-nine, has passed on. And it's so unfucking fair. I stare, longing for a state of numbness, only to be denied. I feel far too much as the fist-sized organ in my chest continues to beat, ridiculing me that his doesn't. It isn't right and it's killing me ... slowly.

The beautiful woman who clings to me as if I could anchor her doesn't belong to me. Cate belongs to *Drew* in the way poets write in sonnets. They belong together, as immortalized in every chick flick ever made.

For him, I do my damn best to hold his widow steady. *Widow.* Shit.

She needs a rock, not the pussy who's lost everything that matters outside of his family. So I mask the emptiness that covers me like a blanket with a pair of useless sunglasses. They hide my red-rimmed eyes as the memories of his last few good days spent hanging at his house burn the backs of my eyelids.

Cate fairs little better as fat tears spill down her cheeks reminding me how life will never be the same. Who will put up with my shit or call me out on it when I need it?

Moisture rolls down my face and I'm grateful for the rain that bursts from the clouds with perfect fucking timing. I open an umbrella and hold it over Cate and me. When the last words are spoken, we shuffle forward, like zombies, and drop freshly cut roses into the hole that's the size of my messed up heart. I shouldn't be so screwed up over losing him. It wasn't like we were secret lovers or anything. But he was my other half in the way only a best friend could be. He had everything I didn't. A good family, a career he enjoyed, and a woman he loved more than his last breath. So why did he have to be the one to die?

I would have volunteered to take his place if given the chance. What did I have to leave behind? A career that I love to hate? A woman? The thoughts make me laugh. My career is currently in the hands of my father. And women have never meant anything more to me than a temporary place for me to bury myself balls deep.

"Ben, I can't."

Cate's shaky words are an echo of my own. Life is far too short and so very unfair. My next words are hollow, but I force them from my throat anyway.

"You can, for Drew."

My memory from that awful day fades as the ice knocks around in the glass that I swirl in my hand. They say it's a woman that always messes with your head. That's not always true. In my case, I'm still royally fucked up over watching Drew die from cancer— stolen from this world long before his time. And that's all I seem to be able to focus on. Not the woman I just finished fucking minutes ago.

She excitedly prances in front of me like she's walking over hot coals, droning on, her voice like nails on a chalkboard as I tune her out. She's striking in a way that any man can see. Yet any interest I ever had in her has long since fled. The fact I didn't get off during our last round of sex is further proof it's time for me to move on. My mistake is making sure she always gets hers, because she's otherwise oblivious to my lack of enthusiasm. But I'm tired of going through the motions. It's time for me to man up and figure out the best way to tell her to lose my number without it ending in her shouting curses at me. Not that I wouldn't deserve it. I just don't have the energy to endure it tonight.

"Ben, did you hear me?" Karen asks.

"Yeah." I clear my throat, dislodging the word from there.

"Anyway, I thought if you could get the day off tomorrow, we could drive up to the hospital tonight."

I don't have to ponder her question as I finally focus on her.

She's putting on the white lacey bra I'd taken off her an hour earlier. My eyes drop and I'll admit she has a great ass. It's even still a little red from my earlier taps. But nothing, there's nothing there but pretty window dressing.

When she glares at me, I finally answer her question with another question.

"Why?"

She stops and scowls at me. "Why what?"

Here we go. Her voice has already started to rise.

"Why would I take the day off? I barely know the woman." The truth is, I hardly know Karen.

"Why?" Her face turns an angry shade of pink. "I would think after all this time together you'd want to get to know my family."

I'm about to say the wrong thing, but I say it anyway. "Why's that?"

Her hands go to her waist and she leans towards me in that *school teacher about to discipline a student* kind of way. She wants a reaction and I can't seem to wipe the bored look off my face. My hope is she gets my meaning without me spelling it out.

"Why?" She stops and takes a deep breath as if that will calm her. But I know better. Three. Two. One. Bingo. I see the change when she finally gets it. Her face softens and her hand reaches out to stroke mine. If she's trying to smooth out my annoyed expression, it's too late.

"The cancer thing freaks you out, I understand that. But it's been ..." she pulls back and taps her fingers against the side of her face, "what, over a year now? Granted, it's sad your best friend died. In fact, it's tragic. But life moves on, Ben." Then as an afterthought she adds, "Sometimes I wonder if you two were more than just friends."

She had to go there, which only proves how little she knows me or wants to outside of the size of my bank account. I try to rein in my anger but fail as I slam my glass down on the side table causing her to jump and her face to pale.

"He was like a brother to me. And he was twenty-nine years old for God's sake. He should be working on having a kid with Cate, not six fucking feet under the ground."

She lifts a hand like she's trying to calm a dragon and maybe I am one. "I'm just saying. We've been together for five months now."

I cut her off. "No, Karen, that's where you're wrong. We've been fucking for five months."

Her back straightens and her eyes narrow. She switches back to school teacher stance and her next words are slow and deliberate, like she's teaching me a lesson or something.

"You fucking asshole. You're a great big jerk who's going to die alone if you don't get your head out of your ass."

Asshole and jerk are just a few of the names I've been called over the years and it rolls off me like water. There are a number of things I could say in response, starting with how I just finished fucking her ass. However, I stay tight-lipped because it appears she's going to leave. *Score.* She pulls up her skirt and yanks her shirt over her head so fast her hair is practically standing on end from static electricity. I smirk because it's somewhat amusing.

"Nothing's funny. And don't bother calling me when you realize what a mistake you're making."

I shrug.

She mutters several more curses as she exits my front door. The noise as it slams is just the punctuation I need to clarify that our *relationship* is at an end. I pick up the drink and take another deep swallow. Karen was a great piece of ass, but that was it. There had never been a moment when I wanted more.

She's right about one thing. Cancer scares me shitless. I can't go through that ever again with anyone. I'm grateful my family doesn't have a history of cancer because one crushing blow is enough. Drew's death shredded me and I'm still trying to piece myself back together. And he's been gone over a year.

I pick up my phone and hit the number I want to dial.

It rings once and my little sister and only sibling, Jenna, picks up. "What's up Benny boy? I thought you would be driving to North Carolina by now."

Inwardly, I sigh because that's where Karen is going alone.

"What gave you that idea?" I ask nonchalantly.

Karen is somewhat of a friend of hers. And I have to do damage control before Karen calls her.

"My phone's ringing. Hold on."

"Wait, Jenna, don't answer. I need to talk to you first."

There is a pause and sharp as a tack, she's putting it together.

"What did you do?"

I bite the bullet and spit it out, knowing she's going to be pissed. "I can't be with her."

Silence. I mark off the time in increments of five. By the time I'm up to fifteen, she finally speaks.

"Why?"

You'd think Jenna was older than me the way she says that word.

"I'm not into her like that."

"Ben ..." she stops and her voice softens even as her disappointment in me is evident. I love my sister, but not enough to date a woman I'm not interested in. "This isn't about Drew is it? Did you freak because Karen's aunt has cancer?"

It sucks how much she knows me.

"I didn't freak." I take another swallow of my Lagavulin. "I'm just not into her. No reason to meet her family when I'm never going to put a ring on her finger."

She's probably crossed her arms by now and is most likely tapping her foot in impatience. I'm no coward, but I'm glad we're on the phone.

"I don't believe you."

"You don't have to," I snap.

She says nothing for several seconds. "Mom's going to be pissed. She likes her. She sees the two of you making little Ben babies together."

I groan. Mom has been on the baby hunt lately.

"You make Jenna babies because Karen's not the one. I'm not in love with her. Not even close."

Jenna sighs. "Ben, I love you. Hell, I love Cate too. And I loved Drew. But if you both don't snap out of it, you might as well have died with him."

If anyone else had said that, I would have hung up or hurled several curse words because what she said is like a slap across my face.

"I know." I barely choke out the words.

"Maybe you should talk to someone, a therapist."

A therapist. I can almost feel Drew standing there in agreement with my sister. He would have choice words for me if he was here. But that's the point. He's not. And he should be. I close my eyes feeling his loss as if it happened yesterday.

"I don't know. Maybe." She sighs like she's won. "Anyway, it's better this way. I'm no good for anyone. I'll never be Drew."

"Ben—"

"Stop, Jenna. Don't set me up with any more of your friends unless they want to be fucked." I mean that in more ways than one. "That's all I have to give."

"Ben—"

"I'm serious."

My sister, the queen of words, is quiet. "Okay," she says, and I know she gets it. "I won't fix you up anymore."

"Good, I never asked you to in the first place."

By the time we end the call, I'm restless. I get up from my chair and walk over to the bottle of Lagavulin on the counter. Pouring myself a double, I realize I can't call Drew and ask him to come over to process all this. I swallow down the liquid thinking what a shit life I have.

My mind wanders to beautiful Cate. She's just as alone as I am. Maybe ... that thought dies a sudden death in my mind because she's like my little sister, which makes me shudder, not to mention I doubt that's what Drew had in mind when he asked me to watch over her.

With that weird idea cleansed from my mind, I head to the shower to wash away the reek of Karen. Passing through my bedroom, I make a quick decision to strip the sheets off the bed to get rid of every trace of her. The act will shock the shit out of my cleaning lady.

After my shower, I call Mark, a guy from work, to see if he's up for hanging out. Maybe poker or heading to a bar will help me forget everything, including the fucking C word, *cancer*.

When he doesn't answer, I assume his ex is back, giving him grief. I flip on the TV and end up watching the *Dark Knight* for the millionth time. Only Drew's there in the back of my head giving me shit about my choices. He wouldn't have approved how I handled Karen. "Then you should be here to kick my ass," I say to the empty room.

The next morning, I crawl out of bed before the crack of dawn to hustle into work. I make it there before the sun has made an appearance, and the office is hopping as I'm not the first one in. Gratefully I'm not the last, either. However, I haven't beaten the old man, my father himself, which has been a goal of mine for some time.

Jeff, my co-worker, spots me as he steps out from the kitchen area. He slings an arm around my shoulders.

"The Money Man's in the house," he announces, getting people to look up from their work stations like I'm some kind of rock star. He leans into me conspiratorially as we pass the cubical pool of first-year recruits and more quietly, but not so much, says, "Ben, my man, it's Friday. Don't make plans for the night. We're taking Mark out to get laid. His wife—"

"Soon to be ex-wife," I counter. I don't know why I bother. Mark doesn't seem to want to let her go.

"Whatever, she's stringing him along by the balls. We're heading to Savanna's after work. And you're coming."

Savanna's is an upscale club in an up and coming trendy part of town. We stop at my small office, the one the old man grudgingly gave me when I decided to come back and work for him after a stint in New York. He's still pissed I went to New York to work for a big firm out of college and not for him. So he's forcing me to earn my place in his firm and not just using my name to snag a corner office. It doesn't bother me. I love a challenge. And getting the old man not to be smug after I decided New York wasn't for me is worth it.

Jeff steps back. "Your dad is in a mood. Watch out."

I nod.

"Anyway, we're taking a cab to the club after work, so don't sneak out." He points at me as he heads to his junior office a few doors down. "We're counting on you."

I don't get two feet behind my desk before I hear my name by a familiar voice.

"Benjamin, late are you?"

Tongue in cheek, I know better than to answer.

"If you think you're up to it, I'd like your risk analysis on the IPO we discussed yesterday."

"I—"

Dad cuts me off. "Ten minutes, large conference room."

He leaves me feeling very much like a chastised child. It's a good thing I worked late yesterday evening, expecting him to put me on the spot. No doubt all the analysts have been rounded up to hear a report I hadn't been asked to prepare. But I had anticipated it.

The meeting runs long and leaves me behind with all the other business of the day, but I nailed it. I deflected every question fired at me with a well-researched answer, giving my father no choice but to be mollified that I'd done the work.

Catching up the rest of the day, I'm busy and out of the emotional shitstorm in my head … which is why I put in at least sixty hours a week.

When Jeff drags me out of the office earlier than normal, I'm grateful for one thing. And that's alcohol. I pay for a few rounds as the guys get Mark good and twisted. I'm halfway there myself, although my tolerance for the stuff has increased, and it's taking more to get a buzz these days.

Downing a shot, I watch as Jeff ropes in a sexy blonde for Mark. A woman with dark hair and clear blue eyes is not too far behind and she winks at me. She has a gorgeous exotic mix of features that makes her a stunner. I buy her a drink or two before I allow her to lead me towards the private restrooms in the back.

She doesn't waste time and works my zipper down as she drops to her knees. I take a fistful of her silky dark hair and wind it around my hand. She works a condom on my semi-hardened cock and I start to wonder if she's a professional. I say nothing and let her work me up from half-mast. Only I'm not into it. She's an attractive woman, but I can't go there. I've had many nights like this and it's getting old.

I pull her mouth away and tuck myself back in my pants. "Sorry, sweetheart. It's not working." Before she can balk and spew curses at me that will draw everyone's attention, I add, "I think I'm too drunk to get it up."

It isn't exactly true, but no reason to cause bad blood.

"Maybe next time," she says with a wink.

I nod. She gives me her phone number, and I take the trouble to program it in my phone, more of the illusion that it's me and not her, which is mostly true. We leave the restroom and I join my friends. I say nothing when they stare at me; I don't have anything to prove to these guys. The night that should have been fun is turning out to be a bust. I eventually cab it home when I finally hit that sweet spot on the drunk scale, and I don't want to wrap my car around a tree.

Somehow I make it to bed, still dressed, which is where I find myself in the morning. A bottle of water and a cup of coffee later, I cab it back to pick up my car. My stomach growls and I pull into the first store I see. It's not where I normally go, but it's right there.

I need to get a couple of things, like bread, milk, eggs, bacon and cereal, for the lazyass hangover breakfast of champions which is a hodgepodge of everything and anything.

I step inside the unfamiliar store and gaze around to determine which direction I should head first to fulfill the small list of items.

That's when I spot her. My dick stiffens and points in her direction like a divining rod. I'm not sure what to make of it. This has never happened, especially considering I can only see her mostly from behind. I do get a view of side boob and her rack is impressive from that angle. I step forward because her lower half is hidden by the display stand in the produce section.

Then I see it. Miles of long, smooth, tanned legs. She looks like she might be headed out to the beach because she wears a loose white tank top with a bright blue bra or bikini top that peeks out from the side where the tank top hangs open. Her tan extends up and under a pair of frayed at the edges shorts that don't have to be tight to make my pulse race.

Blood leeches from my brain and I can barely think. I haven't even seen her face and I could chisel a stone statue with my dick. Her hand lands on a round melon and she turns enough to give me a profile view. Damn if she isn't the full package. Her face is as pretty as the rest of her. Strands of golden blond hair mixed with honey brown are pulled into some messy knot at the base of her neck. I find myself tethered to her like a dog on a leash. Unconsciously, I begin walking towards her.

When I get the full view, she isn't as exotically stunning as the woman in the club last night, yet I find myself way more attracted to the one in front of me.

Her hand is still on the melons and she's squeezing them, or so it appears.

"Excuse me," I say.

Startled hazel eyes flecked with gold meet mine as a smile grows on her lips. "Yes?"

Her voice is like a hand stroking my dick and I have to have her in my bed tonight.

"I'm going to have to write you up for molesting the fruit. It's unseemly with kids in the vicinity. I'll need your name."

This is where she can shut me down because she thinks I'm corny as hell or she'll give me a shot by telling me her name.

"Hmm," she says taking her hand off the melon in feigned

shock. "I could give you a fake name."

"You could or I could ask for ID."

She giggles and that mouth. It takes the strength of ten men to keep my eyes leveled on hers and not take in her extraordinary chest. I wait a few seconds before she says, "I'm Samantha Calhoun, but my friends call me Sam."

She holds out her hand. I take it and lift it to my lips. "Nice to meet you, Samantha. I'm Ben Rhoades."

"Ben? Is that short for Benjamin?"

"Ah," I say reluctantly letting go of her hand. "That's a long story. One you can only hear if you agree to go out to dinner with me."

She raises her brows. "Is that so?"

I shrug.

"Okay, I think I want to hear this long story."

"Tonight?" I ask because I want her in my bed so badly, I'm almost ready to beg. And isn't that some shit? If not for my jeans, my dick would have popped out and told her himself.

"I can't. I have plans."

Of course she does. I remember it's Saturday. I probably look like a total loser for suggesting it. "Monday?"

"Monday?" she repeats.

"Yes, I have a thing tomorrow, and who has plans on a Monday?"

She smiles. "Monday's good."

She pulls out her phone and I have déjà vu for a second remembering last night with the exotic beauty in the private bathroom. We exchange phone numbers and I promise to call her with the details.

"Great," she says and her smile is beautiful.

I turn up the wattage on mine, then leave her after I say, "I should report you to the Produce Manager, but consider it a warning this time."

She giggles again and I know I'm in. I head towards the dairy department and I don't look back. I don't chase women. Never have and I won't start now. If this doesn't work out between us, there are plenty of other women in the world to satisfy my needs.

TWO
Sam

I LOOK AGAIN AT THE MELON I'm still caressing. Oh, the aroma. *Control yourself, Sam. It's a fucking melon. Not a penis, for Pete's sake!*

The dark-haired, gray-eyed god struts away from me as I ogle his goods. Holy melon I'm a felon! The man with the sexiest voice known to womankind who interrupted my fruitporn could possibly be my total destruction as I stand staring, shell-shocked. He is every bit as panty-melting from behind as he was from the front.

Messy-as-hell hair, scruffy face, and a smile that would stop a nuclear war, and he accused me of molesting the damn fruit! How the hell did he know? But he's the kind of man who would make me lose my normally in-control-of-everything-Sam-self. What exactly was that all about? And how cliché is this? Meeting in the produce section of the Whole Foods, of all things? And then he asks me out and we exchange numbers. Jesus tomatoes. I just handed out my number to him like a piece of candy. No background check. Nothing. He leaves and I'm left standing here, massaging the melon like it's one of his balls. And does it ever feel good. Not as velvety smooth as a penis, mind you.

My phone rings shaking me out of my stupor.

"You're still coming, right?" Lauren asks.

"Um, me, miss a day at the beach? What do you think?"

"Where the hell are you then?"

"I took a small detour," I say, tossing the melon in my basket. "I'm at Whole Foods grabbing some stuff for munchies. I'm sure your parents don't want us to eat them out of house and home."

"Oh, that. You know they always have enough food for an army platoon."

"Too bad. I'm here anyway."

"Whatever. I'll see you in a few then. And whatever you do, don't bring any towels. Mom says she has so many out here from people leaving them behind she thinks they're mating and reproducing."

Heading to the register with my haul, I laugh. "Gotcha. Later."

Lauren and I have been roommates since our days at Clemson. We went to high school together and everyone swore it would be a mistake to live together and we would end up hating each other. What did they know? Six years later, here we are, still living together and the best of friends. I'm as close to Lauren as I am my own sister.

As I'm walking to the car with my groceries, my phone buzzes again. Checking it, I see it's my mom. "Hey, Mom."

"Hey, sweetie. What're you up to?"

"Headed to the beach. I'm trying to beat the traffic."

"Well, I won't keep you. I wanted to see if you made your decision yet."

Inwardly I groan. This is something I don't like to think about, but I know she wants me to hurry with this. "Not yet, Mom. I have plenty of time."

"I know you do. Don't wait too long, though."

"I won't. Gotta go. Love you."

"Kisses, sweetie."

It's the perfect beach day—bright blue sky and not a cloud in sight. My windows are down as the music blares.

When I pull into the driveway of the Mitchell's beach house, I mentally push my convo with my mom out of my head as I lug all my purchases upstairs, determined to enjoy the gorgeous day.

"Didn't think you'd ever get here," Lauren says, grabbing some of my bags to give me a hand.

"Hi Sam." Mrs. Mitchell hugs me. "What in the world did you bring this time?"

"Just some fresh fruit to make a salad. I'll get to cutting this up."

"Can I make you a Bloody Mary or a mimosa?" she asks.

"A Bloody Mary would be great, thanks."

When she leaves, I say to Lauren, "You wouldn't believe what happened. I met a god at Whole Foods."

"What?"

So I explain.

"You say his name is Ben Rhoades?"

"Yeah. Do you know him?"

Lauren gives me her scrunchy-faced look. "Not that I know. Mom? Do you know any Rhoades?"

"Yeah. Martin and Julia Rhoades. Why?" Mrs. Mitchell hands me my drink.

Lauren says, "Oh, yeah. Do they have kids?"

"Yeah, two. Maybe three. I can't remember because we were never close with them. I think their oldest is in business with Martin. He owns an investment firm, if I recall correctly. Your father would know more about that. Why the interest?"

"Sam met Ben Rhoades this morning at Whole Foods. She says he's a god."

Mrs. Mitchell arches her brows and leans in. "Really? Do tell."

I giggle again and they both look at me like the melon I'm holding is my third eye.

"Holy hot hunks, Mom. She's smitten. Sam never giggles."

"I know. It's a fact. You all should've seen it. You know how I am at Whole Foods anyway. I ogle the produce like porn, and then he comes up to me and accuses me of molesting the melons. It's like he had a direct line into my brain. And I wish I'd had my damn phone out. I would've snapped a pic of him. Drool-worthy for sure."

They're both eating up my words. "Yeah?"

"Oh, yeah. He had the messy hair thing going from here 'til Sunday and I wanted to stick my hands in it and mess it up even more. Tall, dark, and desirable. End of story."

Mrs. Mitchell, whom I adore, nudges Lauren, "Well, no damn wonder she's giggling."

Lauren asks, "Eyes?"

"Piercing gray. And you wanna hear the best? I gave him my number and he's asked me out for Monday. You don't think he's a serial killer or something, do you?"

Mrs. Mitchell laughs. "I think you're safe on that one."

"And you were going to share this like, when? Tomorrow?" Lauren sticks her lower lip out.

Mrs. Mitchell runs interference. "Lauren, give the poor girl a chance to tell her story. This is hot. Girl meets boy at the fruit stand."

"No! Not at the fruit stand. In the produce section. Just like in the movies," I argue.

Lauren waves her arm. "Whatever. Just finish!"

"That's it. He takes my number, plugs it into his phone, and saunters away. And it was a damn fine view from the rear, too. That man left a trail of smoke behind him, I declare."

"Hmm. I think I need to start hanging out at Whole Foods," Lauren mumbles.

"I don't know. But honestly, he'll probably turn out to be a jerk like the last four guys I've dated. I do have that jerk magnet thing going."

"Maybe you've been demagnetized. You never know."

The rest of the day is spent out on the beach, soaking up the sun, playing beach volleyball, eating, drinking, and having the best time. Berkeley, Carrie, Britt, and Hayley—my other besties, official advisory council, and general I-don't-know-what-I'd-do-without-them-in-my-life—show up later in the morning, and Mrs. Mitchell makes a bunch of sandwiches to feed the troops, like she always does.

We all go out to body surf and the waves are a little rough. Britt ends up flashing everyone on the beach when she stands up sputtering out salt water and her bathing suit top is askew from getting caught in the curl. Carrie and Hayley laugh so hard they can't tell her and the rest of us are behind her, so we don't see it until the nipple show is a done deal. A group of guys give her a standing ovation and offer her a beer as we walk back to our chairs. Britt, being the good sport she is, laughs at their gesture telling them the least they can do is offer her an import instead of the crappy domestic they're trying to give her. That sends us all into fits of laughter, and even the guys love it.

As the day winds down, Carrie suggests Home Team on the island for dinner and drinks, and it's a no-brainer.

"God, I love this place," I say around a mouthful of wings after our food arrives.

We all mmm over the yumminess of what we're eating, and afterward move to the bar area to mingle with some people we know.

"So, Sam how's business?" Berkeley asks.

"Banging, actually." I own an event planning company specializing in corporate functions. I started out right after college, and two years later it's gotten to the point where I'm turning away business.

"That's awesome. I knew you were hiring. I was going to check with you about scheduling something for the electric co-op in the fall."

"Cool. Call me and we can put it on the books."

Turning to set my empty glass on the bar, I glance to my left and notice someone who's been pursuing me like the devil.

"Lauren, he's here," I say.

"Who? Produce god?"

"No!" I elbow her in the ribs. "Trevor."

All the girls lean in. Lauren says, "Where?"

I tell them, "Eleven o'clock. Don't you dare fucking look."

"Too late. He's checking your ass out," Berkeley says.

Britt agrees, "Yeah, is he ever."

"How can he see my ass in this crowd? Wait, is my ass that big?"

"Shut the hell up," Berkeley yells over the noise. "You barely even have an ass."

"Oh, God, I'm not one of those flat-assers, am I?"

"Ugh. Stop!" Berkeley groans. "And no, you're not."

"Oh, crapsickles, here he comes," I say

Trevor is the beach hottie. Kite surfer, tanned, muscular, and the total package kind of guy all the girls want to date. He's also the one who fucked me over about nine months ago. We'd been together for about seven months when I caught him in a drunk moment kissing another girl at a club downtown. I broke up with him, or maybe I should say he broke up with me, as in broke me up. At one time, I thought he might have been *the one*. He professed all kinds of things to me from loving me to us feeling each other's souls, and then *WHAM*! I catch him with his tongue down another girl's throat. Afterwards, he claimed he was out of it, didn't know what had gotten into him, that she came out of nowhere, and he wasn't into her at all, and blah blah endless blah. In his words, it was all one-sided on her part. I called bullshit. If that were the case, why was he deepthroating her with his tongue and why were his arms wrapped around her like ivy? And was he going to do that with every woman he came across when he was drunk? Thanks, but no thanks. I walked away, but about three months later after I'd gotten over him, he started calling me.

The calls were infrequent at first, but then he started doing little things like leaving large Starbuck's lattes and blueberry scones on my porch a couple of mornings a week. And then lunch deliveries started occurring, and not just any lunch. He sends over my favorite salad from one of my favorite restaurants, Cru Café. And the weird thing is it always happens when I'm too busy to grab lunch myself, so I can't help but actually appreciate it. Honestly, he's beginning to put a chink in my armor, and it bothers me.

Lauren and Berkeley both hit my ears at the same time. "Give him a chance," Lauren advises.

Berkeley says, "The word is, he hasn't been with anyone at all since that night."

"How nice. I've heard this from both of you before. I'm not deaf, you know."

"Hey, Sam. Ladies." Trevor flashes his super charming smile.

"Hi Trevor. What's up?" Berkeley asks.

"Same old, you know. Can I get you all a drink?"

"Sure. Vodka soda double lime, for me, please," I say. He gets us all drinks, and we stand smushed up together in the crowded space and chat.

At some point, Lauren gives me the thumbs up. So do the others. Then they fade away into the background. Now my nerves hit. Trevor lifts his drink and we toast. I don't want to be alone with him. I'm not ready for this, because I'm sure he's going to ask me out.

"To a great rest of the weekend," he says.

"I'll drink to that."

"So what've you been doing, Sam? I haven't seen you around the last couple of weeks."

"Yeah, I've been a little busy. A lot of events." I feel like fidgeting, but I manage to keep my cool.

"So, business is good then?"

"Yes, it is. And you?"

"You know, summer is my time so I've been loving it."

"That's great," I say.

"You look really awesome tonight." He smiles. His sun-bleached hair and hazel eyes make a perfect match for his megawatt grin. He certainly is gorgeous. But the trust factor weighs heavily on my mind. I still have that image of him twisted up in that other woman's arms, practically swallowing her tongue. The thought almost makes me gag.

"Thanks," I say, forcing the image out of my head.

I look up to see him staring at me. His eyes zero in on my mouth, like they always do, and it's a little unsettling, so I divert his attention by asking him, "Did you come alone?"

"No, do you know my new roommate, Robert?"

"Don't think so."

"Oh, well, he's here somewhere in this crowd."

Our conversation is a bit stilted, but it could be that it's so jammed in here.

"Hey, can I take you out to dinner Friday?"

He hasn't hidden the fact he wants to get back together, but I haven't hidden the fact that I don't trust him.

"Um, I don't know, Trevor."

"Come on, Sam. It's been almost a year and it's just dinner. You have to eat, right? And people change."

He nudges my shoulder with his own. The teasing tone of his voice and his playful smile has my resolve crumbling. Not to mention I'm such a pushover. Damn it!

"Yeah, I guess. But before I can say it's a for sure thing, I need to check my work calendar at home because sometimes Friday evenings are booked with events. And don't take this any other way than just a meal between friends, okay?"

"Yes, just a meal." He seems sincere.

"Can I text you tomorrow?" I ask.

"Most definitely."

Oddly, as I watch him, a picture of a messy-haired gray-eyed god standing next to a display of honeydews pops into my head. Where the hell did that come from? I give my head a firm shake.

"Sam?" Trevor is clicking his fingers in front of my face. "You with me here?"

"Oh, sorry. I had a momentary brain lapse. It was a really crazy week and I was in the sun all day. You know how that goes."

"Sure. And alcohol isn't helping either, no doubt. Hey, you aren't driving tonight, are you?"

"Oh, heck no. I'm a passenger in the Mitchell's golf cart." I laugh.

"Huh?"

I explain this one. "I'm staying with Lauren at her parents' house here on Sullivan's and we brought their golf cart."

"Oh, right. But still, be careful. They can ticket you even in that thing."

"Yeah, I know. But Mr. Mitchell said they would come and get us if we needed a pick up."

"Lucky you. Oh, to be spoiled by parents like that." He grins.

I make a face and squeak, "I know. And we seriously do not take it for granted."

"That's good."

"So, another round?"

"Sure, and do you mind if we hunt down my friends?"

"Not at all." Trevor buys me another drink but not one for himself. I notice and mention it to him.

"Yeah, I've cut back on the stuff. After what happened when, well, you know, I decided that this," and he holds up his bottle, "had taken the best from me and I wasn't going to let that happen again."

"Oh, well, that's good." But then I have to wonder if he's doing it for show. Again, there's the trust thing.

Berkeley is easy to locate. She's standing right in front of the band, dancing and singing like a groupie. She's throwing off all kinds of signals to the drummer that she'd be a willing partner if he'd give the go ahead. The way he keeps checking her out, I'd say he's interested. I hope she doesn't end up hooking up with him tonight. That could be a little awkward in the morning, trying to explain it to Lauren's mother.

The rest of the gang are scattered. The night wears on and at one point, when I'm coming out of the bathroom, an arm snags me, pulls me around the dimly lit corner and I find myself being kissed. I've no doubt it's Trevor, his lips and mouth still familiar all these months later, but why am I picturing a dark-haired sinfully sexy stranger instead?

"Mmm, that was nice."

"Trevor, that went beyond what I consider just friends."

"I'm sorry. I've been dying to do that forever."

I blow out a frustrated breath.

"I take it I've just blown my hopes of any chance with you," he says.

"To be honest, I don't know what to think. Every time I look at you, an image of you and that girl pops into my head."

"Can't you let that go? I have. That was only a drunk moment. It was nothing."

"But that's just it. It *was* something. To me. And I worry it'll happen again."

He picks up my hands. "It won't. I'll never do anything to risk losing you again."

I shrug. "Let's drop it."

"Will you still consider Friday, then?"

I nod. "I'll text you tomorrow. I'm staying out here, but I'll check as soon as I get home."

"Sounds cool. And thanks, Sam."

I watch as he walks away and any number of women would be drooling and chasing after him. Why not me?

Later that night, Berkeley, who I'm glad came home with us, Britt, Lauren, and I all sit at the counter in the Mitchell's kitchen, eating and drinking. All the girls start quizzing me about Trevor. But the big question is about us going to dinner. When I drop the bomb, they all give me hell.

"What do you mean you don't know if you want to go out with him?" Lauren practically yells.

Sticking my finger over my lips, I say in a very loud whisper, "Hush! You're going to wake your parents!"

"I don't care. You've wanted him to come crawling back, telling you how sorry he was for how long now? And now that he has, you say you're not sure if you even want to go? What the hell, Sam?"

I groan, "That's not exactly true. I've always said I wished he would crawl back and say he lost the best thing ever. I mean, what girl wouldn't after catching her guy kissing another woman? And I've also said I doubted I could trust him again, but that he was starting to get through my wall. It's weird, though because when I was coming out of the bathroom, he kissed me, and nothing."

Berkeley asks, "Whad'ya mean, nothing?"

"I felt nothing at all. It was like kissing the wall. Or my stuffed koala bear."

Lauren answers me. "You don't even have a stuffed koala bear."

"Well, if I did, that's what it would've felt like."

Lauren is quick to reply. "Ugh, you're so damn picky. You

know what? You don't have a jerk magnet. You're just too, oh, I don't know what you are." Her hands fly up in the air.

Berkeley throws an arm around me. It's a good thing I'm sitting or it might have knocked me down. "Hey, leave her alone. If she doesn't like him, she doesn't like him."

I stick out my arm, yelling, "Wait! I didn't say a thing about not liking him. That's not it at all. I don't *trust* him. And now I feel there's zero chemistry. How can you date someone when there's no chemistry?"

"Chemistry shemistry. That's crazy. Chemistry is overrated. That all goes away anyway." Lauren hops to her feet and stands there, looking convinced of her statement.

"Oh, really? When?" I ask.

"When you both have false teeth sitting in dishes on your bedside tables," she says.

"Eww! That's nasty, Lauren! And besides, I brush and floss." This is the first we've heard from Britt. I think she had too many Red Headed Sluts tonight.

"Thanks for that commentary on your dental hygiene, Britt," I say. She stands up and bows. Oh, God, help me. "So, Lauren, what you're saying is that chemistry isn't important. And neither is trust, apparently. I call bullshit on that. How many guys have you dated without either of those?"

"Oh, my. You are getting emotional over this. You even swore and you never swear," Lauren commented.

"Quit trying to distract me. And yes, I do swear, but not very often. I swear all the time in my head, but you know how my mom is. She would always get after us if we so much as got close to saying a bad word, always wanting Laney and me to be proper young ladies. Now answer the question," I demanded.

"A ton. You know what I think? I think your Produce God has your thoughts all skewed."

"Produce God?" Berkeley asks.

"Yes, you know, Whole Foods guy," Lauren explains.

"Oh, right." Berkeley says.

"He has not." I disagree.

"Has too." Lauren argues.

"Whatever," I huff. I notice we haven't heard from Hayley, and when I glance around, it's no surprise to find her asleep on one of the couches. It's probably a good thing because I'm sure Happy

Hayley would side with Trevor too.

Lauren adds, "If he's not important, you should go out with Trevor anyway. If it's not fun, you have a miserable time, or ultimately decide you'll never ever be able to trust him again, then that can be it. Don't see him again. At least you tried. If you don't try, Sam, you might be kicking yourself in the ass. What if Produce God never calls? You don't even know him."

Her point is difficult to argue with.

"Okay. I'll go out with Trevor. Not so much because of what you said. It's more like if I don't go, I'll never hear the end of it."

Lauren jumps out of her seat and yells, "Thank the dating gods, she's seen the light! Now that we have that settled, there's one other thing. Have you made your decision yet?"

I let out a long groan. "Noooo. Did my Mom call you again?"

"Yeah, this morning while I drove out here."

The other girls are quiet.

"Look, I'm not going to say anything other than I wish you'd give it some thought, Sam. Please don't wait too long," she pleads.

"I promise I'm not. I have time."

Lauren offers me a weak smile. "Now Berkeley, tell us all about the guy in the band you practically dry humped on stage. I was worried you'd end up hooking up with him tonight."

I mentally thank her for the segue as everyone's focus shifts to Berkeley. Mine has shifted from Trevor to my looming health issue and then I force it quickly back to the image of the produce dude. I'll be praying to the dating gods he calls me real soon. Because I sure would like to taste a little sample of him. Okay, maybe a big sample.

THREE
BEN

◆

MY PHONE GOES OFF ON SATURDAY morning like there's
a nuclear crisis with texts from Karen. Love me then hate me is the
theme. Warning bells from the sheer number of texts send me
from Whole Foods straight for Home Depot wondering if she's
stolen a key to my house.

When I make it back, I find my father sitting in my living room
watching the U.S. Open, forever the golf fan. I'd forgotten I'd
given him a key. Clearly, I was worried about the wrong person
having one.

"Dad?"

He mutes the TV. "Surprised you're up early. I knocked. You
didn't answer. I figured you might be sleeping somewhere else."

Stories I've heard about Dad from my grandmother suggest he
was a lady killer, so the annoyance in his tone has to be because of
something else he sees I've done wrong. Then again, he always
seems annoyed with me.

"Actually, I made a run to Home Depot." I show him the bag.

"What could you possibly need at this time?"

I hate getting up early in the morning and only do it because
Dad expects it. On the weekends, I try my best to sleep in. But
lately, sleep eludes me.

"You don't want to know." I wave a hand to dismiss this line of
conversation.

"Does it have something to do with that girl showing up at the
house this morning and your mom kicking me out?"

I groan. "Karen?" I wish like hell I'd never introduced her to

25

my parents.

"Yes," he says, holding up his coffee mug in my direction.

My tools are in the garage and that's where I go. I get what I need and make for the door to work on changing the lock.

"You know, I don't think I've had to give you advice about women since you were in high school," he says upon my return.

"You don't have to start now," I mutter, struggling to open the child-proof package everything is sealed in these days.

What Dad thinks won't change how I act. He already rules my career, and the fact that he holds it by my balls doesn't sit well with me. I won't give him power over my dick too. Part of me wants to go back to New York, but even I know that's fruitless. I'm not a big city guy.

"I think it's warranted considering I got kicked out of my own house on a Saturday morning because your mom feels sorry for this girl."

My glare does nothing to stop him from giving me a piece of his mind.

"Don't bring home just a piece of ass to meet your mother." I open my mouth, but his words fill the space before I can. "You're a grown man. I can't punish you like I did when you were a kid. But fair is fair. Every woman you bring home, your mother sees as a possible wife. Keep that in mind because I'm the one who has to deal with the fallout. She's going to give me hell as it is. And I know what's she's going to suggest. Monday night we have a business dinner with potential clients. Your attendance is required. Your mom is going to come as our clients need to know we have the same values. You need to bring a date to keep the balance. And I'm sure your mother would love for you to bring Karen."

I don't bother answering. I finish changing the lock and head to my bedroom where I toss clean clothes in a bag. With gym clothes on, I head back to the living room. I hand my father one of the keys that came in the set continuing to ignore his suggestion about Karen.

"Lock the door when you leave."

At the gym, I punch the heavy bag until my knuckles are bruised and sore despite being taped up. With the aggression I feel, I could kill a man. So I use my time to burn that off. The shower runs hot and when I step out of the locker room, one of my former drunken moments stands there with hands across tits that look great under her shirt. Too bad they feel as fake as they are.

"Ben," she announces my name as if it were a curse.

"Britney," I drawl.

Seeing her makes my dick shrivel. She likes it rough in the sack. And when I say rough, I mean clawing and fighting like wrestling a dude. I should have picked up on the signs. Guys snickered when I agreed to take her out. She'd bragged she could outdrink me and all my frat buddies. I'd taken the bait and lost.

"Don't 'Britney' me. You don't call, text, or fucking acknowledge my presence."

Because I want to forget I ever fucked you. I shrug, keeping my words to myself.

She points a finger in my direction and it fucking sucks to know I'm about to get bitch-slapped and can't do shit about it. The girl can outbench half the guys here, but if I lay a finger on her, I'm an abuser.

"Hey," comes from my beautiful savior. "Are you ready for lunch?"

Jackie, a friend who refuses to date any guy at the gym, sidles up to me, taking my arm. She smoothly diffuses the situation.

"Yeah, let's go."

Jackie's hot. And her tits are nice, even if on the smaller side. She's not who I normally go for, but maybe she's my answer for tomorrow night.

When we get to her car, I take a chance.

"What are you doing tomorrow night?"

She grins at me in that *we're just friends* kind of way.

"You are too smooth for words."

"Then agree to go out with me. You'll be doing me a huge favor."

Before I can explain, she shakes her head. "I'm dating someone now."

I sigh, because having her on my arm on Monday could totally make the evening go far better. I feign shock. "Who is this guy? I have to beat his ass."

She laughs and I can see why guys go for her other than the fact that she's the only holdout from the gym bunnies.

"Yeah, right. Even if I weren't, I so wouldn't go out with you."

Now my shock is real. I'm not conceited, but I don't typically have trouble getting a girl to go out with me.

"You are super cute." I arch a brow, waiting to hear what she says next. "Okay, too cute. And that's why I could never go there. You would completely break my heart. But thanks for asking. You've totally given my ego a boost."

"And now your boyfriend will reap the rewards."

She grins and gets in her car. I watch her pull out before heading to my own. My thoughts switch to the woman I met in the produce section of all places. I'd asked her out for Monday night, not wanting to wait to see her. But I can't take her to a business meeting.

I glance back at the gym. There are a couple of girls there I've hooked up with a few times. They are options, but then again, I don't want to go there. Britney stands in front of the picture window glaring at me. I decide it's time to put in a home gym and let my membership lapse.

Jenna's place isn't far and I head straight there. A sleepy Cate answers the door in flannel pajamas as if it were winter.

"Sexy, Cate," I whisper in her ear as I give her a bear hug. She playfully slaps at my shoulder, so I decide to make her laugh because I know she needs it. "Marry me, Cate, in your minion PJs."

She laughs and it's so good to hear. Jenna's been in my ear about how Cate isn't fairing as well as Drew wanted.

"I can't marry you." I couldn't marry her either. "You're like my brother." Too true, still, I can't help but tease her.

"Oh, I don't know. It could be like Blue Lagoon."

It's the story of two kids marooned on an island and with no one else to fulfill their growing hormones, they eventually turn to one another. For a boy who hadn't seen a naked girl when Drew and I snuck and watched it, we laughed until we were mesmerized by a young and bare-chested Brooke Shields.

She stares at me and I realize she has no idea of the movie I'm talking about. I shouldn't be surprised. The movie is older than us both. My dad had an old VHS player and that was one of the movies there for the watching.

Drew and I eventually watched it again for old times' sake late one night after Cate had fallen asleep and we were both higher than the sky. He'd died a few short days later. The memory shakes me. I pull back from Cate all of a sudden, overcome by Drew's loss again. I see him in that fucking hospital bed near death worrying about everyone but himself. I scrub my face hoping she can't see the wetness from the burn I feel in the back of my eyes.

"Are you okay?"

"Yeah," I say. "Is Jenna around?"

It's a weak attempt to change the subject. Cate isn't buying it. She shakes her head slowly and the room fills with pain and loss.

"Maybe I should go."

She grabs my arm. "No, please."

In her eyes, my grief shines back at me. Then she has me in a bear hug. "It's okay, Ben. I miss him too."

I pull her in trying to hold back the emotion. I miss the fucker like I'd miss both of my kidneys.

We stand there for a period of time that doesn't seem to matter. How can it when we both can't move past the loss? Finally, she steps back and with a soft touch, wipes the tears I hadn't known left my eyes. We don't talk. We find that quiet place between us no one else can possibly understand. She gives me a tight smile and steps into the kitchen. Food. It's what we did a lot of in the end. Mostly, we ate trying to encourage Drew to do so as he wasted away while the cancer slowly ravaged his body.

She fixes us lunch and we sit huddled together watching TV. I hold her hand and she leans into me. And I wonder if Drew is watching us shaking his head. He would so disapprove because we aren't doing what he wanted, and that was to live.

Silently, she turns her head up until I meet her eyes. I can tell she's pondering a question.

"Go ahead and spit it out."

She blushes and I have a feeling what she wants to talk about.

"Jenna tells me you broke up with Karen. I haven't gotten all the details yet."

I roll my eyes begging for patience I don't have. "We were never together."

Cate gets me, unlike my sister. She doesn't press. "Okay, fine. Are you ever going to give someone a chance? Drew would want that."

She has no idea what she's asking. I tried my hand at love twice and failed both times. There is no way I'm doing that again.

Instead, I toss the question back to her. "I could say the same."

"I'm not ready." It's a mantra I've heard from her a thousand times. "I know about the girl from college, although Drew never told me the details."

I close my eyes remembering. The stab in my chest still feels fresh, and I have to squash this idea she has that I'll ever get some sort of fairytale ending.

"That girl shouldn't have happened." That's an understatement. The humiliation I suffered in high school hadn't been lesson enough. "I let my guard down, you know." She had been a stunner, like fresh-off-the-farm beautiful and innocent. "I should have been smarter than to let someone in. But she wouldn't go for my fuck-a-friend rules." I suck in air because I need it for the bullshit part of my life I'm sharing.

"Drew."

I shake my head because Cate knows firsthand what I'm about to say. "He never believed love was synonymous with fucking and convinced me to give it a shot. I liked her more than most I'd been with at the time. I took a chance and followed Drew's playbook."

I grind my teeth together remembering what a fool I'd been. Even after all these years, it still punches at my heart.

"Eventually, she said she loved me and let me ..." I wave a hand.

"Take her virginity."

"God, I love you, Cate."

She grins because even though she is my best friend, it's hard to talk about some of that shit with a woman.

"But yeah. Anyway, we were together for the rest of the semester. I thought I could see myself with this girl in a forever sense. Not right away or anything, but I could picture the white picket fence off in the future."

I swallow. This is the hard part. "A couple weeks after winter break, she wanted to talk, but all she did was cry. I didn't know what to do. The tears shit."

The embarrassment of being dumped burns like a dagger in my chest, even with Cate who knows just about everything about me. I pause, bracing myself to force the next words out.

"She eventually told me she was pregnant." I remember the fear I felt when the words first left her lips. "Despite being scared shitless, I was ready to do the chivalrous thing and walk her down the aisle if I had to. When I told her so, the sad smile she gave me only confused me until she enlightened me of something very important."

I didn't know I'd stopped talking until Cate spoke up.

"What did she say?"

My tongue feels thick. But I finish the story. "She reminded me that I couldn't be the father because we'd always used protection, even though that's not foolproof. It was her way of telling me she'd hooked up with someone else." All my lame moves to be different and better sent her into the hands of another dude, smashing my heart in the process. It had been proof enough that women didn't want the nice guy. "And now you know the rest of my pathetic past."

"Oh Benny. That's terrible."

"It is what it is. And that love shit isn't for me."

She wraps her arms around me, right when Jenna walks in. She gives both of us a harsh glare. A lecture is surely nanoseconds behind.

"What am I going to do with the both of you? Someone has to be the voice of reason. This is not how you honor Drew. He's probably rolling over in his grave. Snap out of it. He wouldn't want this for either of you."

Cate and I look at each other, but don't say a thing.

No one understands Jenna's words better than me, but it doesn't close the open space in my chest that I can't seem to fill.

"You," she points at Cate, "need to take Louise out of hibernation and get with Dr. Mercer."

I try not to react having met the good doctor that Cate says is just a friend.

"Who's Louise? I know Mercer's a good guy, but why do you want to fix him up with this Louise?"

Jenna looks at Cate and they both bust out laughing. Cate doubles over and Jenna snorts.

"What the hell is so funny?" I ask.

Jenna answers, still half-snorting. "Never mind about Louise. But you," gone is the laughter in an instant as her gaze pinpoints me, "need to keep it in your pants. I'm tired of every time women realize I'm your sister they give me that *Your brother is a jackass* comment."

"Would you rather it be like back when I used to come home from college and all the girls would talk about how dreamy I was?" I smirk.

"Dreamy, skeevy." She shudders while shaking her head.

"That doesn't rhyme," I add.

31

"Doesn't matter. Thinking about you and all your shenanigans creeps me out. You can't imagine the earful I got from Karen."

Cate perks up. "Oh, do tell."

"You wouldn't believe." Jenna tells her a story that could only come from Karen's deluded ideas about us. I listen as she leaves out the cancer part which only makes me sound like a bigger ass. However, I allow my sister to make jokes at my expense because it makes Cate laugh. And I feel like I'm doing right by Drew when she smiles.

"The Money Man is a Man Whore. Ben, you really need to settle down," Cate says, patting my arm.

Jenna, on the Ben's-a-bad-boy train, continues on. "Maybe we should shorten that to Money Man Whore. It's got a ring to it."

The girls continue on in a fit of laughter.

By the time I get home, Dad's gone. I pour myself a drink while glancing at my phone, considering making a call so I can lose myself in pussy. But as I scroll, Samantha's name glares at me.

My finger hovers over the screen. I have a way with words, or so I've been told. I could possibly get her over to my house. Who knows, I could even get her out of her clothes and see what she's rocking underneath, which is exactly what I need.

But there is something about her. And it's clear she isn't one-night stand material. That should scare me off, especially since I just pissed off Karen enough that she thought she was the one leaving me.

Fuck, I mutter, mentally swiping left over the pictures of the women I could call. Only Samantha's face continues to pop in my head and my dick jerks. *Fuck me*.

I pour myself another three fingers. It's Saturday night and I can't remember the last time I spent one alone. Normally, I would be balls deep in a willing woman. Instead, I'm suddenly not interested in any pussy that doesn't have Samantha's name on it, which feels like some middle school shit.

By the next day, I decide I need to get her out of my head. I have my regular Sunday dinner plans later with the family, but I have nothing going on until then. And I find myself pulling out my phone hoping I'm not making a mistake.

When she answers, my dick leaps to life.

"Hey Samantha, it's Ben."

"Oh, hey, Ben. How are you?"

I want to ride you like a bull doesn't seem like the perfect response.

"I wondered what you were doing for lunch?"

She's quiet and I hope to hell she doesn't tell me she's got plans with some other guy.

"Um—"

"I'm headed to Husk and maybe you'll have pity on me and not let me eat alone. I know we said tomorrow night, but why wait?"

The well-known restaurant is centrally located downtown in a historic building. Her pause is long and I feel thirteen again, desperate to see a girl. Monday is a bust since I was going to break our date, and besides, I want to see her sooner.

"Sure, that sounds great. When should I meet you?"

"Is one o'clock good? I can pick you up if you like."

"No, it's not far from me. I can meet you."

"Great, I'll see you there."

After I hang up the phone, I realize something about this woman throws me off my game. I want her in my bed, yes. But she's different. I have a feeling my winning smile and usual lines won't work with her.

I find myself at a shop literally smelling the roses and have no idea what possessed me to come here. I've only ever bought flowers for my mother except when I was in high school and thought I was in love with a girl who led me around by my balls. After that failed relationship, I learned not to be a pussy if I wanted pussy. That girl chose a fucktard over me, some guy who treated her like dirt. That was my first lesson I needed in Nice Guys Always Lose. Case in point as my phone buzzes again with another incoming text from Karen. I hit ignore when a sales clerk comes over.

"Can I help you?"

I explain my dilemma to the cute woman who makes sure I get a view of her cleavage. I have to give it to her for figuring out my weakness. Too bad the only tits I have on my brain belong to Samantha. Eventually, I walk out empty-handed. The flirty clerk said that most girls would be put off by flowers on a first date. My head circles back to girls wanting a jackass over a good guy. And the sales woman has just confirmed it.

My wait isn't long before Samantha walks up prettier than a picture and I have to swallow. There is just something about her. She's blissfully unaware that every guy she passes, young or old, checks her out. I want to tie her to my bedpost and have my way with her. But I hesitate because she carries herself like a lady. All of a sudden, I have this urge to open doors for her and drape my coat over a puddle so she doesn't have to step in it. And what the hell? Am I pussy whipped before I even dip my stick in her?

"Ben," she says, as a beautiful blossom of roses covers her cheeks.

I'll be damned. I should walk away right now because I'm not that guy who deserves a woman like her.

"Samantha," I say, taking her hand and needing a reason for touching her. I kiss her delicate knuckles enjoying her subtle scent.

"Aren't you the picture of charm? Hmm, that makes two times you've kissed my hand."

"I try," I say, not letting go of her as we walk inside.

I give the hostess my name and we are led into a narrow dining room to a table for four. The extra place settings are removed while I hold out Samantha's chair. My mother would kill me if I didn't use etiquette at all times.

I sit by the window and stare too long at the vision before me.

"What?" she asks shyly.

Images of her naked on my bed play through my mind like a video on repeat.

"I wonder if the food is safe with you here," I say instead.

She laughs and her whole face lights up. But it's her mouth I zero in on. Her lips are a perfect shade of pink only hinting that she wears makeup. I want to kiss that mouth before I fuck it. An image of her on her knees with my hands all in her hair headlines in my brain.

"You're never going to let me live that down are you?"

I shrug. "Maybe you can convince me you can keep your hands to yourself."

And isn't that a dumb remark? I most definitely want her hands on me.

The waiter comes and we order. I'm surprised by her choices because they mirror my own.

"Maybe one of us should take a chance and order the snapper. That way we can share."

She shakes her head slowly. "I don't share."

And something about the way she says it makes my pants get tight.

"Okay then. Tell me about yourself?" I ask.

"Nothing terribly exciting. I'm an event planner. I started my business when I graduated two years ago and things are good. In fact, I should be down at the Yacht Club getting set up for tomorrow's event."

I'm shocked that for someone not long out of college, she seems to know where she wants to go in life and is doing something about it. It makes me more intrigued than I should be for a casual hook-up.

"Oh. Now I feel bad for taking you away from your business." Good to know her hesitation to accept lunch hadn't been because she wasn't sure about going out with me.

"It's okay. I'll stop over after. What about you?"

I want to know more about her, but give in to her question. "I'm an investment broker, glorified financial planner."

She laughs, which is another win. "Interesting."

"It's more interesting we have a lot in common."

"How so?"

"Well, we both have to do our best to please people in a short period of time and we only have one shot at it," I say.

"True."

"In the spirit of full disclosure, I should mention I'm a little older than you." Her brow lifts. "I left my twenties a year ago. I hope that's not a problem."

"No," she says with a grin and a slight shake of her head. "I'm twenty-four. I hope that's not a problem for you." She smiles.

"Not at all."

Our first course arrives and conversation halts as we eat. I can't help but stare as she puts food in her mouth, making it impossible for a napkin to hide my erection.

"Tell me more about your business," I say in an effort to relieve the pressure in my pants.

Between courses, she tells me all about the impossible older woman in her eighties putting on a tea for her surviving friends.

"I never do social events, only corporate. But she's a friend of my grandmother's, so I couldn't turn her down. On a Monday, she wants. She didn't want the weekend because she and her pals usually have extended family that come around for dutiful visits."

"Sounds like my grandmother. She's a Southern belle through and through."

Conversation is easy and somehow my thoughts clear of her in my bed and I find myself wanting to know more about this woman.

When we walk out a long time later, I'm reluctant to let her go.

"I know you didn't want dessert, but maybe we can go for coffee."

"Oh, Ben, your offer is tempting. But something tells me if I accept, I'll be doing the walk of shame in the morning. Besides, I have work to do."

"Shame?" I feign offense. "Trust me there is nothing to be ashamed of when leaving my bed."

She slowly shakes her head. "No way, Ben Rhoades. I'm not that kind of girl."

I bring her hand to my mouth and kiss her sweet knuckles goodbye. "That's too bad. But maybe you'll pay me a visit there one of these days." I wink unable to help myself.

Her flush makes my balls draw up tight ready to explode. I let go of her hand because I need mine to place it in front of my raging hard on.

"Tomorrow, then?"

"Shit," I mutter. Her pretty face sours. "No, there's nothing wrong. I just completely forgot. I have a dinner thing tomorrow for work."

"Oh," she says and I can see she's as disappointed as I am.

"It's sort of embarrassing, but I need a date. It's not what I had in mind when I asked you out, and it's probably more than a little weird. But I was given very short notice. And I can't imagine anyone else I'd rather have as a companion for the night."

FOUR
Sam

THERE'S SOMETHING ABOUT HIM WITH that damn hair that I want to run my hands through. He stands there looking sheepish as he tells me about tomorrow. It is kind of weird.

"Hmm. A business dinner, huh?"

"Yeah. I'm really sorry. I didn't find out about it until a little while ago when I spoke with my father, who happens to be my boss."

Lauren's mom did mention that he worked with his dad. Good to know she had been thinking of the same Rhoades.

"Will this be one of those stuffy, formal things?"

The corner of his mouth curls. "Probably. But I can make it worth your while. I promise if you go, I will find some way to make it up to you." His eyes quickly sweep over me and I know his promise has more to do with his sheets than anything else. "You name it, and I'll do it. And I'll guarantee you will love it and beg for more."

The way he says those words makes my belly flop. I'm talking take a running jump off the diving board and hit the pool kind of flop. I think back to Trevor momentarily and he didn't even make my toes get close to the edge of pool. "That sounds kind of risqué."

Ben takes a step closer to me. "Samantha, it was meant to sound risqué."

My eyes widen and I swallow the knot of desire that's formed in my throat. "Um, o-okay. I'll go." My voice shakes as I answer.

He leans in and says, "You won't be sorry. I promise."

His fresh, clean scent that reminds me of the beach fans over me. When he straightens, I want to grab him and bring him back closer to me again. He's stepped out of my personal space, and I inhale, trying to get another whiff of him.

"I'll hold you to that promise, Ben Rhoades."

He awards me with a smile.

"Oh, and I assume the attire is business?"

"Yes, that would be correct." He takes my hand again and kisses it. "Until tomorrow. I can pick you up at seven."

"Perfect. I'll text you my address."

"Until then, Samantha."

I head for home only a few blocks away. When I get there, Lauren is waiting.

"Well, how was it?" She practically pants like a dog.

I offer her a secretive grin. "It was nice. Very nice. He's the ultimate gentleman and every bit as sexy as he was in the produce section. It's good to know I didn't have this image built up in my mind, only to be blown to pieces by some douchebag idiot, you know?"

"Yeah, but tell me more. What did y'all talk about?"

"The basics. It was only our first get together. A little about work and stuff. That's it. He's so sweet, though."

"Hmm. Are you going to see him again?"

"Yep. Tomorrow. Like we originally planned."

Her tone conveys shock. "Really?"

"Yeah. Why?"

"That's a lot for just meeting someone."

I shrug. "Not if you like him. At least in my opinion."

"You're giving in too easily."

I plop down on the couch. "What's that supposed to mean?"

"You need to make him chase you. That's what."

"I'm not going to play that game crap, Lauren. If I like him and he likes me, and we want to see each other, then we'll see each other."

She groans. "This is why I want to shake you all the time. You never learn. Guys don't want a girl who gives in so easily."

I lean my head back and close my eyes. "Then fine. If he doesn't want me the way I am, then he won't want me. I am not good at this game stuff, and I won't play them."

Her arms wind around me as she hugs me. "Okay, but never

fear. I'll be here when you need me. And obviously I'm saying things you don't want to hear, so don't hate me."

"I don't hate you, you big goon. It's just that I need to do things my way, you know?"

"I know."

"I gotta run to the Yacht Club. I have an event tomorrow and I need to check on some things. I won't be long."

Monday is hectic at work, and by the end of the day, I'm wiped and having second thoughts about agreeing to my dinner with Ben. When I check the clock, I realize I only have forty-five minutes to get home and change. Luckily I only have a five-minute drive home.

I dress casually for work, so when I get home I take a quick shower and change into a black pencil skirt, royal blue sleeveless silk blouse, and black pumps. As an afterthought, I grab a light sweater as Ben arrives, just in case the restaurant's air conditioning has me freezing during dinner.

"You look the picture of the high-profile corporate events planner," he says.

"Thank you, I think. And you're not so bad yourself." He wears the traditional dark suit, crisp white shirt, and I have to laugh when I notice his royal blue tie. "Looks like we did some matchy matching."

He doesn't get it at first until he realizes what I'm talking about. "Oh, Dad will love this." Then he laughs as he opens the car door for me. It's a two-door sporty Jaguar the color of granite with buttery leather interior. I'm happy he didn't let me climb in unassisted—Ben Rhoades has manners. We drive to the restaurant, and he displays every gentlemanly characteristic while I make sure to check each of them off my list. Helps me in and out of the car, escorts me by taking my arm, walks on the outside of the sidewalk, opens all doors, and stands until the host seats me at the table.

A stately couple stands and eyes Ben then each other. I get the feeling they had no idea Ben would be bringing me.

"Mom, Dad, this is Samantha Calhoun," he announces, giving his dad a handshake and kissing his mother on her cheek. He says something to her I can't hear.

His parents, holy shit, he didn't mention I would be meeting his parents. *Don't think too much of this. It's not like we've been dating and he wants me to meet them. This is business.*

When he introduces me to them, I realize his father has the same name as he does. Ben explains with a wink that his dad goes by his middle name, Martin. That answers one question.

"Samantha Calhoun? Are your parents Randy and Michelle?" his mother, Julia, asks.

"Yes. Do you know them?"

"We do. From the country club." His mother's smile is warm and genuine.

"Oh. Do you golf?" I'm curious to know if she ever golfs with my mom.

"Sadly, no. Do you?" she asks.

I screw up my face. "Not even a bit. I gave it a shot and the best I could do was hit the tee further than the ball."

That gets a laugh out of everyone at the table. We chat for a few minutes and just as I've told them about my work, their clients show up.

Julia leans to me and says drily, "Here comes the fun stuff." I hold back my chuckle.

"You must be Karen," the woman says.

I stare blankly, unsure what to say. Thankfully, Ben steps in.

"No, Mrs. Sadler, this is Samantha, my date for the evening. She graciously agreed to accompany me tonight."

Ben is smooth as he's easily taken the awkwardness out of the woman's misstatement.

"Why don't we order?" Ben's dad says.

We take our seats and I study the menu wondering who Karen is.

Mrs. Sadler leans over from her seat next to me. "I'm sorry. I thought Julia said Ben's fiancée's name was Karen.

My jaw drops, but thankfully the waiter shows up. Ben reaches over and squeezes my hand under the table while I ponder the million and one questions that have popped in my mind.

The Sadler's are interested in converting their investments over to Ben's firm. I listen with half an ear because this is the type of thing I hand over to my dad and say, *Here. Take a look at this for me, please.* I can only hope our solo dinner discussions don't involve this stuff because so far, I've counted six yawns that I've had to swallow.

We finally get to dessert and I think my face almost falls into my turtle cheesecake when Martin asks if anyone wants coffee.

Thankfully, everyone declines. Then I feel a hand on my leg and I jerk to attention, only to see Ben shaking with barely contained laughter. God, did I almost fall asleep? How embarrassing is this?

Mrs. Sadler hasn't given up. "Julia tells me you're a lawyer."

"No, Karen's a lawyer. Samantha here is an event planner," Julia corrects.

Ben's mom didn't sound condescending when she said it. So why do I feel so small?

"That's exciting," Mrs. Sadler says.

I glance over at Ben who looks ready to cut in, but I decide I can hold my own.

"It is actually. There is a certain thrill in seeing the excitement and happy faces when people enter a space I've prepared. And my company is thriving," I'm compelled to say.

"I happen to find lawyers boring. Samantha is anything but," Ben adds.

I blush because the way Ben looks at me sends a wave of lust washing over me. He has no idea if I'm boring or not, but I give him points for the save.

Soon, we're all saying our good-byes, and Julia tells me she hopes to see me again. Is that a message for Ben? I'm not sure, but it sounds as though there's an undercurrent to her words. Maybe it's my exhaustion.

Ben leans over and whispers to me, "Will you excuse me for a minute? I need to have a word with my mother before we leave."

"Sure." I watch him usher his mother aside, and realize what he's going to do. I don't have to hear him to know that angry words spill from his mouth. It's obvious from the way his finger jabs the air and his mouth is punctuated by a scowl. Julia's head bobs and then her eyes droop in what I imagine to be remorse. Ben turns away, his lips pressed into a thin line.

When he reaches me, I ask, "Is everything okay?"

"It will be. Are you ready to go?"

"Whenever you are."

We walk to his car, holding hands. "I'm sorry about the Karen thing. I had a chat with my mom about it." He blows out a breath.

I nod. "It's fine. Who is she by the way?"

He looks uncomfortable, so I know there's a story there.

"She's someone I made the bad choice of introducing to my mother. And Mom thought she would be planning a wedding."

"Oh."

I want to ask more, but decide against it.

"I can't thank you enough for this. I owe you. Huge. And I noticed that investments really pique your interest."

"Oh, you did, huh?"

"Yeah. The little head bob you did was the dead giveaway." His deep laugh makes me shiver.

"Jeez, I'm so sorry." I shake my head in embarrassment.

"Hey, I'm the one who's sorry for making you sit through that. But you were awesome. And don't worry. Mrs. Sadler let out a snore or two," he says with a chuckle.

A gurgle of laugher bubbles out of me. "She did not."

"Oh, I'm pretty sure she did. She was just as into it as you were. Thank you for not snoring."

When we arrive at my place, he opens my door, and helps me out. As we walk to my front door, he asks, "So, I hope this dinner didn't scare you off any future dates with me."

"Well, now that you mention it…"

His brows hit his hairline and I can't hold my serious expression any longer.

"I'm only kidding."

"Thank God." He exaggerates relief. "How about dinner on Friday, then?"

Ugh. Friday! I'm supposed to go out with Trevor. Damn it!

"I can't do Friday, but Saturday works."

His lips purse. "You are the busy one, aren't you?"

I add with a smirk, "I won't deny it."

Suddenly he pulls me into his arms and says, "Thank you for tonight. I owe you and I always pay my debts, Samantha." Then he kisses my cheek and as if he can sense my disappointment his lips land on mine. They are the perfect mix of firm and gentle, and just when I think he's going to push through the seam and deepen the kiss, he does the exact opposite. He releases me, steps back, and says, "Sweet dreams. I'll call you during the week." I watch as he walks back to the car, greatly disappointed that's all he left me with.

FIVE
BEN

---◆---

KISSING SAMANTHA SHOULD HAVE BEEN a prelude to asking her to come home with me. Thanks to Mom and the Sadlers, I couldn't ask without looking like a complete douche. They'd brought up Karen. And Mom and I will have another talk later about boundaries and sharing her wedding dreams with potential clients.

The four walls close in on me as I realize I can't call Drew and complain about my parents. I can't tell him about the woman I met that could be what Cate was to him. That thought stops me. No fucking way. I don't want a woman in that way. I like my space. Still, shucking off thoughts of Drew, I'm left with images of Samantha. I end up jerking one off in the shower as visions of soft curves and honey brown waves that fall halfway down her back flood my mind. She has one hell of a rack too. When I'd pulled her in for a kiss, they pressed against my chest waking my cock to life.

The next several days at work are brutal. One of the admins has a vicious cough that scares the shit out of me. It's June and there is no reason for her to have a cold.

"You should get that checked out," I complain.

"It's just allergies. I swear they get worse every year."

She coughs again and I hear something rattle in her chest. I stand. "I'm ordering you to take the rest of the day off. Go see your doctor. Better safe than sorry."

My growling tone sends her out of my tiny office with wide eyes. *Fuck, it's just allergies like she said, not lung cancer, you douche.*

43

Jeff comes in my open door and I wished I'd closed it.

"What the hell did you say to her?"

He's not my boss. "She's sick spewing all her germs all over the office. She needs to go home. I can't afford to get sick."

That last part is true. The rest I said to save face. Jeff leaves shaking his head and I get back to work. The Sadlers want a five-year plan of how we can invest their money to get them the greatest return. The husband is more conservative than the wife. She, however, is the one with the family money. We are competing with one of the big nationwide firms. I have to prove that going local and having a relationship is better than calling and talking to a nameless person anytime they need to discuss their accounts.

"How's it going?"

My sleeves are rolled up because I've been at it all day. I glance up from my desk and see Dad in my doorway.

"Good. I think I have the right mix," I say confidently.

"Can you present it to me in the conference room?"

I nod. "Give me five."

An hour later, I leave with my father's approval. Jeff and Mark are waiting for me in my office.

"You look like you need a drink," Jeff says.

"Or get laid? What happened to Karen?" Mark asks.

I grab my jacket. "Let's get a drink." I avoid the Karen question.

Somehow she'd wormed her way into my life and acted like a girlfriend. How had I let that happen?

"You guys going out?"

We turn and find several of our female co-workers standing around. Jeff is quick to answer. "Yeah, sure."

We walk to a bar not too far from the office. Jeff is not very discriminating and spends most of his time hitting on anything that moves. His taste is female; shape and size don't matter.

"I think I'm going to head home." I've had several drinks and although I'm not drunk, I do feel a slight buzz.

"Wait, Lisa is into you, man. I'm telling you she's a sure thing."

Lisa is cute and the one who asked to come along. "I don't screw women I work with." I'm firm on that. The last thing I need is for some female to be pissed and be able to show me her displeasure every day.

I wave everyone goodbye and see Lisa poke her lip out. My dick needs service, but I'm not that desperate.

When I make it home, I have a visitor waiting.

"Karen," I say.

"Ben. I think I left my earrings here."

I sigh, not wanting to be a prick. "Okay."

She doesn't bring up the hundred and one text messages she's sent over the past week and neither do I. I unlock the door and almost put my keys in the bowl when I shove them in my pocket instead.

"Where do you think you left them?"

When I turn around, I find her naked from the waist up, dangling her top from her finger. There is no time to react before she's on me.

"Ben, we are so good together."

As much as I don't want Karen, my body reacts remembering what it was like to be inside her. The alcohol flowing in my veins convinces me it wasn't all bad when we were together. And I haven't gotten laid in what amounts to a long time for me, which explains why I'm succumbing to her come on.

"Karen—"

Her lips are on mine and her hand grips my cock through my pants. I groan, because that's all it takes to go from zero to a hard on.

Samantha's face flashes in my head for a second, which only adds fuel to my sex-starved dick. But I hardly know her and she doesn't seem like she's going to let me touch her any time soon. So what the hell? And if I make Karen leave, I'll be forced to remember how lonely this house feels sometimes. And I don't want that. I need the distraction. I need to forget if only for this night. The alcohol and Karen win.

I wake the next morning with a warm body at my back and regret sucker punching my gut. Fuck. Why the hell did I do that?

"Hey, you need to go."

"Huh?" Karen murmurs.

"I've got to get to work and you need to leave."

"But—"

"You came here for a fuck and you got one. Now it's time for you to go. And do me a favor – stop texting me. And stop running to my mom and crying on her shoulder. This isn't her business."

Her mouth drops. "You—"

I shake my head. "When I get out of the shower, I want you gone."

My pants are on the floor and I scoop them up. My keys are still inside and I hope like hell she isn't the crazy type to carry a bar of soap or some modeling clay in her purse to make a mold of them, but I'm not taking any chances.

Thankfully, she takes the hint. She's gone when I get out, which is good because that whole sexcapade has left a sour taste in my mouth. I should have left Karen a long time ago. Or not gotten involved with her in the first place. And I know better than to mess with Samantha. She's a good girl, not the kind that needs a fuckup like me. I should walk away from her and leave her unmolested. But just thinking her name stirs my dick to life as if I hadn't screwed Karen the night before.

Too bad I don't own a crystal ball. If I did, I might have skipped the rest of the week, which sucked ass. To top it off, today is a day from fucking hell. My head throbs migraine style from what I did with Karen. You would think she would have given up by now, but she hasn't. My phone lights up like lightning strikes from all of her texts. And Dad has been all over my ass, trying to get the Sadler account locked up. I've worked like a fiend, not even stopping for lunch. Undoubtedly, that only adds to the cleaving sensation in my head.

Late that night, when I finally get ready to leave the office I recall that the firm has committed to playing in one of those fund-raising golf tournaments on Thursday. Normally, I am all in for these. But the way I'm feeling and my burgeoning workload, I'd rather crawl in a cave and avoid contact with anyone. But that isn't in the cards. So the next day, I find myself at the golf course, bright and early with my plastic happy smile fastened on my face. Dad loves these things for entertaining and increasing awareness of our firm. I'm normally for it too—except for today.

When I finish registering, I look up and wouldn't you know it, my eyes land on a perfect set of tanned legs that go on for days. Samantha stands in a pair of white shorts that meet a plain golf shirt with what is probably her company's logo emblazoned on her chest. What I wouldn't do to be that logo. Damn, she looks good enough to eat. Thankfully, she hasn't seen me yet, so like a stalker I watch her work. It isn't long before a couple of other girls with the same visors on stride over to her. They must be her employees as she shows them something on her clipboard. Moments later, they hop in separate golf carts and drive off, leaving her alone.

There are several things I could do, like go over and talk to her. Instead, I watch as a man approaches her. I know the asshole. He's the fly that buzzes around honey when he finds it. This time he's got the wrong woman. I shake my head as the smooth talking lawyer whose reputation with women is worse than my own moves into her space. I wonder what she would do if I intervened on her behalf and saved her from a guy who would only want to add her to his stats. Shit, what the hell is wrong with me? I have no right to her. So reluctantly, I turn away to grab my golf bag and roughly cram it on the cart.

"Easy with that, dude. What are you trying to do? Wreck your bag or something?" Jeff's comments break through my angry thoughts.

I let go of it and glance up.

"I don't know. Guess I'm not really into this today." My eyes betray me and find my target like a heat seeking missile. Several other lechers approach Samantha. Irrationally, I have a quick notion to go over like a dog and piss on her so they would stay the hell away from her. It's as if they sense her sweetness, and like fucking ants, they're crawling all over her.

"...and I think we can be in the money. So you in?"

"Huh?" I've barely heard Jeff because I haven't stopped staring long enough to focus on anything coming out of his mouth.

"What the hell, man? I just gave you my entire strategy on how we can win some change today in this thing. Are you hung over or something?"

Finally, I give up on staring because she hasn't once turned in my direction, and I face him.

"Or something."

He raises a finger in the air like he's figured it out. I wait for it.

"Oh, I get it. Knocked you off a piece last night, did ya?"

Jeff is clueless. Drew would have called me out by now.

"Something like that," I say drolly before checking out the peanut gallery waiting for a chance at Samantha.

"She's hot. But don't bother. She's colder than dry ice."

Suddenly, he has my full attention.

"What the hell does that mean?"

He holds up his hands. "Dude, she's like everywhere and she

shoots guys down faster than a gunslinger."

I glance over at her and it doesn't look like she's shooting anyone down.

"You look like you could use a drink. Let's go get you a beer. I could use one myself. I hope they have my favorite IPA," Jeff suggests. His eyes trail over to the drink cart girl and it all makes sense. Even though it's the last thing I want, I've dug myself in a hole so I don't have much choice. We walk over and I watch Jeff in action as he tries his best to get the phone number from the girl manning the cart who looks barely legal. After I get a drink in my hand, I stew while finishing it off. I have to admit, I actually feel a little calmer.

"So, we probably should head out. You ready?" he asks.

I check my sheet and say, "Yeah, let's roll."

We load up in the cart and make our way to the first hole. The course is covered in people and well stocked with refreshments every third or fourth hole. By the time we get to the tee, I'm ready to swing. Everything's going great until we get to hole number five. That's where I spot her again. One of the golfers is blatantly flirting with her, and she's doing nothing to stop it. I stand with clenched fists and want to throw my driver at the two of them. Or better yet, I'd like to use his head as my golf ball. *Jesus, calm down, Benjamin. Get your shit together. They're just talking and the guy looks ninety years old.*

Giving my head a good hard shake, I turn away and decide it's not helping to look at her. Instead, I tee up my ball and take a swing.

"Damn, dude, are you trying to destroy the ball?" Jeff asks. "What the fuck is up with you today?"

The ball spins wildly as I slice the hell out of it. It flies right and barely goes anywhere but curves severely into the rough. My yardage is so ridiculously short that I want to crawl *under* the cart. The urge to throw my club hits, only I don't want to look worse than I already do.

Jeff takes his turn and he ends up perfectly positioned in the middle of the fairway. We go to hunt my crazy ball in the tall grass and my next shot sucks eggs too. The rest of my game doesn't fare any better because at every bend in the course, it seems Samantha is there. I do my best to ignore her, but it's next to impossible. She, however, hasn't noticed me once. So why do I keep noticing her?

By the time we finish up, I'm sure I'm bald. I've yanked out every hair in my head and need to pound some straight bourbon. And I rarely drink bourbon. Suffice it to say, we didn't win a dime, and Jeff is not happy. I promise to buy him a bottle of 16-year-old Lagavulin to make it up to him. Thank God he didn't ask for Pappy Van Winkle. That could've set me back a cool grand.

If not for the Sadler account final test run presentation with my dad, I would have worked from home the next day. As it is, everyone gives me a hard time about all my triple and quadruple bogeys.

By the time we call it a day, I'm ready for a Friday night out with Jeff and Mark. We're walking to the bar and Mark is mid rant over his ex and her new guy when I spot a familiar face. She's more gorgeous than she was yesterday. I scrub my face with my palm and wonder why I thought anyone could be better.

Then, the crowd parts and I see a blond guy with his arm slung over Samantha's shoulder. Their smiles make mine falter. When her eyes start to shift in my direction, I force mine forward.

"I'm telling you she yodels, not screams," Jeff says.

Mark glances at me because Jeff and his stories. And I realize I've missed a chunk of the conversation because Mark is now mute and Jeff is spewing the tale of his latest conquest.

"It's true. Every time I'd hit the spot, she'd yodel, no lie." When we don't remark, he adds, "She has a couple of friends," as if that sweetens whatever pot he's boiling.

Mark again looks to me and I shrug. What the fuck am I saving myself for? Samantha is busy all right. She hadn't mentioned she had a date for this evening. I don't know why I'm pissed. I barely know her and I screwed Karen the other night. Only I can't stop myself from glancing over my shoulder. She and the guy are heading into a restaurant. The view of Samantha from behind makes me want to claim her. And the asshole she's with has his proprietary hand around her waist. Who is he to her? If I were a betting man, I would say he's more than just a date. His territorial arm circling her is the first clue. The fact that she isn't shrugging him off is the second. A boyfriend maybe? Well, fuck her.

Jeff makes the call and we head over to his place. Mark doesn't seem sure, so I get the drinks flowing to loosen his morals and forget his soon-to-be ex. When his phone rings with Big Sean's "I Don't Fuck With You," I have to laugh knowing Jeff has changed Mark's ringtone for the guy's ex. Mark looks horrified and ready to snatch his phone. Jeff's there and tosses it to me. We manage to hide it from him and pussy him into drinking until he's lit. When the doorbell chimes, I have to admit any woman who walks through the door would look good to me. I'm that far gone.

A brunette, a blonde, and a ginger saunter in like the beginning of a bad joke. They are more Jeff's speed than mine. But what do I care? Pussy is pussy and I want to bury myself in one and forget the honey-haired beauty.

"Hey," the blonde waves.

I don't waste time. "Ben," I say, introducing myself.

Her breasts look perfect, which is a bonus. The way she smirks when I meet her eyes and the way she curls her finger at me say she's down for anything.

The absinthe I had must have been more potent than I thought, because I keep seeing Samantha's face overlaying the blonde's as I move closer. When she shifts her hand to the front of my pants, my dick isn't confused and won't play nice as much as I want it to. I don't even have to say no for her to realize it isn't happening tonight.

Mark's passed out and Jeff has disappeared. The two remaining girls end up leaving shortly after. And who the fuck knew I could turn down two girls? Something is seriously wrong with me. After I make sure Mark is on his side on the couch, I head out. Only, I'm not ready to go home and face all the shit in my head. So as I walk down the street, I pull out my phone prepared to see if Jenna or Cate are home. When I glance up, Samantha stands fifty feet in front of me ... without the asshole.

SIX
Sam

THE SHOWER SCREAMS MY NAME after the golf tournament and I can't get there quick enough. By the time I finish, Lauren is waiting for me.

"Can I grab you a beer?"

"Ahh, that sounds perfect. I'm wiped."

"Berkeley said it was awesome and that you killed it."

Tipping the beer bottle back, I let its icy contents cool my parched throat. "I hope so. I couldn't have done it without their help. They were awesome. But that's another reason I wanted to get involved with the fundraiser. Well, helping them raise money, but also getting The *Right* Affairs' name out there."

"Looks like it was a win-win for you." Lauren picks up her beer and we clank bottles. "Here's to more success for you, roomie."

"I'll drink to that any day."

After she swallows, she says, "You do realize you'll have to hire someone again."

"Yeah. I think I'm going to contact the college and see if I could hire a couple of paid interns. That would help a lot of people out. The students, the college, and me."

"You know, that's a great idea."

"That's on my checklist for tomorrow."

"Along with your hot date with Trevor, huh?" Lauren's eyebrows waggle.

"Oh, crap. I'd almost forgotten." My head starts to throb a little. After Monday night, Trevor is the last thing on my mind.

"I don't understand you. The guy looks like Chris Hemsworth

and you want to blow him off," Lauren huffs.

"I don't want to blow him off." I know I don't sound very convincing. It's as though I'm trying to convince myself.

"What's the deal here, Sam?"

"You know the deal."

"No, I don't. A week ago, you were willing to give it a go with him. Now you're as cold as a washed up fish on the beach."

I fall back on the couch. "I don't knowwww! I thought I wanted to try. But then when I saw him Saturday and he stealth-kissed me, there really wasn't anything there. Nothing. Nada. And I mean not even the teeniest of tingles. And I used to think he was Steamy Dreamy Trevor."

She leans over me and grabs a wad of my T-shirt. "You swear to me this has nothing to do with your Produce God?"

"Ugh. I don't know." I groan, loud and not so proud.

Her fist eases up on my shirt. "Okay, why don't you look at it this way? You have no commitment to Trevor. Go out and have fun. Even if it goes nowhere, at least you got a free dinner and were seen out and about. If and when you see Produce God again, you can decide if he was worth the wait. Then you have your answer. But in the meantime, don't burn your bridges with Trevor. At least if Produce God doesn't work out, you won't be left high and dry."

"Damn, you're a schemer."

"Not really. I just like to leave all my options open."

I tap my finger against my cheek. "You know what you have that I don't?" That question gets a deep chuckle out of her. For that, I clobber her with a pillow. "Stop being so dirty-minded."

"Well, what can I say?"

"No. You think of the dating scene like a business deal."

I can see her tongue poking the inside of her cheek. "Yeah, I can see why you'd say that and you're right. I do sort of treat it that way. Negotiations and all that."

"Maybe that's what I need to start doing. And maybe I need to leave my feelings out of it, too."

Lauren's arm waves around. "Here's my advice for what it's worth. Don't let your feelings get involved until you know where *he* stands. Then you're much less likely to get hurt."

"Ah, that's how you keep the upper hand, isn't it?"

Scrunchy-faced Lauren gets into my space. "Jesus on a picnic.

How the hell is it that you're just now figuring this out about me?"

I ball my hands up and rub my burning eyes. Damn, I am tired. "I don't know. You know what a slow learner I am in the dating arena."

She pats my back. "Don't worry. I'm a great teacher. And I'll always have your back."

We finish up our beers and I tell her I have to hit the pillow. I can barely keep my eyelids from slamming shut on me.

The next day, the phone at work rings nonstop. But a surprise shows up at lunch, in the form of a Cru Café delivery from Trevor, with a note telling me he can't wait to see me tonight. Just what I need. Shoving all thoughts of our upcoming date aside, I dig into my lunch with a voracious appetite. I'm starved.

After lunch, I start the search process of finding someone new to hire. Checking the calendar for the next week, I make sure everything is completed for our Monday luncheon for two hundred at the aquarium. I call and make the final arrangements. When I notice the time, I realize Trevor will be at the house in less than an hour to pick me up.

My social butterfly of a roommate also has a date, so we cross paths in the living room as we run in from work. After a brief shower, I throw on a sundress and reapply my makeup, then check my hair. Not too bad for the crazy day I had. I finger comb it, going for the messy look, and decide to leave it down tonight. Then I add a touch of gloss to my lips and call it mission accomplished. I grab a small clutch to toss my phone, keys, ID, and some extra cash in just in case, and consider myself ready. When I walk out of my bedroom, Lauren is already in the living room.

"You look great," she says.

"So do you." She's wearing dark skinny jeans, a glittery tank, and strappy stilettos. Her long blond hair is straightened, making her look even taller than her five feet ten inches. "You look like you stepped out of Vogue. So who's the special guy? I haven't had the chance to get the scoop."

She waves her hand, saying, "Please. I barely had time to do my makeup." She tells me his name before quickly adding, "And he's just someone I met through work. Nobody special, if you want to know the truth. But someone to have fun and hang out with."

"At least you don't have to worry or be on guard. And like I've told you a hundred times, you don't need any makeup. You're gorgeous without it."

Two bright spots of pink appear high on her cheeks. Lauren is many things, but she doesn't handle compliments well. She has no idea how beautiful she is. "I'm actually looking forward to tonight. And I love your dress by the way," she says, changing the topic.

"Thanks. I have no idea where we're going so I figured this would suit almost anywhere."

She nods. "Good choice."

The doorbell chimes and we look at each other. "I'll get it," I say.

Trevor stands on the porch looking more than mildly sexy. He's wearing a black button down shirt with black pants. There's something about a guy dressed in solid black that I love.

"Hey Trevor. Come in."

We all chat a few minutes and then he and I head out the door.

"You look beautiful, Sam, as you always do."

"Thank you, Trevor."

"I hope McCrady's is fine with you."

"That's perfect."

"Great. Shall we?" We get into his car, which is crazy because it's only about four blocks, but then again, I'd rather not give him any ideas about coming back here. He parks in the parking garage directly across the street from the restaurant.

"How was your week?" Trevor asks.

"Busy." I explain about the golf tournament and everything else that took place.

He beams. "Sam, that's so cool. It sounds like you're connecting with the right people." We toast each other's success over a bottle of wine. Dinner couldn't be better and we chat about everything, but most of it circles back to our respective business enterprises. Trevor seems like a different person, like he's finally matured into a responsible adult. It's refreshing to see.

"It's funny, isn't it?"

"What?" I ask.

"When we dated before, we hardly ever spoke about our work. And now look at us. I think we've changed."

"Hmm. Maybe so."

"Well, maybe I'm the one who's changed. Grown up some. Realized that what I was doing was a little on the ridiculous side," he says pensively.

He takes in my raised brows.

"Okay." He lets out a little chuckle. "A major lot on the ridiculous side. I'll be honest, Sam. I made a lot of mistakes. I don't know how much you saw, but I wasn't right. Not to you. You caught me at a bad moment, for sure. But I'll confess that wasn't the first. And truth be told, because you deserve to hear it, I slept around while we dated. I got hit on all the time. It's like when I went out alone, it was a free for all. I was a shit and I know it. And you didn't deserve that. My apology comes way too late, but you have it nonetheless."

"Wow." I expel my breath. I'm not even sure what to think. I had no idea he cheated on me and now here he is, spilling his guts. Has Trevor gone up or down in my *do not trust* scale? "I honestly don't know what to say. I'm shocked and disappointed, I suppose."

"Don't say anything. At least not tonight. I wanted to come clean with you because I want us to have a fresh start. I don't pound the liquor like I used to. I'm in control of things now. I realize I have what could be a huge business at stake, not to mention you. I'm not some young idiot running around anymore. I'm sure you don't believe that, but I think on some business level you can relate to what I'm saying. I have a reputation to uphold, and I don't mean the kind with women. I really do want to start on a clean slate with you."

We sip coffee over dessert and he tries his best to tell me he's turned over a new leaf. Perhaps he has. For a moment here, I think he's matured, like he claims he has, but then he springs all that other stuff on me and now I'm wondering about him again. It still stings a bit to know that while we were together, he slept with other women. I'm only half listening to him, because I'm stuck on those words. So that one kiss wasn't a drunken moment but rather a part of a string of infidelities. I'm struggling here, trying to take it all in.

"So, how about heading around the corner for another drink?"

"I guess we could do that." Even though after his confession I'm honestly not into it, I find myself agreeing to go. Once again, pushover Sam allows herself to be dragged into something she really isn't interested in. We leave and head to one of the livelier places on East Bay Street. Downtown is crowded this time of night on a Friday. People are everywhere, ducking in and out of restaurants, trying to get tables without reservations, and going to clubs. Trevor and I slip into a club and meander through the crowd until we reach the bar. He orders us drinks and we hang out for a while. As the time wears on, his behavior becomes less friendly and more flirtatious.

He takes his hand and pushes my hair off my shoulder. "I've always loved your hair, Sam." Then he leans in and kisses my neck.

Whoa. I'm not ready for this. "Trevor, I thought we were testing the friendship waters."

"I know, but you make it difficult."

"Me? How so?"

"You're so beautiful I find it hard not to touch you. Come on, let's go dance."

He grabs my hand and we end up on the dance floor. The music is loud and for a time, I forget about his confession. But then his hands land on my hips and he pulls me against him. His enthusiasm doesn't turn me on like it used to. I'm not feeling this at all, so I try to disengage him in a nice way. But he's become a bit aggressive and his hands move down, cupping my ass. I look up at his face and the glint in his eye does nothing for me. I try to take a step back, but his hands lock down and he holds me in place, grinding his unmistakable erection against me.

"Trevor, let me go." I have to yell over the music.

He shakes his head as if he can't hear me or he's only pretending. I reach behind me and free his hands. When he releases me, he puts his hands on my shoulders and pulls me into him. When I look up, his mouth hits mine. Like the other night, I feel nothing. I squirm out of his kiss.

"What?" Confusion clouds his eyes.

"Really?"

"It's just a kiss, Sam. You're overreacting."

I take a step back from him and say, "Then I'm going to tell you a truth. I still don't trust you. So if you want to remain friends, you need to slow it down."

He squeezes his eyes shut. "Damn. I'm already blowing it, aren't I?"

"If you keep this up, yeah." We're still in the middle of the dance floor, standing among a mass of gyrating bodies. Awkward much?

He nods. "Okay, I got it. No kissing. I promise."

I slant my head, assessing if he's being honest with me. All I know is I need to get off this dance floor. Moving back toward the bar area, I don't wait to see if he's following. I don't understand. He tells me he screwed around on me while we dated, but he's turned over a new leaf. Is that supposed to make me feel better all of a sudden?

His voice comes to me from over my shoulder. "I'm sorry. I guess it was a bit too fast, wasn't it?"

"Look, you just told me how you cheated on me when we were together. I caught you kissing someone and that was bad enough. But now you tell me it was even worse than that and for some reason you believe the slate is wiped clean. Well, it's not."

"But, Sam, I've changed."

"Maybe you have. But I don't know that. I haven't been around you for the last however many months. And you're going to have to prove that to me. Kissing and groping me on the dance floor when we just talked over dinner about starting out as friends isn't the way to go about it with me, Trevor."

He holds up his hands in surrender. "Okay. I get it."

"I'm not sure you do. When I caught you kissing that girl, you broke me apart. You see, I believed you. I believed everything you told me, that you loved me, but your actions crushed me. You betrayed me. I never told you any of this before because it didn't matter. When I saw you with her, I knew there wasn't any reason to talk to you about it because if I couldn't trust you, I couldn't love you. So now you know. And now that *I* know what you were doing, it makes it even worse."

"Jesus, Sam." He put his hand behind his neck and looks up.

"Yeah. 'Jesus, Sam,' is right." I look around a second and then I say, "I think I'm going to call it a night."

"Please don't leave."

"I think it's best that I do."

"Then at least let me drive you."

"Trevor, I only live a few blocks from here and I think the walk might do me some good. You know, clear my head and all."

He eyes me skeptically, and I shut him down.

"I'm not really giving you a say in this, and I'll be fine." Score for pushover Sam. And it's about time too.

As I take to the crowded sidewalks, my brain analyzes what occurred between us. Was I wrong? I'm reeling over the fact that he fucked around on us and I didn't know it. How many times and with how many women? But if I'm honest with myself, I don't care anymore because the real truth is, I don't care about Trevor. And why is that?

Weaving my way through the throng of people, I finally make it to a less crowded section of town and suck in a giant cleansing breath. I make it about a block and that's when it happens. I take my eyes off of my bubble gum pink toenails and come face to face with Ben Rhoades.

SEVEN
BEN

---◆---

BIG HAZEL EYES MEET MINE and for a second, I can't think beyond my next breath. My eyes drop to her kissable mouth and I lick my own until I remember myself. I want her, but more than I should. The weird ideas in my head have to stop, but the liquor coursing through me makes me feel bold.

I kick up my smile, which feels devilish even to me.

"Samantha."

The innocence that turns her frown to a blushing smile makes my dick go on alert like a puppy at the door.

"Ben, I—"

I'm not ready to hear about the asshole she was with. So I cut her off. "It's a nice night. But you really shouldn't be out here alone."

Her chin lifts in defiance and it's cute.

"I don't live far. I'm capable of walking home by myself."

I raise my brows, accepting her challenge.

"Well, it's a good thing I ran into you, because now you don't have to."

Without giving her a chance to argue, I take her hand in mine relishing the touch. "I know all about feminine rights and all that. But my mother raised me to be a good Southern boy. So let me walk you home."

My charm is as thick as molasses. And she shakes her head in amusement.

"You are something else, Ben Rhoades."

59

"That I am."

Remembering where she lives, we walk in the direction of her house. Her hand is soft in mine. And suddenly I feel like a teenage boy on my first date. *Get your shit together, Rhoades.*

"It's a beautiful night," I say breaking the silence.

She shrugs and the lift of her shoulders draws my attention to her amazing chest. I blink because the alcohol in my system is fucking with me.

"Tell me, Samantha, how did you end up on the streets of Charleston this late at night alone?"

It's not really a test because I can come clean and tell her that I saw her earlier. Still, I'm curious what she'll say. She's quiet for a moment, too quiet.

"I could ask you the same." Her eyes lock with mine and I feel lost.

I let her win the staring contest and glance away. Something about this woman makes me want more than I should. I have to get us back on track. Being with her can be fun. So I tell her the truth.

"I was out with friends and decided I'd rather be home dreaming of you than out unsatisfied with someone else."

Her laugh is quiet. "You're dangerous, Ben Rhoades. From anyone else's mouth, that would have been a bad pick up line. But I almost believe you."

"You should. It's the truth, scout's honor." With my free hand, I give her the salute.

She nods and her hair cascades over her shoulder when she looks at the ground for a second. I immediately think about how I can wrap it around my hand and expose her neck as I slide into her.

"We're here."

She tilts her head in the direction of one of Charleston's famous single-styled homes. They're called that because even though they can be many rooms long, they are always only one room wide.

I hold out my hand with the intention of walking her all the way to her door. My motives are clear—to me anyway. When we get there, she fumbles in a small purse and pulls out a key. It dangles on her finger as I cage her in. She is so tiny, I could easily pick her up. Lots of images that have been running through my head like a marathon go on fast forward. I should walk away and continue to traverse this world alone. Closing my eyes for a second, I push back the melancholy of loss. I let the alcohol settle my thoughts because the well of emotions that threaten to rise needs to be tamped down. And there is one sure way to forget. One that works every time.

"You can't get rid of me so easily."

Her lashes flutter and I can tell I'm making her nervous. She doesn't know me, not yet.

"Thank you for walking me home." She looks me squarely in the eye.

I'd been focused on her mouth until that moment. I step closer and fit my left hand to the side of her head on the door. Then I capture her chin in my other.

"Tell me. Did you let him kiss you?"

Her startled gaze dances all over the place. "How did you know?"

It's time to play my card.

"If we'd been playing poker, you would have just revealed your hand. But I saw you with him earlier."

I hold her gaze, curious about how she'll spin it. She doesn't back down.

"I had a date. Is that a crime?"

Oh, I'm really starting to like her.

"It depends." I rub my thumb over her lips. "Did you *let* him have a taste of you?"

Her head moves side to side and she's ready to say something else. But I don't wait to hear her. I have to do what I've waited for all night. I angle her chin to where I need her and press my lips to hers. She's soft just the way women should be. My cock jerks in my pants doing the happy dance.

Her soft gasp gives me the opening to dive in. I sweep my tongue across hers and she melts. And that's not a euphemism. I have to use my right hand to cup her bottom to hold her upright before she can sink to the ground.

She tastes like sweet tea on a summer day. I hold in a sigh of pleasure. She moans and my dick makes a beeline in her direction. When she doesn't slap my hand away from her ass, I use my fingers to gather up fabric so I can get where I want to without letting her go. I have a need to feel if she's wet.

"Wait," she says. "Anyone can see."

Oh, but that would be half the fun ... I don't want to spook her though. Instead, I pluck the key from her and with my eyes half on her, slide it into the lock. Not giving her a chance to leave me on the other side of it once she gets in, I back her in and close the door behind me. I try my best not to lose eye contact for more than a second at a time.

"Ben," she protests.

"Don't, Sam. Can I call you Sam?" She nods. "We're adults. I can see you want this as much as I do. Why deny ourselves?"

"Because I don't know you." Her words are strong but barely a whisper.

I step back giving her space to breathe. Her eyes are heavy lidded and her chest rises and falls with her rapid pulse. But even though my need for her is strong, I have no plans to force myself on her.

Pushing the curtain of hair back from her face, her desires are unmasked.

"So let me get to know you. What better way?" I flash a megawatt grin.

"I'm not that kind of girl," she says finding her voice.

Sighing, I let her go and take another step back and scrub over my face. This situation is so different for me with all her mixed signals. I haven't had a reluctant woman since early in my college days.

"I'm that kind of guy, but I don't judge anyone else."

She moves forward and reaches up. Within seconds, she's pulling my hand free from my hair. When her eyes drop to my mouth, I take control of her hand needing her to understand what she does to me. She lets me and I cover it over my rock hard cock.

"I don't play games. I want you. But I'm not going to force you to do anything. I'm also not going to lie to you either. I want to be inside you so bad. And I think you want me too."

She bristles and slips her hand out of mine. "Ego much?"

There's that stubbornness that makes me stupid as more blood rushes to my dick.

"Just honest. After being so close to you tonight, I know my hand alone won't do." She glares at me, but she hasn't slapped me or asked me to leave. "Tell me to leave Sam." I pause, searching her eyes. Seconds tick by without a word of protest from her mouth. "You won't, will you? Because your nipples are hard under that dress begging for my mouth to cover them. Your skin is hot and flushed. Admit that you want me."

She lifts her head in challenge and says, "People want many things, but you don't have to act on them."

I reach out and cup her cheek. She leans up and I gently bite her lower lip. Then I let my hand slide down the angle of her neck, the curve of her shoulder, and down her arm to grip her waist. "All you have to do is tell me to stop and I will. In fact, I'll go slow giving you ample time to stop and not let this go too far."

Leisurely, I slide my hand down her skirt-covered thigh to land on bare skin. "And I will." I squeeze her leg for a second, but I don't let go. "There is nothing wrong with wanting me, Sam. And make no mistake—I want you."

Her hand clamps on my wrist, but she doesn't try to pull my hand away. We stare at each other, neither of us giving in. I lean in needing another taste. She doesn't fight me. In fact, she fiercely kisses me back.

I take a chance and gradually slide my hand upward under her dress. Her grip on my wrist tightens, but again she hasn't stopped me. When my thumb reaches pay dirt and brushes over a spot on her panties, I groan. Pulling back, I meet her eyes.

"Sweetheart, you're wet. Let me help you get where you want to go."

While speaking, I rub my thumb across her swollen nub a few times. She sucks in a breath and I lean in and take her mouth prisoner again. Soon, her fingernails rake over my skull as she pulls me closer. I slip my finger underneath the barrier that protects her treasure, my goal. She's so ready for me my finger easily sinks into her warm depths. Her eyes are lost as she angles her lower half to make contact where she needs.

"Please," she begs.

"Not yet, honey."

With my free hand, I cup her heavy breast as I continue to work her, pushing in another finger. I have to see her. So I slip the straps of her sundress down and push the material away to expose her bra. The thin material isn't holding her beautiful breasts up. They are fucking perfect. So I shove that material aside freeing one perfect pink nipple. I don't waste time taking it in my mouth. Her pussy clamps around my two fingers and I continue to pump them in and out of her until she's boneless.

My dick is still granite and can't wait to be inside her. I scoop her up in my arms ready to take this to her room. She looks so fucking sweet cradled against me.

"Don't fall asleep, baby. The night is still young."

EIGHT
Sam

HIS VOICE COMES AT ME like a crack of thunder. I jolt in his arms, coming to my senses. What the hell did I just let happen? He just got me off—okay, an amazing vagina-quivering orgasm—but still. He's not much more than a stranger. I met him in the produce aisle, for Pete's sake. I never do anything like this.

"Ben, can you put me down, please?" My voice is barely above a whisper.

His footsteps falter. "What? Why?"

"I really need you to put me down." There is no mirth in my tone. He sets me on my feet so now I am forced to look at him. And much the pity because the man should have sparks flying off him he's that hot. Cliché, but he is.

"What is it? Is something wrong?"

"You might say that." I have no doubt my face is the color of a bowl of cherries.

His questioning expression quickly morphs into a cocky smile and he stands there, all full of himself, like he's the greatest prize ever. And honestly, he is. But I'm not quite ready for this yet. He rubs his chin and flashes a sexy smirk.

"Hmm. You sure seemed okay a few minutes ago."

"Oh, boy. You had to go there, didn't you?" This is such a weird combination of awkwardness and regret. I don't know quite how to handle this.

His forehead crinkles and a tiny V forms between his eyes. Why are men always so damn clueless? Do I need to spell it out?

"I guess I wasn't quite ready for that step we just took."

His jaw opens. For a second he says nothing. "Maybe the fact that you let me get you off, and from the sounds of it, enjoyed the hell out of it, gave me the wrong idea."

And I can feel his growing annoyance.

"You're right. I take responsibility for that and it was great, I admit. But that's as far as it's going for now. I barely even know you."

His eyes narrow for a second before he lets out a chuckle. "It was your choice. And you're lying to yourself for some self-righteous reason."

God, why does he have to act like such an ass? Lying to myself? He's right about one thing; I'm starting to feel self-righteous.

"Is that so? How many women have you done *that* to that qualifies you as an expert in this field?"

Any amusement on his face has totally vanished and his gray eyes darken. "Enough."

"And that makes you an expert?"

"I didn't say anything about being an expert."

"No, you didn't. That was out of line. I'm sorry."

"So what's going on here?" He motions between us with his finger.

Isn't that a good question?

My hand reaches for my forehead. This has been one hell of a weird night. "I don't know. I think we may have gotten a bit carried away, but I think it's best if you go."

He drops his head and that's when we both notice the tent in his pants. He half laughs while adjusting himself.

"You know what? I think you're right. I don't have time to play games with little girls." He gives me a circling salute, which almost reminds me of the *you're crazy* gesture. "Have a goodnight, Samantha."

His exit is hasty and the door slams making me wince. Games? I wasn't playing any games. Things just moved so fast I didn't have time to react until it was too late. I need lessons on how to deal with men. Why don't they have classes for this somewhere? Fuck!

This night certainly turned into a disaster of epic proportions. The first thing that calls to me is the shower. Washing away the touch of Ben Rhoades might help me with the second, which is sleep. Maybe I can dream away tonight.

I crawl into my bed and curl up into a tight ball, trying not to relive the awkward night. But it's impossible as thoughts of Ben making me come as hard as I ever have keep playing in my mind like a video stuck on replay. At one point I find myself so completely turned on I almost have to take things into my own hands. The only thing that stops me is I know if I do, all I'll think of is that messy-haired gray-eyed devil. And he's the one I'm trying my damnedest to forget.

"Ugh," I groan, pulling the covers over my head. He's cursed me for life. Even Trevor didn't spell me up like this. I never had the feels for him this much and the sex didn't come close. Fiddle-fucking-tastic fingers, I can't imagine what a whole night of Ben Rhoades would be like. Probably couldn't walk the next day. Well, no worries on that one. I'm sure I've blown any chance of ever seeing him again.

Shoving the covers off, I climb out of my haven and march into the kitchen for a glass of milk. It's two thirty in the morning and I'm exhausted with no chance of sleep in sight. The glass is now empty and I stare at the bottom of it. About four feet away is the wall my hands were pressed against only a few hours ago as I moaned out my pleasure in the form of one hell of an orgasm.

Stop, Sam. This is getting you nowhere, other than obsessing about BenSex!

"What are you doing up?"

Lauren's voice scares the hell out of me and I let out a scream.

"What the hell, Sam?"

"You scared me."

"I thought you heard me come home. Sorry."

"No, I didn't hear you. I couldn't sleep so I got up to drink some milk."

"Why can't you sleep and how was the date?"

Those are questions I don't want to answer. But she'll wheedle the answers out of me so I might as well get it over with. "Trevor is a jerk and so is Ben."

"Wait, what?"

"Are you drunk?" I ask her.

"Only a little."

"Sit. This is gonna take a while."

After I finish with Sam's saga, she sits there with her jaw sagging. "That's all so fucked up I don't even know where to start."

"Thank you."

Then she gets that sinister look in her eye. "So, he got you off, huh?"

I hit her with pillow. "Is that all you can think of?"

"Admit it. Isn't that all you're thinking of?"

"Well, yeah, but I don't know anything about him."

Her eyes resemble a flying squirrel's. "Where did he do it?"

I point to the far wall. "There."

I can see the muscles move as she swallows. "Holy hell. That's hot."

"Yeah. Why do you think I can't sleep?"

"What about your rabbit?"

"I thought about it, but weirdly enough, I keep having this vision of dark messy hair, a set of gray eyes, with my legs draped over his shoulders servicing my lady garden in the produce section at Whole Foods. No thanks. I'm trying to get all that out of my head."

"Jesus, Sam. You really are a sick person. Do you think he'll call again?"

An awful sounding laugh bursts out of me and then it morphs into a case of ugly tears. And boy, do they ever flow. I don't consider myself a crying sort. In fact, the last time I cried was when I caught Trevor slurping up that chick's tongue. I'm not sure why I'm crying now, other than I think I've just overdosed on too much shit for Sam to take in one night.

Lauren throws her arms around me and shoulders my tears. "Aww, it's gonna be all right, Sammy girl. Trevor is an asshole and we need to figure this thing out with Ben."

I raise my head from the refuge of her body and say, "But that's the point. All I seem to get are assholes. What is it with me? Why can't I attract a decent guy? Someone who genuinely cares about me and not my vagina, for once?"

"Gee, just think about it. You must have one kick ass vagina. Be proud of that thing!" she says.

"I'm serious!"

"I know, sweets. He's out there. I know he is. And when you find him, he'll be the most awesome guy in the universe."

"I'm not asking for the universe. I'll take the world, thank you."

The next morning a gorgeous June day greets me. The sky is crystal clear and the birds are chirping like nothing's amiss. If only.

When I get to the bathroom sink, I look in the mirror and want to curse. Dark purple half moons are sitting below my eyes. Too bad it's not Halloween—I already have the zombie look started, and with a bit of makeup, I could be there in no time. Good thing I don't have any plans today. After a few splashes of cool water on my face, I brush my teeth and twist my hair into a messy bun. Then I stomp into the kitchen to put on the coffee. After I think about it for a minute, I decide a triple latte is in order, so I throw on some shorts and running shoes, and get ready to make the quick run the Starbucks. Only I'm caught up by the coffee and bag that await me on my porch.

"Damn it, Trevor," I murmur to no one. I snatch the goodies up and turn to go inside when I notice the note. As I plop on the couch I almost choke on my bite of scone.

I'm sorry if I acted like an ass last night.
I was way out of line. I hope I didn't blow any chance
I had with you over my stupidity.
I hope you're ready for breakfast.
Trevor

A couple of minutes later my phone buzzes. When I check it, I see it's him. I'm not really sure I want to answer it. But then my curiosity gets the better of me.

"Hey."

"How's the latte?"

"Latte-ish."

He laughs. What used to warm me only makes me want to end the call now.

"And the scone? I suppose it's sconish?"

"Not at all."

"No?"

"Look, Trevor, I appreciate the gesture. It was nice. But after last night, I'm not quite ready…" I can't finish before he cuts me off.

"I'm sorry I scared you off last night. I really fucked up and I'm sorry."

"I guess you and I are sort of running on parallel roads here."

He's quiet for a short minute, then says, "Maybe I'm hoping for too much, too fast."

"Probably."

"So do I have any chance at all? And Sam, be honest with me."

I don't know what to say, so I do what I always do because, even if I have to sacrifice my own, I hate to hurt anyone else's feelings. "Yes, Trevor, you have a chance. Just don't come on so strong, okay?"

"Okay. Would it be too much to ask you to dinner again?"

"No, but can you give me a week?"

"You've got it. I'll call you next week. And Sam, I just want you to know that you're worth the wait. Every single minute."

He ends the call and I groan, wanting to sling my phone across the room. I'm such a sucker and a dumbass.

"What's that all about?" Lauren asks, walking in from her bedroom.

I give her the scoop and she laughs. "When it rains it comes down in buckets, right?" She pats my back and adds, "Don't worry. It'll all work out the way it's supposed to. What we need is a girl's dinner out. Like maybe this week."

"Yeah," I agree.

Then my phone rings again. "Jesus, I bet it's damn Trevor again. He's so persistent.

But when I answer, it isn't Trevor. It's someone else entirely that shocks the hell out of me. My hand automatically reaches for Lauren's and she winces as I crush it in a vise-like grip while I listen to the person on the other end.

NINE
BEN

◆

PRESSING MY TEMPLES, I TRY to stop replaying Friday night with Samantha in my head knowing she isn't for me. It's been almost a week and I'm still scratching my head over her reaction. After every opportunity to stop things, she decided she wanted to continue. But after she got hers, she left me with a stiff dick and only my hand to use instead. And fuck me if my damn traitorous cock doesn't stand in protest every time I think about her.

I shift in my chair when my office door opens after a quick knock. Glancing over my monitor, Lisa is coming towards me. She doesn't stop until she's right beside me. I focus on my computer screen because I should be going over my presentation one last time before the meeting.

Her hand dislodges my own from my hair. "You're going to lose all this gorgeous hair if you keep yanking at it."

I glance away from her expectant face and glare at my hand. I hadn't realized what I was doing until she'd freed my death grip. "I should cut it all off, or shave my head."

Her fingers run through my hair. Her nails graze over my scalp and I can't help that it feels nice. "Don't you dare, Ben Rhoades. Your hair could be famous if you'd leave it be."

She works some magic I'm unable to see. Her face however tells the tale as she grins and steps back to admire her work.

"You look good. Ready for the Sadlers. They are in the small conference room. I was sent to tell you."

Her eyes hold me in place and I have the sense she wants me to

71

say something. Out of the corner of my eye, I catch a flash of golden hair. I whirl in that direction, but see nothing.

"What?" Lisa asks.

I angle my desk chair and backup so I can stand with some distance between us.

"Nothing." Clearly, I can't expunge Samantha from my head despite it all. "I should head over."

Lisa nods and walks away. I grab my laptop and a thumb drive and head in for the presentation. The small conference room isn't quite small. It can hold a dozen people comfortably around the table. The Sadlers sit with their backs to the glass wall at one end of the table. Dad, who sits at the opposite end, watches me approach. He raises a brow in question.

"Sorry I'm late," I announce as I walk in.

I turn on the charm Dad insists could sell any used car on the lot. A couple of times, I swear I catch a glimpse of Samantha, but I plow on.

"Our plan may be a little aggressive, but with no risk there's little reward. We believe that our strategy of personally watching over your investments will keep you safer than say our big New York corporate competitors. We are only a phone call away, not a call center where someone with a script will try to answer your questions, or a large corporation where you have to jump through several hoops before you get to your broker."

My words trail off when I see her. I'm riveted to the view outside the glass. It feels like an eternity since I've seen her last. My gaze sweeps over the curve in her top, down a skirt, to her endless legs.

"... New York is—" Mr. Sadler begins.

"Beautiful." The word slips from my mouth before I realized I've said it.

"Huh?" someone murmurs.

I blink, realizing the word took the fast track from my brain to my lips. The self-destruction button on my brain depresses as I watch Jeff stand twenty feet away talking to Samantha. I know that look on his face, and when she smiles, my vision clouds. I don't know if I'm happy or pissed at seeing her.

"If you would excuse me, I need a drink of water. Does anyone need anything?"

I don't bother to wait for an answer. I'm out the door as my father's glare drills into my back.

Barreling forward, Jeff sees me coming. He holds up his hands in the universal sign of peace while moving a few steps back. I sidestep him determined to reach her. Cupping her elbow, I lead her out of sight of the conference room. Her eyes grow large and I can see the bull I've become reflected in their beauty.

"What are you doing here?" I half whisper, half growl.

She blinks, a frown curling her smile the other way. "I—"

"Have you come to apologize?"

The storm that darkens her expression is immediate.

"Apologize?" Her one word question is more of an accusation. "For your information, I'm not here to see you. I received an urgent call on Saturday from an admin in your office about an event they want me to handle.

I need to get my head checked because something about her defiance makes her more attractive than less. Remembering how our calamitous night together ended cools my jets instantly.

After a lingering pause with our glares locked, I stand up straight and finally say, "Well, by all means, carry on."

As much as I'm attracted to her, I don't have to hedge my bets to know she's not ready for the likes of me. I need to clear my head of her, so I pivot ready to put distance between us. Her hand lands on my bicep and stops me.

She graces me with half a smile. "Ben, this isn't me. I can be the bigger person and not just because it's possible your company will be a client of mine. The truth is I should apologize for letting that night go as far as it did. It was unfair to you."

I shrug as her genuineness takes all the annoyance out of my sails. "You always have a choice," I say in all sincerity before I dial up the wattage on my smile. "Even if I did get hurt in the process."

"Hurt?" The smooth skin across her forehead creases in confusion.

I see no reason to edit myself. It isn't like there will ever be an *us*.

"Yes. My balls were drawn so tight, they'd turned blue. I blame my lack of functioning brain cells for my unfortunate choice of words before I left. And I, too, need to apologize about that." I scrub a hand through my hair because this woman makes me feel off balance, off my game. "It was uncalled for." I lift my hand sheepishly. "Granted, I was pissed because I was hurt."

She laughs, granting me more of her sweet smile. "What is it with men like you?"

"Men like me?"

"Yes. Men like you who are used to all women falling at your feet and ending the night with some sort of sexual gratification."

For a second, I'm confounded by her logic. As I process, I think over all my recent encounters with women.

"I don't need sex from every woman I meet," I say with defiance.

Her smirk is a delicious challenge. "I'd like to see that day."

The smile on her face is wicked with a silent double down dare issued and received. Against my better judgment, my mouth opens and I'm saying shit I wouldn't normally say.

"Let me take you out."

Her lips part and before she can form any type of rejection on her tongue, I keep talking.

"Nothing fancy, just something casual between friends. And no sex," I say with a half-grin. "Just a little makeup dinner. Makeup sex is phenomenal. I'm sure makeup dinner could be good, too."

And what the fuck is that all about?

Her smile blooms and I want to kiss her so bad I have to fist my hands at my sides not to touch her.

"You, Mr. Rhoades, always seem to know the right things to say."

"I think you've proven that's not always the case," I say with a smirk. "As much as I wouldn't mind a good debate, I'm probably going to lose my job if I don't get back to my meeting. I have a client wondering why I left the conference room in a hurry. So you have to agree."

"Is this blackmail?"

"No. But unless you want me to be homeless, you'll answer quickly."

She only hesitates a second longer before she says, "Fine, it's a date."

I reach out and snag her soft hand. The need to touch her is too strong, and I indulge further, kissing her knuckles. "I'll text you. I hope Saturday night is okay?"

I don't wait for an answer, hurrying off to close the Sadler deal. I open the conference room door with a couple of bottles of water and offer them around before I nail the rest of the presentation if their smiles and assurances they plan to sign the contract are any indication.

A couple of grueling days later, Jeff sweeps in my open door. Sometimes, I long for solid walls. The glass fronts don't offer any seclusion unless you turn on the privacy feature, which fills the panes with a gas that turn them opaque. It's kind of cool.

With his arms raised on either side of him like he scored a touchdown, he says, "I hear the Sadler account is in the bag."

I shrug. "The contract isn't signed, but they spoke as if they were leaning towards going with us."

"Then we should celebrate." He claps as if somehow that seals the deal.

I haven't been out since the disastrous night with Samantha, but the last thing I want right now is to go to my empty house.

"How about poker?" I ask.

Jeff's smart which is why he's on the fast track for a promotion. Between Mark and him, they're the closest things I have to friends who could maybe fill Drew's shoes one day. It doesn't take long for Jeff to see through my suggestion. He points a finger at me. "You've been holding out on me. You have something going on with that event planner."

I'm not sure how to answer. Our situation is certainly unique.

"She's a friend."

"Like Karen was a friend?"

I ignore his comment. "Do you want in on poker or what?"

He sighs heavily. "Yeah." He points at me on his way to the door. "You owe me a bottle of Lagavulin."

I nod. "Bring Mark."

"As if you have to remind me. The guy needs luck tonight. He can barely buy lunch these days with that ex of his draining him dry."

Like everything else these days, I lose big that night. It's for a good cause because Mark wins. I can't say for sure whether we let him win or his luck was stellar. Either way, my pockets are lighter.

Days later, when I pull my Jaguar F-Type in front of Samantha's house, I wonder for the hundredth time if I'm doing the right thing. Before I can make a decision, she breezes out the door looking as fresh and beautiful as the proverbial girl next door. The kinds of women I'm used to, normally look like girls gone wild when we go out. Yet my body makes its opinion known as every muscle goes taut with need just at the mere sight of her.

"Hey," she says, opening the door before I can come out of my head and open it for her.

"You're going to get me in trouble with my mother."

She shoots me a grin that hits me right in the dick.

"Why? Because you didn't walk me to the car like I can't do it by myself?" The words drawl out of her mouth, feigning shock.

"I swear, if I didn't know any better, I'd think my sister sent you as some kind of payback."

She pushes her sunglasses to rest on top of her head. Her eyes laser mine. "You have a sister?"

"I do. A younger sister who acts more like my mother. She'd like you."

One flash of her brilliant smile and I'm dumbstruck.

"Sounds like I'd like her. I'm sure she has lots of stories to tell."

I groan for more reasons than one. "You're never ever going to meet her."

"That's sounds like a challenge."

Her smile widens and I shake my head. Tonight I have to channel Drew so I can keep my hands to myself and be the gentleman she doesn't think I can be. And for some reason I can't name, it's important to me.

"Let me get you to dinner before you start getting ideas."

When we reach the marina, Samantha stares out at the car window.

"You're okay with taking a boat ride?"

Startled, she glances over at me. "No." She shakes her head. "I mean yes. It's fine."

I'd texted her what we were doing, but she seems preoccupied or maybe nervous. That's proven when she lets me open her door and help her out without any protest. I use my time wisely and check out her white top that's sheer enough for me to see a yellow bikini top underneath.

Before my dick can get any ideas, I grab the basket I'd borrowed from Mom from the back. Although I'm a passable cook, I picked up dinner I'd ordered on the way.

On the way down the docks, she asks, "Did you charter the boat?"

The wind whips her hair up and she sweeps it behind her ear. The act shouldn't be sexy as hell, but it is. Before my imagination can take me places she isn't ready to go, I answer her question.

"No, we're taking a ride on my boat."

"Your boat. I thought you were practically homeless," she teases.

"Thanks to you, I'm not." I give her a cheeky grin and walk her to my boat slip.

After setting the basket down, I do all the prelaunch procedures before I untether the boat.

"I thought we could watch the sunset on Capers Island."

Her eyes speak volumes as I watch astonishment then suspicion cross her face.

"You are sure full of surprises Ben Rhoades."

I'm full of a lot of things if you'd let me show you I want to say, but refrain.

She climbs aboard like a seasoned pro, which doesn't surprise me. Most people from the area have a boat or have been on one. I finish with the preliminaries and set off. Not too long after, her hand smoothes over my shoulder. I glance up at her and notice she's taken off her tank, leaving acres of creamy tanned skin and a bikini top that does nothing but make my mouth water. I face forward afraid I'll do something like pull her in my lap.

Samantha's not that kind of girl; her own words haunt me. The devil on my shoulder and the dick in my pants wonder why we've given up. I tighten my grip on the wheel if nothing more than to keep my hands off of her. I can do this.

It's a blessing and a curse when she leaves me to go sit out in the sun at the back. My mind wanders away from the beautiful woman who's tempted me in ways I didn't know existed. Staring at the water ahead as the boat slices through it, I'm reminded of one of the times I took the boat out with Drew.

The memory unfolds like a letter with words that leap into life.

Drew is nursing a beer in his hand while I drop anchor. I hand him a pole and he hands me a bottle.

"Women are confusing," he blurts.

"No, they aren't. They have two switches—on and off. Turn them on, get what you want. Then turn them off and send them on their way."

His eyes narrow as if I've said something wrong.

"Dude, your views are seriously twisted."

I shake my head. "You're twisted. Rebecca seriously fucked with your head."

He finishes his first beer and grabs another without even casting his line. I guess fishing is off the table. I sigh to myself, putting my pole down and taking his. I'm sad for my best friend.

Drew's the romantic of the two of us or so the women have always said. Only one woman at a time has his full attention even if it's for a short time. He makes them feel special. So much so if he breaks it off, they remain friends.

"She…" I hate the girl for making him choke on his words. "I loved her."

"And she shit all over you. She played games. You should have known from the beginning when she jerked you around before she gave you a fucking taste."

He looks at me like I'm the one heartbroken. "One day, you'll understand."

I shake out of the memory not wanting to let grief over take what should be an easy evening with Sam. Being here with her, a woman I know Drew would have approved of, forces me to face his loss because I can't tell him how conflicted I am over her.

I try to think of a happier time. I practically spent my high school years on this island. I've never brought a woman out here since. So why now? Why her? I shrug off the thought not wanting to analyze why I'm different with her. Or why that thought scares the hell out of me. What was that saying? Once shame on her, twice shame on me. No way do I want to fall in love again and find out what happens a third time.

I slow the boat to a stop so I can find a place to drop anchor. The tide is high, so it's perfect timing and my luck holds when the anchor gets a good catch on my first toss.

The sun is setting, so I pour two glasses of wine and head to where Samantha's draped over the seat.

"Wine?"

Hidden behind blackened shades, I have no idea if her eyes are closed or open. She sits up.

"Thank you."

I'm not sure how to do the no sex thing with a woman outside of Cate, but that's what I promised her for tonight. The women I've dealt with have been as eager as I was to skip the formalities. And right now, I want to take fistfuls of her hair and devour her mouth. But by our guidelines for this date, I'm not allowed to touch her. So, I fold myself in the seat next to her and shift so the wood in my pants doesn't pierce the fabric.

"It's beautiful out here."

It's true, but the view of the woman before me has stolen all my attention.

"It is."

Letting the wine slowly pour down my throat, I watch her out of the corner of my eye.

I feel collared because I can't touch her and that irritates the hell out of me. But, I have no one but myself to blame. I shouldn't have taken the bait from her dare and asked her out here. *My boat? What the hell, Ben. Did you really think you wouldn't want her bent over the rails screaming your name while you pound her from behind?* I turn away from the line of her exposed throat wanting to scrape my teeth down it to her breasts. I lick my lips and change the topic to business.

"I want you to know I didn't get you the job at my firm. I had no idea they were planning an event. So you earned that spot on your own."

The easygoing curve of her lips taunts me.

"I gathered by your reaction to me showing up at your office. But it's nice to know."

"You've made a name for yourself. That's got to make you proud."

Her smile turns up. "It's been a hard road, taking on clients that were hard to please, but it's paid off."

"It takes a lot of courage to start your own business from scratch. I envy you."

"You work for your family's firm. There's pride in that."

I swallow some more wine, not sure why I got on this subject. The idea that I've crawled back home to work at my dad's company still bothers me.

"Yeah, I guess."

She turns to face me. "There's a story there. Are you one of those guys that got roped into the family business but you'd rather be a starving artist?"

The chuckle that comes out is a surprise. "Not exactly. I wanted to be my own man and not sit in my father's shadow. But I couldn't stay in New York. The city pace was too fast for me and no one cares they have to step over the homeless to get to work." I hold back one of the biggest reasons—I came home because of Drew's illness.

"That doesn't seem fair. I'm sure lots of people care."

I nod. "You're right. It just feels that way. I guess I'm just a small town boy who wants to know the people you run into on the sidewalk."

"No, I get it. New York wouldn't be for me either. I mean, I love to visit. It's a fascinating place, but like you, I'd miss home too much to move."

"So you never dreamed of leaving Charleston for somewhere else?"

She shrugs. "I don't know. I've dreamed of lots of things. But I enjoy my life here and being close to family."

The horizon changes colors from a dusky rose to navy blue. The moment is right and I feel like if I kissed her right now she would let me. Her eyes find mine. Everything is silent except the water lapping at the boat.

"Ben."

She says my name like a prayer and I turn to face her.

"It's okay if you want to kiss me."

My eyes involuntarily drop to her lips before I close them. Hadn't I wanted that?

"I don't think kissing you is the right thing to do." I force the words out in a broken whisper.

Her response is just as soft and a longing as old as time fills the space between us.

"Why?"

There are a million and one reasons if I were honest. Barely controlled, I'm on the precipice of taking everything I want. I've already failed her little test and she doesn't know it yet. I very much want this night to end in sweaty sex.

"Because if I kiss you, I'm not going to want to stop. And we've established you're not that kind of girl."

Her slender hand reaches up as if she plans to touch me and I capture it.

"Samantha, this was a bad idea on my part. I can't give you what you're looking for. I'm not going to be satisfied with just kissing you." I have to fight myself with fisted hands, which proves I'm capable of some control. "And if you let me have you in any way, that's as far as it will ever go. I'm not looking for a girlfriend or a white picket fence with a bunch of mini me's. You deserve better."

When she says nothing to refute my statement, I know my

message has been received. I stand up, wondering who the fuck I've become. Then I add, "I think I should take you home."

TEN
Sam

THE RIDE HOME IS UNCOMFORABLY silent. He's a difficult man to figure out and now I have a case of major whiplash, not to mention a need to run my hands through that chaotic hair of his. One minute he's on fire for me, and the next he's talking some crap about how I deserve better. What's all that supposed to mean? I want to say something, but to be honest, I don't know where to begin or what to say. I don't even know him well enough to think about picket fences and mini me's, so why would he even bring something like that up? He's the definition of confusion.

We finally pull up in front of my house and I make a hasty exit from his car. But he's fast. He jumps out, calling after me. "Sam, wait."

I stop, only because it would be completely rude not to.

I hear him open his trunk so I turn and look to see what he's about. I'm curious now as I watch him pull the large basket out.

Handing it to me, he says, "I want you to take this. I told you we'd have dinner and we didn't, so there's no reason why you shouldn't enjoy what's inside."

"No. I think I've lost my appetite."

"I'm sorry." In the darkness, it's hard to see his features, but his tone is riddled with remorse.

"So am I."

"Please." He holds the basket in such a way that I can't refuse it. I take it from him and he says something that I find very odd. "I wish I were someone else. Someone better than I am. Goodnight,

Sam." He turns with abruptness and jogs the short distance to his car door. Then he's gone, leaving me even more puzzled than before.

I walk inside, reeling from this whole encounter, surprised to find Lauren sitting on the couch.

"You're home early," she says.

I shake my head.

"You look like you've seen a ghost."

"No, not a ghost. Just Ben Rhoades."

"Oh, right. How was dinner?" She wants the details and I need to talk. "Hey, what's in the basket?"

A mixture of a laugh and a huff escapes from me as I plop down next to her. "I have no idea. I think it was supposed to be our dinner."

"What?"

"Exactly. You're not going to believe this when I tell you." And she doesn't.

"So let me get this straight. This is the guy who wanted to bang you the other night, but tonight wouldn't even kiss you?"

"That's right."

"Maybe he has whiplash disorder and forgot to take his meds." Lauren's is the best explanation for his behavior, even if she said it half jokingly.

"I'm wondering the same."

Lauren digs into the basket and oohs and ahhs over the contents as she pulls everything out. "He certainly went all out on this picnic stuff. You have a nice selection of charcuterie, artisan cheeses, and breads for your appetizer. And then an excellent salad along with some shrimp here. Very nice. And I see he didn't leave out dessert. A huge wedge of peanut butter cheesecake, it looks like. Oh, and there are a couple of bottles of white and red wine in here, too. Nice ones, Sam. He's a spender."

I shrug. "A lot of good it does when he acts like he did."

"There's no good reason whatsoever that this food should go to waste, so why don't I open this wine and get us some plates and we eat?"

I peek down into the basket and pull out the plates and silverware she overlooked. We both laugh.

"No self-respecting man who thinks of everything would forget the plates, silverware, and napkins now, would he?" she asks.

"Of course not." And the food is scrumptious.

"You know what we need?"

"You're not off the hook. How was your date?" I push.

"It was fun. But back to the girls' dinner out we've been talking about. We could be your advisory council on this." Lauren practically jumps off the couch in excitement about her idea, and nearly knocks the basket over and all the food. I make the save, wrapping my arms around everything, but in the process, a bunch of cheese ends up down my shirt.

"Damn, Lauren, what the hell?"

She puts her hand down my shirt and grabs the wedge of Clemson Blue that made its way between my boobs and laughs. "Sorry."

"Now I have to take a shower because I reek of blue cheese."

"Yeah, but not just any blue cheese. It's Clemson Blue Cheese. You're special."

"Gah, you are crazy. Make the date. I'm free on Tuesday." I relieve myself of the burdensome basket, and head to the bathroom. I don't bother asking more about her date. Lauren can be secretive about her love life. She'll tell me when she's ready to share. When I rejoin her, she has a weird look in her eye.

"Now what?"

She raises her wine glass and gestures toward the counter. There sits a large bouquet of flowers.

"Where did those come from?"

"A florist."

"Okay, so only about three florists in town deliver after eight. It's ten p.m. Who the hell is sending me flowers this late?"

She shrugs. "They're your flowers. You'll have to look and see."

I walk to the counter and check them out. They're gorgeous, but I love all flowers. I'm not picky in that regard. Ben must've had regrets about the way our date ended. I hope so anyway. I reach for the little card and my hopes are skewered when I read it.

*Can't wait to get together for
dinner with you again.
Trevor*

"Oh this sucks."

"Don't keep me in suspense."

I hand Lauren the card.

"So, you agreed to see him again?"

"Lauren, you know me. I can't say no. I'm such a wimp."

She rubs her hands together, and says, "No worries. Just one more thing for us to counsel you over."

"Very funny." I turn around and head towards my bedroom.

"Where are you going?"

"To bed. I've had enough drama for the day."

The weekend is a bust for me. I'm so backed up at work, I end up spending it at the office. My focus is on hiring someone and I have that event I'm working on for Ben's firm. Apparently they do an annual company party every year and I need to come up with some ideas. The budget is impressive and the guys like to golf, so I need to come up with something for the ladies. A spa option is nice, so I look at several places and choose a couple. Then I go to work researching all the golf courses, spas, and facilities for parties. By Sunday evening, I have two completely different options for them and I'm ready to make my presentation next week.

Monday afternoon, Trevor calls. It's the conversation I've been dreading, but I answer with a cheery, "Hello?"

"How's your day going?"

"Busy and yours?"

"The same. So I was wondering if this Saturday would work for you?" he asks.

"Sure. Sounds fine." I see no way out of this since I basically committed, so I might as well push forward and get through it.

"Okay. I'll pick you up at seven thirty then. I can't wait to see you, Sam."

"Oh, and thanks for the flowers. That was very kind of you."

"It was nothing."

"They're beautiful."

"I'm happy you're enjoying them."

"I am. I'll see you on Saturday."

I hit end, thinking what a sap I am. He's the last person I want to date now. The only man I want to see again is the gray-eyed one that left me a heap of confusion the other night. Tomorrow can't come soon enough. The night out with the girls will help so I can bounce all this craziness off of them.

One of my employees, Nancy, comes in later with a resume and a cover letter of an applicant she thinks would be an asset to the business. After looking it over, I have her set up an interview. Checking my calendar, I look at my agenda for the remainder of the day and my phone buzzes. It's my sister, Laney.

"Hey, sis."

"Sam, you busy?" When she hears me laugh, she adds, "Wait, that was a dumb question. You're always busy. Scratch that."

"It's okay. What's up?"

"I was just checking in. Have you decided what you're going to do?"

"Did Mom put you up to this?"

"Kind of. But can you blame her? I mean, after Grandma and then what she went through ... come on, Sam. You need to make a decision. It's killing her and Dad. But they won't tell you."

A long sigh escapes me. She's right. "I'm sorry."

"Look, I know how scary it is. I went through it, too. But when you get to the other side, I promise you'll wonder why you waited."

"I know. It's just that work has had me swamped."

"Sam. Work is never *that* important."

"Okaaaaay. I'll check my calendar. I promise."

"Okie dokie. I'll tell Mom. I love you, baby sis."

"Love you back."

As promised I take a peek at my calendar and see I have an appointment in the next month, so I push all thoughts of decision making in the far corners of my brain and go back to work. When six thirty rolls around, I drag myself out of there, locking up behind me, and drive home. I'm beat.

As I walk inside, my phone dings with a text, and I grab it, hoping it's Ben. It's not. It's Lauren asking me if I want to meet her for a run. I know I should go, but I'm drained so I text her back begging off. She harasses me to the point I end up changing and meeting her. Damn it, I really can't say no!

The thick, humid air wraps around us as we wind our way through the old streets of Charleston. Once we hit the battery, the salt-laced breeze coming off the water cools the air somewhat. "Can we just put this street on repeat for a while? It's freaking hot today."

"Right?" she wheezes.

"What was so damn important about running, anyway?"

"You needed it."

"Me?" I ask.

"Yeah. Your stress level is reaching the stratosphere."

"Humph." She's right. Thank God I have a roomie who knows me so well.

"Talk to me."

"Yeah, okay. Work. I need more help. But I think I may have found someone. The interview is Friday. Then there's Trevor. I don't really want to see him." I have to stop and pant for a moment. "There's this thing … this, I don't know. I don't trust him for reals. And the no feels thing is bugging me."

"I get that. And?"

"You're going to make me say it, aren't you?"

"Uh huh."

"Ben effing Rhoades."

"I pretty much thought so," she huffs. "Jesus, it's hot."

"So is he."

"All right already. I get that. But so is our Chris Hemsworth look alike. So tomorrow we'll have some liquid therapy and set Sam straight on all that pertains to men. Quit stressing over that. The work thing will iron itself out once you get that new hire up and running. Anything else?"

"Yep. My decision. Laney called today. I have an appointment coming up."

"It's important. You need to do it, Sam."

"I know. I know I do."

"You know we all have your back on this."

I nod.

"And there's something else. Hear this, Samantha Calhoun." She takes a breather. "I am so fucking proud of you. Look at you and your business. You have arrived, girl!" The she comes to a screeching halt so I have to backtrack. I look at her and she holds out her fist. I give her a fist bump and we laugh. She is great at distracting me.

Tuesday night we all meet at The Macintosh. Lauren and I walk in and Berkeley, Britt, Carrie, and Hayley are already seated. We join them to find they've already ordered drinks for us. Thank you, Jesus, for sending me such awesome friends.

Without giving me a chance to say a word, Lauren jumps right in and says, "Sam is in need of counseling. She has a dilemma. She likes Ben but after he wanted to bang her against the wall and she wouldn't let him, now he won't even kiss her and says he doesn't deserve her. And Trevor is in hot pursuit but he got a little handsy on their date and confessed that he slept around while they dated, so she doesn't trust him at all."

By the time she finishes, all the girls have their mouths hanging open. No one says a word, until finally Berkeley begins, "So let me make sure I have this right. Ben is playing hard to get after you gave him a set of purple balls, and supposedly he doesn't deserve you. And Trevor is really the ultimate manwhore."

"That's about right," I say.

"Not all of it because I found out some juicy news today," Lauren adds.

"What?" everyone, including me, asks at once.

Lauren leans in and we all do the same. Right as she gets ready to talk, the waiter comes to take our order. Damn waiters. Why can't they keep their noses out of our business?

We all tell him what we want and he keeps asking us stuff when all I want is for him to get the hell away from the table so I can hear what news Lauren has.

When he finally does, I say, "Go on!"

"Okay. So do you know the girl that works in the cubicle right outside of my office?"

"The one who is sometimes your assistant?" I ask.

"The very same. Well, we got on the Ben topic somehow," and now her eyes dart around the room.

"Hold up. Are you talking about me at work?"

"Okay, I may have mentioned you a little. But that's not what's important here."

"I'll give you a pass this time, but seriously, Lauren, you can't be doing that." My tone is a bit on the scolding side.

"I know. I'm sorry. But listen to this. So Melanie starts telling me about Ben. Apparently he is this major manslut. I mean serious slut of epic status. He has screwed every woman in her gym. She works out over in Mt. Pleasant at Get Fit. You know the place?"

We all nod.

"He has quite the reputation there. And then she has this friend, Karen."

"Karen?" I interrupt her. I remember that name from his client dinner.

"Yeah, why?"

"Just go on," I say.

"From what Melanie told me, they dated for like six months or something, and he was brutal to her. In the end, he acted like she was a piece of dirt. Even his mother thought they were getting married."

"Oh, God." I put my head in my hands.

"What?" everyone asks.

"The client dinner I went to with him. His parents were there, along with that client couple. The woman said she thought Ben was bringing his fiancée, Karen, and thought I was her. When I asked Ben about it later, he only said his mom has a habit of hearing wedding bells when she shouldn't, or something like that. I brushed it off as nothing. I guess he's a real heartbreaker, then. So maybe that's why he said he didn't deserve me."

Lauren nods and says, "Maybe."

Then I add, "But that makes no sense. It's totally out of line with his behavior, if he is a heartbreaker."

"I don't know. Whatever the case, protect yourself from him, Sam. We know he goes through women like beers at a bar. Just be careful."

Berkeley finally adds her own two cents. "Wanna know what I think? I think you ought to fuck him for the hell of it. I mean, if he's a manwhore, why can't you play, too? You're always the goody two shoes, Sam. You never let yourself go. Do it this time. Have fun with the guy without any expectations. He's hot, right?"

"Oh, hell yeah," I say.

"Then for once in your life, have some fuck fun. Make him your fuck buddy."

Happy Hayley says, "I agree. You've been so busy and never do anything like this. You barely sleep with guys and always wait for love. Then you get burned in the end. Let yourself enjoy it for once without the worry of a relationship."

Britt says, "I'm in the fuck buddy camp."

Carrie says, "Me too."

"Lauren?" I ask.

"I am, but with anyone but Ben Rhoades. I don't think he'll play fair."

"Bullshit," Berkeley says. "Sam will hold the cards this time. Do it sister. Free the Sam Slut!"

Everyone starts chanting, "Free the Sam Slut. Free the Sam Slut."

"Would y'all shut up? Jeez, everyone's going to think I'm nothing but a hooker! I'm going to the bathroom."

I get up and go. On my way back, I happen to glance across the room and sitting at the bar, with his arm around a dark-haired beauty, intimately kissing her neck, is none other than my Trevor. The one who said he couldn't wait to see me, and that he'd been faithful to me ever since that night, and that I was worth waiting every minute for. In a moment when I should be fuming, I feel free. So much so, I pull out my phone for a bit of fun and take a picture.

When I get back to the table, I say animatedly, "You'll never guess who's here. And with someone."

"Ben?" Lauren asks with satisfaction.

Shaking my head, I grin. "Trevor." Then I show them the picture.

"No! And he just sent you flowers," Lauren says, disappointment edging her tone.

"Hmm. Watch this." I grab my phone back from the girls and text him.

Me: Hey! Hope you're having an awesome time at Macintosh tonight!

I wait, not really thinking he'll respond, but he does.

Trevor: Hey! You here too? I'm with a friend hanging out.

"What's he saying?" They all want to know.

"That he's with a friend. You know, he seems to have a lot of those."

Me: Uh, I think your version of friend and hanging out and mine must be completely different.
Trevor: Sam, I can explain.
Me: This? I think it's self-explanatory and I believe you and I are through.

And I send him the picture I took. Then I get the radio silence I expected earlier.

"So?" Lauren asks.

I tell them and they all shake their heads.

Berkeley is the first to say something. "Skanks. Men are all skanks."

And why is it okay for men to be glorified whores, but women can't? Screw that.

"I'm going to do it. Free my Sam Slut. I'm done with getting stepped on. It's time Sam has some fun, too."

We raise our glasses and toast my momentous decision to fling my thong to the wind—or in Ben Rhoades's face if he'll accept it.

Then a thought hits me. "Well, one good thing came out of this. I don't have to go on that date with Trevor that I wasn't looking forward to on Saturday."

We raise our glasses for another toast. Tomorrow may be a hangover work day. But now my big question is, how will I approach Ben. I guess I'll have to wait and see him at his firm.

"So, what do you think, ladies? Should I just wait until I run into Ben through work, or should I text him and ask him to get together?"

Lauren has a sly look that sends a shiver up my neck when she says, "I have an idea."

ELEVEN
BEN

—◆—

WORK BECOMES MY BEST FRIEND as I give it my all and then some to avoid going home to an empty house. I can't even muster the energy to hook up with anyone. But I refuse to believe Samantha has a choke hold on my dick. I'm just too busy for the complication of anonymous sex with some random female who no doubt will ultimately want more no matter what they say. Karen is proof of that.

"Dude, some of us are going prematurely bald. And you'll join our ranks if you keep that up."

I release my death grip on my hair and smooth it back. Jeff just shakes his head. "It's one o'clock. I'm grabbing Mark to go grab a late lunch. You in?"

"Nah. A former client of mine from J.P. Morgan Chase reached out to me. He's not pleased with my replacement and wants me to put together a proposal for him."

"Sweet. What does your pops think of that?"

I shrug. "I haven't told him yet."

"Why not?"

I shrug again. "Been a little too busy working to fill him in."

The truth is twofold. I want to do this without Dad's input. I want to land this client and have the papers signed before I tell my dad about it. I need this to prove as much to myself that I can do it on my own without outside pressure. And I trust Jeff not to say anything.

The other part is I'd gotten a call from Drew's estate lawyer.

They need me to provide them an accounting of his investments for the trust set up for Cate. The call is like a sucker punch reminding me again Drew's gone and never fucking coming back. And it's another good reason not to go home.

Jeff and Mark are good guys, but they will never replace my best friend.

Jeff nods. "We'll grab you something."

"Thanks," I say, feeling something lodge so deep in my throat I want to choke.

I wait for him to clear my office by ten feet before I pick up the phone and dial Cate's number.

"Ben," she says and I can hear the smile in her voice.

"Do you have dinner plans?" She's quiet, which is weird. "You there?"

"Yes, actually I have plans tonight."

"It's cool. I was just thinking ..." I trail off because it isn't right. I'm supposed to help her move on, not drag her down with my shit.

"... about Drew," she finishes for me.

"Yeah," I admit.

Her voice cracks and Drew would kill me for ruining her mood. "I'm sorry, Cate. I shouldn't have called you."

"Don't you dare, Ben Rhoades. This is me. You've been there for me, I can be there for you."

Getting to my feet, I stand by the window and look out.

"God, Cate, I miss him."

"Me too."

We're quiet for a while.

"I can cancel my plans," she offers, ever selfless Cate.

"No, I'll be fine," I lie.

"Are you sure?"

"Yeah, I'm good. I'll probably grab a late dinner and crash." Her hesitancy makes me feel more of a shit. "It's okay. I've got a lot I need to get done anyway."

A little more coaxing, including a bad joke that makes her laugh, gets her off the phone.

Sorry, man, I say to myself hoping Drew hears me before I lose myself in my computer screen.

I'm utterly immersed in work until a soft hand releases mine from my hair. Part of me knows, but can't believe. So that's why I end up saying, "I know, Lisa. My hair again."

The hand drops from mine, and I look up, but it's not Lisa. "Samantha."

She nods, looking spooked. The way the light filters around her, she's a vision from heaven.

"Lisa's a co-worker of mine. She's always giving me hell for …," I add, holding up my hands, not sure why I feel I need to explain myself. "Why are you here? Working on our event?"

She holds up the basket. "I needed to return this to you."

I hate the feeling of disappointment that gnaws at me. I'm the one that told her I couldn't be with her.

"You look like you haven't eaten," she says.

Her eyes hold mine and I see as much confusion as excitement.

"Actually, I haven't—"

Before I can tell her that Jeff's bringing me something, she says, "Good, I brought lunch. I thought we could talk."

Talk would evaporate if I allowed myself to look past her eyes at her lovely curves. "Sam, I think all that needed to be said was."

"How would you know until you hear me out? Plus, you need to eat if you plan to conquer the world."

That makes me smile as my stomach rumbles from the smells coming from the basket.

"Fine, a quick bite," I say.

"Is there somewhere we can go eat?"

I pinch my chin as the conference rooms are quickly eliminated from my mind. Then I stand, thinking of the best place to go. Glancing at my watch I see that it's half past one, most everyone would have eaten by now.

Taking her hand in mine, I lead her out the back door to a small patio with two picnic tables shaded by the building from the sun.

Reluctantly, I let her hand go as she grins at me after she glances down at our clasped hands. She sets out a spread.

"A potential catering partner brought more samples than I can possibly eat on my own. I thought I could get your take on them to help me make my decision."

When she takes a seat next to me, my eyes are drawn to her exposed legs from the skirt she wears. I pick up one of the finger sandwiches in order not to touch her. I bite in as she watches intently. It's actually good, better than I thought from what was essentially a deli sandwich.

"Good?" Sultry eyes land on mine.

I nod. "Your turn."

Either I need to get laid or she is purposefully playing the sex kitten. It has to be the former because she's made herself clear that sex isn't on the menu for us. When she opens her mouth, I fucking almost nut in my pants imagining her mouth on me. I have to look away but end up staring at her ample cleavage. Closing my eyes, a picture of her rosy nipples all tight and wet from my tongue takes front stage behind my lids. I groan and shift in my seat to relieve the pressure.

When I open my eyes again, she's staring at me. "What did you think?"

"Really good," I admit.

And I'm not sure what we're talking about anymore. My hand scrubs through my hair because clearly I can't even have lunch with this woman. I would bet money she's sending me a sex vibe. And yet I know I'm wrong.

I clear my throat and focus on the food before I say the wrong thing. Before long, I've polished off most of the offerings with her taking a bite here and there.

"Looks like this company is a winner."

I laugh, "Either that or I was too hungry to taste anything."

She pulls a bag out of the basket and puts the empty containers in there. Then she hands me a Coke and takes one for herself. "I hope this is okay."

I glance at it. "Share a Coke with Samantha, huh?"

She grins, forcing me to smile as my throat dries up. I want to kiss her pretty lips and I can't. This lunch is just as frustrating as dinner was the other night. So why am I here?

"Are you going to tell me what you wanted to talk about?" I ask before I put the bottle to my lips.

She turns her Coke around to show me what's written on hers. Share a Coke with Someone Naughty. "I thought you might want to tell me what's involved with being your fuck buddy."

I turn my head just enough so the liquid that spews from my mouth only hits my sleeve and not her as I choke on more than the soda. Her perfect tits are practically shoved in my face as she thumps my back. I continue to cough and choke, sure I must've heard her wrong.

My nose is lodged in between her breasts and she smells like wildflowers. It seems to be the balm I need to stop choking. She stills a second before her hands cup the sides of my face to dislodge me from her breasts.

"You okay?"

I bobblehead because words are out of reach.

Her mouth turns into a shit-eating grin before she presses her lips to mine. There are many reasons why I shouldn't have dove in like I would find treasure. But her taste is like a magic carpet ride that takes me out of my head and to a secret place where everything in the world is fine.

When she pulls back, I'm the one left with uneven breaths.

"Sam—"

She shakes her head. "Don't ruin this, Rhoades. I'm a big girl and I've done a lot of thinking. Like you said, what's wrong with a little fun between consenting adults?"

"I don't want to hurt you."

Her spine straightens. "What makes you think you can hurt me? Cocky much? I think you should quit while you're ahead. I'm in, only I have one condition."

She stands gathering the remnants of our lunch and holds out the basket to me. I slowly get to my feet, not sure I'm capable of denying any of her requests at the moment. The idea of getting inside her tight pussy makes me stupefied.

"I can do this casual thing, but we have to be exclusive."

"Samantha."

"I mean sexually. You can go out with anyone you want, but if you're sleeping with me, it's only me."

Her request is full of holes and I know in the end she'll want more. But my hard won control is cracking. I want to be inside her with a single-minded purpose. And she's right. She knows what she's offering. Still I have to ask. "Are you sure about this?"

The smile she rewards me with is brighter than the sun. "Absolutely." She hooks her arm in mine and starts to lead me to the back door.

"Actually, I need to get another shirt."

I lead her to my car and open the trunk where I keep a change of clothes. I pull out a shirt on a hanger and place the basket in my car. When I close the trunk, she sits on it. Her brow is arched when she glances at the shirt I hold.

Sighing, I say, "You never know when you need to see a client and you have an accident like this." Of course, there is the other reason … if I end up at an unplanned overnight visit, but there is no way I'm copping to that.

"So, how do we shake on this deal of ours?"

I place my hands on either side of her. The hanger makes a clanking noise against the car. I don't even care if I scratched something. I lean over. "With a kiss." I press my mouth to hers. It starts out gentle until the scrape of her nails glide over my scalp. I pull back a little to say, "You look fucking amazing on my car and I'm going to have you here one day."

She giggles before I lean in again.

"What if I told you I wasn't wearing any underwear?"

I groan and practically swallow her tongue as I grip her hips pulling her into my erection. I hear a car pull up, but I don't care.

"Well, I see you don't need lunch."

I pull back, smoothing Sam's skirt, afraid Jeff would get a glimpse even though she's well covered.

"Isn't that the event planner?" I hear a female coworker say.

That's when I notice another girl getting out the other side of Jeff's car. Mark looks sheepish as if the comment's somehow his fault.

"Maybe that's how she got the job."

I straighten and face Lisa. "I had nothing to do with her being hired. So don't start rumors."

My glare lets her know I'm not up for any bullshit about this. I never use my status as the boss's son. But I will be damned if Sam gets a bad rap for me not being able to keep my distance from her.

Jeff herds the group into the building.

"I'm sorry about that."

Sam gives me a lackluster smile. "It's fine. I really should go."

She slides off my car and I help her because I need my hands on her.

"I won't let your reputation get ruined for this."

She nods. "Maybe we should keep this out of the public eye until after."

Something in me wants to fight the idea. I realize I want her on my arm, but that's foolish. *She's willing to be casual, Rhoades. Don't blow it.*

Before she can get away, I hold her wrist. "When can I see you?"

"Any time," she says, finding that sexy grin to flash at me.

"Tonight at your place?" I practically beg.

"My roommate will be at home."

I forgot about that. "My place at eight."

"I don't know where you live."

"I'll text you."

Leaning in, I kiss her mouth quickly again.

"Later."

As she's walking away, I say, "And Sam?" She turns and the view of her is stunning. I have no idea how I'll be able to get any work done for the rest of the day. "Tonight will be slow and easy for our first time. But I can't always promise that."

TWELVE
Sam

———◆———

THE WALK TO MY CAR is torturous as thoughts of being with Ben tumble through my mind. Slow and easy tonight is what he said. With the way I'm feeling right now, we might have to see about that. Fast and furious may be on the menu for Slutty Sam. I've thought of nothing but him for all this time and to take it slow? What the hell is he thinking?

By the time I walk back in my office, my phone dings with a text from Ben giving me his address. He wants to know if I need directions.

Me: Nope. I've got it. I'll use GPS. See you at 8.

Then I decide to be cute and text him again.

Me: And I expect you to be naked and waiting.

I anticipate a fast response, but I get nothing but silence. After a few minutes I worry I made a huge mistake. Maybe he thinks I'm a crazy ho now. I snatch up the phone and call Berkeley, the specialist in all things slutty.

"Wassup, my girl?"

"I think I just did a total fuck up." I chew my nail as I talk.

"Spill it."

So I tell her and she has the extreme nerve to break my eardrum with her loud cackle of laughter.

After she stops gasping for air, she says, "He is going to so love you. You are his dream girl. Stop worrying."

"Be real here. I'm dying."

"I am real, Slutty Sam. Now get to work and stop the angst. Wear something sexy cute tonight. You know, easy for him to take off, and you're so in with him. I bet the dude is working with a boner." She guffaws at her own little joke. And when I stop to think about it, maybe he is.

"You think?"

"I think. I gotta run. Cheers."

A couple minutes later, my phone dings. It's a text from Ben.

Ben: You do realize I'm trying to close a multi-million dollar deal here, don't you? See you at 8. The door will be unlocked. Don't knock. Just enter at your own risk. And I'll be naked. Count on it.

Oh shit! He took the bait. *Naked.* He's going to be naked. My hands shake at the idea. The memory of him pushing me against the wall rips into me and my face heats.

"Sam, you busy?"

Shit. My admin is knocking on my office door and I'm thinking of orgasms. *Pull it together, Sam.*

"Yes. I mean, no, I'm not."

"Are you okay? You look flushed."

"I'm fine. What is it?"

"Our interview is coming in soon. I wanted to go over a few things with you."

"Fuck."

"Excuse me?"

Jesus, I've got to get my shit together. "Sorry. Just a little unorganized here. Can you give me five?"

"Sure." Nancy gives me an odd glance as she walks out. Probably because I never curse in the office and I just dropped an f-bomb on her.

Five minutes later she comes in and we do a speed run through our interview tactics. Our prospective employee, Nick, arrives, and thank God, I'm able to focus long enough to see he would make an excellent addition to the company. I tell him to expect a call by the end of the day.

After he leaves, Nancy and I talk and both agree I should make him the offer.

Nancy asks, "Do you think he's gay? It's not that I have an issue with it, I only ask because usually you don't see many men as event coordinators."

"I don't know, nor do I care. He has the experience I'm looking for and need."

"Yeah, and I think he'd fit right in actually. And you could use someone with some muscle out there when you have to lug that crap around."

"No kidding. But don't tell him that." We laugh.

When I call him later, he happily accepts. I grin, glad that my day is going so well. I sit in my chair, forgetting about Nancy, when I let out a giggle, thinking that Ben will be the icing on my cake of a day.

"What was that for?" she asks.

"What?"

"That cute little giggle?"

"Did I giggle?"

"Seriously? Sam, you giggled like I never heard you giggle before."

"It was nothing, really."

She taps her pen to her mouth and says, "Didn't sound like nothing to me. In fact, it sounded like anything besides nothing. And I'll go so far to say it has something to do with a man because you've had this secretive little smirk on your face today."

"I have?"

"Yes, you have. Is it Trevor? Are you two finally back together?"

My upturned lips immediately turn south. "Ugh, no. He's a jerk and I don't ever want to see him again."

"Whoa. That's a strong statement."

"Yeah, well, he deserves it." I give her a very brief rundown on that crazy situation.

"Okay, then if not Trevor, who?"

I waggle my eyebrows, saying, "Someone new."

"Is that his name? Someone New?"

I laugh at her little joke. "No, his name is Ben Rhoades."

Her face gets this look of horror on it. "No, tell me I didn't hear you right. You didn't say Ben Rhoades, did you?"

"Yeah, I did. Why?"

"Oh, Sam, be careful. Promise me. I've heard some pretty bad things about him."

"Like?"

"He plows through women like a John Deere tractor."

I wave my hand through the air. "Yeah, I know all that. But after Trevor, I'm not interested in a relationship. I've discussed this with Ben. It's all cool."

Nancy squints at me. "Is this Sam Calhoun I'm talking to?"

"Yep, and I'm just a girl who wants to have some fun."

"Okay. I hear you. But be careful nonetheless. I don't want to see you hurt."

"And I appreciate that. I really do. But a girl has to break out of her mold sometime and let herself free, you know."

She taps that pen against her lips again and then nods. "I think I do know."

After work I go home and I'm a combination of excited and nervous. The mixture has my stomach in one giant knot, so I'm unable to eat a thing. Instead, I take a quick shower and check out my closet for something cute yet sexy to wear. I opt for a dress that hits both and by the time I'm ready, it's seven-thirty.

Lauren is in the kitchen when I come out. "Where are you off to?"

"To Ben's."

The size of her eyes tells me all I need to know. I didn't share what I did earlier today. I'll have to fill her in later.

"Where does he live?"

"In Mt. Pleasant," I say.

"Nice. I can't wait to hear all about it."

"Don't worry. I'll give you the scoop later."

She gives me a little wave, saying, "Have fun, but Sam, please guard your heart."

"I will. I promise."

When I pull into his driveway, I have to say I'm impressed. It's a large two-story house for a single guy. Now it's show time. Will he really be naked? Guess I'll find out. Pulling a tank load of air into my chest, I force my shaking body to calm down.

As I walk up to his front door, I'm happy as hell I wore flats and not the heels I originally eyed, because my legs feel like noodles. My hand goes for the doorbell when I remember what his text said. So I push down the latch and am happy it gives way. With a huge amount of trepidation, I open the door and step over the threshold. Closing the door behind me, I hear him say my name.

The room is dimly lit and at first I'm not sure where his voice is coming from.

Then I hear, "Lock the door, and follow the hall into the great room. You'll find me in the kitchen."

I do as he asks and take the time to notice that Ben's house is an eclectic mixture of modern and traditional. The furnishings look comfortable and inviting and the walls are graced with an interesting array of artwork. When I get to the kitchen, he stands behind the island and asks if I'd like a glass of wine.

"I'd love one." I keep walking. He's shirtless and from what I can see, he's absolutely beautiful. My feet carry me with no thoughts at all. I stop when I reach the island and stand opposite him, since it's the side closest to me. He hands me my glass and I take a huge gulp.

"Thirsty?"

"I am." But not for wine. I want to get this part out of the way, so I take another huge drink and drain my glass. I can't even tell if it's good or bad. I could be drinking vinegar right now and not know the difference.

"Looks like it," he says, taking in my empty glass. "Care for another?"

"Not really." I step away from the counter and move around to him. "Well, I know one thing."

"What's that?"

"You were serious about the naked thing."

"I told you to count on it, didn't I? Only it doesn't seem fair I'm the only one naked."

He grabs something from the counter and covers his dick before I get to see. "Eyes up here. What is it with women who can't keep their eyes above the equator?"

The mirth in his eyes causes me to giggle. I feel nervous and invigorated at the same time.

"Strip, Sam." The amusement is still there, but there is a seriousness to his tone.

Suddenly I'm in the spotlight as his eyes bore into me. I can't seem to remember how to get the damn dress off. My hands shake but he takes a hold of each of my wrists which means whatever he's been holding is gone. He's bare and his heated skin warms me as he pulls me close.

And I can't wait any longer. My hands land in his hair and his end up fumbling with the hem of my dress. Our mouths crash into each other with a teeth cracking sound before we stop a minute, laughing.

"I've ..."

"You ..."

We both start talking at the same time and laugh again.

"You first," he says.

"I'm honestly not sure how to do this even though I've thought of little else all day."

His chuckles are long since gone as his eyes smolder on mine.

"So have I. You are so beautiful, Sam." His hands leave my dress and move to cup my face. "Let's try this kiss again." His lips touch mine, soft yet insistent, and I'm lost. Slowly, our tongues twine together and explore each other. As the kiss deepens, my brain spins with nothing but this man.

His palms leave my face and move to my dress. All clumsiness is gone now as he finds the zipper and tugs it down, so he can free me from its confines. As the dress falls, it seems to take forever as the fabric flows down my skin like a slow moving river, and I tremble.

He breaks off the kiss and says, "I have to look at you. God, if I could only tell you the number of times I've imagined you like this, you probably wouldn't believe it."

He runs one finger slowly underneath a bra strap, making me shiver like it was thirty degrees outside, yet a hundred and twenty inside. Then he slides the strap off my shoulder and presses a kiss there, repeating his actions on the other side. I'm momentarily frozen by desire. And this is only the beginning. I can't even imagine what I'll be feeling later.

"Open your eyes, Sam. I want all of you here."

When I look at him, I get an eyeful. He's erect and his cock is gorgeous. My hand goes on autopilot to grip him, drawn to him. He's smooth and velvety to my touch.

But then his hand wraps around mine.

"Sam, I've been wanting you for so long now. I'm going to have to ask you to keep your hands to yourself or I can't promise what'll happen."

"I like those kinds of promises."

"Normally, I do too, but right now, I want to play with you first." With those words, he takes my hands off of him with a sexy smirk and kisses me. "I have big plans for us. They include the use of your hands, but not right now."

Before I know it, my bra is unhooked and dropping to the floor. "My turn," he says. His head homes in on a nipple and when his mouth hits the target, I moan. I'm not sure I'll be able to stay on my feet with this kind of teasing. My nipple is diamond-hard as he flicks his tongue over it and then sucks it hard. My fingers sink into his shoulders to avoid falling. Pure lust fans throughout my body, scorching my veins. The dampness between my legs grows as he turns his attention to my other nipple. When he moves, a hand slides down the back of my ass, moving the thin string of my thong aside, and starts to rub along my slit from behind. All of a sudden he stops everything and I protest.

"It's okay. I'm only going to pick you up and carry you upstairs to my bedroom."

I sag in relief. And then I feel and hear him chuckle. He bends down and slips off my thong. Then he stands and puts an arm under my knees and picks me up.

"You ready?"

"Mmm hmm." I nod.

His bed is massive and his room is definitely masculine. Dark wood and deep hues blend to make it so. When he lays me down, I sink into a world of comfort. He hovers over me and then kisses me.

"I love your mouth, Sam."

"Hmm." I love his body, but I'm not going to tell him that. Not yet anyway.

His mouth is like fucking magic on my skin. Electric fire. He kisses, sucks, bites, and licks his way down to my thighs. He has this way of using his teeth that is so damn hot. He scrapes them along a certain area until I want to hang from his ceiling fan. What the hell is that all about? By the time he gets to my inner thighs, I am melting.

I've had men go down on me before—so-called boyfriends I thought I loved – and it's been good. But tonight, I experience something extraordinary. Pussy, meet Ben's mouth and tongue. Holy quivering vaginas. This man knows his way around a woman's body. When he gets down to business, we are both speaking in tongues. He's working me in a foreign language I've never heard. And I murmur incoherent words as I lose my grip on my native tongue. Either I have an out of body experience or I don't even know what. All I know is he is a lethal combination of I've-never-had-anything-this-amazing and the-greatest-oral-sex-of-my-life.

"Sam, how are you doing there?"

"I-I'm not sure." And it's the damn truth.

His mouth is on mine and some way brings some sanity back to me. I taste my salt on his tongue and he grabs my leg, wrapping it around his waist. Then I hear him tearing open a condom, and I honest to God want to put the thing on him, but my limbs are still so loose and languid, I can't get them to cooperate and move properly. So I lay there like the dead. He's back and raises a brow, asking, "You with me here?"

"Yeah."

"You look amazing. Tell me you feel as good as you look," he says, as he hovers over me.

"Never better." What I really want to say is, "Stop talking and get to fucking," but I don't want to embarrass myself, so I keep my thoughts to myself.

Then I feel his tip penetrate. I fist the sheet just before he rocks in and out until he's deep seated. It's been far too long since I've felt this. I feel full and stretched in all the right ways. And if I thought I could have slept like the dead after getting off once, I'm now fueled up again and ready to go. My hands cup his firm ass and I tilt my hips to meet him. One hand slides under me and he looks at me. "You good?"

"More," I breathe, holding his eyes in challenge.

He braces himself on one elbow and thrusts in and out, hard and fast. His brow is furrowed and a fine sheen of sweat makes him glow. The man look like an illusion—like something I dreamed up.

"Tell me how you like it, Sam."

He hits a spot that makes me groan, and I pant out, "Yeah, this is good."

A hand moves between us and he finds my sensitive nub, which is still reeling from my last orgasm, and starts to apply the slightest pressure. Then he moves his finger so he's rubbing but not really rubbing.

Oh my God, I'm pretty sure I see heaven as stars explode in front of my eyes and I climax again, moaning out my pleasure. I think I understand why he has a reputation. He knows my body better than I do and this is our first time. I start to realize why women would want to hold on to him.

"You're gorgeous when you come," he says.

"Huh?" I blink before his words register. "Oh." I smile, enjoying the afterglow of two orgasms. "I wouldn't know."

He chuckles at my stupid joke. Then he puts a hand under my waist and flips me over. What? There's more? I feel his cock all over the back of me as he kisses me everywhere. My neck, my shoulder, my back, my ass, especially my ass when he sinks his teeth into me. He lifts my hips, shoves a mound of pillows under me, and spreads my legs. Then his head is back between my thighs, nibbling, sucking and who knows what all. Only I know I'm getting turned on again.

He positions himself at my entrance and plunges in. "You're so wet, Sam."

"I should be. You've just given me two orgasms."

"Hmm. And to think the night has just begun."

"What?" I gasp.

"That was only a warm up."

I'm speechless because two has been the limit of the few guys that came before him.

"And Sam, this one's going to be a little rougher than the last two."

As soon as his words end, he slams into me, deep.

"Oh, God, Ben." It's all I can say.

He presses a palm on my back, pushing me down but keeping my ass raised and fucks me like a mad man. Now I know what I've been missing and why all the bad girls are bad. This is what fucking is all about.

My fingers grab the sheets and clump them up right before I scream out his name and have violent orgasm number three. He isn't done and I ache in the sweetest way. He adjusts his angle as he continues to pound into me building my fourth release.

"That's it, baby. I feel your tight pussy grip me. You're going to come and so am I."

He grips my sides as he nails me to the bed. I come hard screaming out my pleasure as he grunts, coming hard, grinding himself against my ass. Then he pulls out and collapses on top of me, grabbing me close to him.

"That was epic," he says.

I can hardly catch my breath, but manage to utter, "Yeah. It was."

He kisses my cheek and I turn so I can kiss him back. What I thought would be a quick peck turns into a serious make out session. We are nothing but hands, lips, and tongues.

When we finally stop, he looks down and my gaze follows. He's sporting an impressive erection again.

"Jesus, Sam." He shakes his head and laughs. "Don't go anywhere." He gets out of bed and heads to the bathroom but is back before I can think of doing a thing.

"I want you on top." He reaches for a condom and I grab his hand.

"I want to do that."

His grin is one for a toothpaste commercial as he hands me said item. I stick the end in my mouth and use my teeth to tear into the foil packet. Once his cock is fully protected, I prepare to mount. Then I laugh.

"What's so funny?"

"I just thought how I was preparing to mount you. Like a horse."

"And?"

"I thought it was funny."

"Wait." He runs a finger around my opening. "Just wanted to make sure you were ready."

That was nice. Trevor never would've done that.

"The verdict?"

"Mount up, cowgirl." Now he laughs.

I lift up and insert the tip but I don't wait and do it little by little. I fully seat myself on him and he lets out the sexiest damn groan I've ever heard. Then he grabs my hands and puts them on his hips.

"Go. Ride me hard, Sam."

And I do. I hold nothing back. But he tells me to stop and face the other way.

"Why?"

"You'll see."

And he's right. The pressure, holy cow. Or horse. Or whatever. And then he starts to play with my ass. And I freeze.

"No?"

"No."

"Okay." His hands are gone from that spot. "For now. One day I'll change your mind."

I don't pay attention; I'm only focused on one thing.

"Sam, are you close?"

"Yeah."

Then he surprises me when he sits up, but not all the way. His hand reaches for me and starts with a nipple. Then he moves to my clit and that's all it takes to push me over the edge. He follows and after, lays me down right on top of him, and rolls on his side.

"Next time will be like this."

"Mmm." I can't keep my eyes open. I feel him slide out, but I drop off.

I wake up later, after eleven, and the bed is empty next to me. I get up to pee and when I'm done, I walk downstairs with a beautiful ache between my legs, and go hunt for Ben. The kitchen is empty, but I find him outside on the deck, looking over the marsh.

"Hey," I say.

"Did I wake you?"

"No. I had to use the bathroom. I think I'd better get going, though," I murmur.

"No, you don't. You're not going anywhere. Didn't you know?"

"Know what?" Now I'm curious.

"Fuck buddy rules? You have to spend the night."

THIRTEEN
BEN

---◆---

HOW HAD I LET THOSE words leave my mouth? *Spend the night?* When had I ever asked a woman to spend the night? It isn't like I hadn't spent the night with a woman before. Karen stayed over plenty of nights as well as a few others. But it hadn't been planned. It had been because the night ran late and fatigue won out.

"You look like you've seen a ghost," she says.

I blink, feeling my jaw slacken as I grope for words to dissuade her.

She purses her lips. "I can see you really didn't plan on asking me to stay?"

Honesty wins out over reason as I nod.

"Oh," she says.

I watch as she obviously expects me to give her another answer. She walks back in the house and her curves wake my cock.

Watching her leave catapults me out of my stupor. I leave the deck and catch up with her in the kitchen.

"Sam, I didn't mean that. Come, let's get back in bed. I want you to stay."

When she faces me as she yanks her clothes from the floor, I can see I've pissed her off.

"Ben, this is never going to work unless we are honest with each other. Besides, I have to go to work in the morning, as do you. I'm more than okay with going home tonight."

I reach out and pull her to me. "Stay."

Not giving her a chance to respond, I take her mouth as I weave my fingers in her hair.

"Stay," I say again, walking her back to my bedroom.

She eventually relents and lets me lose my mind inside her again. I rush through clean up, afraid she'll bolt, and find myself pulling her close. Her bottom fits against me as I wrap a possessive arm around her.

The next day I wake up from one of the most peaceful night's sleep that I've had in a long time. Most nights some version of Drew in his final days haunts me. I reach out and find air and the spot next to me is cold. After a quick investigation, Sam must've left sometime during the night as dawn has yet to arrive. I'm annoyed that I'm annoyed she's gone.

I go through the motions and end up at work before the sky shifts to blue from its inky blackness. My desk phone begins to light up as I read the headline story of a fake hedge fund manager who siphoned money from his investors for personal use. It's going to be a long day as I put my headphones on to start taking calls from worried clients. Luckily, my father has seen the story and has already determined that we haven't invested any of our clients' money in that hedge fund.

I'm dragged into an impromptu meeting to determine how we will communicate with our clients. We've already had several companywide that wanted to pull their money out of fear. Luckily, my portfolio of investors has been placated so far.

When my dad pokes his head in the door, I almost growl until I realize it's him.

"Benjamin, I'm busy with the fallout from this scandal. I need you to see to a client of mine at two o'clock. Actually, my client passed away and the trust has been reverted to her grandchild. We need to secure this account. So do whatever you have to do to ensure they don't move to another firm."

Before I can ask any further questions he's gone. I check the time and it's half after one. I have no idea how we currently have this client's trust invested. I sit at my desk and send an e-mail to Dad and his assistant requesting the information.

Not too long after, my computer signals an incoming email. And thanks to Trudy, Dad's trusty assistant, I won't be flying blind. Luckily, after reviewing, I find the portfolio mix is similar to another client of mine. I can play off that until I find out more.

I sit back in my chair and absently pick up my phone. Somehow I find myself thumbing through my pictures. When a snapshot of Samantha comes up, my thumb hovers. She's stunning in her bikini top. She didn't know I took the picture on the boat and I'd forgotten about it after the way the date ended.

Her breasts are heaven sent and my dick leaps to life. My eyes close and I remember what she felt like when I was inside her. A knock at my door comes and I see Lisa standing in the doorway.

I sit up and scoot to the desk to hide my bulging erection.

"Your two o'clock is here."

She steps aside and a man walks in. I have no choice but to stand. I lean over the desk to shake his hand.

"Ben Rhoades."

The guy's eyes trail down and I know he's checking me out.

"Well, Ben, it seems you're happy to see me."

"Um," I stammer, not sure what to say.

It isn't often I get hit on by a man. And this time it's a client I need to secure.

"Tongue tied?" He winks. "I get that a lot. I'm Horace. Horace Winston."

It's not lost on me he's still holding my hand. I gently tug it free.

"Nice to meet you, Horace."

The name is an old-fashioned one and doesn't actually suit him. If he hadn't thrown me off with the blatant come on, I might have laughed or joked about it.

We sit and all thoughts of Sam have fled. My dick relaxes back into position.

"I have to tell you, it feels good to be free."

My only response is an arched brow. I feel like a therapist all of a sudden and believe I should just keep my mouth shut and figure this guy out.

"Yes, the old biddy is dead and I can finally live my life."

"You mean your grandmother."

He nods. "I had to pretend to get engaged." He groans. "Not that I don't enjoy Cecily. We've been dating since high school and, well, she's great. You, on the other hand, are more my speed."

I shake my head briskly. "Nothing wrong with being with who you want, but I'm into women." I pause and then mutter under my breath. "Maybe too much."

It's his turn to turn a questioned brow my way. "It's hard to come out. Especially if your family has certain expectations, but you don't have to lie to me."

I laugh, because what else can I do. "No, honestly, I was looking at her picture when you showed up."

Leaning towards him, I flash him my phone screen where Sam's sexy image still graces it.

"Oh." He purses his lips. "Too bad. She is quite nice. Not my type though."

"Your type. I thought you were into guys."

He shrugs. "When you're in my situation, you learn that in the dark, a hole is a hole, especially if the woman has a lot less going on up top than your girl. A woman like that can help the imagination go where it wants to go."

Something about this guy has me asking an inappropriate question. "And your fiancée? Are you planning on telling her?"

"I don't know. Cecily is great. I've tried to get her to accept the truth many times because I do love her, just not enough to give up on pursuing other options. But we get along well enough. She's convinced that I'm confused. In fact she's encouraged me to try out other relationships before I make any decisions."

I can't come up with an appropriate response, so I lift my shoulders in a shrug.

"I know, right? She's a great girl. But ..."

I almost hate to ask, but it's as if he needs a friend to unload on. I need his business, and oddly enough he's fairly easy to talk to.

"But?"

He sighs. "The one guy I'm interested in won't leave his girlfriend. He likes women. Hell, he likes me to go all she-male on him before I blow my load in him."

And then there is such a thing as too much information. I press two fingers on opposite sides of my temples and try not to laugh.

"Yeah, I'm the one that can be your girlfriend and boyfriend too. You should give it a try."

Laughing, I shake my head. "Thanks for the offer."

He waves a hand. "It's okay. Never hurts to ask. Anyway, I had plans to move my money from this ultraconservative firm. But I like you." He winks. "Tell me how you can make my money grow and expand." The innuendo isn't lost on me and I have to chuckle.

We talk shop for a solid half an hour and he's pretty in tune with how he wants his money invested. After he signs on the dotted line, I'm able to report to Dad that I've done my job and made an interesting friend of sorts.

My high from winning a client plummets when I get a call from my potential client letting me know he won't be making any changes with his investments due to the news involving the hedge fund scandal. Even though I've assured him our company hadn't been involved in any way, it's a lost cause that leaves me drained.

Jeff and Mark are busy when I decide I need air and a break from the office. I stroll out of the building and pull out my phone. Scrolling through my contacts, I automatically search for Drew. He was the only one who truly understood the relationship between my father and me. I know Dad wants the best for me. He just doesn't believe I'm the best. And I've spent my whole life trying to prove my worth. Winning a client I had in New York would prove to him that I hadn't left because of failure, but by choice.

Hastily, I shove the phone back in my pocket feeling my mood sour even more. When I turn the corner, I spot the doctor who's been around Cate a few times.

"Ben," Cate's friend says.

"Hey, Mercer."

"Have you seen Cate lately?"

His question makes me feel worse than shit. I haven't been doing my job for Drew very well these days and the guy's accusatory glare is confirmation enough.

"Not in the last few days," I mutter. "But what's that to you?"

Protectiveness overtakes me and I wonder what the good doctor and Cate have going on.

"Can I ask you a question?" His words aren't a request.

"What's that?"

"Is something going on between you two. She's never really explained her relationship with you other than you were Drew's best friend."

I frown. "Me and Cate." I shake my head. "She's like my little sister. That would be ..." I cringe feeling my face pinch in disgust. "Yeah, no, never will happen."

"Oh." The guy's face brightens, then dims. "Do you have a problem with her dating me?"

No one can take Drew's place, but Drew would want me to reassure the guy. He wanted Cate to find someone.

"Not as long as she wants to and you make her happy."

His next words are a total surprise. "I'm falling in love with her."

I take his measure differently. The few times I'd met him, she'd made it clear they were just friends. Jenna hadn't said anything different. "Wow, that's fast."

"Maybe. We may have only started dating a little over a month ago, but we've been friends for a while. And she's easy to love."

"Make her happy, man. She deserves that and more."

When he leaves, I actually hope he wins her over. Cate deserves someone like him.

Back at the office, the sun has long since gone when Jeff pops his head in my office. It's a nightly ritual for him, so I'm not surprised by his appearance.

"It's been a shit day," he complains.

"That it has. The bad guys always seem to ruin it for the rest of us good guys."

"Good guys?" he scoffs, falling into one of the chairs in front of my desk. "I doubt any of the women in this town would call you good except maybe your event planner. Did you nail her last night after your little show in the parking lot?" I scowl at him. "Don't bother answering. You look a little lighter, like gravity doesn't have a complete hold on you."

"What's that supposed to mean?"

"It means that since you blew your load, you're light on your feet."

I can't stop the chuckle. "You are something else," I say evading the question, not sure I'm pissed or amused.

"You want to go out for drinks?" I shake my head. His eyes go wide. "Are you pussy whipped already?"

"Who said I slept with her?"

Mark's voice comes out of nowhere as he steps into the room. "I told you, Jeff, she's not like that."

It's my turn to be surprised. "How do you know her?" Even I can hear the predator in the tone of my voice.

"Her parents live down the street from my dad."

"You ever hook up with her?"

Mark's face pinches. "No." He waves me off. "She wasn't even in high school when I was. But I heard things when I came home from college and they were all good. She's the kind of girl you marry, not bang. So if you're not in for the long haul, Ben, leave her alone."

After they leave, I pick up my phone several times only to put it down. Mark's words haunt me like Drew's ghost would have if he could. I've already fucked up and let my dick rule my actions. I can't play fuck buddy games with someone like her. She'll only get hurt in the end. Somehow, I need to let her go before things go too far.

My decision made, I stay away from Sam for the rest of the week. Good girls aren't in the cards for me. I have nothing to offer them. Even though she says she wants to play fuck buddies, I know how that usually ends up. Karen is the prime example of that.

When Sam calls me from outside my office on a rainy Friday night after hours, I'm ready to say the things that need to be said.

FOURTEEN
Sam

THIS IS PROBABLY THE BALLSIEST move I've ever made, but I have to do something. He hasn't called all week, and I don't know why. After the night we spent and the fireworks display that erupted over his bed, I can't stop thinking about him. And I know he felt it, too. I want some more of Ben Rhoades and I'm willing to take this chance.

My heart is pumping blood through my veins at light speed. I wish I had cruise control for my blood pressure because I totally need it right now.

"Rhoades." His voice is curt when he answers. Does that mean he doesn't want to hear from me?

"Ben, it's Sam."

"Sam," There's a pause. "Hi. I was busy grabbing some contracts out of the printer and had my hands full so I couldn't see the caller ID. How are you?"

Thank God for that. I'm not sure what to make of him yet, but it sounds like at least he's not put off by me. "I'm fine. How's your week so far?"

"From hell or worse." He explains something about a hedge fund, which is purely Greek to me and I tell him.

"All you need to know is that a lot of our clients had to be stroked, petted, and reassured all week that their money is safe and I lost a huge deal because of it."

"Aww, I'm terribly sorry. That sucks because it's not like it was your fault."

"Thanks, but when it comes to money, people don't care. They only want theirs protected. So what's up?"

"I was on my way home and I noticed your car in the parking lot on this yucky rainy Friday night, so I decided to stop and call."

"Wait. You're downstairs?"

I can almost feel his surprise leaping through the phone.

"I'm in my car, but yeah."

There's a long beat and I can imagine him running a hand through his gorgeous hair.

"Come on up … that is if you want."

"On the way," I say, not able to keep the grin off my face.

He meets me at the entrance and stares at me for a long moment before he reaches for my hand. Contact. I feel like I can't breathe when he guides me to his office. "This place is like a tomb," I say.

"Yeah, I'm the only one left. It's been such an awful week, everyone took off earlier than usual, but I had some things I needed to finish up, so I'm the last one here."

"Nice."

"Nice?"

"Yes, Ben, nice," and I wiggle my brows so he catches on.

"Oh." His lips round perfectly when he says the word. "I see, Ms. Calhoun. It appears you may have an ulterior motive here."

"That I do, but I have to say I'm a little confused."

"Confused?" he repeats.

"You don't call, you don't write." I say it in jest, though he knows I want an answer.

His face hardens and I immediately realize I've said the wrong thing.

"Yeah, about that. I think …"

"And that's your problem. You're thinking too much." I don't want him to go into some fuck buddy explanation because I have a sinking feeling that's what he was going to. So I walk into his personal space and lean into him to run my tongue over the seam of his pinched lips. This is so not my style, but I'm willing to give it a shot. I pray he doesn't push me away.

"Sam." He stops me and I would have felt rejected if not for the glazed eye look he's giving me. "I'm pretty busy here if I expect to see my bed at all tonight. What did you have in mind?"

"Do you really have to ask?" He smells so perfect that I shove my face into the crook of his neck to taste and inhale him into my every pore.

"Fuck," he mutters. When his arms circle my waist and his hands grip the cheeks of my ass, I know I've hit gold. "You really want to do this here, now?"

"Uh huh."

"Fine," he grits. "There are rules, Sam. I have to know you understand that I'll give you what you want, but that's all I can give," he whispers in my ear as I nibble on his neck.

Leaning my head back a bit, I lock stares with him and see the pupils of his steel grays dilate slightly. His words are lost with the hardness of his cock against my belly lighting a fire below my waist. His tongue moistens his lower lip and then he takes my own between his teeth and bites down, not too hard but not too soft. He ends the bite with a tug as he pulls my lip into his mouth and sucks on it. When his tongue touches mine, I'm nearly unglued, but his hands pressing into the flesh of my ass keep me on my feet. One hand moves to my waist, holding me steady, while the other slips under the hem of my short skirt, to resume its hold on my ass. The way he grabs me, with his long fingers touching the most sensitive areas of my core, make me even slicker with need.

I'm suddenly hoisted up as he turns me and sets me down on his glass top desk. There's a question in his eyes, and I nod slightly, giving him the go ahead.

For a second when he walks towards the door, I'm struck thinking he's going to leave me there. Instead, he hits what looks like a light switch and the glass wall before me turns opaque.

"Whoa," I say in surprise as he closes the solid office door and locks it leaving us hidden. "I thought we were alone."

"Just to be sure." His lids drop to half-staff as he makes his way back to me and says, "Lift up," in a deep sex-driven voice.

Once my butt clears his desk, impatient hands unzip my skirt and tug it free from my body, depositing it, along with my thong, on the floor. Then he stands and stares at my naked-below-the-waist self as I sit on his desk.

"Hmm. What a sight for my overworked eyes you are. And a lovely addition to my desk, I might add."

"Glad you approve." I don't get time to say anything else because his mouth is on my pussy like it's his next meal. Two hands spread my thighs as his tongue wreak havoc with my control, and he watches as I completely fall to pieces, like a computer that just short circuited. By the time my orgasmic spasms have stopped rocking my world, I notice my hands have left his hair a wreck.

"Sorry about that." I try to smooth the short strands into place.

"I'm not. Not one bit. You were spectacular," he says, his voice husky.

"A nice sexcapade then?"

He chuckles. Then he finds his wallet and out comes a condom. "And I'm saving the best for last." He unzips his pants and drops them to showcase his boxers, which contain an impressive hard on, barely held in restraint by the thin fabric. I watch as he tugs them down and the prize springs free. He takes it in his hand and squeezes it, rubbing it in an up and down motion. Oh my God, is it ever sexy. I want to watch this man get himself off in the worst way.

He reads my mind. "Do you like what you see?"

I can barely breathe as I nod.

"Say it, Sam."

"Yes," I hiss.

"No, say it. Tell me what you'd like."

"I'd like to see you jack off."

"Maybe someday. But not tonight. Tonight you came here because you wanted me inside of you. *Deep.* And now that you're here I want to feel your tight pussy around my hard cock, squeezing it dry."

Oh, hell. I'm almost coming again, and he's not even inside me yet.

His hand still strokes his gorgeous cock, and then he rolls the condom on. With hands on my thighs, he yanks me to the edge of the desk and in one swift motion, enters me. Then he stills. A palm lands in the center of my chest and pushes me back. He bends one leg so my thigh about touches my chest and drapes the other leg over his shoulder. Honest to God, one thrust in this position and he hits every spot that rings my buzzers. I come almost immediately. About three or four pounding thrusts later, I scream his name, but he doesn't stop. He keeps going as if he never heard me. And it builds again until I hit climax number three. That's when I feel his body tense, he stands up straight and slides his hands under my ass and comes. And, Jesus on a picnic, I've never seen anything so arousing in my life. It dawns on me then that we both still have our shirts on, but that was one sizzling romp on the desk, if I do say so myself.

When he looks at me, I'm expecting that sexy-as-hell grin, but instead, I get confused by an ambivalent look. He drops his head back and runs his hands through his hair. I'm not sure what's going through his mind, but it can't be good. And since I've never done the fuck buddy thing before him, I'm not quite sure what to say. So I opt for something fairly comical.

"Hmm... the many uses of a desktop. Workstation, computer space, and hotspot for sexromp."

I'm greeted with silence. Now I feel beyond awkward. I'm sitting on his desk and his dick is still inside of me, and he hasn't said a word. What the actual fuck is going on here?

"Earth to Ben?"

He finally looks at me after closing his eyes for a long second then blinking down at me.

"Yeah?"

"You okay there?" I ask.

"Fine." His voice sounds clipped.

"Did I do something wrong?"

"No."

"Oh, okay, then. Would you be interested in grabbing dinner?"

"No, like I said before, I have work to finish. I'm sorry, but it's been a terrible week."

Maybe it is his work. But he's whiplash Ben again. Or asshole Ben. And I'm too inexperienced to know how to deal with this.

He stands and slips out of me, removes the condom, and ties off the end. I wonder what he's going to do with it when I watch him toss it in his trashcan. In another nonchalant move, he bends down and pulls up his pants, tucks in his shirt and I'm left sitting on his desk bared assed.

I can't keep my mouth shut any longer. "Okay. What's the deal here?"

"What do you mean?"

"You're acting strange. That's what I mean."

"Sam, I'm sorry I haven't been able to connect with you. Work is crazy like that, which is one reason I don't do the relationship thing. You came, you wanted to fuck. I made time and did that. This is what fuck buddies do; they don't expect more."

Why do I just feel like he slapped me in the face?

"Okay. But you're Mr. Hyde. A few minutes ago you were Dr. Jekyll. Why the change? Why are you acting so different? We were fuck buddies the other night and you didn't act cold like this."

His hand is in his hair again.

"I don't know what you want from me. But this is the real Ben Rhoades. As you can see, there are many facets to me. And this is what I have to offer. If it's not what you want ..." He shrugs.

His blunt words sting so I keep my mouth shut, despite the dozen not-so-nice replies I'd like to throw at him. Instead, I hop off the desk and put my thong on and then my skirt as quickly as I can and with a, "See you around," I do a fast walk of shame out of there.

What a douche. I'm not sure what happened after the explosive orgasm, but something surely did. And whatever it was, it wasn't good. I don't know if I want to scream in anger or cry my eyes out. Or maybe both. The damn elevator takes its time getting to the floor as I pound the call button with my fist. When the doors open, I fly through them like I have a firecracker up my ass. And I think I do. His name is Ben Rhoades, resident asshole.

By the time I get to my car, I'm sure my blood is as hot as the surface of the sun. *Slow it down, girl. You're going to crash the damn car.*

As I stomp through my front door, I come to one resounding conclusion. This fuck buddy thing was the biggest mistake of my life. What the hell was I thinking? Clearly, I wasn't. Why can't I be like other girls and choose men who treat them right? And not total twatheads who fuck me over every single time. I am so done with this crap. So done.

Lauren is watching TV and she hollers out to me, so I pop my head in the room. "You do not want to be around me tonight." And I burst into tears. What in the wide world of fucks is wrong with me? I barely ever cry. Since Ben Rhoades, Produce Asshole From Hell entered my life, it seems that's all I ever do. That and curse like a sailor.

"Oh my God, now what?" She immediately rushes to my side.

When I tell her, she just hugs me. In her true fashion, I don't get the old, *I told you so.* And that's what I love best about Lauren.

"Everyone has to go through the worst things to enjoy the best. You'll get your knight in shining armor one day. I swear you will."

That night I dream of my knight, only he has messy dark hair and compelling gray eyes, with a body that drives me to the point of orgasm. I wake up with the sheets all rumpled and my hand in my panties, bringing me to a climax. Damn that Ben Fucking Rhoades.

The next day, my brain is all over the place and I'm supposed to be bringing Nick up to speed on all the current projects we have taking place. Poor guy. I'm sure at various points during the day, he's asked himself why he agreed to come to work for me.

"Sam, are you okay?"

"I'm sorry, Nick. I'm fine. I promise I'm not always like this."

"It's okay. You do seem a little off."

"Yeah, that's an understatement," I murmur.

"Do you want to talk about it?" he asks sweetly.

Oh hell to the no on that. "Thanks, but I'll be fine. What I do want is to review everything I have set up to propose to Martin Rhoades at Rhoades Investment Team. He wants to do a corporate outing for the employees and their significant others and he's offered me the job if I can come up with something that piques his interest. So let me brief you on what I have."

I review the golf and spa options, down to the smallest detail.

Nick looks up and asks, "What do you think he'll go for?"

"I have no idea. I don't know him that well and haven't ever worked with the company before."

"When do you present this?"

"On Monday, but I want you there. Take this home over the weekend so you can be familiar with it. Know the ins and outs so if he directs a question to you, you feel comfortable answering. You good with this?" I ask.

"Yes. Absolutely."

I hand him the folder with all the information. The real reason I want him there is as my shield. Maybe I'm not being fair to him, but I don't want to take the chance of running into Ben and being alone. Ben is my Achilles heel. If I have Nick with me, I'll have to act strong and pretend Ben's only a business acquaintance or possibly a friend and nothing more. Best case scenario would be if I didn't run into him at all, but the chances of that are next to none.

By the time Monday afternoon hits, I'm as ready as I'll ever be. Nick and I head over to Rhoades Investment Team. When we walk into the meeting, Martin is there, along with his admin.

"Samantha, it's nice to see you again. You remember Trudy?"

"I do. Good to see you two again. This is Nick, my newest team member. He's going to be my right hand on this event so I thought he should be here."

After all pleasantries are exchanged, we take our seats. I go over the details of what I've planned.

"This is some elaborate corporate picnic you've planned, Samantha."

My pulse has ramped up to a couple hundred beats a minute. Maybe I've overdone this.

"It is, Martin. But if I were a betting woman, I would imagine that not all the women here, or the significant others of the men, golf. Would that be an accurate statement?"

Martin chuckles. "Yeah, pretty accurate."

"So why not offer them an option?"

"Honestly? The reason I haven't before is because the previous event planners I used never brought it up."

"Then may I say you were using inferior event planners?" I chuckle to lighten my statement, but he knows I mean business.

"So, golf, spa, evening party, and overnight?"

I remind him of the price points. "It's just an option, but with the pricing, the overnight is almost a steal since they throw in so much more as an added bonus."

In the end, after he plays with the figures, over and over, he decides on the overnight option.

"Don't forget, not everyone will attend. Always expect at least ten to twenty percent to say no. So, I have the sign up sheets here and I can send you an email template you can use. If you want to go with this plan, you can shoot this out to every employee and tell them I need an answer by Friday at the very latest, preferably by Wednesday."

"Now I understand why you came so highly recommended. And even on short notice, your plan is well thought out. Everything looks great. Where do I sign?"

I can see where Ben gets his charm as Martin's smile is dazzling. His admin hangs on his every word.

I tap on my phone. "I've forwarded you the email template."

Martin turns to Trudy and says, "Good, when we get it, make Wednesday their deadline. Shoot that out ASAP."

"Got it, boss."

"Once you have the list of attendees, I'll need the names for each of the rooms."

Trudy chimes in. "I can do that."

"And the last thing I'll need is the number of people for golf and the number for the spa."

We finish up our details, setting up another phone conference for Thursday. Nick and I get up to leave, and Martin walks us into the hall and asks us to wait for Trudy to make copies of the contract. As we stand there, my luck runs out and Ben walks in.

"Sam?"

He glances between Nick and me only to flash back to me with a penetrating stare that makes me feel guilty when I shouldn't.

"Are you here to see me?" Even his eyebrows are sexy as one lifts with his question.

"I'm handling the corporate picnic, remember? I just had a meeting with your dad."

"Oh, is that all?" He snaps the question out like I'm there to steal from them or something.

"Of course. Why else would I be here?"

"I think we both know the answer to that."

Flames whip across my cheeks, scorching them. How dare he bring something up like that during a business visit?

I notice how his eyes keep flicking over at Nick, and it doesn't help matters any when Nick puts his arm around me and says, "Sam and I have been working quite hard on this event for your firm here. By the way, I'm Nick Hathaway." Nick extends his hand and at first Ben acts like he's not going to shake it. What a jerkhead. Finally, he grabs Nick's hand. Now it looks like they're hand wrestling.

"Here you go, Sam." Martin's voice breaks through the showdown taking place and I've never been so happy to see someone before.

"Thank you, Martin."

"No, thank *you*. Ben, you should see what she has planned for us."

Ben is still glaring at Nick. "I'm sure it's simply amazing." That tiny muscle in his jaw is twitching.

"Oh, it is, son. The best corporate event we've ever had."

"What's planned?" His dry tone tells me he couldn't give a shit about it. Well, fuck him and his twatfaced attitude.

Annoyed, I cover my frustration with a strained smile and run down the details. I watch as Ben keeps giving his father looks. Finally when I finish he speaks.

"Do you think we should really be spending this kind of money on an event with everything going on?"

Martin's jaw tightens. "And what would you suggest if you were in charge?"

There is obvious tension and I feel like I should walk away gracefully, but I don't know if the event will change.

"Maybe we should host a client appreciation day as a part of the event. Show good will to all the clients and give a presentation about our practices and how we screen for the right investments. And then have an employee-only picnic on the other day."

Martin looks as surprised as I am. "That actually sounds good. It will be easy to add them in. I just need a head count. But I want to stick to the original plan we set up for the employee picnic. Can you put a plan together and tell me how this will affect our budget?" Martin asks.

"I'd like to suggest something. In order to capitalize on your time at the hotel and save money, bring your clients in for lunch and golf, and then have the employee-only party the same night of the golf outing. Then the following morning, everyone is free to leave."

"I see where you're going here. That sounds great," Martin says. "Can you make the changes and have something back to me?"

This whole time Ben has avoided looking at me. So I do the same.

"Sure. I can have something to you this afternoon. And I can send over a modified contract if you agree."

Martin nods. "Thanks, Samantha."

"We'll be on our way. Martin, I look forward to talking to you on Thursday. Have a great rest of the day."

It takes all I have not to run out of here, especially when Ben finally looks at me through cold eyes. When we get in the elevator, I unleash on Nick.

"What the hell was that?"

"What do you mean?" he asks, full of innocence.

"Just what it sounds like. What happened back there? What were you doing putting your arm around me?"

"Oh, that. Sorry, I thought you needed some help back there. I was trying to make him jealous."

"Nick, you're playing a very dangerous game here. Ben runs hot and cold. And it worries me that you pissed him off."

Nick gives me a *what the hell* look. "He seemed like a jerk, Sam, and not worth your time."

"Yeah, well, I need to be the judge of that."

The elevator dings and we walk out. Nick throws up his hands and says, "Women. I'll never figure any of you out."

I'd like to tell him not to feel bad because I can't figure myself out either, but I don't. My head spins with douche-faced Ben. I'd love to ask Nick his opinion, but that would cross the boundaries of employer employee relations. Besides, what would I say? That my fuck buddy is acting like an asshole? No, this one will have to be kept under wraps.

My best bet is to get this corporate function behind me, and then move away from anything that is remotely related to Ben Rhoades. That man has messed with my head way too much and I don't have time for his crap. If this is what being a fuck buddy entails, then no, thank you. I believe I am now on *no* fuck buddy status. I may be horny, but at least I'll be sane.

FIFTEEN
BEN

◆

WHEN I SEE THE EXTRA car in the driveway, I almost hang a U-turn and head back home. Instead, I park and close my door a little too hard in anger. I don't bother to knock; it's my parents' home. Mom's sitting in the living room with Karen drinking what looks like tea from Mom's good china.

"Benjamin."

Folding my arms over my chest, I know I'm being rude. "What is she doing here?"

Mom gasps. "Benjamin Martin Rhoades."

"It's okay," Karen says, getting up. "I should be going."

"No, stay for dinner."

I glare at Mom, and Karen sees me.

"It's obvious he doesn't want me here, and I don't wish to cause any problems in your family."

"I want you to stay and tell me more about how your aunt is doing. And he can help you. He's been down this road before with his best friend, Drew. So sad that story."

I shake my head in disbelief that my mother would actually go there. "Sad? What's sad is Karen hanging around you when I've made it clear there is never going to be anything between us. And the fact that you are entertaining this is beyond sad. It borders on sick."

A knock comes at the door and I take the opportunity to make my exit before I say something I'll regret. I open the door and Kenneth, my sister's boyfriend, is on the other side.

"Hey, man."

I step out of the way and let him enter. "You can hang out in the living room. I'm sure Jenna will be down in a second."

"Jenna," I call towards the stairs before I head to the back. I need air and away from the memory of Drew Mom conjured. The fact that she thinks that I would want to go through that ever again, is ludicrous. And it pisses me off more than I can express that she would even bring it up in front of Karen.

The sun porch is empty, but I step out into the backyard and breathe. I need to calm down because Dad's going to give me shit about upsetting Mom.

My fist connects with the deck railing. Seeing Karen only reminds me of the look on Sam's face after I took her on my desk. I'd been busy, too busy to figure out the right way to explain my deadlines. Instead, I proved I was right about her not being able to make the cut when I gave her the fuck buddy speech. Her pale face proved she'd played with fire and had gotten burned. I can feel Drew's disappointment, which is just as bad as my need for my father's validation.

I need you, brother.

I rake a hand through my hair wondering if I'll ever be able to see past the grief that consumes me. What I wouldn't do for just one more day to kick back and pick at Drew's brain.

What grabs my attention when I look up is the aging structure in the tree that had been Drew's and my fort. How many times had Drew found me back there when I needed time to myself? He'd talk me down from smashing walls or faces. *Take a deep breath*, he'd say. *It isn't worth it.*

I wonder if it will ever get easier to think about him without hating the world for stealing him from us. Leaning my head back, I'm consumed by another memory.

Pressing my fists to my eyes, I hope to ward off the burning that threatens.

I hear him coming up the ladder and I grit my teeth.

"Dude, what the hell happened at school?"

The need not to look like a baby holds back any emotion as I remove my hands and face my best friend. I'd managed to confine my confession in my head thwarting Mom's concern over my state of mind. Only Drew has a key and the words stumble out like my feet had over the threshold of school when I shamefully left for home.

"She dumped me. That flowers, candy, teddy bear shit didn't work for me."

"Whoa, what?"

Drew looks ready to fight for my honor as if one of the guys at school took a shot at me.

"Last night. After the game, I gave her flowers and a teddy bear. I fucking told her, I love her. And today, she tells me we're better off friends. Then she walks off with that jackass."

Drew doesn't mince words.

"Fuck her," he says before with the biggest grin ever adds, "You did fuck her, right?"

He has a way of making me laugh in the worst of times. He picks up the bear she'd given back to me and tosses it in my face. That only starts a war of dodging whatever we can get our hands on. Cans and other garbage we'd left over time. When our laughter cools, I've made up my mind.

"I'm never falling in love again."

"You don't mean that. One day the right girl will come along."

I know he's only trying to make me feel better.

"Fuck that," I say adamantly. "Fuck love."

That memory is just another reminder why I need to stay away from Samantha Calhoun. One of us will break if we continue fucking around together.

"She's not the one," I say to Drew's ghost that continues to haunt me every time I come home. I understand why Cate couldn't go back to their home and sold it. It's too fucking hard. But the need to amend my statement forces the next words out of my mouth. "Because there's never going to be *a one*."

Movement near the tree line catches my eye. Out pops my sister with a guy I don't recognize who's trying to grab her arm to stop her. For a second I admire the tattoos on his arm.

Then the guy draws her close and there is panic in my sister's expression. I shoot off the deck and head in their direction.

"Jenna, please," the guy begs as I near.

He's so focused on my sister, he doesn't see me coming. Jenna spies me as she turns her face in my direction just as the guy leans down to steal what looks like a kiss, but gets her cheek instead.

"Brandon—"

"Am I interrupting something?" I growl, close enough I don't have to yell.

Quickly, he releases her as if he just noticed how fiercely he'd been holding her.

"Sorry." He looks sheepish and ready to bolt. "I should go."

"No, wait," Jenna says reaching out for him. But he keeps moving, not towards the back door, but the side of the house.

"Jenna, let him go. Kenneth's here."

Brandon half turns having heard but doesn't stop. The expression he wears is one of regret. *I should know, I feel it now.* Shame of how I spoke to my mother is starting to weigh on me as if Drew were there as my moral compass.

"I should—"

"Jenna, let him be. Your boyfriend is here. Who is this guy to you anyway?"

"No one," she says and turns away from me.

I stop her and ask, "Why wouldn't you have him meet you at your place instead of here knowing Kenneth was coming?"

"You wouldn't understand."

Her terse words get under my skin stoking the fury that had roiled through me minutes before.

"What's that supposed to mean?"

She spins to face me with an evil smile on her face. "Tell me exactly what you know about relationships." When I only stare, she adds, "Exactly nothing. You know nothing. How can you help me?"

"Try me. Just because I don't want a relationship doesn't mean I don't get them."

A huff escapes her and she flings her hair over her shoulder. "The longest relationship you've ever had is Karen."

"We weren't in a relationship."

She shakes her head. "Bingo. That's why you know nothing. You were with her exclusively for months. You brought her over for Sunday dinner."

"That was a mistake," I interject.

"Mom and Dad didn't see it that way. You took her to business meetings."

"It was convenient. She was convenient. It was easier to fuck one girl."

"Yeah, and I hear you're dating Samantha Calhoun now."

My jaw drops. "I'm not dating her."

She knows exactly what I mean by that.

"You are a piece of work, big brother. And you want to give me advice?"

I ignore her because I need to know. "How do you know

Samantha?"

Jenna gets a gleam in her eye. "You like her."

It was a statement and not a question. "No." The lie burns on my tongue, but I press on. "I'm just curious how you know her and why you think we're dating."

She studies me and I pray she doesn't read my eagerness to know the answers to those questions. Jenna can be a real bulldog about things when she has a scent.

"Mom told me you brought her to dinner. And how do I know her? She's got a business and I've seen her around. She's your type as far as looks go. But I haven't seen her with many guys over the years. I'm guessing she's the relationship type, which you claim not to be."

I almost sigh in relief. For a moment I thought maybe there were rumors about me and her. Charleston is big, but not that big in certain circles. Last thing I would want would be her reputation to be sullied by being involved with me.

She jumps to her own conclusion when I don't answer. "You do like her."

I cover my eyes hoping my next lie will be accepted.

"I don't. There might have been something, but I cut it off. I don't want to hurt her. She's a good one."

"Oh. My. God."

"What?"

"Your lame excuse for not involving yourself with her is actually a declaration that you care."

"I do not."

"Do too. When have you ever cared about whether or not you hurt a girl's feelings?"

"Always."

"Bullshit. You break up with them with silly excuses and they all end up broken hearted. Except I think you met your match with Karen. She's not giving up, dumb girl."

I groan not liking the direction of the conversation and changing course.

"And what about you and Kenneth? It's so obvious you're into Brandon. What gives?"

"Are we talking boys now?"

I glare at her.

"Fine, I like him. I like him a lot. But Dad will never accept him." I open my mouth to disagree then shut it. "See?" she adds. "You can't run away from what you want. Dad isn't the one in a relationship with the guy."

"You sound like Drew."

I become rigid for a second with the reminder.

"Ben, I'm sorry."

I pull her in for a hug and kiss the top of her head. "It's okay."

But it's not. I miss the hell out of the guy. As my sister hugs me back, I think about my advice to her. I know what Drew would do about Samantha if he were me. The question is what will I do, especially since I can't stop thinking about her.

SIXTEEN
Sam

———————◆———————

IT'S TIME TO CALL A MEETING of the minds. Lauren's in charge of gathering the flock together at our place, with promises of copious amounts of food and alcohol. My only wish is that they're waiting for me when I walk in the door from work.

Lauren comes through like she always does. The door's not even closed behind me before Hayley grabs my handbag and laptop bag I'm carrying and Berkeley shoves a shot of tequila and a lime in both of my hands saying, "Bottoms up."

I put the shot glass to my lips and tilt my head back, feeling the burn of the liquid silver run all the way into my stomach. "Thanks. I needed that."

Britt comes up behind me with another one. "Here."

Since this is my liquid therapy session, I don't refuse, and tip shot number two back. "Ahh. Just what the doctor ordered."

"Good. Now go put your comfy clothes on and tell us what's got your thong wadded up your hoohah." Leave it to Berkeley to come up with an image like that. I don't argue but go and change so I can get all this baggage off my chest. The weight of it is crushing me.

When I get back to the living room, Lauren the maestro hands me a vodka drink and begins to direct us all. "There are chips, salsa, dips of every variety and..." She points at me. "Your personal favorite—pimento cheese and crackers."

I dive in with gusto.

"Now, let me get you up to date." Everyone waits as Lauren

goes round robin. "Hayley's still panting after John, like things would ever change there," she says under her breath waiting for a laugh.

"I'm still hopeful he's going to propose," Hayley adds.

"Like I said, things will never change there."

Everyone laughs at Lauren while Hayley pouts and drinks from her wine glass.

"Then there's Britt, our serial dater. Who's the guy this week?"

Britt can take as good as she gets. "Why don't you tell us who your flavor is, Lauren? Two peas in a pod and all that."

"Touché. Moving right along," Lauren says in an effort to not talk about herself.

"And Berkeley's going to see the band again this week. How's your favorite drummer boy?"

Berkeley turns pink, which is actually a shocker. She never blushes. "We're here for Sam. So let's move on to what's important here."

All eyes turn to me, so I finish my bite and fill them in on the fuck buddy situation, ending with my surprise visit to his office and my walk of shame exit.

"That jerkoff is not playing by the fuck buddy rules," Berkeley announces.

"Can you fill me in on those because I never got that email? It must've gone to my spam box." My question is laced with sarcasm.

"Yeah," Berkeley says. "He's forgetting about the 'buddy' part. That's what's great about being fuck buddies. You fuck but remain friends, you know? It's like you don't let the fucking get in the way of a good friendship. He's treating you like a one-nighter he wants to get rid of and that's every kind of wrong in my book. Cut the asshole off. Now. He should no longer be given fuck or buddy status."

I lean back and sigh.

"What? Is there another piece of this we're missing?" Lauren asks.

"He did try to end it, but I told him he was overthinking things."

"Jesus. It sounds like he has feelings for you," Berkeley says.

"What? No! Absolutely not."

Lauren taps her cheek with her index finger. "I don't know, Sam. I'm inclined to go with Berkeley's train of thought. Why else would he act like that?"

"Because he *doesn't* give a damn. That's why!" I insist.

"Well, I think you should pretend you don't give a fuck about him and just keep banging him. I mean, come on. He gives you explo-gasms. What more do you want? Then if you meet someone who interests you, dump the motherfucker." Carrie sits there with a smug expression on her face while the rest of us are slack-jawed. Usually she is the one with the most conservative approach toward men and for her to come out with this is, well, shocking. She twirls a piece of her coal-black hair and giggles. "Y'all didn't think I had it in me, did you?"

I nearly spit out my drink of vodka I just took and the rest of the group howls with laughter.

"Jesus, Carrie," Lauren says.

"I think she may be right," Britt adds. "What do you have to lose, Sam?"

"My heart." I might've just dropped a damn bomb in here.

"Oh, no, you haven't?" Berkeley asks. "That's one of the rules you never break in being fuck buddies."

I screw up my mouth and say, "Not yet, but I'm heading there. That's why I have to do something. Either stop or ..."

"Then you have to stop. If he's a total jackass, which it sounds like he is, your heart's going to get trampled on in a very bad way," Lauren says.

I wring my hands. "I know. I already feel it happening. So here's the deal—we have this event ..."

"Back up." Britt is all business now. "What do you mean by 'we'?"

So I explain. And when I finish, they all look like salivating pups.

"What?" I ask.

"Don't you see?" Lauren asks.

"See what?"

"This can be your chance." Berkeley shakes my arm.

"No! Oh, no. This is purely business." I assert.

"Uh huh. And that's the best thing about this. You can be the stealth event slash romance coordinator," Hayley says.

"What the hell does that mean?"

The group of them starts chattering like a room of old church ladies at a potluck. Not that I would know what that sounds like, but my mom always says it and it sounds fitting right now.

The night wears on and they persuade me to their way of thinking. Putting Butthead Ben in his place will be my mission at that event. But I'm afraid I'm the one that's going to end up paying. Ben is savvy. Way too savvy for me when it comes to women.

The next couple of weeks, I don't have time to think about Ben or his pulsating peen. Or at least that's what I try to tell myself. I'm so busy with work and trying to get his company's event worked out that I leave my house early and don't get home until late.

When the weekend of the event arrives, I'm nothing but a bag of nerves. The girls are helping out, but won't be staying the night. They'll leave after the golf and spa outings are over.

We start things off with the lunch for all the clients and their significant others, and then it will be off to golf or the spa. None of the men chose the spa, only the women—*shocker*.

When Nick and I arrive, we head directly to where the lunch will be held to make sure all is in order. Not long after, Martin and Julia arrive. I introduce Nick to Julia, and go over the menu and some of the other items on the agenda.

Out of the corner of my eye, I see Ben enter the room, followed by two women. I pretend not to notice and grab the attention of one of the staff. Heading to the back of the room, I make sure the water stations are filled and do my best to look occupied. Both women are gorgeous, but one sort of favors him, so I'm wondering if it's his sister. The other one hangs close to him and he has his arm around her. She leans into him and they appear to be extremely friendly with each other. I feel the green monster inside of me show his pointy teeth. If this keeps up, I'll want to tear that bitch's hair out before the day is over.

Why can't I be beautiful like that?

"Hey, everything okay?"

I jump as Nick moves beside me.

"Fine, why?" I snap.

He inspects me for a few seconds, then shrugs. "No reason. Everything is on schedule. Guests are arriving."

"Good." I walk away from him and head to the bathroom. I wish this day was over and it hasn't even begun yet. Forcing myself to leave my little sanctuary, I resume my stance at the back of the room, trying to appear happy.

Nick comes up to me and says, "I think everyone is here. I've got the headcount at one twenty-five."

"Great. Thanks."

I move in the direction of Martin to let him know. When he sees me, I give him the thumbs up to start and turn to return to my back-of-the-room position when I collide with a brick wall of a chest.

"Sam. Sorry."

I'd recognize his scent anywhere.

"Mmm. Right." My tone is off the charts sarcastic. I move to sidestep him and he moves in the same direction. We do this two-step again.

"Annnd we're dancing."

"Hardly. I usually enjoy my dances," I say and I walk away. I'm not sure if he moves or not. I only know I need to get hell away from Ben. Besides, he has a girl waiting for him somewhere. I wonder if it's that lawyer, Karen, his fiancée or whatever she is. This isn't the place for me to worry about that now, but it's difficult with the way he's practically flaunting her in front of me.

By the time I stand in the place I've claimed, Martin is speaking to the group. He gives a nice talk about the caliber of business the firm does, the name they've built for themselves and how they've always done things above board. As usual, I start to daydream because financial matters just aren't my thing. I begin to link the patterns in the carpet together and create new designs in my head when a voice jars me out of my mental vacation.

"I can see you're bursting with excitement to hear Dad's little talk." Ben holds a glass of ice water in his hand as he stares at me smirking. His tanned biceps bulge and I have a flashback of his arms holding my thighs as he pounded into me when I sat on his desk. "This stuff really does put you to sleep," I hear him say.

Keep your shit together, girl. Do not let him see he rattles you.

Since he's the client here, I decide to put on my nice act. "Sorry. You know how awful I am with this stuff."

"You should consider letting us handle your portfolio."

I cock my head and really take a good look at him. He is every bit the sincere guy as he stands before me.

"I'm sorry. That was inappropriate. You'll think I'm trying to strong arm you since you're handling the event here." Remorse tinges his words.

I didn't think that at all, but now that he said it, I can see why he did. And I am utterly mystified by his behavior. He's being nice. But he came with another woman. What the hell is his deal here?

Composing myself, I say, "That's not what I was thinking. My thoughts went down an entirely different road."

An arched brow tells me he has no clue to what I'm referring.

Leaning closer I say, "I think it's best fuck buddies don't mix business with pleasure. But, oh, yeah. Given what's going on here and after the last time, I guess we're not really *buddies* anymore, are we?"

His confused expression intensifies. "I'm not sure ..."

"Sam, lunch is being brought in."

"Thank you, Nick."

I look at Ben and say, "Excuse me, duty calls." He's left standing there watching me. His eyes burn holes into the back of the sleeveless shirt I'm wearing. Instead of heating me up, they send shivers racing up and down my arms, legs, and spine, and my skin erupts in millions of goosebumps.

Once the lunch buffet is running smoothly, Nick and I leave to check on the spa. We make sure everything is set and head to the golf course.

Nick and I, along with Lauren, Berkeley, Britt, and Carrie will be delivering ice-cold beverages on the course to the golfers. The girls should be here any minute.

About ten minutes later, they arrive and I put Nick with Lauren, I go with Berkeley, and Britt and Carrie are paired. The six of us are in three carts with coolers in the back to handle the refreshments and the weather couldn't be better.

The golfers start trickling in and head out. Soon we have everyone on the course so we go to work. I put Nick and Lauren on the front nine holes and Britt and Carrie on the back nine. Berkeley and I travel between the two. And we have an absolute blast flirting, bantering with them, and having them flirt back. Even the women golfers are fun to chat with. The only sour note is Ben. He scowls, glares, and when he's close enough, grumbles about everything from his golf game to the refreshments. Berkeley even calls him Beastly Ben to his face, to which he stops and blinks rapidly several times, looking like a deer in headlights.

"Maybe he has a bad case of hemorrhoids today," she says when he's within earshot.

Her comment makes the guys with him laugh. Then one says, "Dude, lighten up. This is supposed to be fun. You look like hell. You need to get laid."

That shuts us all up. Berkeley and I hop in our cart and drive off. Too bad these are electric carts and drive like those electric shopping carts at Wal-Mart. I wish they could zoom away like a Porsche on gravel, spewing rocks in his face.

The golfing ends and everyone heads back to the hotel to get their rooms. We all want showers before the dinner tonight and all the clients are headed home. The employees will stay for an evening of fun. After Ben brought up the budget, Martin opted for an evening pool party instead of a picnic. My girls are leaving and I hate that, because now I'm on my own, except for Nick, but I don't really count him. I need my support group, damn it.

I hug them all, thanking them and wave good-bye. When I walk up to the front desk to get my room, Nick stands there looking pissed. Ben is also there checking in.

"What's wrong?"

"There's a screw up with the rooms," he says.

"What?"

"Yeah. They didn't book two rooms for us, only one."

"You've got to be kidding me! I went over the list several times with them. Just get another room."

"That's the problem." Nick huffs out a frustrated breath. "They're totally sold out tonight."

"Oh, great."

"Is there a problem?" Ben asks.

"Nothing you need to concern yourself with," I snap. I'm not telling him anything. He's been the biggest ass to me all day. He doesn't need to know crap right now.

I turn back to Nick. "Well, the room we do have has two beds, right?"

"Yeah, it's a double."

I stretch my now aching neck and say, "Then I guess there's only one option. We're going to have to share a room."

SEVENTEEN
BEN

◆

SHARE A ROOM? DID I hear that correctly? No way in hell. All day, I've watched her with that asshole with green coloring my vision. This isn't how fuck buddies act. Never once did I care if Karen flirted or went out with anyone else as long as she was available when I needed her. Everything's different with Sam. I know I have no right, but a possessiveness takes over rational thought.

"Can I get two keys?"

The attendant nods his head while glancing over at Sam. I've had just about all I can take with men checking out my woman.

"Do you mind? I'm here and she's taken," I growl.

The guy looks faintly amused and again glances over to where Sam is standing. I turn and see her gaping at me. She obviously heard.

"If you share a room with anyone it's going to be me," I say in no uncertain terms.

The hotel clerk hands me the keys just as I finish declaring my intention. I take them and snag Sam's arm as that asshole Nick smirks at me. What the fuck is that all about?

Sam, the consummate professional, doesn't cause a scene and waits until after we've turned the corner to snatch her arm out of mine. I stab the elevator button out of impatience.

"I don't appreciate being man-handled."

"No, it seems like you've quickly moved on to your next fuck buddy. I guess I had you pegged wrong."

Her pretty mouth forms an O and I swear I want to fill it with my cock. "You keep looking at me like that and I'm going to take you right here in the hallway."

The whip cracking sound is every bit as bad as the sting across my face.

"How dare you accuse me of sleeping with my employee? And you think I would sleep with you after that comment? What kind of woman do you take me for? Then again, I guess that's your M.O. and you have me confused with how you do things."

I rub my jaw knowing I deserved that. "I shouldn't have said that. But even though you wouldn't, I see how he looks at you. If you'd let him, he would gladly take my place."

"And what place would that be?"

If she only knew how her defiance turns me on.

The elevator dings and changes our focus. She may be pissed, but I haven't given up yet. The doors part as if foreshadowing how I'm going to open her pretty thighs as soon as we get in the room. That's the place I know where Nick would like to be. I press my hand against her lower back guiding her into the cab of the elevator.

"Samantha." That asshole Nick catches up with us. He's rolling an overnight bag as he slips inside with us. "Here is the room key when he pisses you off."

She glances between us and takes the key. I can tell she's calculating what to do as he passes off her suitcase.

When we get to my floor I realize that the asshat didn't push another button. I let the boy get out first because I plan to take Sam with me even if I have to toss her over my shoulder.

The sign directs that my room is to the left in the same direction the boy is already headed. Sam follows leaving me trailing behind them. When he stops, I find that my room is across from his. I have a moment to wonder if the hotel clerks were having a big laugh at our expense.

I open my door and push my bag to act as a door stop while I turn to watch Nick the Dick maneuver his bag and Sam's into the room. Just as she's about to head inside, I stop her.

"We need to talk," I demand.

As if he has some say, the guy grins. "Maybe you should get it out of the way. It doesn't look like he's going to give up until he says what he needs to. No worries, your bag is safe with me."

The fucker winks. My fist balls up and I have a burning desire to ram it in his smug face.

"I'll only be a few minutes," she says to him before turning angry eyes on me.

I push the door open wider and let her step through as the guy watches like he's her protector.

"Don't worry. She doesn't need her bag. She'll be naked most of time."

The guy's face changes as I step in the room and let the door shut behind me. When I turn to face Sam, her arm is in mid swing. Luckily my reflexes are good and stop her from connecting with my face this time. All that training with Drew that I've kept up even after he left … died worked.

"Who do you think you are?"

My mind shifts gears back to her.

"Let's stop playing games. That guy isn't your type."

Her eyes narrow and I'm holding out hope because if she tells me she's with him, I'm going to jail for murder.

"Oh? And who is?"

"Me," I say confidently. "You couldn't keep from eye fucking me all day."

Her head dips back, sending all her gorgeous hair cascading over her shoulders as she gives a belly laugh that rips at my gut. She's been flirting all day and I've prayed it was to make me jealous because it has.

"Is that true? Is that why you brought your fiancée so I would get the hint that we're done?"

It's my turn to gape. "Fiancée?" I ask dumbly.

Her hazel eyes steady on mine. Her face has lost all mirth and they darken into the color of a green-eyed monster. "The gorgeous brunette you had your arm around most of the day. Isn't her name Karen?"

I feel a smirk appearing on my mouth. "I think you mean Cate, my sister's best friend and she's like a little sister to me. But most of all she's my best friend's wife … Well, he's gone now. And he asked me to take care of her."

Her eyes go soft, but I don't need her pity. So I lean in and kiss her mouth. She gasps, taken by surprise by my bold move as am I. Today has been a day of revelations. And I want this woman more than I should.

"You don't have to be jealous. Can't you tell you've got me wrapped around your finger?"

There is no time to waste as I kiss her again in earnest. At first she is stiff, but after my declaration, she relaxes as I circle my arms around her waist. I tug her close, wanting to feel her against me.

"God, I've missed you."

I dip under the hem of her shirt and skim my fingertips over the inches of bare skin. She pulls back breathless and puts her hand between us creating space I don't want.

"Ben, I can't."

The words are like a sledgehammer to my chest, spinning my head around.

"Sam, I'm sorry."

Her face goes soft and I think I've got her.

"I believe you. But you were right. I'm not cut out for fuck buddies. I need more. I want more with someone."

My hands drop to my sides. I've never hated any words more in my life. I have nothing to offer her. As much as I hate to admit this, I'm the one that can't do without her. The game I wanted to play has played me. These last few weeks have been hell as I've been plagued with thoughts about her ... missing her.

I close my eyes for a second and I hear the faint sound of fabric shifting as she makes her way to the door only a few feet ahead. And I know if I want to keep her, I have to play by her rules.

"Wait," I call out.

She stops and I deign to open my eyes to see her looking at me with expectation.

Do or die, my subconscious mind yells at me to do the right thing.

"Sam." All I have is the truth. "I'm no good at the relationship thing. You'll have to set the pace, but I'm willing to try."

There's more in my plea than I'm ready to reconcile. But there hasn't been another woman who's intrigued me in a very long time. I'm not dumb enough to let her go and hope one day when I know I'm ready for this, that I'll be able to find another. I have to man up and give this a shot.

She steps over, but doesn't let me touch her. She rests her palms on my chest and I'm undone.

"Ben, the last thing I want or need is to coerce you into a relationship you don't want."

I reach up and clasp her wrist. "I want this. I want you. I can't get you out of my head."

"But you don't do relationships."

"But what I can't do is be without you. These past two weeks have been torture. I'm sure my palms are chafed because my dick is infatuated with you. I'm not saying it will be easy going, but I want to try."

And there it is. I've said it. I hope I don't live to regret it.

One half of her mouth curls into a lopsided smile. "Are you sure you're not just trying to get into my pants?"

I smirk. "Oh, I want in. And I won't ever lie to you, Sam. You can trust that. I don't think I have from the beginning."

She contemplates this. "So what ... you're my boyfriend now?"

Cringing, I shrug. "Call it what you want, but I'm calling you mine."

I don't wait; it's been too long as it is. I take the wrists that I still hold and move them around me. Then, I cup the back of her neck and draw her to me. Her taste explodes on my tongue like a grenade. I'm lost not knowing how I found myself in this place. What is it about her that makes me want more than I ever have?

She moves closer, creating friction on my dick and I want inside her, now. I release gadgets on her clothes to divest her of them. She's just as eager, nimble fingers working my shirt out of my shorts as she stands in a lacy bra and underthings that aren't more than ribbons of fabric connected together.

"Jesus, Sam, I need to see all of you."

She isn't halfway done, so I help her out by covering her hands and pulling my shirt over my head. Her hands course over my skin and drop to the fly of my shorts. She has me freed before I have to help. Her hand wraps around my dick possessively and, fuck me, I almost shoot off.

"What do you want, baby?" I ask.

She drops to her knees and I lean back on the wall weak with anticipation. She flicks out her tongue and tastes what's waiting for her.

"Fuck, Sam, take it all in, baby."

Her mouth opens and my hand finds her hair as I feed my cock down her throat. I've never felt on the verge of coming this quick in the process. But she's watching me like she wants to see my expression.

"Relax," I say watching her eyes begin to water.

I pull back giving her room to breathe before I cup the back of her head and guide her forward again. I want to see her swallow me whole as I empty myself down her throat. But her eyes plead with me once again and I pull back starting to create a rhythm.

"Breathe, darling."

Her hand reaches around the base and begins to twist, working me as we do this back and forth. I want to last all day but she's too fucking perfect to believe.

"I'm going to come, baby, if you want to pull back ..."

She's different than any girl I've been with. I don't want to presume she'll swallow, although if she doesn't we'll work on that. But she surprises me. Her little hands move in time with her mouth. And I find she's taken over. I don't let go of her hair because, Jesus fuck, my balls begin to pump out my orgasm like a ginormous water gun.

"Yeah, baby, don't stop," I say thinking I will come forever.

When I'm done she swirls her tongue around the crown as if to get every last drop. I draw my hips back from the sensation that's too much for me to handle. I grip her hair and pull her free as my semi-hard cock pops from her mouth.

I bend down and scoop her up. "Your turn."

When I toss her gently on the bed, she lands with a little squeal. It's cute, but not what I want to hear. "Get ready to scream."

I tug her ankles, pulling her pussy closer to the edge as I kneel down in front of her. She's just as pretty down here, all pink and ready for me.

"You're so fucking wet."

"Ben, don't tease me."

It's the first thing she's had a chance to say. "I don't intend to. Hold on."

I part her glistening folds and lap at the sweetness there. I flick my tongue on the tiny bud that's swollen and in need of a little attention.

Her back bows off the bed and I'm only getting started. I curl a finger in her and search for the nub inside. When my finger strokes across it, she lets out a moan. I've found both targets, so I slip another finger inside as I begin to suck at her flesh. I learn what she likes when she fists the sheets in her hands and cries out with abandon. I want inside her, but I need more time. Plus, she needs this first orgasm. I lick and flick and thrust with my fingers as I fuck her dickless until she's begging for climax. My cock surges to life by the sounds she makes. I cover her clit and stroke it with my tongue while furiously finger fucking her. Her tight pussy clamps around my fingers as she finds her release. And as promised, she screams.

Once she goes boneless, I flip her on her stomach and leave her legs hanging over the edge. I reach under her and lift up her hips, urging her on her knees. Then I line up my dick and I'm inside before I realize no condom.

"Fuck."

The word means all kinds of things as I berate myself from the oversight. But I also curse because damn if it doesn't feel like heaven. I pull out and find my pants.

"What's wrong?" she calls out.

"Condom."

She looks sexy as fuck and I feel on the verge of coming again. I find a condom and sheath myself as fast as I can. When I get back and place one hand on her hip, I'm inside her. It's not quite the same, having felt heaven, but it's good enough, especially when she starts pushing her ass into me to spur me on.

"What do you want, baby? You want it hard and fast." She nods. "Then say it."

"Please."

I move languidly, angling to hit the spot that I know excites her.

"I want to hear you say it." With my hands on her hips and swallowing a groan, I command, "Say it."

"Hard and fast," she whimpers.

So I give her exactly what she wants as she cries to the heavens for a release, which grips the both of us and milks me dry. I collapse on top of her and roll us to our side still joined. I circle one arm around her middle and cup her breast with the other.

As our breaths slow, she takes a while before she asks the question. Belatedly, I think being inside her has the calming effect I need to answer.

"When did your best friend die?"

Normally, I don't like talking about it unless it's Cate because she understands. But somehow the words dislodge from my throat.

"Over a year ago," I begin. "He was my best friend since before we were old enough to go to school," I choke out. "He was like my brother."

She tries to move, but I hold on tighter. I know she probably wants to face me and share her compassion, but I don't want to pull out even though I should take care of the spent condom.

"I'm sorry. I'm sure it's been hard on you."

Her sentiment is far different from Karen's. And more thoughts launch out of my mouth as if I'd been holding them back forever.

"I watched him waste away into a shadow of himself."

She nods. "I'm sure he appreciated you being there."

I hope so.

"There were times I didn't know what I would do without him. I still miss him. It's hard losing the best friend you did everything with, you know?"

This is the point of the conversation where Karen accused me of being gay. I brace myself for it.

"Getting over someone who was a brother to you will take a long time. I'm not sure you will ever fully be over it. But in time it will get easier and maybe you'll be able to think about the good without the loss hurting quite so much."

And hearing someone not related to me say it eases something inside me. I whisper the words, "I hope so."

She reaches up and covers my hand and something warms in my chest. I swipe hair away from her neck.

"This girlfriend thing is turning out better than I hoped," I whisper in her ear before I gently bite her lobe. Then I press a soft kiss at the base of her neck. Her eyes close and I nip there before I trail nips and kisses back up to her jaw. I squeeze her breast before pinching her nipple.

Her giggles and moans stir my cock to life and even I'm surprised by my recovery time.

"Is it the girlfriend thing or the fact that you can cop a feel? I'm not sure it's me you like or my boobs."

She's referring to the hand that hasn't let go of her breast like it's the Holy Grail.

"What's not to like about you? You're beautiful, you get along with people, you're hard working and determined, and you don't let me get away with my shit. And your tits are definitely up there. You have to know that as a breast man I can stamp yours as spectacular."

Her grin dims. Before I can question it, her eyes glaze over with pleasure as I move in and out a few strokes before I know I have to take care of business. Girlfriend yes, being a father is a no. Slowly, I pull out grabbing the base of the condom.

"Where are you going?"

I hold up the condom. "To take care of this."

"I should get my suitcase."

Slyly, I smirk at her. "Don't bother. You won't be needing clothes the rest of the night."

EIGHTEEN
Sam

◆

"AREN'T YOU FORGETTING SOMETHING?" I ask.

"What's that?"

"We have a poolside party to attend, which means we need to get our butts in the shower and I need to get ready. Like now." I move to get out of bed, but he pulls me to him and instead, I find my mouth trapped by his lips. He does one of those quick flips and I find myself hemmed in beneath him as he deepens the kiss. All my buzzers are going off, but I have my duties to see to, so I reluctantly pull my mouth free of his.

"You're not making this easy."

"Neither are you."

"What am I doing?" I ask.

"You're naked, in this bed, with your tits pressed against me, and I'm already hard again for you. Now my dick is going to be giving me fits, unless you do something about it."

"Damn, Ben, you're insatiable."

"I wasn't until you pranced into my life."

Steel gray eyes pin mine and my lust for him intensifies. "The shower. But give me a minute. I need to go across the hall and get my bag."

"Not a fucking chance in hell. You stay here. Give me your key and I'll go get your bag."

"No! You'll do something to Nick and I can't chance that. Besides, I have to give him some sort of an explanation."

He crashes his mouth onto mine and his tongue sweeps every

last thought of Nick away. The only thing I want is Ben and his body on and in mine. My head spins from the sensations swirling even after he ends our kiss.

"Get your ass in the shower. I'll join you after I get your bag. And I promise not to hurt Nick. All I'll say is that we've worked out our differences and that you and I will be sharing a room tonight."

"That's it?"

"That's it. I promise." He kisses me again, gets up and starts getting dressed. What a fine body he has, too. His jeans do nothing to hide his extraordinary hard dick and I can only imagine what Nick will think of me.

"Get in the shower, Sam. I'm going to fuck you wet and raw when I get back. Now get the water warm."

He grabs the keys and is out the door. I'm just turning on the shower when I hear the door open back up. Not long after, he opens the bathroom door and enters. Naked Ben is damned impressive.

"Put the soap down, Sam. That's my job."

I hand him the bar and he takes over. Only he's much more thorough than I would've been. By the time he hits my intimate places, my head spins because I'm oxygen deprived. Not much later, he gives me orgasm number one by mouth. Or was that number three? I've lost count. But he doesn't stop. Once I come, I hear the tearing of the condom packet that he conveniently thought to bring, and then his hands are under my ass lifting me. The cool tiles press into my shoulder blades as his cock buries deep into my pussy. His mouth swallows my cries of ecstasy while he captures my lips in a kiss. We breathe as one until he tenses, and I know he's close. But then, so am I. In only a few more thrusts, I'm carried over the edge, and I hear him groan out his own orgasm as he follows.

"I think you've just fucked the sense out of me."

He kisses my neck. "I hope that's a good thing."

"For my body, yes. For my job, no. I need to get a move on before my reputation with a certain older Mr. Rhoades is destroyed."

His deep chuckle sends a wave of heat coursing through me that I force myself to ignore.

"Don't worry, baby, I'll put in a good word for you."

151

A giant gurgle of laughter explodes out of me. "I can just hear it now. 'Dad, she couldn't help being late. We were in the shower screwing and we had to have one more go at it.' Can you imagine?"

He joins me in laughter and seeing him like this, is such a change from the serious Ben I've been exposed to lately.

He adds, "I have an image of my mom's expression." His faces changes and he immediately turns off the water.

"What is it?"

"Oh, you've never faced an angry Julia Rhoades. I have to get you ready. And fast."

Now I really get the giggles. He wraps me in a towel and appears to be on fast forward. I've never seen anyone move so quickly in my life. He dresses in record time and then wants to know what I'm wearing. I am so amused by his comical actions, I can't stop laughing at him.

"This is serious!" Then suddenly he says, "Fuck!"

"Now what?"

"I told Jenna and Cate I would meet them in the bar twenty minutes ago."

I have to clamp my hand over my mouth as his hands twist his wet hair into the craziest style I've ever seen. He grabs my rollie bag, tosses it on the bed, zips it open, and grabs a handful of clothes.

"Here. Put these on."

Finally, I realize the man needs help. I reach for his shoulders and say, "Ben, honey, it's going to be fine. Calm down."

"Oh, just wait. You don't know my sister. Or my mom."

I take the clothes he's holding, set them on the bed, and grab the outfit I had planned to wear. It's a casual black halter dress and I put on the shoes I brought to go with it, a pair of sexy strappy black sandals.

"You're wearing *that*?" He licks his lips as he stares at me.

"Yeah. Why?"

"It's just that, well …" his eyes drop down and I notice the bulge in his pants.

"There's no help for you now, but later there will be. Now here." I run my fingers through his hair and make it look like it should. "That's much better. Now go and meet your sister and Cate. I need a few more minutes to fix my hair and makeup."

He looks me up and down, then eyes the door. "No, I want us

to go down together."

"Are you trying to make a statement?"

"Yes, I am."

"If you're okay with it, then I suppose I am, too."

"You don't mind if Nick knows?"

My brows shoot up. "You're asking me that now? After you charged into the room and got my bag?"

"Oh, yeah." He smirks.

"Now let me finish getting ready. My hair is a bit of an issue since it got destroyed in the shower."

"Looks downright sexy to me."

"You would say that. It's bedhead." I finish my makeup and do the best I can with my hair. I end up putting it up in a messy bun, and pull out several tendrils to hang on either side of my face. Then I add earrings and a necklace.

"All ready."

"Sam, have I told you how gorgeous you are?"

"I don't ..." and before I can answer, he kisses the rest of my words and thoughts away.

When he lets me go, he runs his thumb across my lower lip and says, "When I first saw you, I thought of sunshine. But now I believe you're the brightest star in the heavens. You sparkle like them—you know how they do on the clearest of nights? So distinct you think you could almost reach out and touch them. That's you, Sam."

He's just stolen away every word from my brain.

"Shall we go?"

I nod in stunned silence.

We walk down to the pool together and when I get there, I make myself busy with checking on things. Martin and Julia soon arrive, and Jenna and Cate follow. Nick comes next and his eyes are filled with questions, which I do my best to avoid. But he soon gets me alone and I finally confess that Ben and I were seeing each other but had some issues, which we have now resolved.

"Oh, so you and Rhoades are an item?"

"Yeah, I guess you can say that. We didn't broadcast it, though. We both wanted to keep it quiet."

"Can I just say something? The dude is a major ass."

"I'm sure he was to you. He's the jealous sort. Or maybe I should amend that. Now that he knows you and I are not together, he'll be fine to you."

"I see," Nick says, though I can see he's still skeptical. I don't care. He can deal with it. I give him some things to take care of and he wanders off to handle them.

I'm just about to find the food and beverage manager when Jenna and Cate approach me.

"You're Samantha Calhoun, right?"

"Yes, and you're Ben's sister, Jenna. It's nice to meet you."

We shake hands and she says, "And this is Cate McKnight, my bestie, who Ben also considers his sister."

"Yes, he told me about you, Cate, and I'm so sorry for your loss."

Both women's eyes nearly bulge out of their sockets. Then they look at each other for a second before Jenna asks, "He told you?"

"Yes. I'm sorry. Maybe I shouldn't have mentioned any of this."

"No, no, it's just that he doesn't usually talk about it to many people. Wait, how long have you two been seeing each other?" Jenna asks while Cate watches.

The heat rises from my neck and shoots straight out the top of my head. I would pay for someone to bring me a fan to stand in front of right now, because I sure do need it.

When I don't answer right away, Jenna says, "Oh no. He's not …"

But I don't let her finish. "He's … we're … together." I'm not sure what she was truly implying, but I have a damn good idea. And for whatever reason, I want to protect him at all costs.

She cocks her head and we lock gazes. For a long time. "I love my brother. Very much. So does Cate here. They've both been through an extremely difficult time. Last year was, well, I won't go into it, but let's just say I don't want my brother to get hurt. I know what his reputation is around town, and that it's not very good. But the fact that he's told you about Drew says a lot to me."

Cate cuts in. "What's she's trying to say is that he acts tough, but losing Drew …" her eyes fill and I sweep my eyes for the nearest napkin. I pick one up and hand it to her. "Thanks. Ben doesn't give himself much credit. But without him, I wouldn't have survived. He's got the biggest heart but hates to show it. Please, don't hurt him."

My hand presses to my chest because it suddenly aches for Ben. And when I look at Cate, I blink repeatedly to force the tears back.

The pain these two people endured when they lost the man they loved so much must have been gut wrenching, and still is, from all accounts.

Jenna's back like they are tag teaming me. "To be perfectly honest, I'm not sure he would survive getting his heart broken. And then I'll be forced to kick your ass."

Swallowing to get rid of the giant nugget that's formed in my throat, I say, "I'm not in the habit of breaking hearts." I let out a rueful laugh. "I'm usually the one on the receiving end of the breaks. I'm pretty sure Ben's is safe with me."

Both women smile at me and that's when the subject of our discussion shows up.

"Ah, I see you've met my Sam." And he puts his arm over my shoulders.

"Yes, I see you've changed your mind?" Jenna smirks.

"Where have you been hiding her, Ben?" Cate asks.

He ignores his sister leaving me to wonder what she meant and answers Cate. "Here and there."

"I wish Drew were here to see this."

There is weariness in Cate's eyes, but Jenna's already talking.

"You need to stop that and bring her over for Sunday dinner."

There is some sort of challenge in Jenna's words.

"I will," he says as he leans down to kiss my cheek. I look up at him and smile back. He seems so much happier now than he was earlier. I'd like to think it's me, but I don't want to get my hopes up.

The rest of the employees start trickling in and soon the party is in full swing. Food and drinks are flowing, and the band we hired is playing. People are dancing including Ben and me. It's a great time and I'm even having fun getting to know Jenna and Cate.

We're all standing in a small circle, including Nick, when Ben looks up and says with a scowl, "Who the hell invited her?"

I follow the direction of his gaze and see a gorgeous blond headed our way. She's wearing a short black skirt, stilettos, and a top that bares her midriff. She makes a beeline straight for Ben, wraps her arms around his neck, and says, "Hello, honey. Didn't you miss your fiancée?"

NINETEEN
BEN

IF I'VE EVER FELT LIKE a deer in headlights, it's now. What is Karen doing here? Why the fuck does she think she's my fiancée? Is she completely delusional? I pry her arms from around my neck as Samantha stands there like she's seen a ghost, her eyes large and confused.

"Ben, I've missed you. Now I understand—you were pushing me away. You were planning a proposal. I'm so stupid. But it makes sense you haven't been seeing anyone."

Snapping out of my stunned stupor, I step back, putting space between us. "I'm not sure why you're here, but I never planned to propose to you."

Her high frequency smile falters as she glances around. "That can't be. I got a call from someone at your office saying you wondered why I hadn't come to the client meeting earlier. I hadn't thought you wanted to see me, so I didn't. I was told by the caller you specifically asked about me."

Gears churn in my head as I wonder who at the office made that call. Maybe someone contacted her because she's a client, and Karen read more into it.

"I can assure you, I never asked for you." I pull Sam over. She stumbles towards me, taken off guard by my sudden need to tuck her against my side, apparently as stunned by Karen's appearance as I am. "I don't think my girlfriend would like that."

Karen's eyes bug out before she takes a stumbling step back. "Girlfriend!" she shrieks, garnering the attention of everyone around us. "You told me ... I thought you didn't do relationships."

"Things change."

Her eyes narrow as she assesses Sam.

"You're finally over your best friend's death and you pick the first girl to cross your path. She's not even your type."

And how would Karen know what my type is? Sam is exactly what I want. True, she's different than the others. Her beauty is subtle, natural, and not in your face. She isn't plastic and doesn't need gobs of shit on her face to look stunning. More importantly, she's just as genuine on the inside as she is on the outside.

"Not exactly." I don't clarify because that answer is true for both her statements. "But she's the right girl, and she doesn't compare herself to my best friend."

She fish mouths a few unspoken words before she spins on her heels and swiftly walks away.

"That was Karen?" Sam asks glancing up at me.

I nod.

"That was interesting. I guess I should go find her," Jenna sighs before she turns and strides off.

But it's Cate's face that has gone pale that has me concerned as she walks away and stands against the wall as if she needs it to help her remain uptight.

"Sam, I need to go check on Cate."

She pats my forearm. "Sure, I have some things I need to check on anyway."

I weave my way over to Cate.

"Hey, what's wrong?"

She glances up as though she hadn't noticed me walk over.

"I can't stay here."

I search around to locate Sam needing to tell her I have to leave. "Sure, I'll take you home," I say absently to Cate.

"It's not that, Ben. I need to leave Charleston. I can't stay in South Carolina. I feel Drew everywhere I go, which should be a good thing. Instead, I feel like crying all the time. I need to move so that maybe I can get past this melancholy I feel."

"Cate." But what can I say? "I feel it too." I haven't been doing my job as her protector very well as of late. "I was at my parents' the other day and outside I could picture Drew and me as kids. God, Cate, it hurts like a dagger in my chest knowing I can't call because he's not here and never will be again. I almost hate going to my parents' for that reason."

She clings to me and I draw her into a hug. I think back to so many days we'd ended up in this very position hiding our suffering from Drew. We didn't want him to see our pain as he faded away into nothingness. Our grief has tied us together in a way that only the two of us can share. For that reason, I want to beg her to stay because I selfishly need her. Something I would do, except Drew counted on me. And I can't let him down because I have no way of explaining to him my shortcomings. He would want me to let her go so she can live her life.

When we pull back, her eyes shimmer with tears. "I've been offered a position in Washington, DC, and I think I'm going to take it. It will be a fresh start."

"I don't want you to go, but I get it. And know I'll be here whenever you need me." She nods and I help her to a chair where she sits. I'm not sure a drink will cut it, but I say it anyway. "Stay here. Let me get you a drink."

As I make my way over to the cash bar, I see Horace heading my way and we meet near where my sister stands with Kenneth. I scan the room and Karen is nowhere in sight, which is a good thing.

"Horace," I say with a grin. The guy has a way that makes it hard not to smile in his presence.

"Happy to see me again?"

Automatically, I glance down at my dick, which thankfully isn't tenting my pants this time.

"Haha, made you look."

I shake my head and chuckle because he got me.

"You're a little late for the client meeting."

He pats my shoulder. "I'm actually not here for this. I'm meeting someone and saw you. I thought I'd come and say hi."

"Oh. Too good to come to our meeting?"

He flashes me a smile. "Not too good, just too busy. Besides, I trust you with my money ... and other things if you'd let me."

My jaw hangs loose because what the hell do you say to that?

"Close your mouth, darling. Wouldn't want you to catch flies with all that honey you have going on," he adds.

I actually feel my cheeks burn as my sister takes two steps over seeing my discomfort.

"I must meet the man that made my brother blush. I'm sure

this is a first."

Horace proudly reaches out his hand. "Ah, what a lovely specimen you are."

Jenna gives him her hand and he draws her in for a full on hug. "Well, I can see why your man there is giving me the death glare. You're beautiful. But then you are your brother's sister."

Kenneth glares at Horace with what must be jealousy. When he releases Jenna, he says to Kenneth, "You're one lucky guy. I'm sure you would never leave your date waiting."

Kenneth's cheeks flame pink and I'm beginning to think Horace has that effect on everyone, guys at least.

"Your date stood you up?" Jenna asks, more interest in this line of conversation.

"Not exactly, but he's surely making me wait. And he knows how I so hate to wait."

She takes his arm like they're best buddies.

"Boyfriends suck," Jenna teases.

"Don't they?" Horace says leaning in as if they are sharing a secret just between the two of them. Either that or he's making a joke of the double entendre. "But in all honesty, I have a fiancée. She's out with the girls. I'm meeting a friend."

Jenna, never surprised by anything, says, "Well, maybe he's hung up."

"Oh, I'd say he's hung ... up." He winks at her. "Anyway, it was nice meeting you. And Jenna, a beautiful woman like yourself deserves a ring on your finger. If he's not going to put one there, maybe you should cut him loose."

Kenneth looks on the verge of exploding, so I step between them. "Good seeing you, Horace."

He gives me the once over. "Always good seeing you, Ben. If you ever change your mind ..."

Sam walks over at that precise moment.

"Oh, you're her," Horace says taking her measure. Sam glances between us. He goes on as I cringe wondering what exactly he'll say. "I came into Ben's office when he was having a bit of trouble." He grins at me and I shake my head. "He was looking at your picture, and I must say I can't blame him for the not-so-small problem he had."

Before he can say much more, I jump in.

"Sam, this is Horace. Horace, this is my Samantha."

"*Your* Samantha. Good for you. Nice meeting you. But I think I need to go check on my friend. He might be pissed at me for not being where I'm supposed to be."

Jenna laughs hysterically as Horace saunters off.

"Where'd Kenneth go?" I ask.

She points towards the exit. "He's got a rage-on for some reason. You'd think I stuck a jalapeno in his boxers by the way he's acting. He's gone to the room to cool off."

I turn my attention to Sam.

"Do you mind hanging with my sister for a little while? Cate isn't doing so well and I'm going to take her to her room."

Her eyes soften with understanding. "Is this about Drew?"

I nod, grateful I don't have to explain. I'm more surprised that she gets it and isn't stupidly jealous.

"I might be a while." I don't make it a question, but I do wait for her reaction.

"You take all the time you need. I'll meet you in the room if you don't make it back here."

I lean in and kiss her lips. "God, you're the best girlfriend ever."

She laughs. "I'm your only ever girlfriend."

I kiss her one more time before I have to force myself away knowing I've been gone too long from Cate. I finagle the purchase of a bottle of wine from the bar, though they said they only sold it by the glass. Then, I find Cate exactly where I left her.

"Come on. Let's go to your room and see if this Merlot is up to snuff."

"You don't have to do that. You have someone waiting for you."

"And if she's worth it, or if I'm worth it to her, she'll know how important you are to me. You're my best friend, Cate. And you need me right now. Sam will be fine. She's a big girl and can handle me not being with her every second."

Cate lets me lead her out and to her room a few floors down from mine. It isn't until we're in her room that she finally speaks.

"Am I doing the right thing?"

We sit on the bed with our backs against the headboard. And I know she's talking about moving. I tip my head back fighting the need to beg her to stay.

"I love you, Cate. I always will. And I'll miss the hell out of you, but like I said before, I get it. You just promise me you won't turn into a stranger on me."

She leans over and kisses my cheek. "Never that." Then she places her head on my shoulder.

Finally, I ask. "What about Mercer?"

She sits up. "What about him?"

If the guy hasn't told her what he's told me, it's not my place. Still, I want to gauge how she feels about him.

"I have the feeling he's interested in making you happy."

She shakes her head. "He's just a friend and I like him. But how can I possibly love someone else? And how could you want that for me?"

"I imagine it would be tough to top Drew. But he wanted you to be happy. I want you to be happy"

"I'm not ready," she admits.

I glance down at her, tucking my finger under her chin so she's forced to look me in the eye. "To be happy?"

She agrees and the tears begin to pour out of her eyes. I have a hard time keeping my eyes dry as I hold her.

I pull her into my lap and cradle her like she's mine because tears are my weakness. And I don't know how to combat them. Plus, I don't want her to see me holding back my own.

Long after her tears dry and her sobs becomes restful breathing, Jenna comes in.

"I've got her, Ben."

I lay Cate down on the bed. She doesn't stir which makes me wonder how much sleep she's been getting. If she's anything like me, dreams make it hard to rest these days. I'm again assaulted by the realization that I haven't been around much lately. And that has to change. Cate's moving and I won't be able to see her on a whim like I'm so used to.

Jenna adds. "Go find your girl. I like her."

"I do too."

TWENTY
Sam

MY FEET ARE KILLING ME when I get back to the room. I unbuckle the thin straps of my sandals and am kicking them off when I hear the door open. Ben walks in and his downcast eyes tell me all I need to know. I don't ask him a thing. Instead, I spread my arms wide and he walks directly into my embrace. His body shudders against mine and all I do is stand there and be his rock. Putting myself in his shoes, I can't imagine how I would feel if I lost Lauren.

At last his body calms. "I'm sorry I was gone so long," he says.

"No, it's okay. I was fine and she needed you."

He stares at me in disbelief.

"What?"

"You." He shakes his shaggy hair. "Did Drew send me an angel?"

"I'm no angel." I push the hair back from his face.

"You don't seem real. And I don't deserve a gift from above."

I don't bother answering him. I kiss him to show him how real I am. There is a partial smile on his face when we break apart.

"This has been the strangest day I can recall." His towering frame bends over mine, but he eases away from me and I look up at him.

"How so?"

"First there's you. I was pissed as hell at you because you kept ignoring me and were all over Nick the Dick."

I sputter out laughing, "Nick the Dick?"

"Yeah. That was my name for him when I thought you two were an item."

"An item, huh?"

"Okay, I might have imagined that, but it was only my greed for you. I wanted you all to myself."

His hands reach for my dress and unzip it.

"I wonder why," I say as I shrug the dress off.

"God, you're beautiful."

"I could say the same for you." I reach for his shirt and unbutton it. "Go on."

"And then, you came to your senses." I punch him in his arm which only makes him laugh. "Then there's crazy Karen. I mean, who called her? She said someone from the office called, but still." He goes quiet for a second and I wonder about that too. "And Cate drops a bomb on me and tells me she's moving to DC to get away from all the memories of Drew."

"You don't want her to go."

His head moves side to side and hair spills across his forehead. Before I can help him, his hands are fisted in his hair. "She's all I have left ... of Drew anyway. She's become my best friend."

I nod because I can't help him with that. Cate has to do what she thinks is best. And I don't know her well enough to offer an opinion.

"Oh, and then there's Horace."

"Oh, yeah. He's a piece of work, isn't he? And by the way, what picture do you have of me?"

Two pink spots appear on his cheeks.

"Oh my. I hope it's not anything indecent."

"No! I would never do that without your consent." The combination of sheepish and sexy is irresistible on Ben. I walk up to him, grab his face, and kiss him.

"Show me."

"Huh?"

"The picture."

"Oh." He digs in his pants and pulls out his phone. A few seconds later, he hands it to me with the picture pulled up. It was taken that day on his boat.

"I didn't know you took this."

"I know. I should've said something. I'm sorry."

"It's okay." I hand phone back, a little surprised yet

impressed he went to those lengths.

"You looked so perfect, sitting there, I guess I couldn't resist." Then he reaches behind me and unhooks my bra. "You have the most gorgeous tits in the world." His head drops down and he pulls a nipple into his mouth.

A short time later, after his tongue and lips work me into a quite a frenzy, I say, "I think I need to lie down. My legs won't support me much longer."

He lifts his head up and says, "Don't worry, babe, I've got you."

In one clean motion, he lifts and walks me to the bed and asks, "Have I told you I'm a tits guy?"

"I think I've already deduced that."

He shifts his focus away from my chest and starts to shimmy down my body. "And now you're going to experience what else I fantasize about."

Our lovemaking that night is slow and languorous. Ben touches me in all the right places, making my body come alive like a sparking wire. After he's given me two orgasms, one with his hand, the other his mouth, he tears into a condom packet, rolls it on, and slowly enters me. Our eyes never leave each other's as he slides in and out, seating himself to the hilt every time. His hips rock into me at just the right angle so they press on that certain spot, and soon I'm erupting in yet another explosive climax. He follows as he takes my mouth in a searing kiss.

"I wish I could sleep like this," I say. His eyes are soft and I run my hands through his hair.

"So do I. But I'd better get rid of this to be safe." He gets up and takes care of things.

When he returns, I say, "Ben, I'm on the pill."

He acts like he wants to say something as one corner of his mouth turns up. Then he slides his teeth over his bottom lip. "Spell this out for me, Sam."

"You're the only one I've been with since the last guy I dated, and I've always been monogamous. I'm a safe bet, if you follow. He used protection, even though he wasn't faithful."

"I've never had sex without a condom. Ever. In my life. Except that one stroke slip up with you."

"So what I'm saying is if we're going to be exclusive, and I know *I* am, and I'm on the pill, then …" I let my voice trail off.

"You trust me?"

"Yes. Shouldn't I?" I ask.

"No. I mean, yes. But that's not what I meant. What I meant is that I'm surprised that you trust me enough to offer that, especially considering my past. But I won't betray your trust. I swear, I won't."

"Then I don't think we really need condoms, do we?"

"No, maybe not. But not until after I get tested. I usually do every month. Drew made me start doing it a long time ago and I never stopped."

"Even with condoms?" This worries me a bit.

"Yeah. Nothing's a hundred percent, according to him."

"I guess I should get tested too, then."

He flashes me a smile. "We could go together?"

"Why not? I should've done this a long time ago, but I thought I was good since we used condoms."

"I'm sure you are, but no use in taking chances. Now let's get some sleep, yeah?" he says with a damn sexy smirk.

"Yeah, I'm beat."

I hear his chest rumble as he says, "Isn't that supposed to be my line?"

He pulls me against the wall of his chest and his arms find their way around me. I'm cozy as I've ever been and float away into the land of dreams.

My ringing phone wakes us both up hours later and I jump out of bed to shut it off. I shake my head when I see it's Nick. "Oh, crap!"

"What?" a deep hoarse voice comes back to me from the bed. I smile, remembering all the delicious things from last night.

"It's ten thirty and Nick wants to know what time we're leaving. I need to get downstairs to settle up with the hotel. They need my signature on some paperwork."

Ben gets out of bed and I can't help but stop what I'm doing and stare at the man. He stretches, and I'm not sure if it's to give me the show I want or if it's because he really needs to get the kinks out of his muscles that I now want to run my hands all over.

"You really shouldn't do that, you know?"

"What?" he asks, smirking, knowing damn well what I mean.

I spin and sashay my way to the shower.

"Wait a minute. You can't do that to me."

I giggle as I hear him chasing me down. An arm snags me

around my waist and I'm hoisted in the air.

"You can run, but you can't outrun me." He throws me over his shoulder and swats my ass. Next thing I know, I'm back in bed.

"Ben, I need to go downstairs."

"And you will. Right after I fuck that smile off your face and have you screaming my name."

Thirty minutes later, I run out of the room with wet hair pulled back in a ponytail, wearing a t-shirt, shorts, and flip flops. I don't know if I want to laugh or kill him.

Nick and the sales and banquet managers are waiting for me.

"So sorry. I slept like a log last night. So you have papers for me?" I can feel Nick's eyes on me, but I refuse to look his way.

"Yes. Here are the final bills for everything."

"Thank you. Give me a minute to look these over."

"No problem."

It doesn't take long for me to see everything is in line as it should be. I sign my name on all the pages where designated and take my copies.

"Thank you so much. It's been a pleasure doing business with you, Miss Calhoun."

I stand and shake hands with the sales manager. "Will I ever convince you to call me Samantha?"

"Maybe the next time we work together."

"I hope so," I say as I watch her walk away. This is the part I'm dreading.

"So, you and Rhoades, huh?" Nick says with a hint of a sneer.

"Uh, yeah. Didn't we already have this conversation?"

"Yeah, I guess so. I hope it works out."

I don't like the way he says that, but I let it drop.

He gives me a curt nod and I watch him stride to the hotel doors.

"Where are you going?"

"I'm leaving. I've already had breakfast and checked out, like most of the others." The meaning behind his snide comment isn't lost on me.

"Fine. I'll see you at work on Monday."

Ben is dressed when I get to the room. He can tell something is wrong. So I tell him.

"Let it go. He's jealous."

"But why?"

"Samantha, look in the mirror, sweetheart. You're a prize and he wants you." His words are gentle and kind, yet they don't comfort me.

"I honestly feel he thinks he's looking out for me."

"Maybe. But I'm going to look out for you much better."

I finish packing and we leave. He walks me to my waiting car and kisses me before I get in. It seems lonely without Ben. I roll down the window and he asks, "Tonight?"

"Early?"

"Five?" he asks, laughing.

"My place or yours?"

"Mine." With the way my heart starts to flutter, it makes me wonder if I can hold out that long.

TWENTY-ONE
BEN

———◆———

MY RINGTONE SCREAMS AT ME, waking me from a dead sleep. I bump my head against Sam's, waking her up in the process. We didn't get much sleep after our night together, which seems to be a thing with us. I can't get enough of her and she me.

"Sorry, babe."

Simply silencing that damn thing wouldn't be satisfying enough as I ponder the merits of throwing it against the wall to make it stop. I'm about turn it off when I see my sister's picture flash on the screen. She doesn't call me before the sun is up for no reason. Immediately, I'm awake.

"Jenna?"

"Oh my gosh, Ben."

Rising up on one arm with my heart beating like rapid gun fire, I ask, "What is it? Are Mom and Dad okay?"

My heart stops beating for one minute and it's Drew all over again, waiting for the news that he was gone.

"They're fine."

I exhale all my worry and replace it with no-morning-coffee level annoyance. "What the hell, Jenna?"

"Ben, aren't you supposed to be at work already? It is Monday morning."

"It's ..." I check the time. "Six."

"Yeah."

Shit, what else could she be calling about? "So, what? Did you talk to Dad and he wanted you to check up on me?"

I wouldn't put it past him. There's no law that says I have to be at work at the crack of dawn. And this morning, I have a reason not to be.

"No, I'm calling because Mom and Dad's thirty-fifth anniversary is this weekend and I completely forgot."

"You, who schedules everything? Trying to decide between the stiff shirt Senator, dad's choice," I cough into my fist, "and the tattooed auto mechanic, who you really want, must be keeping you up at night."

"Haha, very funny. Seriously, I dropped the ball and I don't have to explain to you why because you forgot too. Besides, we need to plan something big."

I run a hand through my hair. "And you're telling me, why? You usually handle this. Just tell me how much money I need to give you."

"Of course you would dump this all on me."

"Don't you normally take care of it?" I tug at my hair, ready to pull it out. Sam's smaller hand plucks my fingers loose.

"Yeah, but still. I'm busy, too, you know."

"Fine. I'll make dinner reservations or something. What else do you do for a thirty-fifth anniversary?"

"Is that your sister?" Sam asks.

"Is that Sam?" Jenna asks.

They speak at almost the same time. I nod and Sam frees my hand of the phone.

"Jenna?"

And I'm on the outside looking in. I decide to use the time to mold my hand over Sam's chest. I move in and flick a tongue over her nipple.

"Yes," Sam says squirming. Her voice betrays what I'm doing to her. "No, I'm okay."

I head lower.

"Don't worry. I can help you." As I insert myself in between her thighs and kiss my way to that spot, she says. "Ooo. No. Um … look it's no trouble at allllll."

She forces me to pull back with a fistful of my hair. I give her a toothy grin.

"Twenty guests is a cake in the park. I mean a walk in the park."

She frees me from her bond and I get back to work.

"I do this all the time. I have connections. I'll work something

169

outttt."

Fucking her with my tongue is one of my all-time favorite things.

"No, your brother isn't doing anything. He went to grab something to eat."

I can't help chuckle at that, especially since I'm actually feasting on my favorite thing.

"I'll call you later. I'll get your phone number from Ben."

There's a pause and I'm not sure if I've caused it or if my sister is talking her ear off. I get my answer when she stutters her next word.

"Ggiifftt."

She's close. I'm determined to make her scream while she's on the phone.

"Maybe a trip?"

I stop, unable to hear Jenna's response and say, "Dad will never go for that. He'll say he's too busy."

Sam's face morphs into annoyance. Seems like someone didn't like that I stopped. She grabs my hair and pushes me back down where she wants me.

"True, your dad probably needs a rest. We'll talk."

She ends the call, but I go back to work and get her to the moon and back before we finally leave separately for work.

Although, my day started off pretty fucking awesome, by noon, I'm sure I have scowl lines chiseled into my face. The bearish market is making my life miserable. Everyone is scrambling, trying to mitigate the effects of the down swing today for our penny-watchful clients.

Unfortunately for Lisa, she's getting double the dose of my displeasure.

"Who in the office would have called Karen Spencer?" I ask.

Karen had wanted me to help her get her finances in order for the future, and I'd set her portfolio up, but since we were fucking, I'd passed the torch to Jeff to handle her money so there wouldn't be a conflict of interest.

"No one that I know of, Mr. Rhoades."

My eyes narrow with her use of my surname.

"Is this because I wouldn't sleep with you?" I stage whisper.

She starts to resemble a blackbird with her beady little eyes. "Even though I think you could do better, I have more integrity and respect for this company and my job to do something like that."

I don't know if she's talking about Karen or Sam and don't care to. I don't want to be pissed off if she thinks Sam isn't good enough for me.

"So no one called any of the clients that missed the meeting?"

Her face turns smug. "You should talk to your girlfriend. I personally gave her the list of contacts for the *Sorry We Missed* you letter that went out to all the clients that didn't attend the event."

I chew on that, not believing Sam would've called Karen. It doesn't make sense, unless she doesn't trust me. That thought rolls off me, as I don't believe for one minute she would call Karen.

My day is made worse when I get called into Dad's office.

"Close the door, Ben, and frost the glass."

It's unusual for him to request this. But I do as I am told.

Dad stands older but very much looking like the imposing man he was when I was a kid. I suddenly start to rethink my day and what I might have done wrong. He holds out his hand towards the small sofa and chair he has in his office. I sit on the sofa knowing Dad likes the high backed chair.

His chest rises and falls with aching slowness. "I got the statements from accounting and the bottom line is we didn't make budget and we haven't the last couple of quarters. I had high hopes you would do your part and bring in more high net worth clients from your days at JP Morgan Chase. Unless the real reason you left was due to performance."

Caught by surprise, I think my jaw hangs there As the jab hits its mark. It doesn't take a leap to see I haven't lived up to his expectations.

"Despite that, we aren't out of business. However our fee income continues to decline after the real estate bust a few years ago. The economy may have recovered, but not enough."

Guilt weighs on me knowing I haven't brought in the business I should have.

"So why did we just spend all that money on the employee event? We could have saved that."

Dad sits forward, resting his arms on his knees while he clasps his hands. "This is a lesson you need to learn."

"What's that?" I ask, knowing better but feeling petulant.

"People and perception. If we appear weak, we will be eaten by the sharks. Not to mention all the employees who could jump ship. It's an event we have every year and something the employees remember fondly. That's the case Samantha brought up when talking over the budget in our follow up call."

She's impressed my father. Good for her.

"So what's the plan?" I ask, the heavy burden of his words hanging in the air.

"Quarterly bonuses will be smaller and there will be grumbles about that. We need new business if we are to make the budget this quarter. I don't want people like Mark and Jeff looking for new jobs."

I leave his office after telling him not to give me a bonus. He'd planned to suggest it had I not done so on my own as he'd decided he wouldn't take one either. It wouldn't totally make up the difference in the reduction, but it would make the sting less for some. I work late coming up with proposals for the list of contacts I kept when I left the city.

When I get home in the middle of the night I miss Sam like I've never missed a woman in my bed until now. Selfishly, I text her.

Me: Dinner, tonight? I'll cook.

I don't expect an answer thinking she'll see it in the morning. But my phone dings.

Sam: Love to. What time?
Me: Anytime. My place.
Sam: Now
Me: I wish. Tomorrow? Eight?
Sam: Eight it is.

I lay back getting ready to sleep with a picture of her in my head and my dick in my hand.

TWENTY-TWO
Sam

———◆———

MONDAY AT WORK IS INSANE. Nick acts like an ass towards me. I guess he's still pissed at me for staying in Ben's room. What makes me even angrier is that Martin himself deemed the Rhoades Investment Team function a resounding success. Nick should be happy about that, but when I let him know the great news, all he does is pout.

"It's time to clear the air, Nick. Get whatever it is that's bothering you off your chest."

His scowl speaks louder than his tone. "Okay, fine. This thing you have going with Ben Rhoades ... he's a douche and you shouldn't be involved with him."

Whoa! What the hell is his problem about all of this? I can't believe he won't let this go.

"While I appreciate your concern, like we've already discussed, my personal life doesn't affect you. The topic of Ben Rhoades is closed for discussion."

Nick narrows his eyes until they are practically slits. "You're not serious, are you?"

"Very. Our event was a huge hit with his company so let's move on. We have other business that needs our attention."

"Look, I'm sorry. It's just my sister had a boyfriend that turned out to be worse than bad news. He started out with the dick moves like your Ben, you know, pulling the same kind of crap he is. I took the *do not interfere* route and did nothing. Eventually, things started to get worse and she made excuses for him and told me he wasn't the asshole like I thought he was. Then when things got so bad and she ended up in the ER, she figured out I was right about him. I don't want that for you. All I'm saying is if Rhoades were a good guy, he wouldn't be an asshole to you. I'm only trying to protect you, Sam."

It sort of makes sense, where he's coming from. But then again, he's also taking a huge leap and assuming that Ben's a jerk when in actuality he knows very little about him.

"That must've been terrible for you and I'm sorry you had to see your sister suffer like that. But projecting all that onto Ben isn't right, Nick. He's not that guy."

He shakes his head, throws his hands up in the air, and stomps out. The rest of the day is stressful with Nick's resentful attitude. Maybe I shouldn't have been that hard, but no. The more I think about it, the more I know I'm right. My personal life is not his business, and I need to keep the lines between the two very distinct.

When I get home from the office, Lauren is gone. She's left a note saying she's staying at the beach. I'm not surprised. It's only twenty minutes away and the weather is gorgeous. I get ready to head over to Ben's and pack an overnight bag because I have no intentions of coming home tonight. I also stop at my favorite ice cream shop and pick up a few flavors, some sprinkles, and whipped cream for dessert ... or maybe even to play with later. When I pull up, I grab my stuff and walk to his door. There's a sticky note telling me to come on in.

Music plays, and I can hear pots clanging in the distance. When I enter the kitchen, Ben is busy chopping something. There are worry lines on his face, but I don't ask yet.

"Hmm, busy man, I see."

"Hey. Sorry I didn't greet you. I have chicken going and I was afraid my hands would be a mess to answer the door."

"So considerate."

"Yeah." A smile grows on his handsome face. "That came from Drew. He had me on the hand-washing brigade, I swear," he says absently. Then as if he's just realized what he's said, he stops what he's doing and stands there in silence.

I set my package on the counter and put my hand on his arm. "You know what I think?" I don't wait for him to answer. "I think you're one brave man to be this strong. Because if I lost Lauren, my bestie since high school, I wouldn't be functioning. The fact that you're a successful businessman and have helped Cate this long, despite your own feelings, tells me a whole lot about the man that Ben Rhoades is."

Steel gray eyes meet mine and he holds up his hands. "There are so many things I would do right now if I could, Sam. Only I have fucking chicken juices all over my hands."

And we both start laughing. Which happens to be perfect. I lean in and kiss him and with an arched brow he says, "Risking dirty hands?"

I grab the bag to put the ice cream in the freezer when he stops me with his curiosity. "You'll find out after dinner," I tell him.

That evening Ben opens up to me with stories about Drew and their friendship, how close they were, and talks about his illness all the way to the bitter end. "I really thought he was gonna beat it. I think we were all so sure of it that when it finally came back the last time, we still didn't think he would die. Only he knew. He fucking knew. He was a doctor, you know. An oncologist, of all things. So he goddamn knew he wasn't going to make it. And all of us poor suckers had to sit by and watch the greatest man that ever lived die right before our very eyes. And through it all, you know I never thought it would happen. I fucking lied to myself and him every single day, saying he would find a way. Because he was Drew McKnight."

By the time he finishes telling me everything, his hands are fisted. The urge to hold him is overwhelming, but I don't want to overstep my bounds.

"It's okay to grieve."

"Is it? I feel like I should be able to move on!" His frustration is clear as glass.

He stands and I follow him into the living room. When he sits, he draws me onto his lap.

"There is no time limit on grief, Ben. No one says you only have a year, or a month, or whatever. I imagine losing him was like losing a part of yourself. You can't just sweep it away like crumbs on the floor. You have to learn to live without him. And that takes adjusting. Brushing off your hands and moving on isn't the answer. It doesn't work that way. And if someone told you that, they were lying. When my grandmother died, it took my mother a couple of years to get to the point where she could talk about her and not cry."

He drops his head back on the sofa and I think maybe it's my cue to get off his lap, but I'm wrong.

"Don't go. I need you here."

"Okay. I'm not going anywhere," I say.

"Maybe Cate is right by leaving. Drew is everywhere in this town. I don't want to forget him, but it fucking hurts to remember he's gone. And I'm sorry if I keep dumping on you. It's just until you, no one has understood except Cate, and I'm supposed to be strong for her. So I keep some things to myself."

"I'm here whenever you need me. I've never been through losing my best friend, but I get it."

"Thanks. Your being here helps more than you know."

I rearrange his disheveled hair. "I wish there was more I could do."

What an awful burden to keep to yourself. I don't verbalize this thought, but so many things start to fall into place with him.

"Any time you need to talk, Ben, I'm willing to listen."

He rewards me with a kiss.

After eating around the very charred parts of the chicken, which Ben apologizes for profusely, we decide to shelve the ice cream and save it for some other time. Instead, we end up watching a movie. It was one of the *Fast and Furious* ones, but we both fall asleep during the thing. I wake up sometime in the middle of the night, in Ben's bed, realizing he must've carried me up here.

In the morning, a sheepish Ben apologizes again for the way the night turned out and tells me he wants to make it up to me in the form of a nice dinner as soon as both of our schedules allow.

"Last night happened to be about comfort and support. Sometimes that's what we need." I lift up my shirt and say, "Besides, look at this. Does this look like someone in need of more food? It looks like I swallowed a watermelon."

Ben tumbles me into his lap and cups my breast. "You do not. It's more like a cantaloupe."

"Ahh! You're terrible. I'm not talking about my tits. I'm talking about my gut." I swat his hands away, but not before he squeezes them a few times.

"Why? Your body is fine, your tits are amazing."

I rub my stomach, and it does resemble a cantaloupe. "I need a diet."

"Don't you dare. I want you the way you are, soft with curves like a woman should be."

Well, at least he likes a woman with a Buddha belly. Reluctantly, we leave the bed so we can both go to work. That night when I get home at almost nine, Lauren is back from the beach and all over me for information about Ben.

"I can't believe you haven't called us! The gang is pissed off at you." She jabs a finger at me. Her accusation is loud and clear. Between her job and mine, I hadn't seen her until today.

"I was with him all weekend. There wasn't time. We've both been busy the last couple of days. And I spent the night at his place."

"If the shoe were on the other foot, you would've killed me."

"Okay. Dinner, tomorrow night at our usual spot. All the girls and I'll fill you in."

I know she wants to hear first but I can't stay awake any longer.

The next day turns out to be a killer work day. As I walk into the restaurant that evening to face my cross-examining besties, they all wave at me. Talk about eager. Usually I'm one of the first to arrive, and I'm not even late.

"So?" they all chime in on the big Ben question.

"I'll save you the trouble of asking any questions. He's amazing in every sense of the word."

"Ah, I'm so jealous," Berkeley says. "I knew he could change and be worth it."

"Me too." Carrie speaks out.

"I want John to act like that," says Hayley.

"I hate to be the naysayer here, but do you think he'll go back to being dickfaced Ben? I mean, I want him to be your knight, but I don't want you to get hurt either. And it sounds like your heart is involved now," says Lauren.

"Just listen to this." And I give them a blow by blow of the corporate party and just about everything afterward. I don't give them the details about his friend, Drew. I hold that back, thinking it's too personal to share. Maybe someday, but not today. I skim over it saying his best friend died of cancer.

"You're making him sound like gold, and not the plating kind, which is surprising considering his reputation," Lauren says.

"I think so. I get this super good vibe around him. He's just so ... oh, I don't know. Caring might be a good word."

As we sit, the waiter comes up with two bottles of wine. "Would you ladies prefer white or red this evening?"

We all blurt out, "White."

I don't remember ordering any wine. So I pose that question and he grins as he pops the corks and pours. "This is courtesy of Ben Rhoades. Enjoy, ladies."

They all look at me in appreciation.

"Well, this is a nice surprise. He's stepping up his game. Have you not had sex with the man yet?" Lauren asks.

Everyone laughs and looks at me until Berkeley breaks in. "Well? Is this you dragging him along and him begging, Sam?"

"No! I mean, yes." I lean in and whisper, "We've done it, and the man lives up to the god label I gave him."

"Well, then, I like him more and more." Berkeley laughs and says, "Cheers!" She raises her glass and we all clink ours together.

Lauren adds, "Just be cautious, though. Remember, there are those manslut rumors. I don't want my bestie getting hurt."

"I won't. I promise." And I feel my words are the truth when I say them. With a huge grin, I text Ben and thank him profusely for the wine.

He answers with: **I'm sure I'll think of a way for you to thank me! Enjoy and come over after if you can.**

It puts a silly grin on my face that stays there for a long time.

I have to admit, Ben Rhoades is a tough act to keep my mind off of. Even though I'm running ragged at work, he still manages to keep me smiling. Jenna and I talk several times, planning the anniversary party for his parents, which is coming up this weekend. Ben hasn't been very involved, saying he's leaving all the decisions up to us. Personally, I'm positive this stuff bores him. The glazed look in his eyes is the dead giveaway.

My usually energetic self is dragging lately, but I only have my sex god to blame for that. He keeps me too sleep deprived, but I won't complain.

Friday morning, the day before the Rhoades's anniversary party, I'm at work checking my email, when something pops up. I get a notice from a caterer for the next evening regarding an event that isn't on my calendar. I'm sure I don't have anything booked because I'm attending the Rhoades's party, so I make a phone call and the caterer sends me the email with all the details and the correspondence. It has Nick's name on it. I call Nick into my office to see if he knows anything about it.

"Yeah, I booked it."

"But the Rhoades's anniversary dinner is that night at Margie's downtown. How am I supposed to be in two places at once? And since when do you book events without clearing them with me first?"

His mouth opens and closes, like a guppy desperate for air. "I ... I thought Rhoades was Ben."

Anger diffuses through me and I ball my hands into fists. It takes every ounce of control not to take a swing at him. "You what? You looked at the calendar and assumed it was a date? And even so, that's still taking it upon yourself to book an event without clearing it with me. One, I don't even know this client, and two, I don't even know how to respond to this."

Nick rubs his forehead. "It's a rehearsal dinner."

Now I'm even more furious, if that's possible. "A rehearsal dinner? For a wedding?"

"Yes."

I want to throw something. If I could pick him up, I'd toss him out the window. "Damn it, Nick! You know good and well we don't do these types of events. Our focus is corporate, not wedding or social functions. What in the name of heaven were you thinking?"

The guilty look on his face tells me more than I care to know.

"Say it. I want you to say it to my face."

His face flushes crimson as his eyes darken. "You're doing an anniversary dinner. And to be honest, I wanted to keep you away from him." His tone has become accusatory. I don't like it one bit.

"The anniversary party is a favor, not a job, not that I need to explain that to you. And now I can't attend because you've booked this rehearsal party." I want to add, *You giant fucking turd face*, at the end, but my manners force me to refrain and am way proud of myself for doing so. "And haven't we already discussed that Ben is none of your business?" I don't give him time to answer before I launch into the event he booked. "You are working all these details out yourself for the rehearsal party. And it better go without a hitch. I'm forwarding you the email from the caterer and you're on your own on this. In the future, everything goes through me. Am I clear?"

"Yes."

He leaves my office and I immediately call Ben.

"Hey gorgeous. What's going on?"

"I'm sorry, but I won't be able to attend the anniversary party tomorrow. I'll be working another function."

"What?"

After I explain, he curses up a shitstorm.

"I'm sorry," I say again.

"Can I ask you something?"

"Sure."

"What are you going to do about Nick the Dick?"

I tell him how our conversation went.

"Not as severe as I would've proposed, but it's your business and you're the boss. So I respect that."

"Out of curiosity, what exactly would you have proposed?" I ask.

"Oh, that's easy. I would love it if you'd fired him. Then I could've beaten the shit out of him. Drew did always say I needed to simmer down a bit."

In my silence, he finally adds, "Don't worry, Sam. I won't touch little Nick the Dick. He's safe for now."

TWENTY-THREE
BEN

EVERYTHING IS PERFECT JUST LIKE Sam. I really hate she can't be here to get the praise for pulling everything off in such a short period of time, especially during the wedding season in Charleston. It's nothing short of a miracle. I still want to kick that Nick's ass though.

"What's going on with you?" Jenna asks resting a hand on my shoulder.

"Nothing. How about you? It's strange not having Cate here."

Her smile fades and I know how she feels. It'll be odd not having Cate living in Charleston. I can't remember a time Jenna and Cate were separated. They've done everything together including attending the same college.

"She's looking for an apartment. And because her new job assignment starts in a few weeks and she has to work here until then, she wanted to get out of town."

I pull her in a hug. "Where's Kenneth or did you bring Brandon?"

She narrows her eyes at me before she punches my arm. "Don't say that so loud. You know damn well who I brought."

This is true. Kenneth is everything my dad wants for his princess. His words not mine. "You're going to end up an old woman alone. He's the kind of guy that trades out his wives every few years for a newer model."

"You are so mean." She punches me again.

"God, you've turned violent."

Rolling her eyes, she says, "And I wanted to tell you I really like Sam. She was amazing to work with. Maybe she'll be my new best friend."

Before I can respond, Kenneth shows up. And for a second I think of Horace and all the things he said at the pool party. I wonder if he ever found his friend.

"Ben, how are things in the investment business?" Kenneth asks.

"Couldn't be better. And you, how are things on the hill?"

Kenneth, dry as toast, just shrugs. "Not bad at all."

"Excuse me," I say when a vision of pure beauty rushes in the door.

She searches the room as I head towards her.

When she spots me, her face lights up. "Ben."

"You were able to come after all," I say, drawing her close. I'm obsessed with touching her. It has to be because when she's near, the world quiets and all the shit that's plagued me the whole day disappears.

"I did. There was no way I would miss this. So, I left everything in Nick's hands after all the major stuff happened." She smiles.

I capture her face in my hands and kiss her like we are the only two people in the room.

She pulls back, her hands covering mine. "Ben."

Her face the color of a ripe tomato, I know I'm lost for her. And that's the only four-letter L word I can mutter yet. But it's a word I've never been able to use with anyone else.

"What's going on in that head of yours?"

I finally let go and straighten to my normal height. Some people are looking, but I don't care.

Then my sister is tapping her wine glass with a fork. Time for the reveal of our present, and it turns out better than expected. Jenna does a good job of manipulating Dad in front of everyone to admitting he hadn't taken Mom on a vacation in over a decade. Mom cries about how she's wanted to go to Italy forever. I can only hope Dad doesn't somehow figure a way out of the month-long trip to tour all over the country.

For my speech, I piggy back on Jenna and give honors to her and Sam for a great party. When I take her home that night, I show her how much it meant to me for her to help us pull this off, paying her back in too many orgasms to count.

Monday, bright and early, Dad's at my door.

"This isn't the best time for me to leave. But I'm pretty sure you know that. With that said, don't fuck things up while I'm gone."

I do know that, but I won't admit it. "I can handle it."

"I'm counting on you," he commands as if he's sending me out into combat. And maybe he is. If I don't win this battle, I will lose the war.

After Dad leaves at noon, almost immediately it seems like the shit hits the fan.

Mark steps in my office a few hours later. He and his ex are apparently giving it another go. She'd been at the company weekend event and I did my best not to say anything. He has to live with her, not me.

"What did she do now?" I ask automatically.

He shakes his head. "Nothing. But we may have a problem."

"We?"

He reaches across my desk to hand me a paper and my world spins out of control.

"Who's seen this?"

"Just me, but it's only a matter of time."

I read it again. It's a letter from a large global mutual fund company. It basically says that they invested with the hedge fund that made headlines for being a fake and stealing people's money. The problem is we'd just sent out letters claiming that we'd made no investments in that hedge fund. And technically we hadn't. However, indirectly we had, since we invested with this mutual fund who had in fact invested in the bad hedge fund. That made us indirect investors in that company too, which contradicted our letter. *Fuck*.

As if on cue, my door opens and a familiar face saunters in and my hackles rise.

"Guess what I received today. A letter from your firm and one from my mutual fund company."

Mark pales. I wave him off. "It's okay. I'll handle it."

"Your dad?"

I'm a little annoyed he doesn't have confidence that I can take care of things.

"He's on a plane. I've got this. Get with Jeff and start compiling a list of investors." I wonder how Dad hadn't researched this more thoroughly before making a blanket statement. But the woman in my office demands my attention.

"Ms. Sanders, what can I do for you?" I hide my aggravation at her showing up at my office. I'd hoped that she'd disappeared for good.

She takes a seat and crosses her legs as if to draw my attention to them. But I keep my eyes on hers.

"It's *Ms. Sanders* now?"

"I prefer to keep things professional."

Her eyes brighten. "I know just how professional. Like how you like to spank me when I'm bad."

I close my eyes, not believing that she'd go there.

"Does your girlfriend know how you like to play rough sometimes?"

Her exaggeration of things pisses me off. I manage to ignore her words and say, "Why are you here?" Even though I know damn well.

"See, I don't like to keep my money all in one place. So I have my future retirement accounts with this mutual fund company and they sent me this."

The letter is a replica of the one Mark just showed me. The mutual fund company will send it to all investors eventually. Which means we need to craft a response and fast. I don't have time for this extra bullshit.

"I can go to the press. Hell, I'm a lawyer. I can sue you for misrepresentation. I could have the SEC all over your ass."

The idea of the governing body for corporations and investment companies coming in like the IRS and auditing us makes me shudder.

Words like *we didn't directly invest in that company so technically that's not true* won't do me any good against a lawyer. So I cut to the chase.

"What do you want?"

"Dinner."

I don't quite believe her. My brow lifts in question.

"Dinner tonight, my place, and we can talk this all out."

"I'm going to be busy with everything going on around here."

"Dinner at eight. Be there, or I'll see you in court."

She gets up and makes a show of bending down to pick up her purse as if her ass would capture my attention. It doesn't. I glance at my screen and set up an all hands on deck meeting. When she finally leaves my office, I push my hair back before picking up my phone.

"Sam," I say when she answers.

"Hey, are we seeing each other tonight?"

"No, not exactly." I sigh. This is the part I dread. "I have to have dinner with a client."

"Oh, like the Sadlers?"

"Not exactly. I have to have dinner with Karen."

TWENTY-FOUR
Sam

HIS WORDS MAKE ME ALMOST drop my phone. "What exactly do you mean by that?"

"I guess I need to backtrack a little." He explains about a catastrophe at work. "But that's not the worst of it. Karen showed up right after all hell broke loose. She demanded I take her to dinner."

"What! What the hell does that mean? Can you explain?" I can't hide the shock from my voice nor do I like the direction this is heading one bit.

"By demanded, I mean more like blackmail. She's threatening a lawsuit so I need to check with our attorneys. But she wants me at her place at eight. Sam, I know this sounds bad, but believe me, I have absolutely zero interest in her. Because she's a lawyer, I do have to take her seriously. The company could be at stake. And the fact that she's resorting to threats makes it even worse. For a smart woman I have no clue how she thinks this would make me want her."

My stomach slams to the floor with this news. I know I have no reason to be upset like this. Ben is being honest with me. He could lie and say something totally different and I would never know.

"Okay. I'll deal with this."

"No. There will be no dealing. I'll handle her. I'm waiting to hear back from our attorneys. They may tell me I don't have to do a thing. I just wanted you to be aware of what's going on. And that I may have to meet with her, if not tonight then maybe tomorrow."

"O-okay."

"Hey, I'm not going to do anything to mess with what you and I have going. Tell me you understand that."

"I understand."

"Good. As much as I would rather stay on the phone with you and maybe share some dirty talk, I've gotta go before things take an even bigger turn for fuckmeville. I was hoping I could give my dad something to be proud of while he was gone, but now ..."

"Hey, don't say that. Pull some of your fancy tricks out of your bag. I know you're savvy enough to figure something out."

"Thanks for believing in me. I'll talk to you later."

Even though I try to act like I'm fine, my guts are in knots with the idea of him seeing the spiteful Karen. She's no dummy; I only hope she doesn't hold him over a barrel for something he had nothing to do with.

Later that afternoon, there's a knock on my office door, and I expect to see Nancy's head peek through.

"Mom. What brings you here?"

"I wanted to pop in and see my baby." Her smile is like watching someone yawn—when I see it I automatically grin in return.

"I think I've passed the baby stage."

"Not for me you haven't. But the truth is, I wanted to see if you and your new man can come to dinner tomorrow night." She grabs one of the chairs in my office and pulls it close to mine so she can check out what's on my computer screen. My mom is a curious sort and loves to see how my business operates.

"I can check with Ben, but he's been crazy busy at work. Can you give me another option just in case?"

She clicks her tongue and says, "Tomorrow was going to be perfect because your sister and Evan were free, too."

Shitdiddles! She wants me to introduce Ben to the entire family? What the hell?

"Oh, Mom, we only started dating. Don't you think this is a bit early to do the whole family thing?"

Her hand tucks an errant curl behind my ear. "No, and the reason I don't is that last boy you dated ended up breaking your heart. Your sister and I want to make sure this boy doesn't do the same."

"Oh for Pete's sake, Mom. First, Ben is not a boy. And second,

I'm a grown woman and can watch out for myself."

She clicks her tongue again. "Sweetie, you know you always say that but then end up a sad mess. I think we need to give our approval this time."

"Did Laney put you up to this?" Knowing my mother hen of an older sister, I can see her conniving mind behind all of this.

"No, she did not. It was my idea I'll have you know. And Evan was free, so when I called Laney, she jumped on it."

"I imagine she did. Tell you what, I'll ask Ben, but I will not pressure him. If he says no, then it's no."

"Fine, but will you come without him? We still want to see our baby."

Smiling, I say, "Yeah, Mom. I'll be there as long as my work is caught up."

"You work way too hard, honey."

"I know."

"So, any decision yet?"

"Oh, Mom."

She puts her hands on my shoulders, rotating me so we face each other. "Honey, can I tell you something? Remember when your grandmother died?"

"Yeah. It was awful. You know I loved my Grammy."

"I know you did. She adored you, too. But it took every bit of wind in the world out of my sails for at least two years. Oh, I put up a good front around you girls, but ask your dad about it. But see, here's the thing, sweetie—that's how it's supposed to work. It was hard, but it's the order of things, you know. The parents are supposed to go before the children. I just couldn't bear it if anything ..." Her voice cracks and she stops to compose herself, dabbing at her eyes. "Sweetie, I don't know what I would do if something happened to you, especially since we have all this wonderful information nowadays. You see?" Her eyes pull down at the corners and tug at my heart.

Now I feel terrible when she puts it this way because I can't imagine how awful it would be to lose a child. "Okay, Mom. I promise I'll do something. And let you know about dinner."

We hug and say our I love yous, and I get back to work. When I get home that night, I hit Lauren with all my insecurities.

"I think you're good as far as that vengeful loony Karen goes. She sounds like she's on the crackwagon and Ben wouldn't want anyone like that," she reassures me. "Like you said, he didn't have to say a thing. He could've lied and then said he went out to dinner with a client and told you nothing. You never would've known. He didn't though. He came clean and you can't argue with that."

"I know. It's just that woman was hanging all over him. And the fact that she's a nutjob scares me."

"You also said he acted like he couldn't stand her. If she's that mental, you know he won't go for that."

Lauren's right. I'm beating myself up over this and it's making me as crazy as she is. I need to drop it and move on.

Ben calls me later that evening and he sounds like he's gone nine rounds. Or maybe even twelve.

"You sound awful."

"I feel it. This has been one hell of a bad day. I'm whipped." The desolation in his tone is contagious and his bad mood curls in my chest.

"Hey, you okay?"

"No, but I will be once this crisis is averted."

"When will that be?"

"We're working on it. It's so complicated, and not that you wouldn't understand, but honestly, I'm just talked out right now."

"You don't have to explain. I think you need to go home and rest. Get a good night's sleep."

"I'm heading out of the office now and hope to be home soon. At least I've managed to put that pain-in-my-ass Karen off for another day. I would love your company, but I'll probably be asleep in twenty minutes and then I'm going in earlier than usual tomorrow."

"Be safe driving. We'll talk tomorrow."

"Thanks for understanding."

"There's nothing to understand."

After he ends the call, I sit and worry. Since when did I become so freaked over a guy? I never was like this before. Is this telling me that I care for him more than I realize? And then I become aware of the fact that I didn't mention dinner at my parents to him. Great. I don't want to call him back, because he doesn't need this added demand on his plate. But if I don't ask him, my mom and sister will hound me to death and I'll end up telling them I didn't ask. So I make the hasty decision and call him back.

"Sam? Everything okay?"

"Not exactly."

"What's wrong?"

"It's my mom and my sister. They've done some finagling and want us to come to dinner tomorrow night."

Dead silence greets me.

"You don't have to come. I know it's …"

"I want to. I was just trying to figure out in my head if it would work. The timing and all."

"Ben, I know things at work are rough."

"That's why it took me so long to answer. And then I have that thing with Karen that I need to figure out."

"Oh, right."

"I hate to ask this, but can I tell you tomorrow?"

"Sure. I told my mom it may not work. That's not a problem."

"But I would love to meet your family. If not this time then some other time."

"Okay. G'night, Ben."

And I notice he's managed to put a smile back on my face. But it disappears when I think about why he can't come to my parents and I want to unleash my Kraken and bitch slap the everlovin' hell out of that whack job Karen.

TWENTY-FIVE
BEN

◆

I'VE BARELY HUNG UP WITH Sam when Mark breezes in my office. "Tell me, what's the damage."

"It's not that bad." He hands me a paper.

"So what's this mean?" I see the numbers and figures, but I want him to tell me what's not on the paper.

"Less than ten percent of our clients have that particular mutual fund in their portfolio mix. Most of our clients have a mutual fund from that company, but not that particular one."

"That's good."

He grins which catches me by surprise. Mark has been in the dumps for weeks and seeing him smile when he's not blitzed off his rocker is new.

"It's even better."

"Okay."

"During the last few days, that company has made money for our clients. Not huge amounts, but they didn't lose any. That hedge fund was such a small segment of their investment mix, the other performing investments absorbed the blow."

My mood lightens. "Fucking great news." I can already envision the words I can say to Karen to watch her smug smile disappear off her face.

"All right, have someone prepare an analysis for each of the other clients involved. Then have them work on a narrative for each in layman's terms."

Mark nods and leaves my office without preamble.

"Ben." I glance up and see Trudy, my father's admin at my door. "Your father has a meeting in fifteen minutes I wasn't able to reschedule. I left messages that weren't returned and the potential client has shown up for their meeting time."

"Okay, send me Dad's notes. In fact, can you print them out? Sit the client in the small conference room and have Dad's presentation cued up on the computer. Tell them I'll be there in a few minutes."

She nods. Dad is always prepared, so I have no doubt that he has everything laid out ready to go. I start to get up from my desk when the human resources manager breezes into my office.

"Have no fear, you're the boss now."

I chuckle at her joke.

"What's up?" I sit back in my chair, knowing I don't have a lot of time. However, Janice won't leave before she has her say.

"I've been dealing with an issue with your father."

"And?"

"There have been some complaints from a few people about the number of breaks smokers get versus non-smokers."

I groan, letting my head fall back while pushing hair off my forehead.

"People issues are the number one problem in a company."

"I get that, but this sounds petty, even to me."

"On the surface I can see that. But I've clocked the people being accused and they are taking excessive breaks."

I'm dumbstruck for a second. "So we're resorting to spying on people now."

"Mr. Rhoades, these issues can lead to lawsuits."

There's that word again. No wonder people think this country is sue happy.

"Fine, what do we do?"

"I just need you to approve me sending out this communication to all employees about the Federal and State guidelines in regards to breaks."

"Can you send it to me via e-mail and I'll get back to you?" I ask, getting up from my desk.

"Fine, but I'd like to have this out today."

I nod. After she leaves, I scrub a hand over my face. When I look again, Lisa is there.

"You're messing with your hair again. Maybe you should get it cut."

Her eyes rake over me and the excessive attention says she's still very interested. "I should. Sam says the same thing."

Bringing up Sam is a mean thing to do as I watch her face fall, but I can't deal with anymore crazy women.

Dad's admin steps up next to Lisa. "Don't you have work to do?"

Lisa's face pales before she nods and rushes off. "That girl and her puppy crush," Trudy tsks.

Pressing my lips closed, I hold in the chuckle that threatens to escape. Trudy is in charge of all support staff and just did me an incredible favor.

"Here is what you requested. Let's walk and talk and I'll fill you in what I know."

"Before that, can you send our *sorry we missed you* letter from the client luncheon and this letter," I hand her a copy of the letter from the mutual fund company, "to our lawyers. See if you can get a meeting with them today at their offices or ours."

"Sure. Want to tell me what's going on?"

"Not enough time but there could be a potential lawsuit. I want to know what they think of the merits of any such action against us."

She isn't making notes, but I know she's memorized everything I've said. Dad has sung her praises on a number of occasions. "Okay, let me tell you about the Dunbrookes."

After the meeting, I finally find a minute to text Karen about her planned dinner. And I choose not to call so there would be a record of exactly what I said.

Me: I can't make your blackmail dinner tonight. So you'll have to sue me.

My phone rings and when I pick up she gets right to the point.

"Clever of you, Ben. But I'm not playing your game."

"This isn't a game. I can't do dinner. I have a ton of things I have to finish tonight."

This is true. My office has been a revolving door all day. Most people have finally gone home, and I have to get my own work done. I haven't been able to touch any of my responsibilities yet.

"Fine, tomorrow night, and no more excuses."

"Tomorrow," I say with no certain terms because I very much

doubt I will see her for dinner.

By the time I call Sam and explain that I can't see her tonight, it's late. I do a few other things before I finally head out my office door. I haven't eaten dinner, but decide against it when I stare at my phone where I've pulled up my contacts. I set the phone down on the passenger seat haunted by what I'd been about to do. It's automatic to call Drew when I have a shit day.

It's a good thing I don't live far from work. I breeze through my door and head straight for a bottle of whiskey, pouring myself a healthy glass.

"You fucker, you. I almost think you did this on purpose so you wouldn't have to deal with my shit." My words echo in the empty room after I drain the contents of my glass. "Who the fuck am I supposed to call now?"

I think about Cate and immediately shake my head. She's trying to get her life together. She doesn't need me to bring her down. She left because she wants to move on from her grief. *So don't call her, you asshole.*

The phone is in my hand as if it materialized there.

"Hello," a sleepy voice says.

"Sam," I breathe.

"Ben, is everything okay?"

It is now. "I just wanted to hear your voice. I'm sorry to wake you up."

"My voice?"

You don't know how talking to you soothes me. "Yeah, it's sexy."

She laughs. "Sexy, huh? Is there a reason you need sexy?"

It's way more than your sexy voice. "Is there ever a bad time for sexy?" Her laugh makes a smile form on my face. "Hey, do you think you can meet me for lunch tomorrow? I should be tied to my desk, but I need to see you. Work is hell on wheels."

"Yeah, I think I can do that."

"Great. I would ask you what you're wearing, but then I'd never get to sleep. Goodnight, gorgeous."

"Night."

My morning meeting with the lawyers sends me over the moon. Only, when I get back to the office, I feel like I need people to take a number to stop the pile-up outside my door.

"This is what it's like to be in charge," Trudy says laying out my calendar for the day.

"It's like another full time job."

"That's why your dad comes in early and stays late. It's the only time he has to himself."

Her message to me is loud and clear.

"I need a little more time at lunch." She eyes me like my mother does. "I have something I need to take care of outside the office and I need travel time."

"I'll shift things around, but you need to tell me your schedule in advance."

"Fine, this is all new to me. I never had problems scheduling my own meetings before."

"And now you have me, temporarily," she adds.

When lunchtime comes around, I'm armed with an envelope and drive over to pick up Sam. I find myself in a trance when she walks to my car. She's dressed in an outfit that makes my mouth water and tongue hang out like a panting dog. My dick is on high alert and it sucks I can't act on it.

"Hey, where are we going for lunch?"

"Huh?"

"Are you okay?"

I shake my head because I'm mesmerized by the way her breasts move under her shirt as she sits down. I turn away and shift into gear.

"Yeah, I have a stop to make and I want you to come with me."

All I have to do is think about our next stop and my dick stops trying to poke a hole through my pants to get closer to Sam. Instead, it hides.

"Are you going to tell me where we're going? This is an office building."

"Trust me, okay?"

I take her hand in mine as we exit the elevator and into a reception area. I leave Sam for a second while I announce myself to the receptionist. Then I grab Sam's hand again.

It doesn't take long before Karen comes around the corner all business-like. Her lips thin when she realizes I'm not alone.

"Why is she here?"

"You've met my girlfriend, Samantha. She and I are having lunch downstairs. Since we were close I thought I would personally bring you this letter from our lawyers. And I won't be able to attend dinner tonight or any night for that matter."

I hand her the letter in plain sight of the receptionist who has now become my impartial witness.

Karen's jaw clenches. "I'll be moving my money from your firm."

"I think that might be for the best."

I press the elevator button and am rewarded when the doors open instantly. I walk in with Sam in tow. Both women look shell-shocked. As the doors close forever on a relationship I never intended to have with Karen, I pull a stunned Sam close and kiss her.

"I'm sorry I didn't tell you," I say when I pull away.

"You should have."

Her answer given through gritted teeth warns me I'm in trouble. I back her in the corner of the elevator. "I should have. Let me make it up to you."

TWENTY-SIX
Sam

———————◆———————

"MAKE IT UP TO ME? What the heck were you thinking, Ben, not giving me some kind of a heads up here? I felt much like a fool." My hands fly up in the air.

"No, that wasn't my intent. I wanted her to get the message loud and clear that the two of us are together and that she and I are finished. Plus, I really did need to deliver that letter to her."

"Fine. I get that. But you could have clued me in and not blindsided me. What if I had done that to you? Taken you to a former lover's office? I feel like you used me."

His mouth works, as he searches for something to say. "No! I would never use you. I'm sorry. I should've told you." His hands automatically plow through his hair. "Can you forgive me?"

It's always the eyes. They tell the truth before anything else. And when I look into his, all I see is clear focus and honesty. He didn't mean any harm. He only wanted to do just what he said. The little V between his eyes and the way his mouth turns down shows me how he erred.

"I can, but please don't do anything like that again. I probably would've jumped at the chance to go with you if you'd only asked me first." I walk into his space and put my arms around his waist. "You have to know I'm your biggest supporter."

He leans his forehead against mine and says, "Now I feel even worse."

"And here I thought you were going to make it up to me."

The elevator dings and the doors open. People start to walk in, so we move apart and exit.

"I'd like to do more than what I can right now. But time isn't being very kind to me today. I did say lunch, so let's go eat. Does that sound okay to you?"

As an answer, my stomach emits a huge embarrassing protest at having been denied food so long.

"I guess I have my response," he chuckles. "Come on, there's a great place right over here."

We get seated right away and order. He brings me up to speed on the situation at work, and I do the same.

"I'm glad things are getting somewhat better for you," I say.

"Yeah. It's still crazy, mind you. But at least I feel like we're in control, or maybe have a better fix on things. With Dad gone, I was worried things would go too far south and by the time he gets home he would feel like I was this major failure."

"When I spoke to him, I had the sense he had the utmost faith in you."

"Yeah maybe." He rakes a hand through his hair. "But we're not there yet. This is my chance. And I want to show him I'm capable, that I won't fail. And now this." He rubs his face momentarily, then adds, "Dad always acts like I'm not good enough, not cut out for this, and I bust my ass for him, but … and now this Karen thing. At least the major crisis was averted."

It's nice to see him opening up to me about work and his relationship with his dad. "I can't believe Karen threatened a lawsuit. But you've handled that too. No way your dad won't see that."

His hands start to move towards his hair, but I intercept them and lace my fingers with his. He looks at our joined hands and the corner of his mouth turns up. When his eyes meet mine, they sparkle. "I have a terrible habit of doing that."

"I know. You'll go bald if you don't stop."

"You, Cate, and Drew." A rapid fire burst of laughter escapes from him.

"What?"

"The three of you have all said that. About the bald thing."

"Oh. But it's true. It's a good thing you have thick hair or you'd probably be bald by now."

"Yeah, truth. But to answer your question, she did. Threaten a lawsuit that is. I'm pretty sure it was mostly about her wanting me to continue a relationship with her, sexual or otherwise."

I'm not sure I heard him correctly. "Did you say that she wanted a sexual ..."

"Yeah. I did. You don't have to repeat it. So I had the attorneys draw up a letter pointing out the flaws in any potential lawsuit. They addressed our letter and how we hadn't overstepped our bounds in our language legally. I had to deliver it in front of an impartial witness. Turns out I had two, but I didn't plan on bringing you there. And yeah, I should've told you in advance. I was overly focused on getting her off my back, I guess. So let's talk about your newest client. That's pretty exciting."

It's so amazing to see his eyes and face light up when I tell him about my latest contract that I almost preen. His full attention is focused on me, unlike when I dated Trevor. He didn't give a damn about my business. Not only did Ben feed me lunch, but he also nourished my ego. But then his expression crashes when he checks the time.

"I hate this. I need to get back. Filling Dad's shoes is a lot more than I bargained for."

"At least it gives you a good idea of what it will be like if you ever decide to take over for him one day."

"I hope that's not for a long time," he says.

He kisses me good-bye and I long for so much more than what he gives.

When I get back to my office, I'm checking my calendar and notice my doctor's appointment for the day after tomorrow. I hadn't realized it was this week. My mood sours, as apprehension and fear take hold and their roots grow deep within me.

I hate to do it, but I hit my mom's number on my phone and wait for her to answer.

"Mom, I'm calling to reschedule our dinner. Ben's schedule will be freed up in the next couple of weeks after his dad returns from Italy. I'm sorry I didn't make it the other night. It was a bit crazy here for me.

"Oh, sweetie, that's fine. Why don't you come and eat with Dad and me tonight?"

"I can't, I have plans. I'm sorry."

"Well, let me talk to your sister and we'll figure out another night? Oh, and I know I'm pestering you, but do you know when your doctor's appointment is?"

Every muscle in my body tenses in a very bad way. "Yes. It's the day after tomorrow."

I can almost hear her relax. "Good. I'm glad with your busy schedule you didn't let that slip behind."

"No, Mom, I didn't."

After we end the call, I think about the shit hand of cards my family has been dealt in this issue. I wish it would magically vanish. It's no use pushing it under the rug, with Mom and Laney here to remind me. I wonder how hard it was on Mom when she became ill herself. Dad must've gone crazy with worry. I was a self-centered teenager at the time, and though Laney and I were scared, my parents did one hell of a great job at shielding us from the horrors of her surgery and treatment. I don't know how they did it.

The constant ringing of my phone pulls me out of those distant and unpleasant memories. Nancy is a godsend when it comes to screening calls. She handles most everything, sending Nick what he can take care of. He's still not happy with how I left him at the rehearsal party, but that was his fault for scheduling it in the first place. He has one more chance to prove himself. If he doesn't, then I'm going to replace him.

After my teleconference, I go to meet Jenna. We made plans the night of the anniversary party and we're finally getting some time to hangout. Jenna is waiting on me when I arrive. I give my name to the hostess and she seats us in a posh private booth, a perk of knowing the manager.

"It totally pays to be in your line of work," Jenna says after we sit.

"Yeah, sometimes it can come in handy."

"I want to say thanks again with all your help for my parents' anniversary. They were thrilled and I couldn't have pulled it off without you."

She smiles but it doesn't quite reach her eyes.

"No problem, I loved helping."

"You should know, you make my brother happy. And my parents love you. So maybe you'll be planning your wedding one day soon."

I hold a hand up. "I think it's way too soon for that."

Thankfully, a waiter comes over and puts the brakes on an awkward conversation. It's after we order drinks and appetizers that I really get the sense things aren't good. She's staring off in the distance, frowning. Add that to the purple bruises under her eyes telling me sleep has been a stretch for her.

"Hey, what's up? You look like you've got something on your mind."

She grabs her glass of wine, takes a huge gulp, and folds her arms, hugging herself. "If I tell you this, can it stay between us? I mean, I don't want you to say anything to Ben about it."

"Sure."

"I'm having man issues."

"Ahh," I nod. "Kenneth."

"Not exactly."

My brows lift because Kenneth is the only guy I've ever seen her with.

"Okay, yes, Kenneth is part of the problem. He's great and everything I could want in a man."

Our waiter busts up the conversation by delivering our appetizers, but Jenna doesn't seem to be very interested in food. As she picks at her plate, we resume our discussion.

"If Kenneth is the man for you, then what's the problem?" I ask.

Her face lights up like I flipped a switch. "There's this guy, Brandon, who I'm positive my parents wouldn't approve of. Not that it's a problem because he's just a friend. It's just ..." Her eyes go dreamy. "When I'm around him, he's interested in *me*. Not in what my family does."

"Life's short, Jenna. You have to be happy, and if Kenneth doesn't make you happy, sometimes you have to cut bait, you know?"

"You don't know my dad very well. I can hear him already."

"So, what? Are you going to marry someone to please your dad, and then get divorced a few years down the road?"

She shrugs, as if she's considered that route.

"Holy crap! You can't possibly think that! Does Cate know?"

She grabs my hand and says, "No, and you can't say a word about this to anyone."

"I won't, but promise me you won't do anything foolish. You need to hang out with my friends. I swear they would set you straight."

That night, as I lie in bed, I can't help but think about Jenna and her dilemma. I wonder if Ben knows how this is rolling out with his dad. For that matter, if Ben and I go down that road, what would Martin think of me? Would I be good enough for the Rhoades family? I'm thankful for my parents. They would never expect that of me. And now that I think of it, Martin didn't seem the type that would do that to Jenna either. Maybe she's overanalyzing things. I hope so. I also pray she finds the answers to her problems and chooses the guy who makes her the happiest.

The following day at work drags, and so does the evening. Ben is tied up, as he is the next night, too. His phone calls are a poor substitution for the real thing. I miss him, but I don't want to intrude on him either. He's exhausted when he gets in at night and he needs sleep so he can function at one hundred percent during the day.

The day of my appointment arrives too soon for me, but I face it with all the courage I can muster. I've buried my head like an ostrich over this visit for as long as I can, so this is my day of reckoning. The sad thing is, my doctor's not going to like what I say. My stress threshold is at maximum capacity without me rupturing my own head gasket. As I sit across the desk from my doctor, he looks at the computer screen, tapping the keyboard and hmming repeatedly.

"So, Samantha, you had the genetic testing as we discussed at your last appointment and we talked about all your options. We said that for six months you could think about what to do. I know you've probably given it a lot of thought in that time."

"To be honest, I don't know what to do." Right now, I swear my stomach is actually quivering.

The lines around his eyes deepen and he frowns. He obviously isn't happy with my answer. "Okay, Samantha, this is very important. I know you're young and a twenty-four year old usually doesn't have to make these types of decisions. But given your family history, particularly your mother, aunt, and grandmother, I would strongly suggest you give this a little more urgency. You've tested positive for the breast cancer gene, and not just any gene, but the most aggressive one. Your last breast ultrasound was normal, which is great, but now I urge you to decide on the other issue. Prophylactic mastectomy and reconstruction is a very viable option, and even though it's extremely traumatic, with the removal of the breast tissue it would cut your chances of getting breast cancer down immensely." He starts scribbling something down on a piece of paper and hands it to me. "I would love for you to talk to these people. One is a plastic surgeon who could discuss your reconstruction and what your breasts would look like afterward, and the other is a not an individual but rather a group of young women who have gone through what you are experiencing right now. They could answer a whole host of questions you may have. The big thing we want to do here, Samantha, is to prevent cancer from happening."

"I understand. Thank you for giving me these." I hold up the paper. Maybe they'll help. I don't know. "My mom and sister have been on my back. I know it's time." I'm smart enough to know that this can affect me. My mom fought it. My aunt did too. My grandmother tried and lost her battle. Laney opted for the surgery. What's the matter with me? Why can't I just say "Let's do this thing"? My heart, gut, and instincts all tell me to go for it, yet they're my breasts, my boobs, and I still grieve for the part of me that will be missing after the surgery. Is that so wrong of me?

I leave with all kinds of thoughts of the three B's swirling in my head. My business, my boobs, and Ben. As I walk back into work, my phone rings and it's Laney.

"Hey, sis. Mom wanted me to call to let you know she has a date for family dinner. Can your boyfriend make it two weeks from now?"

"I'll ask. Give me the date so I can put it in my calendar." It's a Wednesday night.

"You okay?"

"Mmm. I'm not sure. I went to the doctor today. Tell me something, do you like your boobs?"

She laughs. "You mean my new boobs?"

"Yeah. New and improved boobs."

"I really do. I can't tell the difference at all, except for the scars under the nipples and the lack of sensation, but that's insignificant. The only thing that bothers me is that I won't be able to breastfeed when I have kids. But it beats dying, you know?"

"Yeah. It does."

"You still trying to decide?"

"I just ..." I hesitate for a second.

"Tell me you're not serious. You carry that fucking gene, Sam. You don't have a choice."

"I know." In a small voice, I add, "What will Ben say?"

"What do you mean?"

"I mean, he loves my boobs."

"If he cares anything at all about you, he'll support you in this. And he'll love your new boobs. Just talk to him," she urges.

I bite my lip, thinking about her words long after the conversation has ended. Work consumes me again and after I get home, I'm changing my clothes when my phone buzzes with a text.

Ben: Can you come over?
Me: You ok?
Ben: Yeah. Just miss you. Got home early for a change.
Me: Sure. On my way.

Traffic isn't too bad, and he's waiting at the door when I get there. He pulls me inside and kisses me like it's the last day for the earth to exist.

"Miss me, huh?"

Steel gray eyes meet mine and I'm unsure what I see. "You have no idea. I left with a series of requests for meetings and more meetings. But I needed a fucking break. I need you."

Bunching up my tank top he pushes it out of the way while his mouth takes over mine, making me senseless for him. He cups my breasts with his hands, using his thumbs to flick my nipples through the fabric of my bra. Soon, he pushes it up and over my breasts so I'm exposed for him.

His reverent hands make it impossible to think. Only his next words spike straight to my gut.

"You have the most perfect tits I've ever seen or sucked. God, I love these." And my stomach spirals straight to the floor, crashing at my feet.

TWENTY-SEVEN
BEN

◆

HOW CAN I BE SO fucking lucky? "Most women have to buy what you have. And I hate fake tits. Why ruin what is naturally created? You can't recreate how they feel. Don't get me wrong, they look great, but they don't feel the same at all."

Something about her silence tells me to stop. "What's wrong?"

She pales and glances away. I tuck a finger under her chin to get her to look at me.

"What's going on?" I try again.

"Nothing."

She scrambles to her feet and puts distance between us. I mentally run down what I've said and I don't get it. Finally, she faces me and I'm pretty sure what I see is fear in her eyes.

"So if I didn't have these," she glances down at her amazing breasts, framing them with her hands, "you wouldn't want me?"

It's obvious I'm clueless when it comes to women, but I can swear I've done nothing wrong. So I make my move and stand before her again.

I cup her and squeeze gently. "You have spectacular breasts that money can't buy, more than a handful. You must be a C, probably a D."

She shrugs. "Large C, small D. But you didn't answer my question."

Okay, maybe she's hormonal. I know better than to ask. Instead, I give her the truth and hope I find the right words and don't fuck this up.

"I love them. I'll admit when I saw you, it was your legs and the side view of your tits that caught my eye. It may sound shallow, but it's true. However, it isn't your beauty that keeps me here. Hell, I've had many beautiful women in my life and none of them captured my attention like you have."

I stop because I have the shits of the mouth. Drew told me I would fall one day and I'd be begging some woman to see the good in me. And here I am. All I have is honesty, so I give it to her.

"You've seen Karen. She's something to look at, yet her attractiveness is buried under all of her conniving ways."

"She's prettier than me."

Something's off. Sam isn't vain, but she doesn't have low self-esteem either.

"She has nothing on you, baby." I place my hands on her arms and stare in her hazel eyes. "You've got it all. And she doesn't. Whatever she's got going on will fade one day and the only thing left will be spite."

I search her eyes hoping she'll see the truth in what I have to say. "That and rubbery tits." I laugh at my own joke. "She wasn't even that small to begin with. I think a B, she said. She didn't feel like she could compete. And now she can't. You are perfect just as you are. And when you get older, you won't look like a clown. I bet your breasts will still be amazing, just like you."

Her smile is still mysteriously missing. Her arms are crossed over her chest like she's hiding from me. What the fuck am I doing wrong?

"What really happened between you and Karen anyway?"

Thankfully, I manage to hold in a groan. All thoughts of sex have fled the building. I'm still up for her in more ways than one. But she doesn't look anywhere near ready for me to touch her. I turn for the couch and sit down. I've done this to myself, bringing Karen up. Talking about her and the reasons I'm not with her isn't going to help whatever is going on.

When Sam doesn't come over and sit next to me, I pat the cushion, praying I'm not making another mistake. Hopefully, she doesn't call me an asshole for treating her like a puppy. The fact that I think of it means I've probably fucked up again. I scrub my face remembering all the reasons for not wanting a girlfriend. The main one is women are too complicated. And I'm not smooth enough not to mess it up.

I glare up at the ceiling missing my best friend like crazy.

Her hand pulls mine free of my hair jarring me from darker thoughts. "Ben."

"I know. I know." Cue in heavy sigh, because I don't know what to say that won't set her off.

"Just tell me," she urges.

Her quiet words make me meet her eyes. Sadness is still there and frustration builds in my chest. I lean back holding her gaze. I know when I tell her the truth things will change between us. She'll see me for the dick I am because there isn't a way to pretty up what I have to say if I plan on staying honest with her.

"She was convenient. A steady screw so I didn't have to waste time at a bar or a club looking for someone to fuck when I had a mind for it."

Sam's brows rise and I close my eyes, gazing away. I stare at the blank screen of the TV because I can't look at her when I say the rest of it.

"She's a lawyer, busy like I am. She wasn't clingy." I laugh at that. "Or so I thought. She cleaned up nice when I needed a date and I let it go on longer than I should have."

"Is that what you think of women ... of me?"

I snap my head in her direction and focus on her. "Not exactly and definitely not you. I'm not going to be ashamed of who I was." As her eyes go wide, I add, "I'm not proud of it either. But I've always been honest. Even with Karen. I guess somehow she believed she could change me. I don't know. My five-year plan has never included a relationship. My goal has been to make something of myself. Have my dad be proud of me for once. Then you came along."

Shaking my head, I wonder who's talking. When have I ever been into monologues? Only, she doesn't look convinced.

"Sam, you're beautiful. God, you're beautiful. But that's not all that attracts me to you. Your spark, that you don't put up with my shit, you're independent and not needy. I'm not going to lie and be totally altruistic—I fucking love your body, especially your tits. But you are more than that."

"Thanks for noticing." She gives me a sad smile. "You had to know who she was. What made you walk away when you did?"

I have no fucking clue why she's zeroing in on Karen. This has to do with looks and her tits, but I still can't piece it together.

"You think I left because she had fake tits?"

She shakes her head. "No, but why did you finally leave?"

"I didn't leave because I was never hers," I snap, suddenly angry that I seem to be defending that Karen and I weren't together. "She was never mine." I pause taking a deep breath. *Just tell her, Ben,* I think to myself. "She wanted me to go with her to visit her aunt in the hospital. And I didn't see why I should go."

Her forehead crinkles. "That doesn't seem like the Ben I know."

"What? I felt bad the woman was sick, but I had nothing to offer. Karen and I didn't have a future together. There wasn't a reason for me to confuse a bad situation by getting the awkward questions about a relationship that didn't exist."

"Bad situation?"

And here it is. She's going to think I'm a jerk.

"Her aunt had cancer." I run a hand through my hair. "But even if she didn't, I still wouldn't have gone. But that cancer shit scares the hell out of me, Sam. I'm not going to lie. I can't do that again. I had to smile while watching my best friend die because he didn't need to carry my pain when he had his own. And I won't do that again."

That last part comes out a little more bitter than I mean. I shake my head getting to my feet. I need a drink and head to find the bottle of Lagavulin.

Sam is right behind me. She places a hand on my back and her warmth seeps into me.

"Ben, I'm sorry."

I turn to face her. "No, I'm sorry." I sigh. "It's just I can't seem to get the fucker out of my head. I miss him like crazy and I should be over this. I bet you feel like I've said it a thousand times."

She shakes her head, cradling my face. "Who says you should be over this? There isn't a timestamp on grief. Say it as many times as you need to."

I glance up, but she hangs on, bringing my head down to meet her gaze. There is a fire in her eyes that melts all my resistance. Words explode from my chest giving me the freedom to breathe.

"It's been over a year and I feel like a fucking pussy for needing him. But since we became friends, he was there almost every day of my life until he went to medical school. And even then, we talked a lot. When he moved back, I practically lived in his house the last few months of his life. And now nothing. He's gone and everyone assumes that I should just be able to go on like he never fucking existed. But I can't and I certainly will never willingly put myself in a position to watch someone die again. Once is more than enough for a lifetime."

The air I suck in manages to hold the burn in the back of my eyes from spilling over.

"It's okay."

And this is part of the reason why I'm falling for her. She pulls me close to cover my mouth with hers. Somehow she knows enough words have been said. I have to be close to her in a way I've never been close to another human being.

"I need you like crazy, Sam."

She nods, taking my mouth again and smothering my words with heat. Her hands pull my shirt from my pants and it's as if she's close to orgasm the way she claws at my clothes. She leans up with a glint in her eye. I have no idea what's she's about to do.

She splits the fabric of my shirt, sending buttons airborne, and fuck, if I'm not turned on faster than a Porsche 911 turbo engine.

"Want to play that game?" I ask.

The smile she flashes me lights up the room. Clothes are taken off with no care to their destruction. Soon, we're standing in front of each other naked, like two bulls ready to lock horns. She makes the first move taking a flying leap at me. Only I take it one step further. When she tries to lock her legs around my back, I shake my head and lift her higher.

"Hook your legs over my shoulders. I want to eat that amazing pussy of yours."

As I hike her up by her spec-fucking-tacular ass, she wiggles and works her way into position as we stand in the middle of my living room. I bury my head in between her legs. There is an art to eating pussy. And as much as I like her where she is, I need more use of my hands without fear of her falling down.

Good thing I know my house. I take several side steps until my leg hits the edge of the sofa. I carefully sit and Sam pulls free. I take advantage of the moment and lie back.

"Sit on my fucking face, baby. I'm not done yet."

I get her off twice before I flip our positions and get her on her hands and knees. There isn't anything gentle about the way I ram into her. She doesn't complain, only screams out for more. When I blow my load, I'm so spent, we lie in a heap on the couch until I can catch my breath.

By the time my alarm goes off the next morning, I've managed a couple of hours sleep. It has been days since I've had Sam in my bed and I've made the most of our time. We christen many rooms in the house except the bathroom, which I plan to rectify.

"Wake up, sweetheart. I have to go to work and I plan to smell like you when I get there."

By the time I make it to the office and sit in my chair, I've done things with muscles I haven't used in a while. It's time to get that home gym installed if I plan to keep my pretty little girlfriend happy. The sheer number of times we went at it, if I'd gone bare my dick would have been chafed if not for Sam's wet pussy. I'm for sure out of cum. Which reminds me of our test. We haven't gone yet with everything going on, and I want to be inside her bare.

I send her a text.

Me: Testing, tomorrow morning?

It's not a question even though I've phrased it that way.

Sam: Afternoon?

I growl, not wanting to waste another minute.

Me: Sure

I make the necessary appointments and send her the time. Then I focus on work. All the correspondence about the confusion with the mutual fund company and the effected parties has gone out, with another letter still to review.

"Do you think you should call your dad?"

Jeff sits in a chair across from my desk and I have to stop myself from telling him to go fuck himself, since my door is wide open and I'm the acting boss. It would not be a good look.

"Not happy with my leadership, because I think it's working for me?" I ask with a raised brow instead.

"It's not that, but shit, man. If things go tits up, this is all on you."

He doesn't have to tell me. Men were made by the tough decisions if you look back in history. And I don't need my dad to tell me if I'm being a good boy or not. Not anymore.

"I know. But trust me, I've got this."

I hit the send button on the letter I approve which isn't apologetic. Mistakes happen, but it isn't ours. We hadn't directly invested in that slime ball who gives a bad name to all investment bankers. We trusted the information we had at the time that our clients' money was free of the fraud. And unfortunately for us, mutual fund companies don't always disclose every investment they deal with on a daily basis.

"You've got balls, my friend."

He's right. All my chips are on the table, and if I bust, I'll lose everything.

There is a ruckus in the hall. Jeff turns around just as a woman barrels through my door with Lisa in tow.

"Ms. Spencer," I say dryly, wondering why she's still invading my life like a carpenter ant infestation until I break.

"I may not be able to sue you, but I want the person fired who called me to come to your event."

I glare at Lisa who is supposed to be the gatekeeper in our office. I can see a talk with Trudy in my future. How did Dad deal with all this shit and still get things done?

"You're no longer a client, Karen," I say slowly, hoping she'll get the message.

"I haven't pulled my money. And I haven't decided if I will. Just because you're an asshole doesn't mean your firm hasn't made me a shit ton of money. And don't worry—I want nothing to do with you. I've moved on. But whoever tried to use me for the fool should be fired."

I push at my hair knowing I need to handle this. "I'll deal with it. Now if you excuse me, I have work to do."

Her eyes narrow and it's easy to see she wants the final word.

"Just so you know, you may have made me a ton of money, but you weren't the best man that's been in my bed."

She spins on her heels leaving my office in a huff. If she thinks her words will eat at my ego, she's mistaken. The last thing I want is for her to think about me at all. So if she has to lie to herself, so be it.

"Wait, who did you give the client list to?" I ask Lisa.

"After the event?"

I nod, already knowing the answer but needing to hear it to one more time. "That cute guy that works for your girlfriend."

"Nick?" I ask.

She nods. "He's not going to get in trouble is he? He asked me out. It would suck if I get him fired."

"Thanks. You can go, and make sure Ms. Spencer leaves the building."

Lisa glances at Jeff as if he can overrule me. I am going to have to have a meeting to remind people I am still in charge the next several days until Dad returns. When she leaves, Jeff whistles.

"I don't envy you, man."

Certainly I don't either. I have to determine whether to tell Sam in person or over the phone. When I dial her number, I still haven't decided.

TWENTY-EIGHT
Sam

◆

WHEN MY PHONE RINGS, I can't keep the smile from forming on my lips. "Can't get through the day without hearing my voice, huh?" When he doesn't immediately respond, the curve drops from my mouth. "Ben? Are you there?"

"Uh, yeah." A heavy sigh explodes out of him.

"What's wrong?"

"Honestly, I'm not even sure how to begin this conversation."

The way my heart is hammering, this can't be good. "Okay, why not try talking for one thing? You're scaring me."

"No, no, don't be scared. I'm sorry. I just hate to bring this up to you, because it's not good. But I guess I just need to spill it. It was Nick."

"Nick? What about him?" I ask.

"He was the one who told Karen to come to the party."

"Wait, what? You're telling me that Nick called Karen and told her to come?" My face must be a thousand degrees right now because my blood pressure is boiling. "Why the hell would he do something so presumptuous as that? And who gave him the authority?"

"Sam, calm down, baby. You're yelling."

"You're damn right I'm yelling."

"Do I need to come over there?"

His question stops me in my tracks. "You would do that?"

"Of course I would."

"Thank you, but no, I can handle this. And Nick."

His gentle chuckle comes to me over the phone. "I imagine you can and will."

"And what's so funny about that?"

"I'd like to be a fly on the wall when you do your handling. I can envision you handing Nick his ass in his hands."

"Oh, Ben, I'm so screwed though."

"What do you mean?"

"Other than his meddling in my personal life, he's a good employee. He does a good job and knows this business. And now I'll have to find a replacement." My head is pounding at the thought already. "Do you think I should give him another chance?"

"You don't want me to answer that, do you?"

"No. You want to beat his ass, don't you?" I already know his answer.

"He's intentionally tried to ruin us. He pisses me off to about ten on the Richter scale, so, yeah, I'd like to kick his ass into the next county."

Ben's absolutely right. Nick has done some terrible things, and stuck his nose where it never should've been. If I'm smart, I'll do the right thing and fire him. "I don't blame you. I'm having problems with that myself."

"Listen, my sister knows a lot of people. Maybe she can help you find someone. Or even knows someone looking for work in your area."

"Well, if she does, that would be awesome."

"Unfortunately, I've got to get back to work, but let me know if you need me."

"Ben? Thanks for letting me know. It wasn't an easy call to make."

"No. I didn't want to tell you, but you need to know these things. I'll call you later. But Sam, I'll be around, just call."

This is just great. How am I going to handle this? Nick isn't here yet, but I won't give him the opportunity to settle in. As soon as he arrives, I'll confront him.

As I wait, I open up my work calendar so I can get even more depressed. The schedule is packed and without Nick, how am I supposed to handle everything? I hear Nancy come in, and she pokes in her head to tell me good morning.

"Nancy, can you send Nick in here when he arrives?"

"Sure thing."

As I continue to inspect the workload, I notice I've checked a date off in two weeks. I cross reference it with my personal calendar and it's the day I'm supposed to get back to my doctor. He's expecting me to talk to that plastic surgeon. *Damn!* This is the last thing I need right now. With the business the way it is, I don't have time for this. Not to mention, do I really want to face this right now? And that would be a big N-O! I'll do what I can be very good at doing and that's burying my head in the sand, like the proverbial ostrich. I quickly make a reminder note in my calendar, and push it back for four weeks from now, just so I'm not completely negligent and idiotic.

A few minutes later, I hear Nick come in. This is one conversation I am dreading, but it's best to move on. I can't continue to deal with his mothering.

After a knock on my door, he walks in. "You wanted to see me?"

"Yeah. Have a seat."

This is unusual and his frown lets me know he gets something's up.

"I may as well get straight to the point. Why did you call Karen Spencer and invite her to the Rhoades Investment Team party?"

It's always the eyes. His grow into enormous orbs and then his lids shrink them into slits. "What ... how?"

"Doesn't matter. Just answer the question."

"She's a client of theirs. She was on their client list."

"I see. And she got a call late in the day. A call that said her fiancée wanted her there, or something to that effect? And now that we're on the subject, how did you even know Karen and Ben had even been in a relationship?"

He shifts in his seat. Not once but three times. Then he raises his hands in the air and says, "Rhoades is an asshole. He's only going to hurt you. Like he hurt her. I overheard Lisa talking to someone about it at the event. I was trying to protect you."

"I thought we'd covered this. You don't have the right to protect me, Nick. You're not my brother, father, sister, or mother. You're not my friend. You are my employee, or I should say were. You overstepped your bounds on too many occasions and this one went way too far. You need to clear out your desk."

His eyes bulge again. "You can't be serious? I was doing you a favor. The guy's going to fuck you over."

"That's enough." I stand and point to the door. "It's time for you to leave, Nick."

He actually looks shocked, which on one dimension is slightly comical to me.

"I ... I can't believe you'd let me go over this. I did this for you—to save you from him."

"Perhaps you should've concentrated more on saving your job and not meddling in other people's lives. You nearly cost Rhoades Investment Team a lawsuit over this. I hope this teaches you something at least and that's to keep your nose out of other people's business."

Okay, so I did exaggerate that a bit, but he does need to be scared. This type of thing is intolerable and he could get into serious trouble down the line if he persists with this behavior.

"I'm sorry if you think having someone trying to help you is meddling. You'll see, Sam. He's going to hurt you. And bad. Then you'll be wishing you'd listened to me."

With that, he stomps out of my office. I follow him into his and watch as he cleans out his desk into a banker's box. As he leaves the building, I say, "You probably don't believe this, but I am sorry it turned out this way. If there's anything you left behind, I'll see that it's returned to you."

He nods and continues out the door.

Nancy approaches and wants to know what happened. I have to tell her the truth. When I do, she believes I did the right thing.

"He was so intrusive, always asking personal questions about you. I think he had a thing for you."

I shrug. "Maybe, but in the end, he still needs to learn that he has to stick to the job. Personal feelings be damned at work. But now I'll be underwater with everything we have going on."

"Hey, if you need me to fill in, just say so. And let's make good use of those interns. They haven't been doing much lately. I can put them on all kinds of assignments."

"What would I do without you?"

"Oh, I don't know. Cry?"

We both start laughing. Nancy's right. We have enough coverage to squeak by. Granted, it's not ideal, but we can make it work.

Late that afternoon, my phone buzzes.

Ben: How'd it go?

Me: He was shocked. Thought he was my hero. Lol
Ben: Yeah? How so?
Me: He thinks you're an ass! Btw, he overhead Lisa talking about it to someone at the event.
Ben: I guess he's one in a long line for my ass kicking. No doubt she was jealous about you. But I can't fire her for office gossip. Can I see you tonight?
Me: Love to say yeah, but I don't think I can do it.
Ben: No worries. I'll call you later.
Me: Sounds good.

Sure wish I could make it work, but by the time I leave here, it'll be at least nine and I'm still feeling tired from our sexcapades last night. What a night that was. Just thinking about it gets me wet.

"You feeling all right?" I didn't hear Nancy enter my office.

"Huh?"

"Your face is awfully flushed. Are you coming down with something?"

"Oh, no. I'm fine. Just a bit warm is all."

With pursed lips, she says, "You need to take care of yourself, honey. You work too hard."

"Nancy, I love you for caring so much."

She smiles and hugs me. "Well, I'm outta here for the night. See you in the morning. And don't stay too late."

"Okay, Mom!"

We both laugh because Nancy is a lot like my mom. She's not quite as old, but she acts a lot like her.

It's dark when I finally shut everything down and make my way home. My neck muscles scream and it reminds me of how much I could use a good massage. The house is empty when I get there. No doubt Lauren is staying at her parents' beach house again.

I shovel in a few bites of a quick dinner and change my clothes desperate for bed when my phone buzzes.

"Ben." My face brightens as I imagine his messy hair and steel gray eyes on the other end.

"Hey, gorgeous. Tell me, what are you wearing right now?"

After a throaty chuckle, I say, "A white tank top, tiny boxers, and that's about it."

"Oh, God, you're killing me. No bra?"

"Why would I do that when I'm in bed?"

He groans and I smile even more. "Do me a favor. Take a selfie and text it to me. I need to see you."

"Seriously?"

"As a fucking heart attack."

I do as he asks, and shoot him the picture.

"Jesus, Sam. You look perfect. What I wouldn't do right now to kiss your perfect tits. Look at you in this picture. I want you to do something else for me."

"What?"

"Take your shorts off."

What is he thinking? "Oh no. I am *not* sending you naked pictures."

"No, that's not what I want you to do. Just take off your shorts, please." His gruff voice has me doing as he asks. "Are they off?" he wants to know.

"Yeah."

"Good. Now touch yourself. And when you do, I want you to tell me how you feel."

My inhale is shaky as my hand brushes against my core, fingers delving into my slit.

"Well?"

"Good. It feels good," I admit.

"Are you wet?"

"Yes, Ben. I'm wet."

"What else?"

"Warm, slick."

"Move your finger around your clit. I want to hear you make yourself moan, Sam. Can you do that for me?"

"Yeah."

"Pretend it's me doing it. Remember how I did it to you? Mimic what I did. Can you do that?"

"I-I think so." I circle my clit over and over, then run my fingers up and down, back and forth.

"Harder, Sam, and now I want you to slip a finger inside."

I do as he tells me, but now talking isn't an option anymore.

"Tell me how you feel."

My voices seizes in my throat as I shudder. "I want to come," I pant.

"And you will. Make yourself."

"You...only if you make yourself, too."

"Already doing that, baby."

"Oh, God, why can't I be there watching you?" I swallow, my mouth suddenly dry. The visual of Ben with his cock in his hand is almost enough to push me into my climax.

Ben's voice brings me back. "The same reason why I can't see you. Are you close? Because I am." The huffing from the phone lets me know just how close he is.

"Very," I eke out.

"Come on, baby, do it now." And at his urging, and after a few more rapid strokes, I climax and hear him do the same.

About a minute passes when his voice finally comes at me. "Sam, pull the sheet up to cover your pussy and take another selfie. I want to see you post-orgasm."

I do it and send it to him.

"Just as I thought. I love the look on your face after you climax."

"Ben, what's fair is fair. I want one, too."

"You sure about that?"

"Yep."

"Don't say I didn't warn you."

I have to wonder what he means. A couple of seconds later when his picture arrives, I'm not at all prepared for what he sends. I get the full scale of Ben, but he's naked and one hand is wrapped around his cock. Hmm. Very naughty Ben. How delicious is this?

"Well?"

I can tell he's holding back a laugh.

"I guess you could say we've passed the test of phone sex then?" I ask, trying not to laugh myself.

Now his laugh explodes through the phone. "Passed? We fucking aced it, baby."

As we get ready to say goodnight, I remember the family dinner my mom wants to do. I ask him about it and he seems to be okay with the date.

"Two weeks is good. Dad will be back by then and things will be much calmer. Tell your mom it's a go."

"Great. I'll let her know. And Ben, thanks for the great phone-gasm."

"It was totally my pleasure, but Sam, I'm always happy to lend a hand. Or a mouth. Or a tongue."

TWENTY-NINE
BEN

MY DAYS HAVE BEEN HECTIC and my nights lonely. I haven't seen much of Sam between my work and hers. The sound of her voice cradles me and I miss her warm body next to mine. The phone is wedged between my ear and shoulder as find myself on the verge of begging as I shut down my computer.

"You wouldn't believe the clients today. Apparently the constant rain over the last few days is making everyone crazy." I say.

"What happened?" And the humor in her voice makes me smile.

"One of Dad's clients called me to tell me her psychic said red is bad. So I need to dump any investment where the company's logo is red."

That gets a laugh out of her and it feels good. She's been stressed and I want to make her feel better. "And how can you possibly do that?"

"Exactly. I think I've convinced her to hold off and see if the psychic meant something else. And that's not the half of what's happened today." I pause, but when she doesn't speak I switch gears. "Sure I can't convince you to come to my place tonight?"

"I wish, but with Nick gone, I'm afraid I'll be working from home tonight."

"I can come over there," I coax.

"You'll distract me and I'll never get anything done."

"Okay, but that means I'll be texting you to show you how

lonely I am."

Her giggle has a husky note to it. "You realize you're giving me blackmail material."

My brow rises. "So, the good girl is actually bad. You'd do that?"

"Don't test me, Ben Rhoades." She laughs again. "But I really have to go. I'll see you on Wednesday."

I sigh. "My hand is getting such the workout."

"I'll make it up to you."

A few parting words later and she's gone.

"Who would have ever thought the great Ben Rhoades would be pussy whipped?"

My head snaps up so fast, I might have given myself whiplash. There, leaning on the doorframe, is Jeff.

"Who's pussy whipped?"

"You, my friend, unless you agree to hang with us tonight."

Before I realize I'm even doing it, I'm shaking my head. "Nah, man, I'm tired."

"Exactly, you sound just like Mark."

I pause for a second realizing he's right. I shrug. "It's been a long day."

"Yeah, and that sweet little event planner with the great rack has you all wrapped up."

My eyes narrow as my heart begins to accelerate. "Keep your eyes to yourself and don't talk about her tits. Not cool."

"So it's official—you and Mark are being led around with a leash around your necks."

I counter quickly. "I thought you and Mark were going out tonight."

He shakes his head. "No, I hoped if you got on board you would convince him. Instead, I find you practically begging some woman to get laid. That's how it starts, man. They want to give it to you all the time until they know they have you. Then they tease you with it and use their cunts to keep you in line. I'm telling you, variety is the spice of life. They don't really respect you until you show them you can get it somewhere else."

His words sound so familiar. I'm sure I've said something similar to Drew over the years.

"Don't knock it until you try it."

With his head cocked back, he lets out a belly laugh. "That's the best you've got? You should hear yourself, man. She's got you so fucked in the head you can't even give me a proper comeback."

I ponder his words for a second until I realize I don't care what Jeff thinks of me. Sam makes me happy and I don't want to lose that.

"Dude." Jeff says, forcing me to glance up. "Look, is there a rule that we can't tap a client?"

"There isn't anything in the employee handbook if that's what you're asking." The human resource manager and I have become fast friends these last several weeks since Dad has been out. "But it is strongly discouraged. Why?"

He shrugs. "I'm out. Later." He pushes off the doorframe and disappears into the darkness of the office. Almost everyone is gone and I get to my feet and leave too.

The rain is coming down so hard, I have my wipers on the highest speed when my phone rings. I almost don't answer because I need to concentrate on the road. When I see who it is, I answer using the in-dash Bluetooth.

"Cate."

"Ben." Her voice doesn't quiver. However, I can't be sure.

"Is everything okay?"

"Yeah." Her sigh is heavy. "I just miss you guys and Jenna's out."

Good, she's okay.

"Hey, can I call you back when I get home? It's raining like crazy."

"Oh, yeah, sure."

I hate how she sounded with that last comment. "I'll be home in ten. I'll call you right back."

My plans had included sending Sam a picture of me and my hand, but that will have to wait. When I get inside, I pour myself a glass of Lagavulin before I call Cate back.

"What's going on, little sis?"

"It's nothing really."

But I know better.

"You can always come back home. Jenna still has your room vacant or you can stay with me. My house is big enough for the both of us."

She's quiet and I realize this is the second time tonight I'm trying to figure out the right thing to say to a woman.

"I can't."

Her words are soft, but their meaning is loud and clear.

"He's there and I see him everywhere. I hate to say it, but it's easier being here in DC in that respect."

I drain the contents of my glass. "I get it."

"Ben, I'm sorry. I didn't mean to bring you down."

So she'd heard that. I push my hair back.

"Take your hand out of your hair, Benny."

"God, you know me." I pull my hand free and start to pour another two fingers.

"Everyone knows you. But I didn't call for us to be sad. We've had enough of that. How's Sam?"

I take a quick sip and bite down on the warmth that's spreading through my gut.

"She's good."

Just like Cate knows me, I know she's nodding her head in agreement.

"Good, I like her. She seems good for you."

"She is. I'm going to meet her family for dinner in a few days."

"Wow, you *are* serious about her."

I shake my head. "I am. It's weird—I don't think I've met a girl's parents since high school. And it should scare the shit out of me. And in a way it does. But I'm also kind of looking forward to it."

"I have a good feeling about you two."

When my next words spit out, I know I've been holding them in without anyone to talk to about this.

"I think I'm falling for her."

A squeal rings my eardrum. "Oh, Benny, I'm so excited for you. Drew knew one day you'd fall in love."

"Hey, I didn't say the L word. I remember when Drew told me he was in love with you."

The conversation fills my ear as if he were there.

"Ben, I think Cate's the one."

"Don't fuck around, Drew. She's like my little sister."

"I'm not fucking around."

"You're right. You're a serial monogamist."

"There's nothing wrong with that."

"There is. Look at your last relationship with Rebecca and she turned out to be a class A bitch like I warned you."

"Are you saying Cate's a bitch?"

"Hell no," I spit into the phone. "My little sister, remember?"

"I know, but I don't get your point."

"My point is maybe you need time before spouting the love shit. Are you even sure you're over Rebecca? You know I saw her the other day."

He pauses. The answer sometimes lies in the silence.

"I thought I was in love with Rebecca. But fuck, man, I got over her. I don't think love is something you get over ever, not real love at least."

"Now you sound like a pansy. Dude, how do you ever get so much pussy being a pussy?"

He laughs. "One day my friend, you will fall."

"Never." And I'm so sure of that.

"You will."

"Okay, how do you know you're in love with Cate? I feel like as her big brother I have to make sure you're the right guy for her."

I'm teasing. The only friend I would ever have allowed to get close enough to date Jenna was Drew. If he hadn't seen her like a sister, the way I saw Cate, I would have wanted them to hook up.

"She's my first thought in the morning and my last thought when I go to sleep."

"Damn, man, you don't have to use that poetry shit on me."

"It's true. You'll see. It's like my mission in life to see her smile."

"Okay, that shit isn't contagious, is it? I feel like I'm talking to a girl."

He laughs. "You'll know when you've hit bottom when a gorgeous girl practically begs you to screw her and you aren't the least bit tempted because she isn't 'your' girl."

"So have you been tempted?"

I shake off the memory. Had I just told Cate all of that? But the truth rolls off my tongue.

"No."

THIRTY
Sam

———————◆———————

BEN PICKS ME UP AT six thirty and as soon as I open the door, I'm in his arms and our mouths devour each other's. The kiss turns into much more and he walks me into my bedroom as he briefly pulls away from my lips.

"Do we have time?"

"Barely."

"I can be fast and I know you can." He's already unzipping his pants and then reaching for mine. He tears mine off so fast, I'm surprised he doesn't rip them. A giggle rushes past my lips.

"You think this is funny? I'm a desperate man. My cock has missed that pussy of yours, baby."

"I can tell."

His hand reaches for me, and he doesn't have to tell me how wet I am. I already know. But the smirk that curls his lips tells me he's happy with what he finds. Then the humor is gone and a seriousness takes its place.

"Sam, you're gorgeous." His mouth crashes against mine again as his hands reach under me lifting me onto him. In one movement he plunges into me, filling me deep the way I love. "I'm not going stop until we both come." True to his words, we're both fast and find ourselves exploding in simultaneous orgasms. "I think we were both overdue."

"I'd have to agree. I hate to break up this party, but if we don't get a move on, we're going to be late."

He groans as he lifts me off of him. "I need to clean you up.

And I love having you without a condom. I'm glad we did the testing thing."

"Me too." He kisses me again.

We get dressed again, and when we're finished, I ask, "You ready?"

"As I'll ever be."

I sense something odd. He keeps adjusting his shirtsleeves. "Hey, are you nervous?"

His hand furrows through his hair. He's totally on edge. "Not exactly nervous. I look forward to meeting the people that created such an amazing woman."

"Flattery will get you everywhere."

"Thanks for telling me now. I do have to admit, it's a little daunting meeting them too."

"Why's that?"

He shrugs and I get the sense that this is important to him. "It's just that I hate being judged."

"They're not going to judge you." I take his hand and rub a small circle on the top with my thumb.

A heavy sigh puffs out of him. "I guess I'm used to my dad's high expectations. Growing up, he was critical of everything I did. I figured that's what I should expect from your parents -- that no guy would ever be good enough for you."

"Okay, I get where you're coming from now. But let me assure you, my dad isn't anything like yours. All my dad will be concerned about is that you don't rip me to shreds or throw me off the Ravenel Bridge. Other than that, you'll be fine. Got it?"

"What about your mom?" he asks.

I'm confused. "My mom?"

"Yeah. Is she one of those nose in the air Charleston bluebloods?"

Now I chuckle. "You are going to laugh so hard at yourself after you meet my mom. Yeah, she was born privileged, but you'd never guess it." I give him directions to my parents' house as we go. They live downtown, not far from me. It only takes a little over five minutes to get there from my place. Even though they live close, I don't see them as often as I'd like.

When we pull in the driveway, he says,

"This place is awesome."

"We love it. I grew up here."

It's an old three-story brick home, located south of Broad Street, that's been here since the eighteen hundreds. It exudes the kind of Old World charm that tourists flock to.

We park and walk up the back of the house. Mom is waiting to greet us and I observe Ben as she folds him in her arms. Mom is one of those people who you can't possibly dislike. She warms you up, no matter how cold of a person you might be. Her hair is still honey blond, like mine, and I inherited her hazel eyes. She has Ben grinning with that hug of hers.

"Ben, Sam has told us so much about you. It's wonderful to meet you finally. Come in and please make yourself at home."

"Daddy!"

"Angel Pie! Give me some of that heavenly sugar of yours." Daddy wraps his bear-like arms around me and lifts me off the ground in one of his trademark hugs. They always make me giggle. When he puts me down, he turns around and says, "You must be Ben. It's a pleasure meeting you." And they shake hands. Ben eyes my dad's stout frame. Both men are tall, but Dad is much broader with a dusting of silver in his brown hair. His friendly brown eyes smile at us and I know he's happy to see us.

"Same here, sir."

"Call me Randy. And come on in. What can I get you to drink?" Dad corrals Ben, and Mom pushes me into the kitchen.

"Why, Sam, you didn't tell me how good looking that boy is."

"Mom! He's not a boy, and yes, he is good looking." I grin. "What did you cook?"

"Daddy's grilling filets and I have a salad, my special potato casserole, haricots vert, and I made peach cobbler for dessert."

"Oh yum. Vanilla ice cream too?"

"You know it, honey."

"Laney and Evan?"

Mom says, "They should be here in a few minutes."

When I join Dad and Ben, they're laughing and Ben appears to be at ease, which makes me feel relieved.

"I was just telling Ben about the time I tried to make you girls pancakes for breakfast," Dad says.

"Oh, they were awful. He could've used them for pavers out back."

"See? I told you."

Ben laughs. "I enjoy cooking," he gives me a pointed look,

"when I don't get distracted."

"Well, this one," I shake my head, pointing at Dad with my thumb, "Mom only lets him get close to the grill."

"What's that about the grill?" Laney asks as she and Evan join us. I can see Ben eyeing them, and he's probably noticing the similarities in us. Laney and I have the same color hair only I'm taller and a tad bit slimmer, but not by much.

I make all the introductions and then explain Dad's kitchen ban. After Dad takes all kinds of ribbing from us in his good-natured way, Mom informs him it's time to light the grill, to which we all die laughing.

"Whatever did I say?" Mom asks.

"We were telling Ben about Dad's culinary talents," I explain.

"Oh, dear," Mom sighs.

"At least he can grill," Ben says.

"Yeah, but you should've seen the time that one grill exploded on him," I say.

Laney and Evan start laughing. Evan says, "I remember you telling me about this."

Dad rubs his face and gets this sheepish look. "It was on Christmas Eve and I did have a bit too much eggnog."

"A bit?" Mom asks.

I look at Ben and say, "He turned on the gas and forgot then he went to light the grill and thought the gas was off, but he put the lighter to it anyway and kaboom. He's lucky he's still here."

"I am. And that should teach you all a lesson," Dad says.

"What? Don't drink?" I ask.

"No. Don't drink and cook!"

Now we all really laugh. Mom adds, "How about you stay away from the grill while drinking?" and she clears her throat loudly because Dad stands there with a drink in hand. Now he looks adequately chastened, and Mom goes up to him and ruffles his hair.

"I've only had one, Michelle."

"I know, Randy," Mom says. "Now go light the grill."

Ben pipes in, "Care if I join you, Randy?"

"Sure, come on."

Ben follows Dad out and that gives Laney the opportunity to attack.

"Dang, sis, he's freaking hot!"

"Hey, what am I?" Evan asks.

Laney looks at him and says, "You're my husband."

"That makes no sense," Evan says, pouting.

"Yes, it does. You're hot, too, but we're not talking about you. We're talking about Ben."

But that was enough to satisfy Evan so he smiles.

Laney turns her attention back to me and says, "So what gives? He looks like a real catch."

"Wait a minute, you're basing that on his looks only?" I ask.

She does have the decency to look ashamed. "You're right. That was a leap, wasn't it?"

"I'll say. But, to your point, he is a catch, and not because of his looks. But you need to get to know him. So talk to him."

"Okay, I will. But on another note, have you scheduled anything yet with the doctor?"

Shit. I've done such a great job of sweeping this aside, I've forgotten all about it.

"Samantha Calhoun, what the hell are you thinking? Oh wait. Clearly you aren't thinking at all. This is your life you are playing with. You understand that, don't you?"

Evan says, "Laney, keep your voice down."

I look at my brother-in-law and say, "Thanks, Evan. Laney, I've been really busy. Work is ..."

"Too busy to save your life? Have you told Ben yet?"

"No! And I don't want you to either. Now drop it. This isn't the time or place. This is a family dinner where he's supposed to be meeting you all, having a good time. I'll tell him, but I certainly won't do it tonight at the dinner table."

Laney's eyes droop. She and I share the same hazel eyes. But now instead of hers being bright, they are dimmed by sadness. "I just don't want to lose my baby sister to something she could've prevented by a procedure that she keeps putting off."

Guilt weighs heavily on me. "I promise I'll do something about it. I swear."

"It doesn't have anything to do with Ben, does it? Tell me it doesn't."

"No. He's great," I lie. He is great but I know I risk losing him with all of this. And right now, a broken heart on top of all this is something I truly don't want to face.

Dad and Ben come back inside and Mom hands them a platter with the steaks. All the men traipse back outside to grill them while the women do kitchen duty.

"Mom, she hasn't scheduled anything yet." Laney is a tattletale.

"I had my appointment just the other day," I defend.

"Oh, Sam, it was so hard on your father when I was sick. Please, I'm begging you, don't put it off. If anything happened to you, I'm not sure he could handle it. And I don't know if I could either. Just do it. Please. I know it'll be hard. But look at Laney." Mom's eyes are almost ready to spill water, and I don't want to ruin tonight.

"I won't. I need to make another appointment is all. I lost an employee at work and I'm swamped, but I'll take care of it."

"You're too precious to me, Sam. Please do it."

Soon the men are back with the cooked steaks and we all head into dinner. I paste on my happy face, as does Laney. Ben sees right through it, though. He rubs my leg under the table, and his eyes question me, only I can't provide the answers he seeks. I grin and laugh and act appropriately to make things appear normal. But dinner drags as my dilemma burdens me. I would love nothing more than to be able to talk to Ben about it, but that's the one thing I can't do. The thought of it has me cringing in fear, as I know it would him.

"Michelle, this is delicious," Ben says. My mom glows under his compliments.

"Yeah, Mom, you outdid yourself," I add. Then I tell Ben, "Save room for dessert. You're going to die when you taste her peach cobbler."

And when he digs into it, all he does is "mmm." And who can blame him? It's warm, gooey, and covered in creamy vanilla ice cream.

When he scrapes his bowl clean, he says, "Michelle, that was way past good. Thank you for such an excellent meal."

"It was my pleasure, Ben. And you come back to eat here with Sam any time."

"Thank you. I hope to do that."

Laney and I help Mom clean up while the guys hang out with Dad. I'm sure Dad is entertaining them with all kinds of stories, as is his usual way.

Mom leans over and says, "Ben seems to fit right in with the men. He doesn't hold back or seem at all immature." I can't contain my laughter at her statement.

"It's okay Mom, you can say it. Trevor was an overgrown teenager and Ben is the complete opposite of him."

"Oh, honey, I didn't mean that in a bad way."

"Of course you didn't. But I agree." She hugs me and Laney pipes in. "I think Ben is a much better catch."

"Duh," I add. They both start laughing as I join in.

"It's nice to see you happy, Sam," Mom says. We finish up and join the guys.

"I hate to break up this party, but working girl here," I announce as I enter the room. All eyes hit me at once.

Dad says, "You work too hard."

"I have to if I want my business to succeed."

"Angel Pie, I've told you a dozen times, you can come to me and I'll front you the money."

"Daddy, I've told you a dozen times, not happening. Besides, I'm past that already. Now I need another employee or two and I'm good."

Ben's hand flies up in the air. "My bad. Jenna's supposed to call you. She has the perfect match for you, Sam."

"Yeah? Really?"

"Yes! I was supposed to tell you today, but everything at work derailed me."

"I'll give Jenna a call in the morning," I say.

Mom asks, "Who's Jenna?"

"My sister," Ben says.

"How wonderful." Mom beams.

Then Ben explains. "Jenna used to run the sales and marketing for banquets at Charleston Spaces. So she has all these connections and when Sam needed another person, I asked her if she knew anyone."

"This is going to help me so much." Now I'm excited again. "However, I'm still working girl, so we need to leave."

I laugh as Daddy's lip pokes out. "You'd better watch out, Daddy, you might trip over that thing," I tell him.

He shakes his head. "I get no sympathy around here."

I spread my hugs around and Ben ushers me out the door. When we get to the front of my house, he shuts off the car.

"Are you going to tell me what happened back there?"

"It was nothing. Just between sisters, you might say."

He's silent for a moment and picks up my hand. "You can talk to me, you know. I'm a great listener, at least that's what Drew said. I'm here if you need me. I care about you, Sam; you can count on me." He raises my hand to his lips and kisses it.

"Thank you, Ben." I lean in and kiss him, praying he means what he says. "Will I see you tomorrow?"

He palm cups my cheek. "I hope so. And you were right about your Dad. He's nothing like mine. And he sure loves his Angel Pie."

"Yeah, he does."

"I personally think she may have wings and a halo." He runs his thumb along my lower lip. What should've been a teasing comment all of a sudden makes me feel heartsick. I know I need to tell him the truth about my possible surgery. What's ahead and what I'm hiding from him looms over me like a darkening cloud threatening hail.

He gets out of the car and walks around to open my door. When we get to my front door, I fumble with the keys. But he's right there to steady my hand. I know he has it in him to be my rock, but can he?

"Are you sure everything's okay?"

No, it's not okay. There's a possibility I could get breast cancer, which will have you running for the mountains with that messy dark hair of yours on fire!

"Fine, all's good and fine here, Rhoades. Just open the door so I can get inside."

He slants his head for a second, but then proceeds to unlock my door. "Sweet dreams, gorgeous, and I'll call you in the morning."

I watch him walk to his car and give him a little wave as he drives away. I make it the several steps into my room before I allow myself to break down.

THIRTY-ONE
BEN

———◆———

GETTING THE CALL FROM MY dad's admin to come to his office makes me feel like I've been called in to see the principal. I have no idea how he feels about the way I handled things while he was gone. When I enter the room, I wipe my palms on my pants.

Dad stands behind his desk and gestures for me to sit. I can't read the expression on his face.

"Have a seat, Ben."

I sit in the chair he indicates, trying not to feel five again.

"So how did things go?" He sits at his desk.

Shrugging, I say, "Good. Fine."

I have no plans in detailing the shitstorm I went through. I did a good job, but when he folds his hands together, I know I'm sunk.

"Full disclosure, Trudy's been sending me daily reports."

Keeping my game face on, I don't know whether to be pissed off or not surprised at all. So I nod.

He's always been good at maintaining a poker face. Something I try my best to mimic. He taps his fingers together almost in a prayer pose while I wait for the verdict on my job performance.

"I might not have chosen the direction that you took on certain things that happened, but I can't deny you resolved all issues swiftly and without legal consequence."

I exhale the breath I'd been holding.

"Thank you, sir," I say, almost military style. It's probably the best compliment he'll ever give me.

"You can relax, Ben. I do think there is room for

improvement."

Of course he does. The relief I feel dissolves.

"This company needs your fresh approach."

I blink. Did I hear him correctly? Had he meant the company needs improvement and not my performance?

"It's time for me to take a step back. Your mother never looked happier in the last twenty years as she has over the past month. And I realize I've put this company before her, before you, and Jenna too."

I'm so stunned I can't think, let alone speak.

"I want you to take on more responsibility. You don't know how long I've hoped for this day. I'm proud of you."

He stands and the next thing I know I find myself enveloped in a bear hug with my father. Fuck, I feel like the world's been lifted from my shoulders. His approval is something I've worked for my entire life.

When he pulls back, my mouth opens spewing words I've longed to say. "I have ideas."

Although a cloud has been lifted from my chest, I still feel dazed when I leave his office. He listened to me and even agreed to some of my plans. I feel like Neil Armstrong as I float across the floor as if I'm walking in zero gravity. And the office suddenly feels like a strange new world.

Back at my desk, I pick up my phone. My first thought is Sam and how much I want to share this development with her. It's only after that thought do I realize I can't tell Drew. Fuck. I hit the desk with my fist, the solid surface absorbing my blow. How many conversations did I have with him on this subject? If only he were here to share this news.

I push the emotions back, not wanting to lose the high from attaining one of my goals in life.

It's early, but I have to see Sam. Talking to her on the phone won't cut it. I grab my keys and head out the door. I wave at Jeff who's giving me a curious look. He probably thinks Dad's pissed me off. I don't bother to stop. I've been working sixty plus hours a week and I deserve to see the sun for once when I walk out the door.

The air is stifling, yet I draw in a lungful as I take my first step into the light. My heart fluctuates between loss and lightness, but I know Sam can make everything okay.

I make a quick stop before I show up unannounced at her office. From where I stand in the front, I see her head bent as she types furiously on her keyboard. God, she's beautiful.

It's that moment of perfect clarity. And I see it as though I'm looking through crystal. I'm in love with this woman.

"Can I help you?"

Glancing down, I realize I've been mesmerized by Sam.

Hastily, I ask, "Is she free?"

Her admin's face lights up with mischief. "Go right in."

So fucking eager to touch the woman who quite possibly may be the one I spend the rest of my life with, I don't waste another moment.

Lightly, I knock on her door before I breeze in. "Hey, gorgeous."

When she lifts her head, her lips curve in a smile that makes me feel like the most important man in the world.

"Ben."

My name rolling off her lips makes my dick leap to attention like a dog waiting for a bone. Shit.

My legs move independently of my mind, as I find myself around her desk drawing her to her feet. Her shock melts away as she surrenders her lips to mine when I devour her like she's my last meal.

Her cheeks are as red as the roses I present her. She takes them from my hand and lifts them to her nose.

"I know they aren't exotic. I thought about which flower I could bring you that no other man has. In the end, perfection can't be improved upon. You are my rose. And damn, Sam, if you aren't everything my world's been missing."

Damn boy, slow down, I think, as her eyes grow large. I kiss her again unable to resist.

"Tell me you can leave early."

Her eyes drift over my shoulder. I turn in that direction and find we've gathered a small audience. Then her staff starts to clap.

When I glance back at her, I smile.

"I didn't think you could get any redder," I laugh. "Let's give them an encore."

I wrap her in my arms and kiss her long and hard. For show, I dip her to the sounds of more applause and whoo whoos.

"What do you guys think? She deserves a break, right?"

They all nod. I turn back to her to find reluctance on her face.

"Ben, this is sweet, but I can't. I'm swamped."

She sweeps her hand over her desk, which is littered with a few stacks of paper. Nothing that looks too daunting.

"You can," I tease, holding on to each of her arms so she can't walk away.

Giving her employees my back, I draw her closer. I grip her ass, pulling her tight against me.

"For the love of God, woman. If you have any compassion ..."

"Believe me, you're making this hard."

I chuckle and whisper in her ear so our audience doesn't hear. "No, I believe you've made me hard." In a regular voice after stepping back, I say, "Come on, I have news."

"You do?"

Her smile is like a sunburst in my heart.

"Yes, I want to celebrate. I have so many things I want to tell you." *Including that I'm so in love with you.* I manage to keep that thought to myself. I want it to be the last thing I tell her . I don't want her to think I've said it because I'm horny or stoked about my father giving me props.

"And what about these?"

The dozen roses end up between us.

"Exactly! They need water, which is another reason for you to come over."

She inhales and her chest lifts with the movement. Silently, I groan almost unable to wait to get my hands all over her.

"I can get water here."

"You could," I nod. "Or you can take an hour, or two." I cough that last part. "And make my day."

She gives in with a sigh but her eyes spark with lust. "Okay, but I have to drive because I can't stay all afternoon. I'm behind as it is."

I poke my lip out which earns me a grin and a slight shake of her head as she laughs. But I end up with her on my arm as we leave her office to yet another round of applause.

Once I have her just inside my door, I cage her in.

"Fuck, Sam," I study her face.

She has the eyes of a saint as she looks at me. She makes me feel like I can do no wrong, like I'm a fucking superhero. "It's like I haven't seen you in years."

She giggles, which makes my dick hammer at the front of my pants.

"It's only been a few days."

She has no idea.

"Way too long, we need to fix that," I answer.

Her pause makes me think I'm going too fast. The silence stretches between us as I figure out what to do.

"What are you saying?"

I search her eyes a second longer realizing I need to dial it back. I don't want to scare her. "Nothing, I just need you naked."

Pulling her shirt free of her pants, I scoop a handful of her amazing tits.

"Take off your clothes before I rip them off," I command

I step back eager to watch the show. Her eyes heat with desire and feel like laser beams as she stares at me. She smiles while moving at the pace of a turtle in order to torment me.

A growl vibrates my throat. "No teasing."

She spins around and glances over her shoulder. Her hair creates a sexy curtain covering one of her hazel eyes. Her thumbs work in the front before reappearing in the back. She tucks them under her waistband before wiggling her ass in an eye-catching way. I salivate at the sight trying to keep my tongue in my mouth. I plan to use it a lot before she heads back to work. Her pants fall, leaving her in white lacy underthings that frame her ass as pretty as a picture.

"Sam," I warn.

She lifts her shirt and spins back around to flash her perfect breasts which are barely contained in the matching bra she wears.

I can't wait any longer. I move in and lift her up. She's on board with my plans and wraps her legs around me, shoes left somewhere behind.

Our eyes are locked as I march us into my bedroom. When I spill her across my bed, her hair fans out in invitation.

"God, you are so beautiful."

Her eyes light up and her lips part as if she's about to say something. I'm not a mind reader, but I swear she was about to tell me she loved me. Then again, maybe that's wishful thinking on my part, considering I'm going to confess my feelings to her later. I want there to be no doubts in her mind why I say it. So I continue to hold back until after I've had her. This can't wait.

As the seconds tick by I continue to stare at her gorgeous body. And I've never been more sure in my life that I want her by my side for the long term. She slides a hand down past her navel and underneath the lacy panties.

"Too bad I'm going to spoil that beauty," I growl.

"Why?" she asks concerned.

"I don't have it in me to go gentle right now. I'm going to fuck you until we both feel dirty."

I yank the material away from her body, not caring if they rip. I need to see what she's doing. The damn things give without resistance as I tug them down her bare legs.

"Part your thighs, baby. And let me watch you touch yourself."

She does as I ask, her submission given with a heavy lidded stare.

"That's right. Show me where you want me to touch you."

She parts her lips and her pussy hints with moisture. Without preamble, I dive in. I give her a good lick before I tease her clit with my tongue. Her hand moves into my hair giving a good tug as she guides me where she wants me to go.

"That's right, sweetheart. Let me know what you want."

She moans and squirms on the bed as I thrust my tongue inside her. I add a finger into the mix as I suck at her swollen clit. When I curl another finger in her pussy and rub that spot on the inside, she begins to scream as her orgasm bursts into my mouth.

I continue to finger fuck her as she rides out her pleasure. After she releases my head, I lift up to see her face relaxed, sated. And doesn't it make me want to thrust inside her.

"I'm so glad we were tested. I can't wait to slide my bare cock into your sweet pussy. But first take off your bra."

Her obedience to my demands is a major turn on. She sits up, her tits straining to be released from their confines. When her breasts are free, I can't help but lean in and suck one nipple into my mouth as my fingers tease the other.

"Lay back."

With complete trust, she complies. I draw her arms over her head. "That's it, baby, I'm going to take care of you again, but first…."

I settle over her with my legs on either side of her. I cup her tits while moving forward. Her eyes fill with amusement.

"What are you up to, Ben?"

"I think you know exactly what I'm going to do, don't you?"
She nods. "I've been wanting to do this since the first time we
met."

My hardened cock drags over her as I move it into position in
the valley of her chest. I push her tits to encase my dick in their
warmth. And fuck me if it doesn't feel good. When the head pops
out the other side, she shows me her naughty side. She lifts enough
to flick her tongue across the crown.

"Fuck," I growl.

I squeeze her tits thrusting slowly in and out. The friction is
almost as good as being inside her. As an added bonus she sucks in
the head of my cock. My fingers dig into her flesh as my eyes roll
back from the sheer glory of it. A second or two later, it feels as
though the world implodes as the magic shatters. My mind blanks
as I pull free of her mouth and release her as if we've gotten an
emergency evacuation notice. And maybe I have. Quickly, I
scramble off the bed to find my shorts, and maybe my voice.

"What?" she asks, sitting up "What's wrong?"

Words constrict my throat like a steel band as my dick goes
completely limp. I shove it into my boxer briefs as I hastily pull
them up, finding everywhere to look except at her.

"What?" Sam asks louder.

The quick glance I give her shows she's pulled the sheet up to
cover her tits. "You look like you've seen a ghost. Are you feeling
okay?"

I shake my head.

"You're scaring me, Ben. Tell me what's going on."

From the floor I find her eyes. My voice comes from a far off
place. "I have seen a ghost," I begin. Echoes of the past fill my
head as I try to get out the words. "I found something hard."

She grins, not getting it when I meet her eyes. "You mean your
dick?" she teases.

I snap out the word, "No," and her face turns paper white.
"Whatever it is, I felt it in your breast," I say shakily.

Immediately, her trembling hands cup her breasts and search
for what I found. The act, which should have been seductive, is all
of a sudden clinical and scares the hell out of me.

"Right one," I croak out.

And I know exactly when she finds it. Her head lifts and abject
fear mars her pretty face.

"Oh my God."

The words come out as a sob and she's right about needing a higher power. She continues to probe it as if the thing isn't large enough to feel or if she's hoping it will vanish beneath her fingers. But there is no denying what I felt. I tested it twice before I let her go as though she'd scalded me.

"I should've known better," she mutters.

Before I can ask a question, more words spill from her lips.

"The doctor warned me." She rocks back and forth, hugging her breasts with her hands.

There is no way I heard her correctly. "Warned you about what?"

Although she's been looking at me, her pupils seem dilated, unfocused. They finally adjust on me as terror takes its ugly grip on her.

"About my family history with breast cancer."

"Your what?" I stutter.

The horror that crosses her face pains me for a minute as the sound of my voice ricochets through the house. I hadn't meant to yell those words, but I'm sure I didn't hear her correctly.

"I have a long family history with breast cancer. My doctor suggested that I have preemptive surgery."

A long family history. Cancer. I feel like I've been injected with ice as I stumble back, my body chilling from head to toe. I point an accusing finger at her.

"And when were you planning to tell me all of this?"

My voice sounds detached and that should worry me. But the ghost of my best friend spurs me on.

"Ben."

Funny how when she said that earlier, I felt hope. Now I just feel numb. She gets off the bed, the sheet falling away. As she steps towards me naked, it should remind me of what we were just about to do. But all thoughts of sex have taken a back door to the fact that I need to breathe and can't seem to remember how. I take another step back finding the wall and hold out a hand to stop her forward progress.

"You lied."

The words destroy my heart and everything I thought I could have.

"Ben, I didn't lie."

The plea in her words eclipses the worry hidden beneath. Her eyes shine with what will turn out to be tears. I've seen it a thousand times before.

"Omitting the truth is the same as lying, Sam. You knew how I felt about cancer and you hid this from me." My voice breaks and a familiar sense of loss invades my soul.

"I didn't."

She reaches for me, but I shake my head. My eyes burn like the words in the back of my throat. I ache with pain I thought I'd overcome.

"You did and we both know it."

I don't know which of us is more upset. She creeps closer as if she's approaching a wild animal.

"Okay, but I wasn't keeping it from you. I wanted to find the right time."

"And the right time was when?" I demand.

I put more distance between us, heading for the door. Taking the hint, she picks up her bra and panties and then starts putting them on. I leave the room as she speaks.

"I was planning—"

My hand shakes as I pour the golden liquid into a crystal tumbler. I've downed the first glass before she makes her way into the living room. She snags up the rest of her clothes and puts them on.

"Were you waiting until after you trapped me in a relationship before you spilled that little bomb on me?"

My harsh tone does nothing to stop her from looking like she wants to calm the raging bull inside me.

"Ben, I had every intention of telling you."

"You could have done that before ..." I pause, not adding *I fell in love with you.*

She glares at me. "Before what?"

I wave her words away as anger takes control over my mouth. "Before everything, instead of walking around like a false advertisement."

Her expression morphs into something I haven't seen before.

"You arrogant bastard. You found a lump in my breast, and I tell you I'm at high risk for breast cancer, and you make this all about you."

I pour myself another drink before I face her.

241

"Sam." I stop and remember that despite it all, I don't want anything bad to happen to her. "The last thing I want for you ... for anybody is to have to deal with that hell. But I can't do this, and you knew that."

"It's not like I set out for this to happen."

"No, maybe not. But you could have shared this with me long ago. And then we wouldn't be having this conversation."

Her mouth drops.

"What? You wouldn't have dated me?"

She thinks better of me than I am. I nod.

"It's not like I haven't ended things before because of cancer."

It's easy to see she gets my Karen reference. It doesn't matter that I wouldn't have stayed with that woman even if her aunt hadn't gotten sick.

"And that's it? You're going to let me face this alone?"

Her question is as quiet as the tears that stream down her face. There's a finality to it that punches a hole in my chest. Yet, I'm a statue unable to move.

"Sam, you have family and friends. You aren't alone." I swallow as a flash video plays in my head of Drew slowly dying in front of me. "I can't do it again," I choke out. "I just can't. And it's not fair to you for me to pretend otherwise."

I wait for her to storm out. But she just gives me the saddest look.

"If I told you I love you would that make a difference?"

She loves me. For a moment, my heart soars only to plummet to the ground in a sickening thud.

"Sometimes, love isn't enough," I mutter, before downing the contents of the glass.

Her spine straightens and her face clears of empathy.

"You know what, Ben Rhoades?"

I know better than to answer. But I do anyway as I pour myself another three fingers. "What?"

"You can go fuck yourself, you asshole."

The worst part is not the door slamming in her wake as the exclamation mark on her storming out of my house. The worst part is she didn't yell the words, she said them with pity and regret.

A thousands thoughts circle my brain in a matter of minutes. If Drew were here, he would punch me in the face. Knowing I could have handled our parting words better, I toss back the last of the drink before hurling the glass at the door. It breaks into a million shards just like my blackened heart.

I've let the only woman I've ever loved walk out my door, yet I can't make myself run after her.

"I love you," I whisper for the first time and in place of goodbye. I can only pray we both survive what's to come.

"Don't give me that look," I say to no one. Only the echoes of Drew's memory seem to continue to glare at me from beyond the grave. The contents of my stomach churn and it won't be too long before the liquor takes me to a place I can't get to alone. "I can't, Drew!" My shouted words go unanswered. So I whisper the next ones as I stare at the ceiling wishing for Drew's apparition to make an appearance just this one time. "I can't watch someone I love die again. It will kill me."

THIRTY-TWO
Sam

———————◆———————

THOUGH MY CAR ISN'T EVEN fifty steps from his door, it feels like fifty miles. Stumbling through blinding tears, I finally make it. When I get inside the heat is stifling, but I'm chilled to the bone. It takes several stabs with my key to hit the ignition and the engine finally comes to life. Driving in this condition is impossible so I make a call.

"What's up, baby sis?"

"Laney ..." I choke out.

"Sam? What's wrong?"

Sobs explode from me like a cannon.

"Sam! Talk to me, please. You're scaring me!"

"I ... I ..."

"Where are you? I'll come to you."

I hiccup out my answer. "B-b-ben's d-d-driveway."

"Is he there?"

"N-n-no. He hates me." I rest my head on the steering wheel.

"Just stay put. Sam, don't you dare drive. I'm calling Lauren."

The scene replays itself over and over, like a broken movie projector. The accusatory look on his face, and the pain, but not only that—it's the fear in his eyes that I keep seeing. Oh my God, what is happening here? My hand shakes as I cup my breast. Why did I wait so long?

My phone buzzes. It's Laney.

"Yeah."

"Stay on the line with me. I'm meeting Lauren at your place and we're coming to get you. I'll drive you home. Can you tell me what happened?"

Her simple question brings on a new barrage of tears.

"Oh, Jesus, Sam. I'm sorry. Just stay calm. I can't stand to hear you like this."

"L-l-laney, I'm so s-s-scared."

"What happened?"

"I have a lump."

"A lump?"

I fill my lungs with a shaky breath. "In my right breast."

"Oh, fuck," Laney says. "How did you …?"

I don't let her finish before blurting out, "Ben found it."

"Ben? When?"

"A few m-m-minutes ago."

"I don't understand. Hang on, I just got to your place and Lauren's getting in the car."

I can hear the car door closing. Then I can hear Lauren's voice in the background, but Laney hushes her. "Okay, Sam, so Ben found it. But then why are you in his driveway?"

Her question has me going numb. The entire scene replays itself again and I want to hate us both. Him for calling me a liar. And me for my denial, my intentions. But am I a liar? When was I going to tell him? My fear of losing him had me frozen, paralyzed, and look where it got me.

"He accused me of lying to him about everything when I told him about our family history."

"He what? What an asshole!"

"It wasn't like that."

"Wait, you're defending him?"

"Laney, you don't understand." And I break down into another round of tears.

"Okay, hang tight. We'll be there in fifteen minutes. Promise me you won't go anywhere."

"I won't. I promise."

She makes me stay on the phone until she pulls in the driveway behind me. They both get out of the car and when they see how broken I am, Lauren threatens to go to the door and break it down to get at Ben.

"No, Lauren, leave it be."

"He needs his ass kicked. This is when you need him the most."

I know she doesn't mean it, but her words bring on yet another round of sobs. I have to stop this. I'm not the sobbing type, but I can't seem to break this cycle.

Laney says, "You need to move to the passenger side so I can drive."

Nodding, I get out and shuffle over to the other side of the car with Lauren holding my hand. Before I get in, she hugs me, saying, "It's going to be all right, Sam."

I crumple into her hug and wrap my arms around her, tears raining down my face. "I wish I could believe it, but right now, my world is collapsing." I feel as though I'm being sucked into a bottomless pit and everything is fading in my life.

"It's only temporary. I promise." And she tucks me into my seat, buckling me in. Is this what it's come to? I feel like a child needing to be taken care of.

Lauren leaves and then Laney backs the car out. I lean my head against the warm glass and close my wet and swollen eyes. "I wish I had a time machine so I could go back and do everything over again."

"What would you do differently?"

"I would tell Ben about our breast cancer history."

Laney is quiet for a moment. Then she asks, "And what do you think it would change?"

When I think about it, I don't have an answer. Would he have run? Probably. He's so scared of cancer, it's crazy. And I can't blame him. It wasn't about the breasts all along. It was the devastation of losing his best friend to cancer and his fears of going through that all over again. He would've run, no matter what.

As Laney drives, she makes a call. I'm not totally with it, so when she starts talking, my ears perk up.

"Yes, I need to make an appointment for my sister, Samantha Calhoun. She found a lump in her right breast and needs to be seen soon."

Laney glances at me and I nod.

"Friday?" She looks at me and I nod again. "What time? Ten thirty?" I nod. "That would work out fine. And thank you."

"Thanks, sis," I mumble.

"Do you want me to call Mom or will you?"

"I can do it, but not now. I'm not in the right state of mind."

"I get it. But Sam, don't wait too long. She loves you too much not to know this."

"I know."

We pull up in my driveway and Lauren is already there. When we get inside, I drop onto the couch and Lauren shows up with a shot of Jack Daniel's Tennessee Honey. "Down this right now."

I don't bother to argue because I need it badly.

Lauren sits on one side and Laney on the other. Lauren says, "Start at the beginning, sweets."

So I tell them the whole ugly truth. Every single bit of it. By the time I finish, they both want to get back in the car and kick in Ben's door, strip him naked, and castrate him.

"It's not like that, you all."

Lauren looks at me like I belong in the psych unit. "The man just ripped your heart out, shredded it in front of your eyes, then stomped on it and kicked you out of his house, all when you were at your lowest point. After, I might add, you told him you love him. How can you possibly defend him?"

"He didn't kick me out."

"He didn't exactly cuddle up to you and call the doctor either, did he?" Lauren asks.

"There are things about him you don't know."

"Things? What kinds of things?" Laney asks.

"I never told you all this because it was so personal to him, but a over a year ago, his best friend since kindergarten died of cancer. And they were super close. Closer than even brothers. It really threw him for a loop. He's just now getting past all that. The cancer thing totally freaks him out."

Lauren thrums her fingers on her legs. "Okay, I get all that. But still. It's even more important that he not abandon you now, when shit is really falling apart. He, of all people, should know you need his support more than ever. So in my humble opinion, that makes him an even bigger douche."

"Exactly! He's the ultimate doucheface," Laney says.

I hug my body. "I can't explain it."

Lauren sighs. "You don't have to. But I should've let my instincts about him rule. The rumors were rampant. Anyway, what's done is done. Now the important thing is to take care of Sam."

Laney hands me her phone and says, "Call Mom."

"Now?"

"Please."

As soon as I tell Mom, she immediately starts sobbing, which induces another round of tears with me. My heart is crushed as she tries to pull herself together, yet fails. Then she wants to rush over, but Laney grabs the phone and explains that I'm going to try to sleep. She informs her of my appointment so she can be there, too.

In the meantime, Lauren has called in the gang and they will be arriving at the house later.

Suddenly I'm frozen with fear as I think about the ramifications of what's happening and violent tremors shake me from head to toe.

Laney grabs my hand. "What is it?"

"I don't want to die." Tears bubble out of my lids faster than I can blink and I feel like I'm suffocating. "I shouldn't have put this off," I stutter. "This is all my fault. And now I'm going to put you and Mom and Dad through all kinds of hell because I was so selfish."

"Hey, hey, hey, who said anything about dying? And you don't even know what this lump is. It may be nothing. You just had an ultrasound so I'm thinking it's a cyst or something. Don't go jumping the gun here, Sam." Laney always was the calm one, the one that thinks about things rationally.

Lauren hands me another shot and I throw it back, letting the burn find its way to my gut. My hands can't stop shaking as I hand her back the shot glass. "Sorry."

"For what? Being afraid? Who wouldn't be? But Laney's right. Let's take this a day at a time. And don't worry."

I give them an unconvincing nod. Then I remember my business. "What am I going to do about work?"

Laney, who's lucky to not have to work because Evan has family money, says, "I can help. I'm not busy with any of my charities right now. What do you want me to do?"

"You don't mind?"

"Of course not. I'm your sister, Sam. I'll do anything for you."

"What would I do without you?" I throw my arms around her. "Nancy at the office can tell you what needs to be done. I can go in tomorrow. But then I don't know if I'll be worth a thing on Friday."

"Don't worry. Let me go in now and handle what needs handling for the rest of the afternoon."

After she's gone, I ask Lauren, "Why is it always me that needs the pieces put back together?"

"Because you're beautiful and kind and loving. And Sam, don't change."

My body sags at her words. "I think I'm going to lie down for a while."

"Okay. I'm here for the day. Call if you need me."

"Have I told you that I love you lately?" I ask.

"You just did."

My tear-stained smile is weak, but it's all I have to offer right now. I trudge to my bedroom, with the weight of the world on my shoulders. When I get to the bathroom, I stare at the woman in the mirror and the haunted eyes reflected back tell me how frightened I am. I wipe off the mascara that's made its way down my cheeks, and then strip off my clothes.

As I stand in front of the mirror, I examine my breasts. They look fine. But they're not. Why do they have to be sick? Why can't my breasts be healthy? I'm only twenty-four. I don't want to lose my breasts. My fingers quiver as I slide them over the right one on the area where the lump is and that sinking sensation explodes in my guts. I try to pretend it's not there, but it is. Small and hard, I can feel it. And it doesn't hurt a bit, which is even scarier. Over and over, my shaky fingers explore it, hoping against hope it's not there. But it always is.

I hang my head and the burn of tears fills my eyes again. The same shaky hand that felt the lump now moves to my mouth to shield it so my cries are muted. I'm not sure how long I stay like this, but soon, my legs fold beneath me and I end up on the floor, curled up in a ball.

"Sam, sweetie, wake up." Lauren crouches by my side in the bathroom.

Lifting my pounding head, I stare at her for a second, confused. I'm naked but for my panties and lying on the bathroom floor.

"What's going on?" I ask, confused.

"I was going to ask the same of you. What are you doing on the floor?"

I swipe the wet mess off my face and sit up, crossing my arms over my chest. "I don't want to lose my boobs," I cry.

"Oh, Jesus, Sam." And she pulls me into her arms. "I don't want you to either. But I'd rather you lose your boobs, than lose you. I wish I could give you mine."

"What's going on in here?" Berkeley sticks her head in the door.

Lauren answers, "Sam's having a rough moment."

"I'm sure she is. But if she'd get dressed and come out of there, she could have her rough moment with the girls and we could help her get through it."

I lift up my head and say, "I don't want to lose my boobs."

"Is that what this is all about?" Berkeley asks.

"Yeah," Lauren and I say at the same time.

"Then let's have a titty party," Berkeley yells.

Lauren asks, "Don't you mean pity party?"

"Hell no. I mean titty party. Get your ass off the floor and put a shirt on or you're gonna have to party naked."

"You'd better do it," Lauren says.

She's right. Knowing Berkeley, she'll drag my naked ass in the living room, boobs bared, and won't give a shit what I say.

I go to my closet and start putting on a bra.

Berkeley snatches it out of my hand. "Nope. You won't be needing that for a titty party. Just put on a T-shirt." I grab one and throw it on. And some boxers. Then we all go out to the living room and all the girls are there.

"Yay! She's up," Hayley says.

"That's right and we're having a titty party. Everyone has to take off their bras." All the girls look at Berkeley like she's lost her mind. "Come on. Sam doesn't want to lose her boobs, so we're having a titty party. Bras off."

Everyone takes them off and hangs them on Berkeley's extended finger.

"Excellent. This is what we're going to do. Sam doesn't want to lose her boobs, but we don't want to lose Sam. So we're all going to take off our shirts and then each of us is going to tell Sam why we'd rather lose our boobs than lose her. Who wants to go first?"

Lauren steps up to the plate. She rips off her shirt and stands naked from the waist up.

"Sam, first off, I'd give you my boobs, but you probably wouldn't want them since they're a quarter the size of yours."

Everyone boos her and I laugh.

"But second, I would gladly give up my boobs to keep you around because life without you would be like mashed potatoes without the gravy. You have been my best friend since I can remember. You are the sweet to my tea and I can't even imagine taking one step without you beside me. I would wander the face of this Earth like a lost soul without you. And boobs, what are they anyway? Just two humps on your chest. So you can't breastfeed when you have kids. Big fucking deal. If that's the only price you'll have to pay for your *life*, Sam, then by God, take it and run. Take it, Sam, and live. Please!"

She wipes her face when she's done, and so do I.

I stand and give her a big hug. "I love you, too, you big goon."

Next comes Berkeley.

"Okay, Miss Calhoun." She rips off her shirt and shimmies. "How do you like them apples?"

Everyone claps and whistles.

"If you for one minute are worried about keeping boobs over life, then fuck that shit. I, for one, will kick your skinny ass all the way over the Cooper River. I mean, we're all together in this. This is not just you, sister. Those are not just your boobs. They are our boobs. And if getting rid of them is going to save your life, save our group, then we are kicking their asses out. Got it?"

Everyone whistles again and cheers.

"And we'll get you a nice and shiny new pair that will look as pretty as can be. Because in the end, the only thing that matters is that you're here, Sam. That's it. We don't give a shit about anything else. Got it? We love you and we're going to be with you one hundred percent of the way in this." And she grabs me and hugs me, squishing her boobs against me so hard, I'm afraid they'll pop.

The rest of the girls give their own testimonies, one by one, telling me how much they love me and refuse to let me walk down this road alone. By the time Hayley goes, it's decided that we are all one giant set of boobs to be shared by all. I have this image in my head of two tits taking over Charleston, and I die laughing.

"What's so funny?" Lauren asks.

When I share my image with them, we all snort-laugh. Then the shooters come out. And I brace myself for what is coming next.

Berkeley asks, "So what happened with Ben?"

Silence hangs heavy like lead in the room.

I groan, saying, "Do we have to talk about it?"

"Yes," Berkeley insists.

So I give them all the dirty details of how we were having sex when he discovered the lump. "He froze and I didn't know what was happening. He backed away from me like I was some sort of contagious thing. And the look on his face." I can't stop the shudder that rips through me. "But the worst thing of all was when I told him about my family history, he pretty much accused me of being a shitty person. Called me a liar. And then, fool that I was, I told him I love him and asked him if that made a difference. Obviously, it didn't." And a riot nearly breaks out. God, I love my girls, but I'm not in the mood to handle this tonight.

"I say we lead a brigade to his home and beat the shit out of him," Britt suggests.

I'm shocked. "Britt, I can't believe you would encourage such a thing, being the peacemaker that you are."

"He destroyed you, Sam, in your worst nightmare. He's a fucking bastard." I can't contain my shock. This is so unlike Britt. "In my opinion, that's worse than fucking around on someone."

"Oh, holy shit," Berkeley says.

"She's right," Hayley agrees. "He inflicted a mortal wound. It's a disgrace and he should be ashamed of himself."

I hold up my hand, palm facing toward them. "Whatever he did was bad, but that's that. I'm not leading a charge against him. It won't do anything but worsen things."

"He's going to go forward in life then with no accountability whatsoever?" Hayley asks.

I shrug. "I guess so. Look, I don't really want to talk about this anymore."

"I know," Lauren says. "But you have to face these facts and not defend him."

"I told you all why he did what he did."

"You're too nice. I still can't believe you defend his actions, Sam," Lauren says, giving me the saddest look.

"Okay. I know. End of story. Let's move on. Can we have more alcohol?" I ask with much more enthusiasm than I feel.

They all eye me with suspicion, but that's okay. I just want off this topic.

Berkeley sets us up another round of tequila. Eventually, I'm smashed, and weaving around the house like a car with a flat tire.

"I think it's time for me to go to bed." I try to focus on one of the two Laurens I see. I say goodnight to everyone and crawl into my bed, but before I pass out, I decide to text Ben.

Me: I'm so sorry for holding out on you but I sware I mean

to tell you. I relly did. I was tryng to find the rite time. I guess I waited too long. I have an appointment on Friday to get cheked out. Ben, im so scarred. Why does if have to be me? I hate that my boobs are sick. I ment what I said when I told you I loved you. Im so sory.

My finger hovers over the send button, but then I hit it and it's gone. I lay my head on the pillow and close my eyes.

The morning comes and along with it a throbbing headache. Why did I drink that crappy tequila on top of vodka? Oh yeah. To forget what I'm facing. I barely remember climbing into bed last night. What I need right now are two Advil. When I move to stretch, I push my phone out from under the covers. Picking it up, it opens to my text messages and that's when I see it. Oh, fuck. I drunk texted Ben last night. But he didn't respond. No surprise there.

I reread the sent message several times and decide to text him again, explaining.

Me: Hey. Sorry about that text last night. The girls came over and filled me with a lot of tequila. Anyway, I thought an explanation was in order. I am totally and completely sorry for not telling you about my issue sooner. I didn't do it to withhold information. I did it because I was waiting for the right time. I didn't expect you (or me even) to find a lump. Please believe me. I'm not in the habit nor do I make a practice of lying. Sorry, I didn't mean to have diarrhea of the mouth—fingers. And I do love you. PS. I do have an appointment tomorrow and I am scared. Out of my mind.

I hit send before I lose my nerve. I wait. And wait. And wait. No response. Did I expect one? Yes, I suppose I expected something. Anything. I thought he would at least tell me not to be scared. Or that he hoped everything would turn out okay. I'd be the worst liar now if I told myself it didn't matter, if it didn't bother me. Because the truth is, it does. Horrifically. I've bared my heart to him twice now—three times if you count my drunk text, and he hasn't even told me he hopes things turn out okay. It cuts deeper and harsher than anything I've ever been through.

The throbbing in my head makes me get out of bed. I down two Advil and drag myself into the shower. It's there I let my tears flow again. Is this how I'm going to be for the foreseeable future? I hope not because this is miserable.

I don't know if I can function enough to go to work. I go through the motions of drying my hair and then I call my sister.

"How's the office?"

"I have it under control. Nancy is awesome and your other employees are doing great. I have you covered for today, too."

"Oh, Laney, thank you! I don't think I can make it in today. You're my savior."

"I've got it covered, baby sis."

My day passes in slow motion but I cannot recall what I've done. It's as though my brain has gone to sleep even though I'm awake. It's a strange sensation, one I can't remember experiencing before.

During the day, I try to call Ben, but he doesn't answer. I try again that night, and again it goes to his voicemail. I end the call before leaving a message both times.

In the morning, my stomach feels like I'm riding the rollercoaster from hell. I'm so nauseated any thought of food has me running for the bathroom.

"How about a cup of hot tea?" Lauren asks.

"Maybe that would help."

Lauren makes one using our Keurig and one sip has me gagging.

"It's my nerves. I'm so scared."

"It's going to be fine, sweets. I have a feeling right here." She lays her hand over her heart. "You just had that ultrasound. You're not going to suddenly develop a tumor. It's probably a cyst or that fibrocystic stuff."

"You're right. I'm trying to stay positive, but it's so hard when I carry the gene."

Her arms hug me tight. "I know."

"And I wish Ben were here. I need him now."

"And that's why he's such a jerkface douche."

"I know."

"What time are they picking you up?" She's referring to my mom and sister.

"Nine thirty."

"Good. I'm ready for you to get this behind you."

"Me too," I say.

I walk into my room to finish getting ready. While I'm in there,

I decide to send Ben another text, although I don't know why.

Me: I'm getting ready to go to my appointment. Please answer me. I'm so damn scared right now. I could use your support. Please help! :/

I wait but get nothing. I guess he truly is showing his colors. I know he struggled with Drew, but I'm not asking him to go through cancer with me. All I want is a simple text of encouragement. How can he do this? Was I really that terrible to him? Am I that horrible of a person?

My whole body trembles as I dress. I tug on my jeans and even zipping them is difficult. Hooking my bra proves impossible. I fall back on my bed and force myself to take deep breaths. Inhale. Exhale. After a few more, I try my bra again, and still no luck.

"Lauren, can you come in here, please?"

She comes in and sees me sitting there.

"What's up?"

I hold up my bra in tears. "I can't get this hooked. I'm too shaky."

She presses her lips together and takes the bra from me. "Stand up."

I do and slip it on so she can hook it behind me. "Thanks."

"You bet."

I just pull my T-shirt on when Mom and Laney pull up. I inhale and force one foot in front of the other as I make my way to the car. When we get to the doctor, they usher me straight to the ultrasound room. Since this isn't a new experience for me I know what to expect. The gel is cold and I shiver when she starts. It's not long before the girl is finished.

"You can get dressed and have a seat in the waiting room."

They must have put me on the rush list because I barely put my ass in the chair when Dr. Hastings calls us to his office.

All three of us are his patients so he knows us.

"Please, sit."

Once we're seated, he begins. "So, Samantha, everything appears to be fine, but I stress the word *appears*. I'm about ninety-five percent sure it's benign. But we won't know without a biopsy. It looks like a cyst or a cluster of microcalcification. With that being said, we have two options, remove the lump, or do the mastectomies. You already know my opinion on this, and I believe you've gotten other opinions as well. I would suggest whatever you decide that we get this scheduled as soon as possible."

I blow out a huge breath and say, "I'm going to have the surgery. The bilateral preventative mastectomies." This is the only viable option for me and the abject fright I've lived with over the last couple of days has formed this decision. Though I hate it, it's almost liberating to get it behind me.

"I think you're wise, given the fact that you carry the gene." Then he launches into the most detailed description of my nipples that I end up tuning him out for half of it. The medical jargon makes my head spin with the facts in trying to make a nipple decision. If I keep them, there's still a slight risk of getting cancer.

"Laney?" I ask.

"I kept mine," she says. "They are slightly numb but I figured I could always have them removed later, if necessary. But I have ultrasounds every six months."

"Okay. Let's do that."

"Samantha, I realize this is a big step, a huge decision you're making. But remember one thing. You're choosing life over your breasts," Dr. Hastings says.

"I know. I realize that now. This lump has scared me to death."

"Let's get you set up with your surgery and reconstruction then." I've opted to have it all done at the same time.

Again, relief and worry flood me. The logical part of my brain knows this is the right thing to do, but in actuality, I'm scared shitless to go through with it. My sister senses my fear and grabs my hand. "It's going to be all right. You're going to be all right, Sam." I squeeze her hand back.

We walk out and head to the surgery scheduling office with Dr. Hastings. He gives the admin all the information so she can get things started. When we leave, I have an appointment with Dr. Wilson, the plastic surgeon, on Monday and my surgery is set for a week from today.

Before we go to the car, I excuse myself to use the restroom. While there, I send Ben another text.

Me: Please call me. I have news. I'm leaving my appointment and I have surgery scheduled in one week.

Optimistically, I text him the time and place of my surgery.
On the way home, I ask my sister, "Laney, what do you like

best about your new boobs?"

"The thing I like about them the most is I don't think they're going to kill me like my old ones were going to."

THIRTY-THREE
BEN

◆

I WAKE IN A POOL of my own despair to the sound of my front door unlocking. For a second, I think it's Sam coming back to me, only the sound of Mom's voice sending me scrambling to hide the evidence of my rock bottom.

"Benjamin."

She moves into the kitchen and hasn't caught sight of me yet. I slide the last empty bottle under the couch before I say, "Mom, what are you doing here?"

My voice, catching her off guard, makes her jump out her skin.

"There you are." She sets a heavy bag on the counter and heads my way. "Your dad said you called out sick. I brought some food including some homemade soup."

She bends down and lays her cool hand on my forehead like I'm still a kid.

"Mom," I say shaking her hand away. "You can't just show up. What if I had someone over?"

Someone? *Is that how it is now?* I ask myself.

"You look like hell, Benjie. And I don't see anyone here. Is Sam coming over to take care of you?"

The question burns in my chest like a motherfucker. I shake my head stiffly.

"Well, then you need me," she declares, getting back to her feet. "So what's happened now?"

I can hear the disappointment in her voice. She knows I fucked up.

258

"Nothing, but I need my key back."

She spins around, a frown wrinkling her forehead.

"Ben," she pleads.

I shake my head again. "You and Dad can't just show up when you want. I'm a grown man."

When I'd bought this place, giving my parents a key considering I had been a bachelor seemed like a good idea. But Dad making himself at home several weeks ago and Mom showing up unannounced has changed that idea to a bad one.

I hold out my hand. She sighs and fishes in her pocket to produce a key she lays in my palm. Then she turns and sees the TV screen frozen with Drew's teenage face along with mine.

Her face softens as she draws her own conclusion. "Is that what this is all about?"

There's no way to answer without spilling my guts, which I have no intentions of doing.

"The two of you were inseparable. He was the brother you didn't have. We all miss him, Ben. Have you considered talking to someone?"

I don't look to see the video Mom made for our high school graduation party. It's the scene with Drew and me and our arms slung over one another looking like we're ready to conqueror the world, frozen in time.

"Mom, I don't want to talk about this. Thanks for the food. I need to get up and hit the shower."

She kneels back down and pushes hair out of my face. "Oh, Benjie, promise me you'll at least eat something."

I nod and she bends to kiss my forehead. And as much as it makes me feels like a child, there is comfort in her touch.

"You should call your sister. She's bound to show up if you don't," she says while getting to her feet. Good thing Jenna doesn't have a key. "I'll put away the food, then I'll leave."

"Before you go, what day is it?"

She's startled by my question, but quickly smoothes away her distress, no doubt putting together how far gone I am.

"It's Friday afternoon." *Friday?* I'd lost two days by drinking all I could. "You realize there is broken glass by the door."

If I want to pretend that two nights ago didn't happen, I can't answer. So I listen to her getting the broom out of the closet and sweeping it up. I push at my hair and turn to bury my face in the cushions forgetting the horrified look on Sam's face as she left me.

After Mom's gone, I sit up and gather the bottles I'd hastily shoved under the couch. There is no way Mom didn't see them. I manage to get them all and pull myself to my feet. I drop them unceremoniously into the recycle bin, creating a melody of breaking glass.

My heads pounds as I make my way to my bedroom. The bed sits unmade as it had been when Sam left. I crawl on it only to rustle Sam's fragrance. And damn if that doesn't jerk my cock to life with the image of her sprawled naked burned into my brain.

Still horny as fuck, it takes mere seconds with me doing nothing other than lying on my dick to send it shooting ribbons of cum on my bare chest as I roll over. Cock in hand, I finish the job, longing to be inside her.

You should call her, asshole. I find my phone near the bed. When I turn it on, I get a flash of a text message from Sam before my phone goes dark. I don't get a chance to read it, but I'm certain she's calling me every name under the sun, none of them good.

I head to the shower, something I haven't seen the inside of in days. I'm surprised Mom didn't mention how rank I must smell. My headache continues to pound away and I don't deserve relief. I want to be there for her, but something stops me. What am I going to say? Will I have to lie to her like I lied to Drew? The memory is faster than I can stop it.

I'd driven hours to reach his place. His call had scared the shit out of me. Drew was always the optimist. And his words had freaked me the fuck out.

"Drew," I called out.

"Here."

I glanced over to see him sprawled over the couch like a wayward blanket.

"What's going on?"

I planted myself before him on the coffee table.

"What do you think? I'm going to fucking die."

"No, you're not. You're going to beat this." Whatever this was. Had he gotten the results back? "Where's Cate?"

"Cate's in school where she should be. Where I should let her stay."

"What the fuck, man? What's up with all the doomsday talk?"

"I have Ewing Sarcoma."

"Yeah, and?" Because I had no idea what that was. It didn't sound good.

"My chances of surviving this are somewhere between nil and none."

"That's not true," I said, even though I had no idea.

"Okay, you're right. If I were say ten to fifteen years younger, I would have a fighting chance. But at my age, the prognosis is far worse."

For a second I watched him stare at the ceiling with fate kicking his ass. But I wouldn't let him give up. "You said worse, not no chance. You can beat this thing. Have you told Cate yet?"

That's when the first water drops leeched from his eyes. And fuck if I had to grit my teeth to not break down myself. There were only a handful of times I'd seen Drew cry. And most of them were before we were out of elementary school.

"I have to let her go, Ben. I have no right to hang on to her. She deserves better than to watch me die."

"You're not going to fucking die Drew. We'll figure this out. You can't give up yet. And you can't break Cate's heart. She's one of the good ones. You fight this for her."

"For her," he echoed.

Slowly, I come back to myself realizing the water had turned tepid on its way to cold. I shut off the shower and get out, wrapping a towel around my waist. I can't go through this again. The lies about his chances of survival and how I was coping with it had spilled off my tongue as I watched my best friend slowly lose his battle with cancer. The disease didn't seem to care he'd been the best guy there was out in the world. It still choked the ever-loving life out of him.

I stare into the mirror where Woolly the Fucking Mammoth has taken up residence on my face. I have no desire to shave. So I brush my teeth and towel off, only to find myself standing in my room with no place to go.

You could go apologize to Sam.

That thought sends me into my kitchen with only a pair of boxer briefs on. I yank open the refrigerator door, mad at myself, mad at the world. I pour some of the soup in a cup and put it in the microwave, nuking it until it's scalding hot. I don't wait for it to cool off. Instead, I take my punishment like a man and drink it down before fanning myself like a little bitch.

Fuck.

I head to the stocked cabinet and find a bottle of vodka. It burns worse than the soup. But at least I've kept my promise to Mom. I've eaten something.

The sofa calls to me as the vodka dulls my headache. I pick up the remote and press play. At some point the Drew on the screen seems to be talking to me.

Call her.

Squinting at the TV, that day when we were happy flashes there. He'd said one day we would rule the world. And that was the biggest bullshit ever. I reach for the half empty bottle of vodka.

Shit.

My conscience won't let up as the words *call her* keep repeating in my mind.

"For what?" I yell, hoping that will stop the incessant mantra in my head. "Sorry for being an ass? But, oh, I still can't fucking be with you."

I get a firm grip on my hair and tug. The pain reminds me I'm still alive. I let my head fall back and glimpse a picture of Drew, still young with a head full of hair. And I remember.

The phases of Drew flash before me. Healthy Drew, Sick Drew, Recovery Drew, Relapsed Drew, Realistic Drew, Dying Drew ... Dead Drew.

"How am I supposed to go through that again?" I say out loud.

If anyone heard me, I'd probably be locked up. And maybe that's for the best. I can't imagine Sam losing her hair, her tits ... her life.

"Wasn't there a bald chick who sang sad shit?"

Drew isn't here to answer me though.

"Yeah, that's right. Sinéad O'Connor. She was kind of cute. I bet Sam would look even better bald." What the hell am I thinking?

My dick tents my shorts as a bald Sam sings to me when I should be singing that chick's song "Nothing Compares to You" or something like that to Sam. I sit up and find my laptop. I fire it up and google the song needing to hear it. The song streams through my speakers as I pick up the fucking vodka.

Shit.

"You were right. Look what a pussy I've become," I say to Drew's phantom.

When the song is over, I feel just like the bottle of vodka—empty.

I wake the next day or so, drool on my cheek, head pounding. Glaring at me on the TV is Drew and on my laptop the singer's eyes. And more empty bottles stand around me in accusation.

Knowing what I need to do, I stumble into my room, not sure how many more days have passed. The bathroom light yells at me, so I turn it off and take care of business before staggering back to my room to plug in my phone.

On my laptop, I fire off a message to the office that I'll be working at home this week. I can't face anyone right now. They're bound to see through me, but I can't handle anyone asking me about Sam.

Five minutes later, I hear my phone fire to life. I sit with it tethered to the wall as a barrage of messages flash. I read them feeling shittier after each one. She's called. She didn't even sound mad. The first one is cute as she's obviously drunk. Seems like we both turned to the bottle when we couldn't turn to each other. Then her next is a hasty explanation.

There's more and she seemed eager to forgive me. I don't deserve her, my angel. She mentions news, but doesn't tell me what. I have a few missed calls, but no more messages from Sam. That she's scheduled for surgery puts the fear of God in me. Had they confirmed cancer? My fingers hover over the phone, but I put it down like a chicken shit.

I slip into memory like a drowning man.

We were high as shit.

"Is she gone?" Drew asked, laughing.

I nodded. "She's going to get snacks."

Drew guffawed like I'd said the funniest thing in the world. Only the smile died on his face.

"I want you to do something for me."

"What?" I asked, chuckling.

He straightened and I frowned. He pulled a couple of envelopes from behind the seat cushions.

"Give this to Cate." He pointed at one. "And give this to the guy she falls in love with."

"What? No?"

"Benny, stop. I'm going to die. I probably have a week."

"What?" My heart stopped in my chest. "No. I won't accept that."

"I'm a doctor, man. Don't make this hard. Cate will be back here any moment and I need you to promise me."

"Promise you what?" I snapped, anger killing my buzz.

He sighed. "I want her to move on. I want her to fall in love and be happy."

"And how the fuck do you propose she does that? She fucking worships the ground you walk on. That's asking too much, man."

"That's the thing. I love her so fucking much, I want her to be happy. I took these years from her. I owe her the world. And there is some guy out there that can give her all the things I wanted to."

"There are miracles, man."

"Not for me. I'm a dead man talking."

I glared at him. "You're an asshole. You know that?"

He nodded. "I should have let her go."

I jerk awake as my phone shrieks to life. I get up to get it if only to silence it. The sound punches at my head like a heavyweight boxer. Sam's picture in the yellow bikini flashes on the screen a second before it goes dark.

There is no way I can call her back. Hearing her voice will only make me lose my resolve. So I open a text message box and start to type. I erase it several times. I'm about to start another one when a message comes through.

Sam: This is my last message. I'm sorry about Drew. But I'm mostly sorry about us. I get it. We're done. Don't bother to write back. Lose my number. I'm deleting yours. I hope you have a happy life.

I'm doing us both a favor, I think. You are good people like Drew. You would want the same for me just as Drew wanted for Cate. I'm just skipping to the end because I can't watch you die.

Me: I'm sorry.

I hit send and turn off my phone. With a fresh bottle and my laptop, I set up shop in my office to take care of business before making friends with Jack. Mr. Daniels and I haven't spent much time together. But we will.

The knock at my door won't stop. I blink several times from my place on the couch. I haven't slept in my room, not having the heart to smell her or remove the sheets. The rap gets more persistent.

"I'm coming, I'm coming."

I groan when I see the figure through the peephole. I unlock the door but walk away, hoping to lie back down before the yelling starts.

"What. The. Hell. Ben?"

Jenna bursts through the door like the little fireball she is.

"Please stop yelling," I beg softly.

"Like hell I will. I've called you for days. Mom said you were sick, so I gave you a pass. But Dad said he hasn't seen you all week. This isn't like you."

I cover my head with a cushion hoping she'll take the hint and go away. Unfortunately, for me, my sister is a tenacious bitch. She pries the throw cushion from my hand and glares at me.

"You reek and look like Sasquatch." She chuckles for a moment and I have no idea why, but it rings church bells in my head. I close my eyes against the pain. When I don't laugh, she sobers. "Ben, tell me what's going on. Have you been listening to this?"

She points to the YouTube music video that's paused on the screen and the story of what happened between Sam and me regurgitates out of my mouth with a life of its own.

When I'm done, her face holds a pensive look. She bends over and wraps me in her embrace. And my body suffers through the shuddering emotion that pours out of me. I'm no longer able to hold it back.

She pulls back. "Ben."

I shake my head. "Don't say it. I can't do it. I won't watch her die."

"Ben," she says again. "You don't know if she's going to die. Have you called her?"

"It's too late for that. She told me to lose her number."

I close my eyes reliving the stabbing pain I got from her last message.

"She's angry, Ben. But if she loves you as much as you love her, she'll forgive you."

"I never said I loved her."

Her head moves side to side like I'm delusional.

"Your reaction is answer enough," she says softly. "Take a shower and stop drinking. You're not doing anyone, most of all yourself, any favors. Get your head out of your ass and go be with her."

Long after she leaves, I turn my phone on. One message from her says it all.

Sam: Sometimes sorry isn't enough.

I slam the phone down as an echo of the words I said to her are tossed back in my face. Later, I will feel fortunate that the phone landed on my mattress.

Fire burns in my gut for an unspecified time. Somehow I manage to get work done in sober moments. Then the grief over loss cripples me and forces my hand to poison my blood with a bar's worth of liquor. It isn't until I finish my entire supply that I get up.

My head rests against cool tiles as I let water meet my flesh in too many days to count. I've disappointed everyone. Dad probably regrets offering me more responsibility. Me not being in the office has only meant that he's had to keep his old hours. The piece of Drew that I keep within me is ashamed of my behavior. And Sam ...

I sit on my sofa turning Drew's letter over and over in my hand before I finally open it. Not that I need to. I know the words by heart.

Ben,

You didn't think I'd leave this world without giving you any parting words of advice, did you? After all the years we've been together, and everything we've been through, you know I never would do anything like that. Damn, I'm sounding more like your lover than your best friend. This is the part where you're supposed to laugh.

*But seriously, dude, you've meant more to me than any friend ever could— you **are** the brother I never had. And I'm telling you now, if I didn't tell you before, that I have loved you ever since you stuck your popsicle up that asshole, Mickey Master's nose in the third grade. You were my hero then as you are now. All these years you've said those words to me, but honestly, Benny, I have looked up to you in more ways than I can count. You are a mountain to me and always have been. Hell, you got me through those tough nights in med school when I didn't think I could keep my eyes open to study for the next exam. Your stupid jokes had me laughing until tears ran down my cheeks. You were the one that always told me I could do it, but I knew you had the balls to do anything too.*

And you were there with me during my rough spot, when I went through that shitty break up. But you were right. She wasn't for me and you said so from the start. You picked me up and pieced me back together, promising it would be better and damn if you weren't right. But then, you always were.

Now it's my turn to impart a few bits of wisdom. You told me I had a special knack to talk you down from the ledge. I don't, not really. You talk yourself down, only you don't realize it. I just get the conversation started and then you, in your Ben way, take it over and run with it. That's what you're gonna have to do when I'm gone. You're gonna find a way to figure it out and run with it. I'm depending on you, man. My girl will depend on you and I know you have what it takes to get the both of you to the happier side of this shit.

Now here's the deal. Don't worry about the little shit. It always takes care of itself. Don't let your damn dick run away with you either. I know how you are sometimes, dude. Fucking every piece of tail in sight won't help you at all. It'll only be the band-aid for all your wounds and end up getting you into some shit you don't need. Put that awesome brain of yours to work and let it do some magic. And add your heart to it too. You have one of the biggest hearts I've ever encountered. Use it—not just for keeping yourself alive. Open it up and let yourself fall in love, man. It will be the greatest gift you can give yourself—and me.

Now do what I told Cate—go and live. Don't you dare let yourself wallow in misery and self-destruct, like I know you have a tendency to do. And have the greatest life you can. Don't look back, but only forward. And know my life would've been half of what it was without you as part of it.

Love, your brother in this world and the next,

Drew

And take care of my wife. I don't want to come back and have to haunt your ass. This is where you're supposed to laugh again.

I was never the hero. And if he could see me now, he wouldn't say that.

I'm dressed and in my car not truly knowing where I'm going. But when I get there, instantly I know this is where I'm meant to be.

The doors slide open and I catch a glimpse of her. She's flanked by her family as she walks towards an awaiting nurse.

"Samantha," I call out.

She freezes, but doesn't bother to turn around to face me. I get a precious view of her profile.

"You're right—sorry isn't nearly enough. And telling you how much I love you and need you isn't enough either," I choke out. "No matter what, I'm going to be here for you, even if it's too late."

She gives me no acknowledgement as she faces forward and disappears behind the windowless double doors.

Three pairs of eyes turn to glare at me. I can feel the eyes of the other people in the waiting area as well. Their judgment doesn't matter. Laney makes the first move.

She's on me before her dad can wrangle her away. Her fist connects several blows I take, knowing I earned that and more.

"You asshole. You don't get to show up now. You're too late."

"Laney," her mom says. She rests a hand on my forearm. "She's going to be a while. You don't have to wait."

"I know. And I'm sorry my appearance is causing your family distress. But I have to stay."

Her lips compress in a thin smile. She shuffles her family to a far corner. I slump in a seat and rest my arms on my legs as I cover my face.

"He shouldn't be here," I hear Laney rant.

"The bastard has a lot of nerve," one of her friends adds.

I look up to see four more pairs of eyes that could only be Sam's friends giving me death by castration looks. I fist my hand in my hair as I find the floor for solace and push their words away. There isn't anything they could say to get me to leave.

Time passes like a slow leak. Hours later a man in blue scrubs comes up. When her family stands, I wait until he reaches them before standing and moving close enough to eavesdrop.

"She's fine," he says in greeting. I can't see his face, so I can't anticipate his next words. "Although the tumor looked …" His words are drowned out by Sam's mother's gasp. "Her breast tissue didn't look very healthy." I rock on my feet wanting to find a chair, but force myself to stand to try to hear anything else he has to say. "She'll be in for a little while longer before she's taken to recovery. You guys might want to go get something to eat. It probably won't be until later this afternoon before you can see her."

I go back to my seat where I plan to wait it out until I know she is safe at home.

"You should leave," one of her friends spits out at me as they head out.

"I should," I whisper. "But I'm not."

"She's not going to want to see you. But you don't care do you? It's all about you."

She's right about part of that. I don't care that she doesn't want to see me. Still I sit. Night comes and I watch her family escorted through the patient doors. And hours later, I watch them leave.

"She says go to home," Laney hisses at me before telling her friends they can go back.

Still I wait.

I overhear her mother tell Sam's friends she's being moved to a regular room. She glances at me as if she'd hoped I would hear. I wait before following them to that waiting room where I plant myself as a fixture.

As time passes, several nurses feel sorry for me in my rumpled clothes and overall disheveled appearance. They bring me bottles of water and tell me they don't want me to end up in the emergency room. So I drink the water, but I refuse food. I just need to see Sam leave this place. Nothing else matters.

I continue to wait, only answering e-mails while Mark and Jeff cover for me.

It isn't until late a couple days later that the doors open and Sam is ushered out in a wheelchair. When our eyes connect, I wait for any reaction.

THIRTY-FOUR
Sam

———————◆———————

LANEY, GOD LOVE HER, CLAMPS my hand in a bone-crushing grip, all the way to the hospital for my surgery. How in the world did she go through this alone? Okay, she had Mom to guide her, and Dad and Evan were with her, too. I was off at school with my head up my ass my senior year, and not a care in the world. I could kick myself in said ass right now.

"What would I do without you?" My words are choked.

"What do you mean?" Her eyes pin me.

"You've done so much for me this past week. Work, the rescue from Ben's, the surgery. I mean, I seriously don't know what I'd do without you."

"Sam, I'm your sister. It's what families do for each other."

"Yeah, but when you had your surgery …"

"You were in college. Did you think I would pull you out of school to help?" She laughs. "I had Mom. And Evan was my savior."

"Yeah. You didn't have an asshole boyfriend who dumped you like a hot potato the first minute he found a lump in your boob."

"Jesus. I wish I had something better to say than I'm sorry, Sam. If I'd known what a jerk he turned out to be, I would've kicked him in the balls that night at Mom and Dad's."

"And I would've let you. But I guess it's best he showed his colors now rather than later. Can you imagine if this had happened after we were married?"

Her hand squeezes mine tighter, if that's even possible. "You guys talked marriage?"

"No! It was only a hypothetical comment."

She relaxes her grip and I flex my hand.

"Sorry. It scared me for a minute that he had the potential to do that much damage."

"Oh, he had the potential. I just never saw it coming." My hand automatically goes to my chest and absently rubs the place where my heart is. Like that's going to ease the ache that seems to have permanently lodged itself there. "I wish life had a rewind button, you know?"

"How so?"

My hand moves from my chest and slashes through the air. "I'd like to erase what I said to him. I humiliated myself, when I told him I loved him. And then I gave him all those chances with my idiotic texts. It's a terrible feeling and I want it to go away."

"Listen to me. You did nothing to humiliate yourself. If anyone should feel that way, it should be Ben."

"Easy for you to say, but I'm at the receiving end of an emotional cannon and I'm getting bombarded here. Have you ever been in love and had someone do something like this to you?"

Laney shakes her head. "No. Not to this degree."

I'm silent because there really is nothing else for us to say. We arrive at the hospital and Mom and Dad are waiting on us. They both hug me, but relief marks their eyes. Mom has been ready for me to get this over for about a year now. And who can blame her when she's a breast cancer survivor herself?

Trying to be as upbeat as I can, I say, "Let's get this show on the road."

Mom says, "What about the girls? Aren't you going to wait on them?"

"They know where to meet us. Fourth floor."

"Okay, let's go." Dad takes my overnight bag from me.

"Did you bring everything they told you?" Mom asks.

"I did, and I even have my toothbrush." I'm famous for forgetting that and end up having to buy one wherever I go. I must have dozens of toothbrushes at home.

"Good girl," Mom says.

We get upstairs to the surgery check-in and not long after, the whole crew arrives. My doctor has reviewed everything with me, start to finish, so I know exactly what to expect. The girls also know, but they're here for me—to cheer me on when I go in and to be here when I wake up. I should be in the hospital for two days, three at the most. Since my surgeon doesn't believe I have cancer, I won't have any lymph node removal or anything like that, thank God. I'll be in a lot of pain and discomfort, especially since I'm having immediate reconstruction. But I decided I'd rather get it all over with at once, than do it in two stages, and get my spectacular new boobs going ASAP. That's what Laney did, so I'm following her footsteps.

We're all sitting in a group when I hear my name being called. Everyone hugs and moves to walk with me as far as they can toward the double doors, eager to convey every ounce of support possible. And that's when I hear his voice calling my name. I don't dare look at him. I can't do this. Not now. Why did he come here?

Then he starts talking. What is he doing? I don't—can't—acknowledge him.

My feet keep moving until I'm safely behind the double doors. What happens next is a blur. I'm given an IV and meds, and then my Mom, Dad, and sister are allowed back, but my head is swimming with the effects of the drugs. My surgeon comes in, smiling. And soon, I'm rolling down the hall and being pushed into the operating room.

A nurse talks to me, and asks me if I'm in pain.

"No, but my throat is scratchy," I tell her. "Can I have some water?"

"Not yet, honey. You just woke up. We need to wait a little bit."

"Woke up? Was I sleeping?"

"Yes, Ms. Calhoun, you had surgery. Do you remember?"

"Yes, but I thought I was getting ready. It's over already?"

"It sure is and you're just waking up. Can you tell me what day it is?"

"Friday. It's Friday." I rub my neck because my throat really burns.

"Your throat will feel lots better later today. It hurts from the tube they put down it during your procedure."

"Oh. Okay." All I want to do is sleep. As soon as I start to drift, the doctor's there.

"Samantha, how do you feel?"

"Tired. I want to sleep."

"You can sleep in a bit. I have good news. No cancer."

"Oh, that's nice. Can I sleep now?" I'm too tired to give even a tiny rat's ass.

Dr. Wilson, my surgeon, chuckles. "Not yet, we want you to wake up for us. Don't go back to sleep."

Oh. I was hoping to take a nap. "But my eyes don't want to stay open."

"Samantha, your surgery went extremely well. Both Dr. Bains and I couldn't be more pleased."

"How nice. Will you tell my family?"

"I'm getting ready to do that. And in a few more minutes, I'll let your mom and dad in to see you."

When he leaves, I hope to take a little snooze, but the nurse pops over and won't let me. Pretty soon, Mom, Dad, and Laney stick their heads through the curtain to check in on me.

It seems like a week passes before they deem it okay for me to sleep. And I conk out like I've been hit on the head with a hammer. The next thing I know, I wake up in a room surrounded by family and friends. My mouth tastes like I've been on a weeklong bender and my throat is still scratchy.

"Ugh, I have skunk breath."

Lauren shakes her head. "She goes in for major surgery and comes out complaining about her breath. Only you, Calhoun."

"Water," I croak. Mom shoves a plastic bendy straw in my mouth.

"Thanks, Mom. That tastes heavenly."

Everyone stands around my bed, grinning. I feel like a goon. "What? Do I have a booger on my nose?"

They laugh. Then Laney says, "We're all just so giddy over the outcome of your surgery, Sam. And you're booger free."

"Oh, thank God. I was worried there for a minute."

I look over toward the window and there is a monstrous flower arrangement. "Aww, who sent that? It's gorgeous!"

They all shift their eyes away from me and no one answers.

"What?" I press.

Finally, Laney seems to be the chosen spokesperson. "They're from He Who Shouldn't Be Named."

"He Who Shouldn't ... oh shit. He sent me flowers?"

Lauren says, "Boy, did he ever. And that was after we all basically treated him like the dog he is in the waiting room."

My head is super fuzzy from the pain meds, but I know I heard her correctly. "He was in the waiting room? He didn't leave after I wouldn't talk to him?"

"Nope. He stayed throughout the surgery and I think he's still in the hospital somewhere," Laney says.

"Why would he do that?" I wonder out loud.

Lauren answers this time. "Beats the hell out of all of us."

"Now everyone, maybe we should treat him a little better," my mom, the quintessential peacemaker says. "We don't know what he's been through."

Laney looks at her like she's lost every last marble in her head. "What *he's* been through? What about your daughter? Hasn't she been through enough?"

"Laney, don't use that tone with your mother," Dad says.

"Hey, let's not talk about this or He Who Shouldn't Be Named in my room. And Laney, dump those flowers in the trash or give them to the nurses. I don't want them in this room."

"You got it, sis."

Mom scowls and Dad smiles. I have a feeling that Dad is on the Ben haters list too. We haven't talked about it, but I'm sure he's caught enough of our conversations to know that he hurt me terribly and since I'm a Daddy's girl, that's a huge no-no in his book.

Two days later, my surgeon signs my discharge papers and I'm getting ready to go home. Mom and Laney are taking me. Two more gigantic bouquets of flowers have arrived from Ben, but I had the lady take them directly to the nurses' station after I read the cards. I want nothing more to do with him. He made it very clear that his journey with me was finite, so I'm doing everything possible to prove to myself there's no road to travel with him.

The nurse enters my room with a wheelchair.

"Oh, I'm fine to walk," I say.

She laughs. "Everyone says that. It's hospital policy. Unfortunately, you don't have a choice. It's ride or stay."

Even though my brows shoot up, I have a seat. Laney says she'll get the car and pull it around the front to the patient loading zone. Mom walks with the nurse and me, and we ride the elevator down to the main lobby. When we exit, we're walking past a waiting area and that's when I see him.

He's disheveled, wearing the same clothes he was the day I came in for surgery, and he resembles a homeless man. His beard is filled in and his hair—well, it looks completely unkempt, just like the rest of him. Ben Rhoades is truly a mess, as he stares at me with those steel gray eyes, pleading for what? Mercy? A chance to speak and say what? Another opportunity to rip my soul out? He can't damage my heart anymore, because I don't have one. He burned it to ashes when I left his house the last time we were together.

I look away as my chair rolls on by, straight for the entrance where I glimpse Laney's car through the sliding doors. Just let me make it there before the tears hit. Because as much as I want to deny it, he's still a part of me, infused in my soul. He's wrapped around my beating heart—the heart I try to tell myself doesn't exist.

A brief thank you to the nurse is all I can stammer out before the sobs rupture from me.

"What's wrong? What happened?" Laney asks.

"Just drive." In thirty seconds, I've gone from a smiling, cancer-free patient to a blubbering wreck all because of a pair of beautiful gray eyes and a tangled mop of dark brown hair.

Mom tries to hold my hand, but I need it to constantly swipe my face. When she crams a pile of tissues in my hand, I cough out my thanks between sobs. How can I explain what's going on to the question in her concerned expression? My house isn't but a short drive from the hospital so we pull in the driveway and I do my best to compose myself. When I hear my sister yelling, I get out of the car to see Ben pulling in behind us. I have to give him an "A" for persistence. But damn it, why can't he leave me the hell alone? I don't need this shitshow right now.

"Get the hell out of here, Rhoades," Laney shouts. "Haven't you done enough damage to her already?"

"Yes, I have. But I want to make amends and prove to her I'm ..."

"You're what? A piece of shit intent on destroying what's left of her?"

"No! I ..." He tries to say, but my sister cuts him off.

"Shut up and get the hell out of here."

"Laney, please." Mom is shaken up. It may be time to step in.

"Laney ..." I begin.

"Samantha, go inside with Mom. Now."

"Samantha, please. I need to speak with you." His voice is raw with emotion.

Laney steps between us. "Rhoades, if you so much as say one more word to her, I'm calling the police and taking out a restraining order. You're harassing her and stalking her. Now get off the property."

He holds his hands in the air, palms facing us, and slowly backs away with sagging posture. I can see it's the last thing he wants to do, but I have to side with Laney on this. She only wants to protect me, and he did the perfect job of shattering me and is bringing me to tears again.

Before he gets in his car, he says, "Sam, please don't cry. I'm sorry. More than I can say, but please don't cry."

"Like you give a damn? Where were you all those days and nights when she was sick with worry and crying her fucking eyes out over you and what you did? Oh, I forgot. You were throwing yourself a pity party. And now you stand there and tell her not to cry? You're nothing but a pitiful piece of shit. Get out of here." Then Laney turns to Mom and says, "Sorry for that terrible language, Mom, but it needed to be said. Come on, Sam. Let's get you inside." She puts her arm around the disaster known as her sister and we walk into the house.

Mom brings in my overnight bag and Laney paces in the living room. I head straight to my bathroom so I can blow my nose and rinse off my face. When I catch a peek of myself in the mirror, I want to laugh. My eyes are red and swollen, my lips puffy, and I look like something that cat dragged in to display as a trophy kill. I need a shot of Jack Daniels in a glass of tea.

When I mention this to Laney, she hollers, "You can't drink! Are you crazy? You're on pain pills. Remember?"

"Oh, crap. I forgot."

"Swear to me you won't drink!" Laney says.

"I swear."

She holds out her pinky and makes me pinky swear. What the hell?

"Laney! What do you think? That I'm going to OD on Jack?"

She offers up a shaky laugh.

"I think the whole world has gone cuckoo," I say.

"It's all because of that fucking Rhoades," she says.

"Laney, please," Mom admonishes her.

"Sorry, Mom."

Right then, Lauren barges in the door, with a toothy grin that

A MESS OF A MAN

should be an ad for a chewing gum commercial. But one look at my swollen face stops her dead.

"What happened? Are you okay?" She runs to my side and puts her hand on my forehead.

"I don't have a fever, if that's what you think."

"Then what?"

Laney spills everything, down to the very last detail.

"Jesus crackers. I don't believe it." Then she grins. "He's in love with you."

Laney turns on her. "Are you crazy? That's the last thing she needs. That asshole bugging her and bringing another shitastrophe home to roost and then pulling the rug out from under her."

Mom says, with her hands over her ears, "Laney, language."

Lauren shrugs. "Not saying anything about that. I was just making an observation. If he was as unkempt as you say, and still in the same clothes as what, two days ago? That means he never left the hospital. And you've got to admit, it takes some damned sizable balls to follow you all home like that. He's flipped over her. In a bad way. The boy is in L-O-V-E. Just sayin'."

"He told her that at the hospital. Right before she went into surgery, if you recall," Laney says.

"I don't want him. I can't trust those words, at least coming from his mouth, anyway," I say. "And they came too late."

The doorbell rings.

Laney practically growls. "If that's him, I'm going to rip his balls off."

"Laney Calhoun Harrellson. You may be married and not living under my roof anymore, but I am still your mother and if you don't watch your mouth young lady I'm going to ..." then she clamps one side of her mouth together and I guess she realizes there really isn't anything she *can* do, so she shuts up.

Laney pulls the door open and a flower delivery man is there.

"Oh, thank you." She brings in the flowers and hands them to me. It's another gorgeous arrangement and I have a feeling I know who it's from. I look at the card, and sure enough, it's from Ben.

There are many flowers that are beautiful but none as perfect as you.
Love, Ben
Please call me. Give me a chance, Sam.

I hand the card to Laney and she screams, "That son of a

bitch!"

My mom's hands cover her ears and Lauren laughs.

"I don't know what to think about all this, but I need some rest so I'm going to lie down."

Mom immediately hugs me and tells me if I need her to call. Laney says the same and they both leave.

Lauren eyes me for a second. "You know I'm right. This is the real deal for him."

"Maybe. But it doesn't matter. I can't go through that pain again."

"I know. But what if you don't have to? Men who only care a tiny bit for women don't jump through hoops and don't do cartwheels and backflips like he obviously is doing for you. If this is a man you have deep solid feelings for, you need to consider this."

"I'm too tired to think about this now. I'm going to rest some."

"Okay. I'm here if you need me," Lauren says.

When I crawl in bed, it's difficult to get the image of Ben out of my head. He looked so *awful*. That couldn't have been a façade. No one does that for shits and giggles. He is proving something, but I don't know if it's to himself or to me. I drift off and I'm not sure how long I sleep, but when I wake up, I hear voices. Female voices, so I know someone is here with Lauren. I get up and wander into the living room. Lauren sees me and gives me a wink.

"Sam, you need to meet Sadie."

"Sadie?" I ask, confused.

"Yeah. Sadie is going to be cleaning and cooking for us until you're able to do it yourself. Like for the next two to three weeks, courtesy of Ben Rhoades."

"Hi, Ms. Calhoun. It's a pleasure to meet you. I'll come late in the morning so I'm here to make you breakfast or lunch, or both if you want. And then I'll leave after I have your dinner prepared. And I'll do your housekeeping while here."

"Oh, but I ..."

"Sadie will only be here for two or three weeks. Just until you can do these things for yourself. It's a gift from Ben, Sam." Lauren's grin is so large, it's almost obscene.

"Thank you, Sadie."

I walk into my room and call Lauren in.

"I can't do this," I whisper.

"Why not?"

"You know why. It's ridiculous."

"So what? Make him pay, Sam. It's nothing more than he deserves."

"But I feel guilty." And I do. More than I can tell her, but I don't know why.

"Just shut the hell up and let Sadie do her job."

"Okay. Okay, I will. But I don't like it." Only I change my mind after day one. Sadie is amazing. Her meals are excellent, and I wish I could afford to keep her forever.

In the two weeks that Sadie is here, I feel extremely spoiled and pampered. I wake up to the smell of coffee and homemade bread every morning. I get a full breakfast, then a made to order lunch and a dinner that's out of this world every day. Not to mention Sadie does all our laundry, including sheets and towels. This is the life. On her last day, I'm practically in tears. I don't want her to leave and I tell her how much I will miss her.

"I've enjoyed being here very much, too, Ms. Sam. Maybe we'll see each other again."

I seriously doubt that, but I nod anyway. Because it would be rude to do otherwise, I send Ben a note thanking him for Sadie. It's brief and to the point.

Ben,
Thank you for sending me Sadie.
She was a big help and was wonderful.
I appreciated her very much.
Sam

The next day, I go to my surgeon for my first follow up visit. When he examines me, he's very pleased with my healing. Laney was right. My new boobs look great. The only things different are the scars and the nipple sensations are diminished. They are still reactive, but not as much. But it sure beats dying.

When I get home, there's a card in the mail from one of the local spas. Apparently I have a home massage coming tomorrow, courtesy of Ben. It's one of the hot stone massages, and it will be an hour and a half long. He also sprung for a facial. Boy, he's totally going for brownie points. I can't say that I'm not happy about this. A massage is just what the doctor ordered.

The masseuse arrives on time with her table and supplies. The only problem is I can't lay on my stomach yet with my new boobs, but she is able to work around that by concentrating on other areas with me on my back. I feel like a new woman. When I tell her what happened to me, she gives me a gift certificate to come to the spa when I'm healed and can lie on my stomach, so I can get a full massage. I tip her fifty bucks.

Lauren and the rest of the girls come over that night. Berkeley brings pizza and we sit around and discuss Ben.

Berkeley wants me to call him. Not to see him but to hear him out. Britt is on the fence. Carrie and Hayley are on the *hell no* team. And Lauren is quiet for a long time. She finally says, "He loves you, Sam. Like has it for you in the worst way. You're going to have to do something because he'll continue until ..."

"Until what?" I ask.

"I don't know, honestly. He's trying hard, for sure."

"Why have you changed your mind about him, Lauren?" I ask.

She taps her finger against her chin. "I'm not sure I have. He totally feels remorse for what he did or he wouldn't be going to these lengths. And like I've said, he's crazy, head over heels for you. I'm just sayin', you know?"

Berkeley adds, "Give it a few days to mull over, Sam. There's nothing that says you have to act now."

"There's nothing that says I have to act at all. After what he did, I'm not sure I have the nerve to take the first step."

"You do. You're the strongest person I know." Lauren smiles when she says it.

The next day, I'm watching TV and wondering when I'm going to go back to work. The doctor said three weeks, minimum. Work is super busy with a stacked schedule. Jenna's help in finding Nick's replacement was a miracle. Laney has put all her charities on hold for me and is basically filling in full-time. But that can't last forever because she holds some high ranking positions and they need her to fulfill her role. Mom has even pitched in a time or two. There are a few things coming up this weekend that Berkeley and Carrie are helping out with, but my doctor is adamant about me not doing anything for three weeks, so that leaves me out.

I decide to give Nancy a call to see how things are panning out.

When her cheery voice answers the phone, I can feel my lips curl into a smile. "How's my favorite admin doing?"

"Sam! Oh my gosh, it's so good to hear your voice. Can I tell you how much you've been missed?"

"I wish you wouldn't because it's going to make it harder to stay away. I can't come back until next Monday," I groan.

"Don't you worry about a thing. We have you covered on all ends here. You wouldn't believe what we have going."

That's an odd comment coming from her. "Okay, I'll take the bait. Tell me what's cooking over there."

She snickers. "Well, at first it was World War Three. I thought Laney was going to call in the SWAT team to tear gas the place."

"What are you talking about?"

I'm getting to that," Nancy says. "But then there was a huge stand-off. They yelled and screamed. Threats—oh my God, you wouldn't believe how they went at each other. And that sister of yours—she sure has your back."

Now I'm totally confused. "Nancy, would you get to the point?"

"Right. So after the shouting match and the SWAT threats, we finally pulled them apart, and he convinced her he could be a huge help."

"He? Who's he? Nick?"

"No, not Nick. Ben. Ben Rhoades. He's been working his butt off here, helping. Between your sister and him, they have kept this business running like a well-oiled machine, Sam."

Holy fucking shit. Ben? Laney and Ben? In the same room? And she hasn't killed him?

"I can tell you she wanted to at first."

I hadn't realized I'd spoken those words out loud.

"Jesus. He's been working for me?"

"Not only working, but doing about fourteen hour days here. I'm not kidding, Sam. He and your sister make quite the team. It was tense at first, when she had him doing everything from fixing the toilet to manning the phone, but now they've come to some sort of agreement. Oh, and I'm not supposed to tell you so don't rat on me."

"What? What's that supposed to mean?"

"Apparently he doesn't want you to know he's doing this."

I have no words for this. I can't even think straight.

"Sam, are you there?"

"Yeah, Nancy. Hey, I've got to go. Thanks for telling me. And I won't breathe a word to Laney."

"Thanks. And we really do miss you and can't wait for you to get back here."

"I miss you, too."

I end the call and stare off into space, thinking about everything that Ben is doing for me. What about his job? If he's spending all that time at my business, how is he managing his own work? What is his father thinking about all of this? And he's doing it with me not supposedly knowing about it. My brain is exploding with all this knowledge and I would be lying to myself if I said my heart weren't warming to it.

There is a pad of paper and a pen on the coffee table so I start to list everything that Ben has done for me. As I'm reviewing my list, the mail comes and when I sift through it, Ben strikes again. He's sent another gift in the form of food. But this time it's an open ended credit for take out from the Carry-Out Concierge, a pricey delivery service from many of the downtown restaurants. I'm shocked. There is no spending limit on this, nor is there an expiration date on it.

When Lauren gets home from work, I show it to her.

"Woohoo, you hit the jackpot on this one, girl!"

"I can't accept it. It's too much."

She looks at me like Yoda from Star Wars just rolled up. "Are you nuts? You have to accept it. After what that douche did to you, he deserves to empty out his bank account pampering your ass."

"Okay, one, he already has. And two, I have to explain." Then I fill her in on what he's doing for me at work. "And three, with all the signals you've been sending me lately, I sort of thought you were Team Ben."

She cocks her head and says, "Let's get one thing straight here—I am always and forever Team Sam. And while I think Ben Rhoades is madly in love with you, that doesn't negate the fact that he crushed my girl. Since he did that, the douche must pay and this is one way for him to do that. With this being said, do I think he needs to pay forever? No. There is a limit to my revenge. Take advantage of this for a while and then stop using it. If you want to see him, or talk to him, then call him. But Sam, you can't string him along forever. That will only bring you down to his level when he hurt you and you don't want to be like that. As far as your business is concerned, that's one more area he's proving himself to you."

She's right. If I'm going to make contact with him, I need to do something soon.

A couple of days go by with Lauren and I enjoying my latest gift in the form of fancy dinners every night. I'm not gonna lie and say I have zero guilt when spending oodles of Ben's dollars on this stuff. But as Lauren says, payback can be hell.

Once more, the mail delivers another Ben attack. Only this time, it's in the form of a letter. No gift from a fancy spa. Nothing from a fine dining establishment. This is a handwritten missive through and through. My hand trembles as my finger slides under the flap to open it. Am I willing to take this step? I feel my heart thumping in my chest. I know it's pieced back together where he's concerned, but has the glue dried sufficiently to hold all them in place? I'm so fucking scared, sometimes I think that taking a breath will shatter it all over again. If that's the case, what will Ben's words do to me?

THIRTY-FIVE
BEN

———————◆———————

THE KNOCK AT THE DOOR isn't much of a surprise. I've been a hermit over a week and I'm shocked it's taken this long for my sister to do a follow up.

Only when I open the door, Jeff and Mark stand on my stoop. Jeff holds up a six-pack of beer and I step back to usher them inside.

"Damn, man. What happened to you?" Jeff comments before flopping on my sofa.

"Sorry we showed up unannounced," Mark says, putting a hand on my shoulder.

I give him a weary smile and nod as Mark sits in the chair. Part of me isn't up to company. But there's a part of me that misses having someone I can confide in that's not my sister or Cate. I take a chance and sit on the opposite end of the couch.

"I fucked up," I confess.

Mark and Jeff trade glances.

"This has something to do with a woman. The cute event planner I'm guessing," Mark says.

I nod, feeling her loss as much as the finality of Drew's death.

Jeff lets out a long-winded sigh, but I don't care. "You know we are about to cross into pussy territory talking about women the way they talk about us."

Shrugging, I say, "You walked into this shit pile. I didn't ask you to come."

"Yeah, because I thought your old man gave you hell about

284

how you handled things."

I scrub a hand over my face. "Actually, he gave me a promotion." They both gape. "It doesn't matter. Not coming into the office will end that career move."

Mark gives me a sympathetic smile. Jeff, on the other hand, wears a clownish expression with wide eyes and an open mouth.

"You're going to let a pair of tits ruin your career."

He has no idea how close to the truth he is, except the tits in question ruined my relationship. Pushing my hair out of my face, I meet his gaze. "She's worth far more than that."

Silence takes over until Jeff leans forward and starts passing out beers.

"You two fucks have caught the pussy virus and there is no cure. I'm glad I'm immune to that shit."

"Jeff, let it go," Mark says sullenly.

"How's the bitch?" Jeff asks him.

"She's not a bitch."

Jeff has the decency to look startled. "Really, after everything you've told us?"

"I haven't told you everything."

Jeff throws an incredulous gaze my way before asking, "So, what did you do?"

The story unfolds from my mouth like a badly constructed paper airplane destined to crash mid-flight to the ground.

"Damn," Jeff says. "That's messed up."

"Thanks, Captain Obvious."

"What have you done to win her back?"

"Outside of her sister threatening to call the cops on me?" He nods. "Flowers, paid for a housekeeper, food, a massage." I toss up my hands. "I don't know what else I can do."

"Did you tell her how you're feeling all pussy whipped?"

I roll my eyes knowing what he means, but not rising to the bait.

"She'd likely delete any e-mail or text message I send without reading it."

Jeff shakes his head. "Write her a note or something. Women eat that shit up."

"You know what, you might have an idea there," I say to Jeff.

"How's her business holding up with her being out?" Mark asks, drawing our attention to him. "What?" He shrugs. "She's probably going to be out of work for a while."

Several beers later, a crazy plan forms in my head. After they leave, I sit at my desk with a pen in my hand and a blank piece of paper before me. I stare a long time, before I put the pen to paper and begin.

Sam,

I could say sorry, which I am, but that does nothing to erase the pain I caused.

I could tell you how much I love you, but it's meaningless because I wasn't there when you needed me most.

*They say love is blind, and in truth I **was** blind to how much you meant to me until I let you slip through my fingers.*

The days are long and the nights cold without you. Please don't give up on me. I know we are meant to be together.

If you give me another chance, I promise to be the man worthy of you.

I know now that all I need is you. The alternative means a solitary existence for me.

I once told you I believed you were the brightest star in the heavens. I still believe that, only now without you, my life is lonely and dark—nothing but a black hole.

There is no one else on this earth for me.

B~

I slip it in an envelope addressed to her, but hold off on sending it. I have a few things I need to do before first. In the morning I make one of two necessary calls before my plan falls in place.

"Dad."

"Ben," the pause is so thick, and I'm too sluggish with my response. He beats me to the punch. "Do you plan on coming into work today?"

"Actually, I'm going to take a leave of absence."

Silence. I hear my neck crack as I straighten my spine.

"I'm sorry to do this. But there is someone who needs me." Even if she doesn't want my help.

"What about your workload?"

"I've got it covered. Jeff and Mark will handle the day stuff. And I'll log on at night and handle the rest."

Dad's displeasure when he ends the call is something I push to the furthest reach of my mind as I get myself presentable for the first time in weeks.

My second call is much easier.

"Jenna."

"Ben."

She says my name as quiet as a whisper.

"You alone?"

"Not exactly. Give me a minute."

I hear rustling and the pad of her feet against the floor.

"Is Kenneth in town?"

Her pause is enough answer.

"Since when did I answer to my big brother about who I bring to my bed?"

"Is it Brandon?" I ask, ignoring her deflection.

"None of your business. Now why have you called?"

"Take it from me, baby sister, follow your heart before it's too late."

"Shit, who body snatched my brother? Did you fix things with Sam?"

"Not exactly," I sigh. "I need your help. Did you ever refer that person to Sam for her open position?"

"Yeah, she started, I think."

"Can you find out if Sam needs an extra set of hands?"

"Oh, Benny boy, I like how your thinking. Give me a minute, I'll call you back."

"Thanks."

"Don't thank me. You owe me."

Not quite an hour later when I walk into Sam's office, everything's going smoothly until Sam's sister spots me. Laney isn't happy and throws every kind of threat imaginable at me, but I hold my ground. Eventually, we come to a sort of unspoken agreement, all in the name of helping Sam. Over the course of a couple days, her attitude toward me begins to soften, as I believe she sees I only have Sam's best interests at heart. Or at least that's what I keep telling myself. The next two weeks I burn the candle at both ends but each morning I show up with a smile on my face. I wasn't there when she needed me the most, so now the least I can do is help keep Sam's business clicking along.

The day Sam's due to return, I show up at my office for the first time in about a month. It isn't long before Trudy informs me my father wishes to see me in his office.

It feels like I'm taking my last steps on death row as I walk past a hallway of offices with everyone watching me like they know my father's about to give me the boot, not that I can blame him.

"Ben, have a seat."

Dutifully, I do as he asks.

His demeanor is rather calm and I expect the worst.

"Am I to assume you've joined us for the foreseeable future?" I'm not sure how to answer that. When I don't, he adds. "Is your leave over?"

I nod.

His exhale of breath is heavy with a prepared speech to come.

"When you left your job in New York, your mother and I knew it had a lot to do with Drew. We understood and supported your decision."

I'd planned to leave the city anyway. Drew's illness only made me change my plans sooner. But I say nothing to correct him because I'm dumbstruck. All that time he made me feel like a failure, and he already knew.

"Did your recent leave have anything to do with Samantha Calhoun?"

I dislodge the word, "Yes," with a croak.

"I assume she was worth your absence from work."

I clear my voice. "Very much so. I needed to help her out for a while."

He nods. "Do you love this girl?"

"Yes."

Relief washes over his face. "Finally."

Stunned, I say, "What?"

He sighs. "You've been great in your career; there is no doubt about that. But I was young and single once, too. I wasn't sure if you'd ever settle down. And I'm grateful we're not having this conversation about Karen. I would have referred you to the best lawyer in town for an ironclad pre-nup if your mom had gotten her way." He pauses while I blink, flabbergasted by the turn of conversation. "Samantha is smart and not dazzled by the limelight. I like her."

"I don't know what to say."

"Say that you fixed whatever it was that needing fixing."

"I doubt it. But I owed her."

Nodding, he adds, "Don't give up. Did I ever tell you about how I met your mother?"

He launches into a story about meeting Mom, but ended up dating a different woman with all the right surface qualities, even though Mom was the shit, too. His words not mine. In order to win Mom back, he had to get creative.

Baffling me further, he sends me home to make my last play for Sam, with the expectation that I'll be back at work bright and earlier the next day.

I search high and low for what I need before I head to my final destination. The intel I gathered during the time spent in her office was that she's only working half days for the first week. I want to get there before Lauren shows up.

Armed, I manage to knock on her front door.

"Coming."

Her voice sends all kinds of emotions racing through my four stages of awareness of her on the track of the Indy 500. Lust, Loss, Love, Lonely.

The door opens and she's startled and stops from opening it wide. "Ben."

I take a moment to drink her in. She looks gorgeous with hair haphazardly pulled back wearing a loose T-shirt that could be mine for its size. She's also wearing tiny shorts that show off her great legs.

When my eyes meet hers again, I breathe her name, "Sam."

She looks at my arms. "What do you have there?"

"A present for you." I kneel and set the puppy down at her feet.

I stay in that position because she comes down to pet the dog sniffing at her. Her smile is wide for the little guy which causes a pang of jealousy to stab me.

"Hey, little fellow."

Her twinkling eyes meet mine. "What's his name?"

"Benjie."

She grants me a smile before turning it back to the Jack Russell Terrier I'd brought her.

"Such a cutie. Too bad I can't keep you."

"But you have to," I say.

She meets my eyes. "Why?"

"Because you deserve unconditional love—" As if on cue, the dog leans up and licks her face, sending her to giggles. "Lots of kisses." She glances back at me while the dog decides to roll on his back so she can pet his belly. "Someone to keep you company and to protect you. And if I can't do this for you, I want you to have someone who can."

She laughs again because Benjie is a ham for her affections. The sound of her happiness soothes my soul. And I know she's going to be okay.

"Even if I wanted him, I can't take him. You've done enough. And I'm too busy to properly take care of this guy."

She gets to her feet to the dismay of the puppy. He stands on two legs begging for more attention. "I'm sorry, sweetie. I can't keep you."

"It's fine. I'll keep him for you until you're ready. You can come over and get him, or text me and I'll drop him off."

I scoop him up and get to my feet. "It was great seeing you, Sam. Whatever you need, let me know, even if it's to set you up with a guy who deserves you."

At her astonished expression, I run my last play with three seconds still on the clock. Only it's truth, not a game.

"Through all of this, I remembered the most important thing Drew taught me."

"What's that?" she asks cautiously.

"I love you so much that your happiness means the world to me, even if I'm not the one giving it to you."

I turn and head to my car. I'm not going to lie; I hope she'll call me back and tell me she wants me too. But she doesn't. I drive home, filled with a deep sadness I haven't felt since I lost Drew.

Behind my closed door, I use my tub for the first time in forever. I sink into the heated water and man up. I'd lost the best thing I've ever had. And I learn an unforgettable lesson. My heart still beats even if I don't want it to. I have no desire to go back to empty hook-ups. I'm considering joining the priesthood when a knock comes at my door.

Benjie barks a moment too late. We'll have to work on that. As much as I hope it's Sam at the door, I called Jenna to tell her the bad news on my ride home. She said she would stop by with pizza and wine.

I hastily pat myself dry as the knocking gets more persistent.

"Hold your horses, Jenna" I call out slinging the towel around my waist and padding to the door.

THIRTY-SIX
Sam

◆

THE DOOR SWINGS OPEN AND Ben stands there with damp hair and a towel loosely wrapped around his waist. Benjie shoots out the door and I quickly chase him, gathering him in my arms before he has a chance to get very far. I'm rewarded with puppy kisses as he gives my face a thorough scrubbing.

"Sorry about that. The little guy is pretty fast."

"Yeah, I'll say." I try to hand him to Ben, but he only has one free hand as he's holding his towel with the other.

"Hey, do you mind?"

I follow his glance and chuckle. "Not a bit. Benjie is too cute for words."

"Give me a second while I throw some clothes on." He disappears upstairs, and it's a shame, because a peek at naked Ben would've been a nice treat.

A couple of minutes later, he's back, running down the steps, wearing faded jeans and pulling on a T-shirt. Damn, he looks good.

"So, I didn't think I'd be seeing you so soon," he says.

"Yeah, you left so quickly and I was a little shocked by your visit. By the time I collected myself you were already gone. Can we sit?"

He throws his hands up in the air. "I'm sorry. I don't know what I was thinking. Yes. And let me take him from you."

He reaches for the puppy, but I stop him.

"I kind of like holding the little guy." I follow him toward the couch. When we sit, I begin. "You said a lot of things back at my house."

Our eyes lock and his are as intense as I've ever seen them. "I did," he whispers.

"And you said a lot in your letter."

"Yeah?"

"And the things you did for me at work." He starts to speak but I stop him with my hand on his arm. "I know I wasn't supposed to know about that, but Nancy told me. And don't be upset with her. She is your biggest supporter. But I can't thank you enough for what you did. That was … well, you totally went beyond anything I ever would've expected."

"It's what you do when you love someone, Sam."

"I know. And that's what I want to talk about. The last time I was here, I don't have to tell you how I felt. You already know. I can't ever go through anything like that again."

"I can't make excuses for my behavior because there are none. If you give me a half a chance, I swear I won't ever make you. The time I spent without you has been hell. Work," he shrugs. "I'm surprised I still have a job. But none of that matters. I'll do anything for you. You have to know that. I love you more than my career or even life itself."

He fists his hands in his hair and I gently tug the offenders out from his gorgeous, but over grown, locks.

"I learned a huge lesson. You can't replace the ones you love. I should've learned that the first time around. But with you—I know it here." His hand moves over his chest.

I study his eyes first before I move to his stooped posture. His hands are balled up as if he's fighting himself. I've been on the fence since I made the decision to come here. I had to see him, but I hadn't been sure what exactly I was going to say.

"How can you be sure?"

His eyes fiercely hold mine. "Because when you walked out the door, my life ceased to be. I was a mess. Ask my mom or Jenna. I didn't eat, I couldn't sleep, I couldn't … be, knowing I'd lost you.

"You mean that." It's a statement and not a question.

"I do. But I get it if I've destroyed us. And your happiness is the only thing I live for now."

The agony in his eyes is real. I remember Trevor's pleas to get me back. He never looked at me the way Ben is now. I lift a hand and stroke his cheek.

"I had to know. And I have to know you won't ruin me again."

"I couldn't. You've ruined me for anyone else. I've worked hard just remembering how to breathe without you." He huffs out a distressed breath. "I don't know how to prove it to you other than with my words. But I swear I won't."

I lean in and press my lips to his. He doesn't move and I pull back trying to figure out if somehow I've misjudged. He licks his lips, then cups my face before planting the sweetest kiss on my mouth. I open for him and allow our tongues to tangle in ways I hadn't known I'd missed. Far too soon, he pulls back.

"I want you to know I'll be with you for your treatments. I don't care how long it takes. I'll take another leave of absence if I have to."

I feel my forehead crease as confusion clouds my head.

"Treatments?"

"Yeah. You know, chemo."

My fingers fan out across my chest as my eyes widen. "Chemo?" *Holy shit! All this time he's thought I have cancer!* "I ... you don't know, do you?"

Now he's the one with the confounded expression.

"Know what?"

I inch closer to him so our thighs are touching.

"Ben, I don't have cancer. That lump you felt was only a cyst. I had the surgery as a prevention, like my sister did, because we both carry the BRCA gene, but I'm cancer free. Having the mastectomies reduces my risk of getting cancer in the future."

A thousand emotions pass over his face. Shock, relief, and joy are just a few. His movement surprises me as he kneels on the floor and spreads my legs. I can say my lady parts get excited as he buries his head in my lap and his arms circle my waist. It should be another good sign of things to come. Only muffled words come from his mouth that I can't understand.

His body shakes, scaring me until I realize his trembles are the result of overwhelming emotion.

My eyes fill knowing the relief he must feel. I'd felt it too. Where my family has felt loss but is also full of survivors, he'd lost his very best friend. I say nothing, letting him be. My hands dive into his hair, realizing the depth of his feelings for me. He came back, even though he was under the impression that I had breast cancer. He'd been willing to go the distance with me and stand by my side. That fact is only more proof that he won't make the same mistake twice. I can trust that he will be there for me, no matter what.

Benjie decides he's tired of hanging out on the couch and takes of mouthful of Ben's hair and chomps down, tugging on it.

"Ouch," Ben cries. He lifts his head to face his attacker and I notice the shimmer of tears left on his cheeks.

I place my thumbs under his eyes and wipe away at some of the moisture before dabbing at my own eyes.

"He's certainly a fierce canine," I say.

Lifting his shirt sleeve, he swipes at his face before he says, "Yes, he is. And those teeth of his are like needles."

"I've noticed."

A whisper of a smile returns to his face. "You have to know I'm happy for you. But I would have been there no matter what."

"I know," I whisper.

He places another gentle kiss on my lips. "Let me put him in the pen I have in the kitchen."

He scoops up Benjie and is gone a moment.

When he comes back I say, "I want to show you something." This is the final test. This is the reason I put off telling him and delayed the surgery. But so much has happened between us and I'm much braver these days. So with a deep breath, I lift my T-shirt.

"What are you doing?" he asks.

Taking off my shirt hadn't been a scary prospect before. But I stick to my guns. He needs to see all of me before he can truly commit.

Sucking in a breath, I tell him, "I'm showing you my boobs."

"But I don't need to see them."

With my shirt half on and half off I pause half a second before continuing.

"Yes, you do. You were so in love with them, it was one of the reasons I kept putting off telling you about it. Well, that and Drew."

"Jesus Sam." He looks torn to shreds. "God, I loved your tits, but I'm *in* love with you ..." His eyes confirm everything his mouth voices.

"It's time to put it behind us. You've proven you're much more than just a boob man."

"I never meant to make you think I couldn't live without your boobs. It's you who I can't live without ..." His head drops as it oscillates slowly.

I need to divert him, so I cup his face in my hands. "Let's move past this. I have." Then I kiss him lightly before I reach behind me and unclasp my bra. His lips are pressed together, telling me he's nervous. I'm not sure of what he's going to think. The scar is not so significant, but it's there, and I have to own it. So here goes. I drop the bra and sit here, bared from the waist up.

His eyes open up, his mouth follows, and then the corner of his mouth lifts. At first it's a slight curl. But then he's grinning full out.

"Holy fuck. I wasn't sure what to expect, you were covered up. I just assumed ... But they're awesome, Sam."

"Yeah? You really think so?"

His eyes slide back to them and his tongue peeks out only to disappear back in his mouth.

"Yes. Yes, they are. I don't want to sound like a creep, but can I touch them?"

I hope like hell we get past this stage of awkwardness.

"When have you ever had to ask before? Just be gentle. I'm still not totally healed."

"Okay." He reaches out tentatively and brushes the backs of his fingers across them. Then he turns his hands around and only ever so slightly, cups them. "They're beautiful. Just like you."

"But the scars," I point to them.

Slowly, he shakes his head.

"I don't give a fuck about any scars. It's you I love." His finger touches the juncture between my breasts. "I have you healthy and alive. That's all I care about. You want to know something?"

"What?"

"First, I thought you had cancer and would have to go through treatment. When you said you didn't, I thought that was the greatest thing in the world. Then when you said you had mastectomies, I assumed that you didn't have any breasts at all, and here you sit with two amazing tits. Who cares about scars?"

A ripple of laughter bursts out of me and I throw my arms around him. "I love you, Ben Rhoades."

"Samantha Calhoun, I love you more than words can tell you."

His mouth hovers over mine for a second, lips brushing back and forth. And then his tongue tastes my lips, right before it slips past the opening of my mouth. We are soon devouring each other.

Heat shoots out his eyes as he tentatively asks, "Can you have sex?"

"Yeah, why?" A slow wicked grin grows on my face.

"I ... um ... didn't know if you were on any kind of restriction."

"What do you have in mind, Rhoades?"

He stares at my mouth like a starving man, which only serves to make my smile sprout wings.

"It's just Ben Jr. is so fucking happy to see you and your new tits."

I can't help the laugh that leaves my throat.

"Naughty boy. Did you miss me?"

"Fuck right I did. And it's been over a month, Sam. If you can't, that's fine. But I'll beg you for a hand job."

I toss my head back. Never have I felt so empowered.

"I think you've earned the full on deal. Just be easy on my boobs."

His head bobs with a sly smile on his face.

"Can I at least kiss them?"

"Oh, I think that can be arranged."

Just when I thought he was about to lunge at me, all of a sudden, he stops and pins me with his steel-gray gaze.

"I missed you so much. There were times I didn't think I could make it without you. The fact is you set my world to rights. . Not seeing your smile, or hearing your voice was like the sky without stars. And when I look at you, you make me feel healed inside. Drew taught me many things about life. And he was right about something really important. He told me to open up my heart and allow myself to fall in love because it would be the greatest gift I could give myself. Only I didn't realize how epic it would be. I give you credit for that. You taught me how to love. And now that I know, I don't ever want to live a day without you. Promise me you'll live each day with me. Be my one and only, Sam."

"Don't you know?" I ask.

"Know what?"

"I already am."

EPILOGUE
BEN

———◆———

I TUG AT MY COLLAR for the millionth time. I shouldn't be nervous, but I am. Cate's wedding is done and soon I'll be out of this monkey suit as the reception is dying down. Speeches have been given, the first dance done and cake eaten. Mercer stands next to me patiently waiting for me to spit it out.

"Are you sure you're okay?"

I nod. "I should be asking you. It's your moment."

He stares at me with good humor on his face before he claps me on the back. "You're on."

I watch as Cate, pretty as can be, turns and gives her back to a gaggle of women. It's almost scary the fierce expression they give one another as if this moment could win them the key to life. These are the times I'm grateful I'm a guy.

"One, two, three," Cate calls out before launching her bouquet over her head. She spins around to watch what happens next.

As the surreal event unfolds, I swallow wondering if a catfight will break out. Once I might have relished that prospect, but my Sam stands in the middle. The idea of her getting hurt makes me want to leap in the fray and tell all the other women to back the fuck up.

But as if the man-hungry group is the Red Sea, they part and the bouquet arcs beautifully to land into Sam's awaiting hands as if by destiny. Only it wasn't destiny, but by design.

She glances around unsure of what's going on. I get a few more reassuring pats as I step towards her. The music has stopped. But the sound of my blood racing through my veins mutes everything around me. Lights flash and I wonder if Sam has figured it out yet. When I reach her, she still looks confused. But in a second, it will all become clear.

"Samantha, you are the breath that fills my lungs. You are the blood that rushes through my veins. Without you, I would cease to exist. Knowing you're mine isn't enough anymore."

She covers her mouth as I bend down on one knee and gaze up at her radiant face. I see the shine in her eyes as the puzzle of what I'm about to do pieces together for her.

"I want to give you my name... the keys to my house... my car, my boat. Whatever it takes for you to agree to be my wife." I wait a beat. "It's kind of time for you to say something, sweetheart," I beg.

Her hand comes down and she pushes my hair back. Her grin lights up the room and she knows that she has my number. And I don't care.

"Well?" I ask, taking my first breath and hoping it won't be my last. Because if she denies me, I won't have the heart to go on.

"You need to ask me first."

I blink. "Oh, right."

The sounds of laughter all around us rushes into my ears, but I ignore it. I take a deep breath.

I reach in my pocket with steady hands because there's no doubt in my mind she's the one. I pull out the box and open it before I say the words I've wanted to say since she took me back. I'd wanted to give her time, time to forget and see my actions as true.

"Samantha Calhoun, will you do me the greatest honor and become my wife?"

She nods and I take quick notice of her family and friends. Cate and Mercer agreed to it all and helped with the plan. The time for Sam's parents, sister, and best friends to show up had been given so that they could witness this moment. The hard part had been when I faced her family in secret weeks before to ask them if I could marry her. Her mom had been quick to hug me with happy tears. On the other hand, I got an uncomfortable speech from her father and made promises under penalty of castration to her sister before they agreed. It was worth it because having them here at this moment is important to my soon-to-be bride.

Her face is more beautiful than a painting as her smile etches in my heart. When she says the words, it relieves the pressure on my lungs.

"Yes, I will. I thought you would never ask."

A Little Over A Year Later

I lift my bride-to-be in my arms. "Sit here," I demand.

She nods, used to my moods and knowing just what I need. I head upstairs and grab several things from my drawers. When I come back, she's sitting, waiting, and doesn't that make my dick want to punch through my pants.

"Do you trust me?"

Her answer is quick and always the same with a nod of her head in the affirmative. I draw her to her feet and take reverent care to strip her of all her clothing. The sight of her pink cheeks only stiffens my cock further. Her embarrassment when I get this way only makes me want to tattoo the word *mine* across her chest.

"I want to do something. Something we've never done before," I say.

Her silent acquiescence continues to stir the heat between us. I've brought a myriad of items I can use with my lack of having the right tools for this little endeavor. I settle on a pair of brand new cashmere socks. I think they would cause the least discomfort. Goosebumps rise on her skin when I hold them up to her. I walk around her admiring the view of her curves before settling behind her. She remains still, ready for whatever game I want to play. I gently draw her hands behind her. Then I use one long sock to bind her hands together. It's not tight enough that she couldn't get loose if she wanted to. That's not what this is all about. When I stand before her again, she's taken by surprise when I begin to blindfold her with the other long sock.

After I admire my handiwork, I guide her back down onto the sofa. I place her to sit as comfortably as she can with her arms bound behind her. This isn't a bondage thing so much as I want to take away her ability to touch me or control the situation. Her loss of those should heighten her pleasure.

"Am I the only one that's going to be naked?" she asks quietly.

"For now," I groan.

If she only knew how bad I wanted to be buried to the hilt in her, she might be afraid. The need I have for her is all consuming.

I head in the kitchen for the one other thing I need. With glass in hand, I head back to the living room and strip off my shirt. Before this is over, I want to be skin to skin with her. I want to remember every curve. And I don't want to take too long to be free of my clothes.

Planting myself between her legs, I take an ice cube from the tumbler I brought. Placing it in my mouth, I lean in. I press the tip of the frozen cube gently against one of her nipples. And after a second it draws tight.

"See, it's still responsive," I say, as if I needed another experiment.

She sucks in a breath as goosebumps erupt on her skin. It isn't as if we haven't tested her nipples a million times before, every chance I get. But still, I say the words. With my hand, I cup and massage her perfect tits. No, they aren't the ones she was blessed with originally. But they're even better. And not because they feel better, because they don't. Don't get me wrong, they are so much more real than I expected. The reason they are better is because they won't be the cause of her death.

And even if one day she's diagnosed with cancer, we will fight it together. And God forbid it steals her life from me. Thankfully the chances of that are small. But if it happens, I will rejoice in our time together. I will celebrate her life, not mourn her death. Like I know she would mine, if fate takes me from her first.

I continue to squeeze and tease her breast as I head lower with the ice to settle between her legs. I plan to spend an eternity here. Or whatever time we have. I've learned my lesson on that score.

I force all other thoughts away as I push what's left of the ice inside her. Her back arches off the chair as I suck her clit into my mouth. I stroke my tongue over it and suck it again for however long it takes until she shatters around me screaming out her pleasure. Because even though I will have a bad case of blue balls for the next several weeks, this night is all about her.

One Month Later

The wedding is fast, but not fast enough. My cruel sister convinced Sam it was a good idea we abstain for a month before the wedding. I sit and fidget in my chair as my cock decides to make another protest by beating at the fly of my pants. Sam's delicious tits are practically spilling out of the top of her dress. I'm afraid I'm going to drool and the photographer is going to catch it. Every time I've seen her, she's been in loose fitting clothing. She told me it was so she wouldn't tease me. But I say just the opposite. Imagining what lay beneath has had me practically investing in a lube company. She'd taken our month long vow of chastity to another level. I blame it on my sister's encouragement. My lovely but somehow sadistic fiancée found it funny that my hand developed blisters that have now turned into calluses.

The joke is on me, but the results are incredible. The first time I kissed Sam in a month is today at the altar. I have to admit, I will probably remember that moment more due to our abstinence. And I had to fight myself not to squeeze her ass during that kiss while my groomsmen made jokes behind my back.

I look down the long table of the wedding party and notice my bride is too kind for her own good nature. The sheer number of our wedding party nearly overwhelms me. She had to have her sister, her best friends, plus Jenna stand up for her, which meant I had to recruit two other guys for my side.

When my best man, or should I say, best woman, taps her wine glass with a spoon, I know we're in the home stretch.

I watch as Cate stands in her fitted tux. What I don't expect is for her to pull out a letter. And immediately, I know whose words she's about to read.

Benny,

Well, dude, you finally did it. I knew this day would come, even though you had your doubts. You never had faith in yourself, but I always did. I would've placed all my money on you any day of the week—that's how much I believed in you. And do you know why? Because no matter what happened, you always had my back. Even when the chips were down, and you know what I'm saying here, you always looked for the brightest spot. That includes the time I decided to learn how to skate. I think you were the only one who thought I could do it. I told you that you were my mountain. And it's true. You were when I was five and you stayed that way to the end. That's why I loved you so much.

You have no idea how much I wish I could be with you today to celebrate, but know that I'm here in spirit. There are so many things I'd like to say to you right now but the number one thing that stands out the most is—damn, I wish I could've seen your face when you said, "I do." All those times I told you how you'd know when you found your one and only—brother, what I wouldn't give to have seen your eyes shine with love when you looked at your wife walk down the aisle. She must be one very special lady to have landed you. Treat her with kindness, Ben, like the most precious bird. Be gentle and caring and love her with everything you have.

To that special lady my brother married—I know he can be an idiot and hardheaded at times, but be patient with him, and trust me on this—you will never find a man who is more generous with a bigger heart than Ben Rhoades.

And to both of you—live life to its fullest. Cherish it like it's your most prized possession. Never take each other for granted or the time you share together.

Now if everyone can raise their glasses so we all can share a toast. To Mr. And Mrs. Ben Rhoades. May their journey of life together be long and filled with much love and happiness.

When she finishes, there's not a dry eye in the house including her own.

Damn you, Drew, I think as I hold back the emotion that swells out of me. I refuse to cry. Two times since I met Sam is more than my quota. However, his words will live with me forever. Cate leans down and kisses my cheek before handing me the letter. Immediately, I know I will keep it with the other for the rest of my life. No doubt, I will read it over and over again as the years pass, especially when I can't share with him all the things in my life he believed I could do.

When the night is almost over and guests are about to leave, I snag my bride.

"Time to go," I say tugging her towards the exit.

"Wait, I need to say goodbye to my parents."

I shake my head. "We'll go over to their house tomorrow before our flight. I need you right now."

She indulges me with a salacious grin as we exit the hotel. Our limo waits out front, our driver opening the doors. We decided not to stay in the same hotel for many reasons that don't seem to matter now. I wish now I could have taken a quick elevator ride before I unwrapped my bride. Instead, I signal the driver to head off towards our hotel. We have about twenty minutes before we get there.

"What does this do?" Sam asks with a wink.

She presses a button, but if the wink isn't clue enough, the smirk she sports tells me she knows exactly what she's doing. Her next move after the privacy window raises is to scramble off the seat and look up at me from the floor as she positions herself between my legs.

"Jesus, Sam, you don't have to do that. I want to taste you."

She shakes her head as she undoes my belt.

"It's my turn to have my way with you, Rhoades. Hands behind your back and no touching," she demands.

Who am I to argue about a blow job, but I'm not very good at taking instructions. I lean down and cup her face.

"I have to kiss you first."

When I pull back, I add, "There's something you need to know."

She tilts her head to the side. Not in fear, but in curiosity.

I've said thousands of words since I've known how much in love I was with this woman. But I feel I've missed saying one important thing.

"Even though I may not have looked like it on the outside, I was an accident waiting to happen when you met me. My life was on a path of slow self-destruction. I'm not perfect, and never will be. I'm sure I'll make a hundred mistakes as we grow old together. But you, Sam, are the crew boss who put a stop to my wrecking ball. You make me better. You make me less of a mess of a man."

A THANK YOU

We'd like to thank you for taking the time out of your busy life to read our novel. Above all we hope you loved it. If you did, we would love it back if you could spare just a few more minutes to leave a review on your favorite e-tailer. If you do, could you be so kind and **not leave any spoilers** about the story? Thanks so much!

COMING SOON
BY
A.M. HARGROVE & TERRI E. LAINE

A BEAUTIFUL SIN

Canaan Michael Sullivan is a man of God, a model student, a faithful seminarian, and eventually a respected priest. He follows the rules and asks God to forgive his sins and the sins of others, like Catholics priests are taught to do. To the outsider, he's what every Catholic parish seeks for in their priest. Only he has something to hides from everyone, a sin rooted so deep he can't find absolution despite all his penance, until *her*.

Haven is an island all her own. She's independent and focused on achieving her career goals even if it means going back to the city she fled the first chance she could. The memories she kept hidden, she'll have to face. Only she doesn't expect to run into the boy who changed her life all those years ago.

Unknown to the both of them, they been bound together by a few simple words he'd spoken when she was just an eleven-year old girl and he wasn't must older, a mere boy himself. Those words will soon change everything, including his chosen path. A beautiful sin will tie them together, threatening the future he'd worked so hard to create and his past he'd worked so hard to bury.

ABOUT THE AUTHORS

A.M. HARGROVE

Reader, Writer, Dark Chocolate Lover, Ice Cream Worshipper, Coffee Drinker, Lover of Grey Goose (and an extra dirty martini), Puppy Lover, and if you're ever around me for more than five minutes, you'll find out I'm a talker.

A.M. Hargrove divides her time between the mountains of North Carolina and the upstate of South Carolina where she pursues her dream career of writing. If she could change anything in the world, she would make chocolate and ice cream a part of the USDA food groups. Annie writes romance in several genres, including adult, new adult, and young adult. Her books usually include lots of suspense and thrills and she sometimes ventures into the paranormal, sci-fi and fantasy blend.

TERRI E. LAINE

Terri E. Laine, USA Today bestselling author, left a lucrative career as a CPA to pursue her love for writing. Outside of her roles as a wife and mother of three, she's always been a dreamer and as such became an avid reader at a young age.

In her early years, she and her best friend would tell each other stories over the phone when they were bored. They called them their "soap operas" and generally revolved around whatever boy they liked at the time.

Many years later, she got a crazy idea to write a novel and set out to try to publish it. With over a dozen titles published under various pen names, the rest is history. Her journey has been a blessing, and a dream realized. She looks forward to many more memories to come.

You can find more about her books at www.terrielaine.com.

other books by Terri E. Laine

Chasing Butterflies

Catching Fireflies

Ride or Die

other books co-authored by Terri E. Laine

Cruel and Beautiful

A Beautiful Sin

One Wrong Choice

Sidelined

Fastball

Hooked

Other Books by A. M. Hargrove

Cruel and Beautiful
A Beautiful Sin
For the Love of English

The Guardians of Vesturon Series:
Survival, Book 1
Resurrection, Book 2
Determinant, Book 3
reEmergent, Book 4
Dark Waltz, A Praestani Novel
Death Waltz, A Praestani Novel

The Edge Series:
Edge of Disaster
Shattered Edge
Kissing Fire

The Tragic Series:
Tragically Flawed, Tragic 1
Tragic Desires, Tragic 2

The Hart Brothers Series:
Freeing Her, Book 1
Freeing Him, Book 2
Kestrel, Book 3
The Fall and Rise of Kade Hart

Other Standalone Novels:
Sabin, A Seven Novel
Exquisite Betrayal
Dirty Nights, The Novel

Stalk A.M. Hargrove

If you would like to hear more about what's going on in my world, please subscribe to my mailing list at my website. Please stalk me. I'll love you forever if you do. Seriously.

Website – www.amhargrove.com
Twitter - @amhargrove1
Instagram – amhargroveauthor

Links to other social media can be found on website.

Stalk Terri E. Laine

If you would like more information about me, sign up for my newsletter at my website. I love to hear from my readers.

Website – www.terrielaine.com
Twitter @TerriLaineBooks
Instagram – terrielaineauthor

Links to other social media can be found on website.

CPSIA information can be obtained
at www.ICGtesting.com
Printed in the USA
LVOW12s1806230217
525233LV00004B/878/P